SCUM
VALLEY

MATTHEW ELLKS

To my brudda. Fox!

SCUM VALLEY

Book One

All the best mate. Keep Charging.

MATTHEW ELLKS

Matt

ISBN: 978-1497313200

CONTENTS

Dedicated to my lovely wife Putu

and two young grommets,

Selina & Raymond

Epigraph

THERE WAS TROUBLE IN THE OCEAN
FROM A WAVE THAT JUST WENT PAST,
IT SNAPPED YOUR LEASH, BROKE YOUR BOARD
AND BLOODY KICKED YOUR ARSE.

KARMA MATE, IT DOES EXIST
IT'S CAUSED THE STATE YOU'RE IN,
SWIMMING INSTEAD OF PADDLING
'COS YOU WERE DROPPING IN.

YOU STUMBLED ON THE TAKE OFF
LIKE A RAG DOLL YOU WERE TOSSED,
SMASHED REAL HARD AGAINST THE REEF
THAT WAVE SHOWED YOU WHO'S BOSS.

SUCKED OVER THE FALLS AGAIN
THEN HELD LONG UNDERWATER,
THAT WAS JUST NO NORMAL WAVE
IT WAS THE DEVILS DAUGHTER.

FINALLY ONE GULP OF AIR
BUT ONLY ONE YOU SEE,
YOUR MIND IS GETTING TESTED
BY A WAVE FORMED OUT AT SEA.

YOUR EGO'S COPPED A HIDING
AND YOUR BODY'S SORE AND BRUISED,
YOU SHOULD PULL OUT WHEN YOU DROP IN
BUT YOU STAYED ON AND CRUISED.

SO WHEN YOU GET YOUR BOARD REPAIRED
AND YOU'VE RECOVERED TOO,
SEE IF YOU LIKE SOMEONE DROPPING IN
AND DISRESPECTING YOU.

Stuart SCAR Camp'

Foreword

I first met Matt Ellks in the early 70s. We were both hookers (no, not male prostitutes … well not yet anyway) for opposing school football teams. We were about 10 years old and, coming from a big family of boys, it was not beneath me to sledge while packing down for a scrum. As Matt's school was Catholic, most of that sledging was related to paedophile priests, and on more than one occasion Matt chased me in a furious rage … when I wasn't even carrying the ball.

You might have thought this experience would have repelled Matt from my family but the opposite was true. And this tells you a lot about him. While the rest of the kids from his school obeyed the orders of the Mother Superior and crossed the road twice to avoid passing "the heathen house" Matt made a beeline right for our front gate. The first time he came in he had a five foot nothing G&S twin fin with a smashed nose he wanted repaired. He also had a ten dollar bill and asked if this would be enough. I had never seen a kid of my age with a ten dollar note before and invited him in. We have been best friends ever since. Matt was one of many "only sons" who gravitated to our mad household of testosterone-fuelled creativity and adventure, but no one spent more time at our place at Rose Bay than the grommet who had by now become known as Ellksy. We had many early morning surfs together, walking in darkness down to Bondi, or out to Nielson Park when the swell was big enough, and soon began spending weekends and holidays at our grandparents' houses on the Central Coast. This would usually require us to catch the train from Sydney's Central Station to Gosford, a trip which awakened in both of us a spirit of adventure that has never left. I even remember one time looking out the window of the old red-rattler onto the train yards of the inner city and Matt saying, "Doesn't it make you feel like a Hobo, travelling the lines and living life on the road?" I think I experienced more of that wondrous sense of discovery with Matt than with anyone else.

We had many fantastic trips together, up the coast to Angourie camping and surfing, and even over to Lord Howe Island where, I am told, we two were the first to surf the outside reefs in 74. In the late 70s Matt changed schools to where I was goi⸱ Cranbrook, and while I had a bad influence on his studiou⸱ for a while, I will never forget the day he came to me and ⸱ he was giving up "playing up" at school and was going ⸱

work harder. I thought, well good luck to you, and watched as he dedicated himself to improving his scholastic achievements and all of his results improved dramatically. He has always been one who knows how to get a job done.

What followed were many great surf adventures through Indonesia and Hawaii where Matt made his mark, and even, with echoes of knocking on our front door decades before, knocked on the door of "Fast Eddie" Rothman, and became very tight with the "Black shorts" and even became a franchisee of the "Da Hui" surf-wear label in Australia. For many years Matt also worked hard at his trade as a tiler and amongst other things ran a very successful surf shop in Bondi.

Throughout our childhoods Matt also made forays into many different worlds, and would always return with rivetting tales about the adventures he had been on. I particularly loved his stories about working for his dad at the races, his many holidays to the ski fields of Thredbo and holidays overseas with his parents. But nothing could prepare me – not even his time as an exchange student in Japan – for the story of his first trip to the USA. He surfed in Hawaii and Maui, and on the mainland hitched across the Utah Desert from Aspen to California. He was still in his teens.

Unlike me, Matt has always been interested in politics, and I remember him arguing red-faced with right wing "Silver tails" at High School as if the future of the planet depended on it. Hell, maybe it did. He proved to be a great debater at school and while he had a broad knowledge that reached far beyond the curriculum he also continued exploring other worlds and dimensions, including Eastern philosophy, fitness and health, and even mind-expanding drug use.

Matt has always had an insatiable appetite for experience and knowledge and had a love of working his way into different groups and social circles. He has also always been one to "give back" to the community, perhaps a trait he inherited from his extraordinarily generous and warm-hearted mother. He has, at various times, been a surf club director, boxing trainer and environmental activist. He has a "David and Goliath" complex that has worried me at times, but which I have also been thankful for, as it is a philosophy he believes in so passionately; that it is not beyond him to "become physical" when backing someone up. He never shies away from taking on "The Man" and lobbies constantly against corporatisation and injustice. There is almost nothing he likes more than tearing into hypocrisy and greed, or sticking up for battlers. There have been a lot of battles in Matt's life and, luckily for us, he has also, for as long as I can remember, been a great story teller and avid writer.

In 2004 as I was finishing up a stay in Indonesia I caught up with Matt who, having just arrived, told me he thought his future might be somehow entwined with Bali. He has since married a beautiful Balinese woman and had two incredible little kids. He has also built, with his own hands, a family villa on the more remote northern coast of Bali. Here he lives – when he's not back in Jindabyne earning money tiling to continue his interests – and surfs and writes. He also remains active with various groups dedicated to environmentalism and corporate watch-dogging.

For a long while I have been encouraging Matt to pen his "Long Awaited Memoirs", but always his reply is that he is still in the middle of living. Just today I logged onto Facebook and saw his status update that he was surfing alone in the wilds of West Java. I have in fact been impressed sufficiently by his travails to make him one of the key characters in my first novel. Still, maybe this collection of short stories, drawn from real life, will let us in on the real secret of what makes Matt tick, far more than anything anyone else could ever write.

Monty Webber

Bondi: A Morning Swell

There was a distant tropical thunderstorm on the horizon, which seemed to propagate a pulse destined for the shallow reefs of an exotic Pacific atoll. A lone surfer named Dan was complacent in waiting for the marching swells to enter the magnificent bay that he'd discovered on his solitary surfing expedition. It would seem that the ancient lava flows, which formed these perfect surfing reefs, conferred with a surfer before they spewed into the sea. The configuration of the atoll's sharp corals and the uncanny perfection associated with them was a surfer's dream. Mother Nature definitely had the surfer in mind when creating this part of the planet.

As the set of waves approached him, he paddled wide in anticipation of a larger beast. He paddled over the first lump and was temporarily blinded by the strong offshore trade wind blowing a swirling spray off the back of the wave. It rendered him incapable of sizing up the monster shadow of the next lump steaming towards him. He knew it was big, by the way it dwarfed him. As the spray subsided, he knew this looming, dark, foreboding contour was the one he'd been patiently waiting for. He positioned himself and started paddling frantically to find its G-Spot for take off. As he launched into the 10-foot monstrosity, he turned under the thundering lip like it was a cakewalk. His senses had become rhythmic with the turbulent ocean. He rode deeper and deeper, seemingly lost inside the curtain of mystique and rapture. As the cylinder kept pearling along the perfect right-hand reef, he stood casually in the engine room of its smoking rotating shaft. As he neared the end of his exhilarating ride, there was a clanging getting louder and louder interrupting the euphoria of the moment.

All of a sudden, he regrettably woke up to the sound of his phone as it penetrated his flimsy dream membrane. It was hard not to hear the 'bling bling' in his blind-drawn, one room apartment. It seemed to echo in his dark recovery cave.

"Fucken' b-jesus!" he swore, as he reached over, blindly, to pick up the old school receiver.

He had to pull it hard towards him as the cord was tangled. Upon holding it to his ear there was a crackling noise due to a bad connection followed by, "Yeah, it's Cookie. Are you there?'

There was a slight pause as Dan's brain was yet to respond. "Are you there yet?" His mate Cookie knew Dan was currently on a three-day bender. "Earth to Dan, come in … If you can hear me the waves are cranking, so you'd better get your arse outta bed."

Dan's brain still wasn't ready to put out in the word department. He clutched his face and ruffled his hair. Cookie knew Dan had picked up and was hoping the yellow cumbersome plastic earpiece hadn't been dropped on the floor.

"You still there? You didn't pull a root, did you?" pried Cookie, wondering if last night's girl was keeping him occupied.

"Nah, mate, no trophy, just a shockin' hangover." He tried to clear his throat, which felt like someone had wedged a fur ball in it while he was sleeping. "What time is it?"

"Time to get up, ya drunk! The surf is six-foot solid with bigger sets and the right-hander behind the Baths is as good as it gets!" The surf at Bondi was good and it was Cookie's mission to get his friend up out of bed and into the water. There was nothing better to Cookie than surfing good waves with a few mates. Being a keen surfer he had already walked the short distance from his aunt's unit down to "the hill" at South Bondi to check the surf before the sun had even peeked its head over the horizon.

"Looks like the waves are getting bigger, so no time to 'uck around; we're out there!" Cookie was originally from Maroubra Beach, a few miles further down the coast. During his childhood, his mum had her hands full bringing up six kids by herself in a small, red-brick, State Housing Commission unit. She was a staunch matriarch, who tried hard to care for all her kids. But two eyes can only cover so far, so they were always destined to make it on their own from an early age. Cookie, the second eldest, was in his mid 20s. His missing front tooth and shoulder-length unkempt hair gave you the impression that he was a knockabout kind of guy. The sun and sea had bleached his hair in parts and his lack of applying sunscreen had made his face a breeding ground for freckles. His eyebrows were dark and prominent, edging towards joining up in the middle. Usually unshaven and sporting camel breath, he was rough around the edges, but a gem of a bloke to get on the "piss" with. A couple of drinks in him and nothing was sacred. Bagging sessions were conducted with no conscience. No stone was ever left unturned. Beer to him was like mother's milk, rum was nectar from the Gods, food was something consumed between drinks and he'd kill you for a cigarette. His talent for hustling came naturally and deservedly so. He had served his street apprenticeship in the back lanes of a shifty neighbourhood. His background of attending a lax NSW state public school also helped refine his rebellious nature. Many a school day was spent absent whilst refining his surfing skills at Maroubra Beach's infamous "Dunny Bowl".

"Well, I'd better get my arse outta bed if the surf's up!" Dan rubbed the crusty sleep from his eyes, then continued grinding his fist into his sockets. It felt therapeutic, as it massaged the alcohol-soaked mass behind his frontal lobe. Cookie knew Dan was always aroused by the prospect of classic waves pounding the coastline.

"Many guys out?"

"Andy and Sloth are getting some great rides already!" Andy and Sloth worked construction together. But being hardcore surfers, they were always managing to fit a surf in before and after work. They had been bobbing in the ocean since dawn, enjoying the large waves. It seemed both these surfers lived and breathed in time with the ocean. If the waves were up, they were usually out there before anyone.

The towering "Sloth" was nicknamed after the lazy South American tree-dweller. Around the same age as Cookie, he was tall, about 6'4", beach-weathered and always lurching, which gave him an uncanny resemblance to the forest primate. But he was more of a slow moving amphibian than a jungle bludger. He may have been slow moving, but he was never one to bludge, unless it was on his own time. He was a responsible worker, but embraced chilling out. You see, his elder brothers were well respected in Bondi and he was fortunate to be living within the family blueprint they had forged. Their well-cut path of paid dues gave Sloth a comfort zone to bask in. His brother's experience gave him sight of boundaries that he knew he could keep within and avoid retribution—a privilege of being the youngest in his tribe.

On the flipside all you had to do was talk surf with the guy and you would think he was related to the "Road Runner". If anyone could get you psyched to surf two-foot onshore shit it was Sloth and of course always in his corner backing him up was his five-eight and work buddy Andy. Blonde haired Andy was an unassuming but very motivated kind of guy, especially when surf was mentioned. Being smaller in stature, the quiet achiever

3

walked in Sloth's shadow, but he was never dwarfed by the big man's presence. Andy had a lot in common with Sloth, but was far from a "Yes" man to him. They agreed to disagree on many occasions and could put shit on each other like only friends can. They did a lot of things together and, in true Aussie mateship, always covered each other's arse.

"They've been out there since first light and Andy's last wave towered over him like the Poseidon Adventure!"

Cookie had pushed the right buttons for any surfer to want to get up and head down to the beach. Dan stretched his eyebrows and lowered his jaw, letting out a loud yawn as his body twitched. "What about Fitz and Porky? They around?"

Cookie lowered his voice so as not to wake his aunty or announce to the world that he was smoking marijuana, "We're all here punching cones getting psyched up." Patronising the bong before a surf was a ritual for these lads. It was a daily ritual for most of the beach crew.

"Fuck, what about waiting for me?"

"You can't come over. You know my aunt doesn't like you and you know she's punched out my mates before."

"Okay, okay, whatever," Dan mumbled.

"Don't okay me. I'm protecting you, ya knucklehead! With me aunt's Nazi background and your habit of rooting girls in her lounge room you're lucky she hasn't stuck one of her Doc Martens up your loose arse yet. Actually she's probably scared of losing her boot."

Dan winced. That was enough to terminate the conversation. "OK, Cookie, see you down the beach in 20 minutes."

He threw the covers off and pulled himself up past horizontal. The weight of his head meant it took a couple of turns to actually reach sitting position. As he sat on his bed, the night before was starting to come back to him. He focused his brown, bloodshot eyes on the mess in his room. His eyes were now fully opened to witness what looked like a bomb site. The room was littered with last night's leftovers—pizza box, tinnies, stubbies, a spilt bong complete with stained carpet, a cocaine mirror, a smelly ashtray, a sink full of dirty dishes and parts of Dan's brain cells scattered everywhere for good measure.

"Shit." he muttered. His mind started wandering back trying to piece last night's memory together. He recalled dancing the night away at a dark and dingy bar with a few nice chicks on some really good acid. He remembered a girl named Kelly, who he fell in love with because she had incredible green eyes and sensually moved her hips like an uninhibited porno queen. Dan fancied himself as a dancer and a bit of a stud. Surfing every day gave him good abs, and boxing contributed to some of his flowing moves on the dance floor. He had nearly worked for Studs Afloat cruising Sydney Harbour. He just couldn't quite get his head around parading his dick in public. Sure, he'd be flaunting it in front of girls and he was proud of his manhood. But all he really ever wanted was the sex trimmings the cruise had to offer. He had been teased by pornographic stories from his mate Jake, who told him about the job. Tales of hundreds of imprudent women running up to the stage, like bees to honey, and stroking his mate's dick gave him half a fat.

Dan's main hobbies focused on fun, sex, freedom and surfing. To Dan they complemented each other. Surfing toned his muscles for sex and vice versa. But he was by no means an exhibitionist. He would only get in the nude after a few ales, which was classified as rather shy behaviour in the Bondi social world, especially when the main boardriders' club was named RBS for "rude boys surfing".

He got up and washed his face in the adjoining bathroom. He looked in the cracked mirror above the porcelain basin. His dark brown hair was sticking up all over the place from the way he had slept. He wet his hands and tried to press down the pointy bits. He stood there for a moment patting his hair. "Good boy, Rover," he murmured to himself. He spooked himself when he focused closely and found himself looking into his twitching eyes. He soon was gazing into them deeper and deeper, recounting images both real and hallucinogenic, all relative to his shaky state. He snapped out of his short trance and started fraternising with the person in the mirror. He thought about his crazy indulgent life, then smiled. He was a happy man. Living in Bondi was a happening thing with its surf, sun and babes and he was glad to be in the thick of it. Returning to his living area, he searched for his wallet and keys.

"Twenty bucks!" he exclaimed, as he checked his pockets and came up trumps. He could now afford some breakfast and a couple of cones. Amazing how cash in the "next morning's" jeans can bring so much joy or so much grief depending how little is left. Dan scratched his head and tried to do his sums on the night

5

before.

"Spent 50 at the Kardomah Club, 20 for that acid, mmmm …, ah, shit! I lent some to someone, I think." Dan cringed as he pondered who he lent cash to. He was in no state to remember. His wallet came to hand in his jacket, his keys, after a few minutes, were found still in the door and he even managed to find a small bud on the floor.

It was time for a quick cuppa, so he put the kettle on, got the tea bag ready and pulled the blind to access the day. The sun's rays were being shot out from the horizon in all their morning glory, the wind was offshore and there wasn't a cloud in sight. He leant out the window and could clearly see gilded swell-lines stacked to the golden horizon. As the old rusty kettle whistled, he strode towards it knowing that it was going to be another epic day's surfing. He poured his cuppa and chopped up the little bud he'd stumbled across. As he exhaled huge wafts of cannabis smoke, his thoughts were starting to think how good the surf was going to be. The month-late electricity bill—due that day—never entered his train of thought. He visualised the view from inside the tube, looking out. How deep would he ride today? With his excitement level rising, he packed the last cone in the bowl and engaged. Taking one more swig of his tea, he grabbed his wetsuit and 7'2" big wave board and headed out the door.

Emerging from the bottom of his stairwell, he entered Hall Street, which was a cold awakening. The street was dwarfed by blocks of flats, which kept it in shade till mid-morning. Being winter, Dan could feel the strong westerly, blowing off the mountains, on the back of his neck. It put a shiver through him. He was glad he had placed highly in the Bondi Boardriders' Open Championship the previous year, winning a new steamer from the local surf shop. To Dan, the full length rubber steamer was worth its weight in gold on a chilly winter's morning. He walked past the numerous cafés and shops, as he headed on down the beach. The early birds were starting to gather. Like any other sunny morning, the golden sand invited people to start their day. His connection with the beach was deeper than most. His passion for this stretch of inner city sand was evident in the thousands of hours he had put in the surf, honing his skills as a waterman.

From three years of age, he became involved in the local North Bondi Surf Club, as his uncle was the sweep for the club's

6

surfboat. His uncle, Paul, had a big influence on Dan from early childhood. Paul was also the first-grade hooker for the Roosters and Dan idolised him. The thrill to be the team's ball boy each week was hard to surpass when you've just turned five. No wonder a young Dan's dreams revolved around footy and surfing.

Every Sunday morning, Dan and his good mate, Porky, would attend the young Nippers' swim and flag competition. They both enjoyed and excelled in their surf club's activities. But their main reason for being there was their pursuit of surfing. At around 11am, Nippers would finish and Dan and his mates would bolt over to their mums, grab their coolites and head into the surf. North Bondi's surf was always small, as it was the sheltered part of the beach and therefore ideal for a youngster to learn. The area was well patrolled so the length of rope cut by mum was loosened considerably. Dan cherished his newfound freedom amongst the waves—a freedom of spirit that would stick with him for the rest of his life.

Footy had been parallel with surfing till he broke his arm in a U/14s rugby match. He was playing halfback for his school when he made a clean break down the blind side of the ruck. The fullback was coming across in cover and cleaned Dan up, landing on his wrist and snapping it in two. The injury kept him out of the water for a couple of months, which proved very testing for his character. During those two months there were three good swells and all he could do was watch in total frustration for a super-keen grommet. He concluded from the experience that unless an injury occurred whilst surfing, he could not justify the time spent out of the water. Footy was out and surfing took priority.

Dan turned the corner onto Campbell Parade and felt the full brunt of the icy wind. He could now see swells entering the bay and his tempo increased as he headed for the hill. The southern grass hill was a meeting place for the local surf culture. It was a large park, on the foreshore of the beach, providing a vantage point to watch the surf from. Bondi was so big and diverse there were several crews to hang out with. The stretch of sand from north to south was at least a mile in length.

In the southern corner, down near the rocks, the aptly named "Rock Crew" strutted their stuff. They were a stylish offshoot of the Bondi Icebergs' swimming club, who demanded respect. These guys were older and some of them didn't even surf, but were recognised as elders and that was good enough. No one fucked with them!

Dan was cool with them, but they were a bit too old to hang out with. He identified more closely with two other crews further up the hill, these being "The Hill" and "The Wall". Members of "The Hill" comprised your ex-public-school stock, whilst "The Wall" was mainly your ex-private-school crew. Dan was comfortable with both, as he had gone to both types of school. All these surfers were young men surviving what inner-city life could throw at them. Their passion for surfing was the common thread in their lives, for the majority of these guys lived to surf and didn't like to work too hard. They embraced the Aussie larrikin lifestyle and loved their beach. Surfing was their non-conformist means of escaping the mundane shackles of society. It was an escape from SCHOOL, from THE BOSS and from authority in general. Work was something which stood in the way of a new swell. It was an infringement on their fundamental freedom to surf. To these guys the pulse of the ocean was all that mattered. Fuck the establishment! The boys were going surfing!

Dan's jaw dropped as he saw Sloth pull into a massive closeout tube behind the Baths and somehow come out. The monstrous 10-foot lip missed the back of his neck by inches.

"Struth! Did you guys see that?" he shouted, pointing. Crew were hooting down third ramp way.

"Third Ramp boys liked it!" said Cookie, as he greeted Dan in a brotherly bear hug. "Third Ramp" was halfway between the southern hill and Bondi Surf Club in the middle of the beach. It was the third pedestrian access ramp from the southern end of the beach. In the early 20th Century, a large promenade was built along the beach's foreshore to protect the area's sand dunes and provide a spectacle for the public. Men, dressed in hats and suits, used to drive and park their Model-T Fords on the promenade, to enjoy a stroll with their sweetheart. A picnic or swim on the beach was also fashionable. So, a series of ramps were built for access.

Third Ramp's crew were mainly guys from North Bondi. Most of these guys belonged to working class families—the same families who had lived in Bondi since the days of the Model-T Fords. They always seemed to have big families and were well connected in the community. They were always winning games of footy for Bondi United and were most likely to end up with a good job on the Council. Their dads were running local politics and if anything got too outta hand, they had control in the area to fix it. Their forefathers were diggers, whose reputations had been etched in the golden sands long before Dan was thought of. There were plenty of elders at this beach. The beach was built on raw Aussie culture. From your lifeguard to the local garbo, Bondi was a vibrant cross-section of folk.

"I'm out there!" exclaimed Dan. He started pulling his wetsuit the right way out. The Sun felt warm, the sparrows were chirping and Dan felt alive and complete. This was his home beach, his domain, and there were fun waves to be ridden with good mates.

As if to heed to a command, all the boys used Dan's words to move them into action. As set waves peeled perfectly behind the Baths, the boys' hurried movements became more frenzied.

"We're goin' to get sooo barrelled!" was repeated over and over.

"You got wax, anyone?" someone shouted.

"Lucky I'm fuckin' sponsored by the yuppie fuckwit who just opened that new surf shop," was Cookie's answer, as he threw the wax up in the air for any of the boys to claim. "Suppose youse want a wax comb too?"

"Nah, me hair's just fine!"

The lads put their towels and bags together under one of the tall pines which overlooked the hill. As they ventured down to the water, other surfers were coming out of the woodwork and doing the same. However, by the time they had paddled out into the line-up, there were only a couple of surfers accompanying them, because a few had changed their minds after finding it impossible to paddle out past the breaking waves.

Corro had paddled out by jumping from an easier position off the rocks around at "the Boot". The Boot was a rock slab situated beyond the Icebergs. You only jumped off the Boot when the waves were big and timing was critical. To jump when a set approached meant getting smashed back on the rocks. Corro knew what he was doing. He was a local surf hero who showed World Top 16 talent during his junior career only to give it away to hang with the boys. His ability was highly respected and his loyalty to the boys always admired. He had a sense of order for the beach, which had been handed down by his elder brother. His eldest brother was a radical surfer and similarities could be seen in Corro's mature surfing style. Sporting a trademark moustache and surfing a colourful red and yellow board with matching wetsuit, he paddled over to the crew and took his place in the line-up.

Dan's hangover was taking its toll, as he breathed deeply in

order to get his lungs working properly. The paddle out had been
very heavy, resembling a mine field. He had paddled hard through
the breaking waves, which were pitching and exploding with tons
of water behind them. He had almost been turned around a few
times, copping several 8-foot monster waves on his head. As he
paddled past the breakers and inched towards the safety of the
pack he looked over to Corro, who hadn't even got his blonde
curly hair wet, and wished he had jumped off the rocks as well.

Andy had already racked up several barrel rides and couldn't
help asking, "Where've you guys been?"

"Fart-arsin' around as usual," said Fitz. "Nice couple, you and
Sloth been pullin' into! Must be my turn ..." Fitzy, as he was
affectionately called, was a true blue North Bondi boy, growing
up in the family home in Brighton Boulevard. He was an A1
student and excelled in any sport he undertook. He was reared like
most Bondi youngsters, at North as a coolite kid, and was also a
very keen skateboarder. He was also known as the Colonel,
because of his resemblance to Colonel Sanders, of the Kentucky
Fried Chicken Empire. From his golden curls to his penetrating
azure eyes, the Colonel was your typical blonde surfie. His love
for the ocean ensured his destiny was to advance to the south end
and to ride a fiberglass board. The transition from North to South
Bondi was the norm for any local kid who aspired to become a
real surfer. North Bondi was protected from big swells, so it was
the optimal place for a kid to learn on a soft foam board called a
coolite. It was many a surfer's dream to work in a surf shop when
you got older and Fitz was also living that dream. He had acquired
a job at the newly-opened surf shop in Lamrock Avenue and
loved his job: selling surfboards. At 24 he had seen enough
surfboards to know a good shape. He understood the mechanics of
the rocker, rails, tail and so forth and what conditions each shape
would go well in. He ripped in the water and was well liked. He
was another hardcore local.

"Did you bring this crew with ya?" joked Sloth, nodding his
head towards Dan. "Couldn't help yourself—had to bring all ya
mates!"

"Yeah, mate, at least I've got mates. Brought 'em just so they
could drop in on you." Sloth was like an older brother to Dan. They
had lived behind each other at North Bondi when they were five
years old. Sloth's elder brothers took Dan under their wing at an
early age. They all surfed and would regularly take Dan off his

mum's hands for a day at the beach. The 15-minute walk to the waves seemed like an eternity to a small kid with an oversized coolite under his arm, but it was always worth it. The board rash, the sunburn, the fear of sharks, scary stories of the tidal waves of "Black Sunday", stubbing your toe, bindiis and thorns, hunger pains and the long walk home were all mere formalities of becoming a keen surfer. The fulfilment far outweighed any hardship. It was like he had found his purpose at a very early age. The equation for this youngster was simple: surfing equals happiness.

"How big are the sets?" Dan asked Sloth.

"About ten feet and I need every inch of my 7'8"."

"Yeah, I'm on me seven-two. I lent fuckin' Alex me 7'6" and it hasn't fuckin' boomeranged yet." The surf was easily big enough for Dan to be riding the board he had lent to his forgetful cousin. It was a Brewer Surfboard that he had brought back from Hawaii and he slapped the water in frustration, knowing he needed the extra length. He flashed on the possibility that it would end up in some pawn shop and let out a grunt.

"Four inches makes a lot of difference when you're trying to stroke into these gnarly faces! That's what happens, lending ya shit to crazy cousins. Come to think of it, you've always been short a few inches ..." Sloth's words dissolved as he was distracted by the large set approaching. He immediately started paddling further out in earnest. The other surfers caught wind of it and started to scramble. The pack consisted of seasoned locals, except for two unfamiliar guys who should never have been out there in the first place.

"Paddle faster, Porks!" screamed Fitz. He had Corro paddling one side of him and Cookie on the other and all he could see in front of him was Porky's big fat arse. This was certain to be the biggest set of the morning, if not the year, and it would be touch and go whether half of them were even going to get over it. He didn't want to get tangled up in the lip and go over the falls with Porks, so the Colonel veered around him, hot on Sloth's scent.

The overwhelming size of the set was clearly visible, as the pack reached the summit of each wave and anxiously peered out to sea. Fear was gripping each surfer as they scratched for the middle of the bay. Sloth led by example with his long arms stroking like pistons. The fear each surfer was experiencing was the thought of millions of tons of water coming down on them. As the boys paddled onward they hooted to each other to try to keep

11

their nerves under control. After all, this was a life and death situation and their spiritual strength was being summoned. As crunch time drew near, it seemed everyone was going to miraculously make it to safety. Everyone, that is, except for Porks and the two guys who should never have paddled out in the first place.

As the first wave stood tall, everyone scraped over it, except the doomed three. Crew watching from the beach knew their fate was sealed and waited with bated breath. Grown men gasped as Porky tried to push through the thickest twelve foot lip Bondi's ever seen and got absolutely smashed. He became a human projectile, as he was launched from the lip onto the two guys below. It seemed to take an eternity for him to fall out of the sky and hit the bottom of the wave. Some spectators shielded their eyes, others gasped, but the local crew that had assembled on the hill were in hysterics. The pack outside were oblivious to the mayhem and were still paddling frantically to make it over the remainder of the set. Fortunately, the boys had experience on their side. They had frequented Hawaii and Indonesia over the years, so although their equipment lacked size they were more than ready to have a go. Already half a mile out to sea they prepared themselves for possibly a freak wave.

Down the middle of the beach the lifeguard tower had been keeping a close eye on what was unfolding. The head lifeguard was a local lad named Laurie, who had grown up surfing with the boys. He was watching through his binoculars. He knew the boys were always out there when it got big, so when a junior lifeguard asked him, "Do those guys know what they're doing?", all he could reply was, "Hey, if we needed rescuing you'd be wanting one of those guys to save us." He respected their global surfing experiences and regarded their ability to be greater than his. He knew they were experienced in big powerful Hawaiian or Indonesian surf similar to these conditions. Laurie also knew he wasn't in the same category and wasn't going out there to rescue any mad motherfucker. The beach was closed, so the boys were now responsible for their own actions. Like the building crowd, he was there to enjoy the spectacle.

The first wave of the next set was rideable but had a big chop in it. Sloth was the furthest out and let it go. Corro was keen but also paddled over it in anticipation of the next wave. This was a mountain which Andy and Dan couldn't refuse. They swung in

12

unison and paddled into it. As they felt the wave pitching, they jumped to their feet accumulating speed as they descended. Everything was going to plan until the chop rose up the face to meet them. As both riders were jolted from their boards the massive lip threw over both surfers. The throwing lip obscured them from the pandemonium they had caused amongst the number of surfers and people watching from different vantage points on the beach. Crew were hooting them all the way to the kiddie's pool at North. Spectators looked on in amazement as both surfers reappeared for a split second as they were sucked over into the abyss. The wave snapped both their legropes and Dan's board got hurled twenty feet in the air, showing firsthand the awesome power involved. The 380 bus full of passengers heading into the city gazed in horror as they witnessed the board spiral skyward. People walking on the promenade seemed to sense the drama and searched offshore for some sign of what was going on. Was it another Black Sunday about to happen? As Dan and Andy got thrown in all directions, at the mercy of this watery beast, the rest of the pack were still thinking of survival strategies.

The next wave of the set towered over all. A fifteen-foot monster, at least twenty-five feet in the face, presented itself for anyone who dared. With a strong feeling that it was part of his big-wave-conquering destiny, Sloth strode into a position to take on what felt to him like Everest. Cookie and Fitz paddled wide towards the safety of the shoulder. As most would have paddled over it Corro had other thoughts. Like Sloth, he saw it as his moment of reckoning and was ready to push his limits. Sloth breathed deep as he double-stroked into the monster. Corro swung around further inside on a boil and shoved his board beneath him to spring him forwards and down the face. He had left it late and reaching his feet was dropping at a rate of knots. On tippy-toes and arms outstretched to compensate the free-fall, he kept descending for what seemed ages for those privileged to see it. Sloth was now also up and riding the rogue swell on the outside of Corro, his large frame now dwarfed by the mountainous wave. Both men embraced the moment as though they had been waiting all their life for this wave. Their sheer determination to win with this wave had the beach's large, vocal audience in awe. To the people on the beach, Corro and Sloth disappeared for a moment, while the crew from the hill watched them synchronise bottom turns. It was poetry in motion. Both surfers rode the wave with a

13

series of well-executed turns under the wave's cavernous jaws. Hoots and shrieks were exploding around the beach. As another peak-hour 380 bus drove past the hill on its way to Bondi Junction, some grommets at the back were hanging out windows coo-eeing with excitement. They were going for an early morning skate down Bondi Road because the waves were too big for them to surf.

Porky's dad cleaned the Icebergs bar during the morning shift and had been occasionally glancing out the window to try and see what was going on in the bay. On sight of Sloth and Corro's effort, he couldn't help but acknowledge their bravery with a hearty cheer.

"My God! Those guys are legends!" he said to his co-worker unaware his son was getting washed into the beach full of water.

Sloth and Corro managed to ride the freak wave and keep out of each other's way until the wave jacked up on the inside section ready to close out. Both lads wanted to flick out and escape the perilous ending but unfortunately Sloth left his kick-out too late for Corro to follow him to safety. All alone riding the giant mass of water, Corro decided to do what any legend would and pull into the massive closeout tube. As a salute to those who were watching, he raised his arms in defiance of what was to come. To the screams of the completely captivated audience, he corrected his line so he had totally committed himself to riding the wave for as deep and as long as he could. The massive jaws of the barrel engulfed him like a black hole. The crowd went quiet. The wave's entrails were shot high into the air as the wave internally combusted. Seconds seemed like minutes as people searched for a sign of life. Like the invincible hero he was, Corro popped up twenty seconds later in the white-water washing machine to cheers from the crowd.

The full force of the Pacific had been behind these sets of waves. The sequence of events that transpired was the stuff Bondi was made of. After their wave, Corro and Sloth were given a repetitive Hitler-like salute from the boys on the hill; a praiseworthy salute practised by surf-nazis the World over. People were scanning the white-water for bodies. A couple of local grommets were salvaging any washed up surfboards on the shoreline. One by one, everyone was accounted for. Cookie and Fitz were shaking way out to sea. They started laughing at each other in fits. They were stoked to be alive. They knew they were

14

heavily under-gunned riding 6'8"-sized boards. So they did the smartest thing and paddled to North where the swell was smaller to come in on. After avoiding a big set, which broke wide of Ben Buckler, they finally made it to the safety of the beach in the northern corner.

Sloth had other ideas and decided to try his luck again. The swell was building by the minute and he knew he couldn't wait too long, for the conditions were deteriorating quickly. As a grommet found a piece of someone's board on the shoreline, Sloth sized up a ten-foot lump. Paddling into position he could see it was going to be a fast fucker. With all of Bondi watching he lunged to his feet and began dropping. The local firemen clapped in joy at watching their friend take the challenge. Like everyone else who was there that morning they had stopped to watch the event. They had unlocked the gate next to the 322 bus shed and driven their fire truck onto the hill for front row seats. They all knew Sloth because they were tight with his elder brothers. They revelled in the thought that he was their mate's younger brother who was up to the task at hand.

As all watched on, Sloth's big frame punched off the bottom and pulled into the mouth of the motherfuckin' pit. From the beach, the lip looked like it was racing too quickly for him to handle. He had to put his foot on the throttle if he was to come out of this pearler. His speed accelerated as his board drew a precise line behind the curtain. Using his lanky frame, he pumped continuously to keep up his momentum. He was so deep that huge foamy fingers were reaching out and touching the tail of his board, trying to pull him back into the void and smash him. All the time they niggled, he stayed true and focused to his commitment. His body was being charged by the millions of positive ions caused as the lip exploded beside him. He felt in tune and was confident of coming out.

From the beach, crew had turned away thinking he had been swallowed up. They were trying to see where his board would pop up to gauge the length of ride. A few, who knew better, kept following the peeling tube hoping to see the impossible. No one was disappointed. Sloth rose to the occasion and got spat out with terminal velocity miles down the line in front of the lifeguard tower. The beach erupted as he claimed the barrel and then straightened out to come in.

As the hands of the Hotel Bondi's clock showed 9am, the

15

drama which had already occurred would be just one of many crew would be talking about over Sunday dinner. There was still the whole day in the 'hood to get through and sometimes that was more dangerous than what the boys had just encountered in the water. As the onlookers resumed their daily routines, the surfers were congregating at different vantage points to continue checking the swell. As it pounded the coast, grommets were scamming lifts to go and surf inside Sydney Harbour at the protected novelty wave at Nielsen Park.

Dan and Andy were the first to walk up the hill to a standing ovation. The fire truck sounded its siren in praise. A local contingency had flocked to the beach upon hearing of the morning's events. Mates with wenches getting home from a big Saturday night in the city were pulling up in taxis. The Hill's spectators, comprising of hardcore surfers, drunken bums, crack whores, groupies and grommets, welcomed their gallant comrades with open arms. Porky was carrying one half of his former surfboard, trailing Dan and Andy. A cheeky grommet named "Big Ads" made squealing noises from a safe distance testing Porky's tolerance level. The grommet had lodged the other half of his board way up in one of the pine trees and was pointing to it as he grunted. Porky soon dismissed the grommet till a later date and joined the excitement of the celebration going down.

Corro was talking to the Coleman brothers down on the promenade at Third Ramp. He was nonchalantly shrugging off the brothers' accolades. He took it all in his stride. Young grommets were riding their bikes past him trying to fathom why he shouldn't be dead. After all, if they suffered the same beating they would surely perish. With his red and yellow attire, he stood out like a superhero to them.

"Are you invincible?" one young bike rider asked. Corro blushed as if he was put on the spot in front of the boys. "It's more like I don't give a fuck!" was his eventual comeback. The grommets loved having legends like him to look up to. Someone who didn't give a fuck was cool! Some Japanese tourists wanted a photo with him, oblivious to what had just happened in the water. They obviously liked his red and yellow outfit. As if they had infringed on his world, he told them frankly to "Fuck off". It wasn't a personal thing. It was more of a coming down from the moment thing and he didn't want his train of thought to be interrupted. The brothers questioned Corro on his firsthand

16

account and he seized the opportunity to bag Sloth. "Yeah, the big bloke was screaming 'Mummy' for the entire drop." He had all of Third Ramp chuckling to themselves. He turned around to the gang hanging over the railing on the above landing and asked: "What a big poofta, aye?" He then burst out laughing, but was cut short by a barking cough taking over. After spitting up a few oysters, he asked politely: "Has anyone got a ciggy?"

Sloth grabbed a shower at the ramp in the southern corner before proceeding up towards the boys. It was like Jesus Christ walking into Jerusalem. Crew were hooting at him from all corners of the beach, as he strode up the grassy southern parkland. Some grommets, who had skated down Bondi Road, whistled at him from up near the old Astra Hotel. As he reached the pine trees on top of the Hill, he was feeling kind of special, though he knew if he let his ego run with the moment, the boys would bag the shit out of him. Still buzzing from the euphoria he just smiled, said nothing and let all the hype go over his head. He and Andy had work to finish off and even though it was a Sunday, they needed to get there fairly early. After a few high-fives, they headed to the car for a towel and some dry clothes. Several good mates tried to persuade them to take a detour for some herb, but they were late for work and keen to get the job done. After all, they didn't need to get high: They were already there!

Cookie and the Colonel were slowly making their way back to South, chatting with young girls along the way. Their life-and-death experience behind them, it was back to business with their next challenge. Bondi's young beach girls were plentiful and the boys had just acquired hero status for the day and were keen to cash in. They were in no hurry to go anywhere in particular, except home with a fair maiden.

The surf was now so big it was unrideable. The wind had turned onshore from the south and it was hard to distinguish a decent wave in the white-capped soup. Just as quickly as the scene had appeared, it disappeared. A few bodies were left on the Hill, like always, but mostly everyone went their separate ways.

"Well. S'pose it's time to head home, Porks," said Dan, as he pulled on his sweater. The southerly change had a bite to it. "And I've got twenty bucks to buy us a well-earned rock of hash for breakfast and there's cuppas and toast at my joint to help wash 'em down."

"Sounds too good to be true, mate. After my luck of breaking

17

my favourite Indo board, I'm ready for a whole hearted brekkie!"

They gathered their belongings, said their goodbyes and headed to Dan's place for a well-earned rest.

Sloth and Andy threw their boards in the back of their Holden Kingswood station wagon. A cream coloured, typical work truck with scattered trowels and plastering tools all over the place: a classic surfer's work truck, with Honey Wax and Tracks surf magazine stickers plastered on the back window and bumper bar. They jumped in the car and Sloth kicked it over after a couple of attempts. It backfired in fine style and the crew still left on the Hill laughed. The sun had warmed the inside of the car considerably, so he told Andy to wind down the passenger window and let some air in, because his driver-side handle had broken.

"See youse this arvo, lads!" he yelled out the window, as he waited for a pause in the traffic. Once available, he put the pedal down and screeched off to work.

Corro never made it back to the boys on the Hill, because an older groupie had kidnapped him in transit on the promenade. She had lured him into her car with the offer of a hot shower followed by free bongs and breakfast. With some booty on top, how could he refuse?

Cookie and Fitzy cruised by the Hill. They were both smiling after setting up "drinking dates" later that arvo at the Regis Hotel. They grabbed their stuff and headed home for a hot shower and a cuppa. They were taking their time and enjoying the moment. There was no rush for them to do anything, as they had no job to go to that day. Once back at Cookie's aunt's, they made toast and recalled the morning's events as they'd unfolded. They were happy they'd survived and were now soaking up the sun in the backyard.

The two enigmatic guys who should never have been out there in the first place went their way vanishing up Bondi Road and were never heard of again.

As usual, it was the start of another day in Bondi!

East meets West

It was another bleak winter's afternoon. Dan and the boys were hanging at South Bondi on the Hill watching the onshore, messy surf. Thick, grey rain clouds were quickly moving in from the south-east and the boys could see that it wouldn't be long till they copped a drenching. The surf was mostly closing out and the steel-blue water looked cold. The weather was becoming wilder by the minute, as the wind howled and whined over the sand and up the parkland. The foreshore was desolate and the wind blew anything away that wasn't anchored or tied down. A couple of young lifeguards, under Laurie's instruction, ran down from their tower to close the beach by crossing the fluttering red and yellow beach flags. The tops of pine trees lining Campbell Parade were bending in the gale. Snapped branches and pine cones were sailing through the air and blowing onto the adjacent road. The ocean was starting to look like a washing machine with the increasing swell and lower tide. Some of the crew scattered as the rain closed in over the bay, blanketing the headlands. Campbell Parade was nearly empty except for some hurried pedestrians running to take cover. No-one was outside sipping lattes.

"If we don't split quick we're fucked!" said Porky. "What are we doing?"

"The footy's on soon. How 'bout we go to Ken-san's? I heard he's got some killer weed ..." Dan didn't have to do much convincing. The remainder of the boys looked at each other, raising their eyebrows, as if Dan's words were spot on—the scent trail ultimately leading to a warm lounge room, footy on the box and a bowl full of mix.

"Fuck, yeah! Let's go and smoke with our little Jap mate before we get soaked!" yelled a jovial Fitz. It didn't take much to get him excited. Eating regular sheets of acid every couple of years had kept him on knife's edge.

"Who's playing anyway?" asked Alex. Alex was Dan's thick-headed cousin who lived at Maroubra. He had a goofy face, a big, dented nose and an unwavering mouth that sat comfortably, stoutly, below his brown, misleading puppy-dog eyes. He enjoyed mixing with Dan's mates and used to play Rugby League against some of them. Whenever his team—the Wombats—ran onto the park against Bondi United, he had extra incentive to prove his merit. From the sidelines of Waverley Oval, the Bondi boys watched on, as Alex displayed his passion for tackling hard. He loved how physical the game was and he always managed to involve himself once a bit of biff started. Unfortunately, his A-League football career ended abruptly, when he started a brawl at Coogee Oval against the Paddo Colts. During the melee, he received a ban for life, after hitting the ref "... accidentally, of course!", explained the big fellow. Fighting was in his genes as his dad had been an above-average boxer. From a young age, Alex had sweated it out at the Woolloomooloo Police Boys' boxing ring and Ern McQuillan's gym at Newtown. Twice a week, he would go to training and occasionally he'd drag Dan along with him. However, Dan soon lost interest in accompanying him, preferring to train with other crew, after Alex kept pummelling him. Alex's height and reach advantage made certain he was regularly smashing Dan in the face. It wasn't anything personal. Alex just enjoyed punching anyone in the head. Alex was a formidable figure standing about 6-feet tall. His neck was thick and sat on muscular shoulders. He had a wide, pigeon chest, which stopped his large shoulders hunching over his body. Occasionally, to his mum's disgust, he would sport a Mohawk, exposing his rough-dented melon. He had numerous bumps and scars from all the hits he had taken over the years. His mum always preferred that he wear his light brown mop of hair over his earlobes, as it stopped them from getting sunburnt at the beach. He had "Fuck you" tattooed on his right shoulder, but he wasn't a big ink fan. "Fuck you" was his only tattoo and summed up, pretty much, where Alex was coming from.

Throughout the ages, both Maroubra and Bondi surfers had always got on well. There was a mutual respect. Growing up in the same environment meant they had a lot in common. Inner-city beaches were frequented by many shady and colourful travellers. These beaches were easily accessible for people visiting the city and fallout from Kings Cross and Surry Hills often graced their white sands. Skulduggery was common, so Southside surfers had to be apt and on their toes. Dealing and rorting, rapes and murders, cops and robbers, were all part of the city beach lifestyle. It took a lot to shock these surfers. They were a different breed to their Northern Beaches' counterparts. The Harbour Bridge, and the miles of road in between, protected northside beaches from a lot of city heat. Bondi had once been labelled, by the surfing fraternity, as "Scum Valley" and part of

Maroubra Beach was called "the Dunny Bowl" and these names had stuck. Southside beaches were sewage-infested, rundown and patronised by lowlifes. But that gave the place its spice. It was an area where street credibility went a long way. Shabby apartments were aplenty. Bondi's beachfront was comprised mainly of dark, red brick multistorey facades built in the 1920s, 30s and 40s. These old buildings dominated the landscape along Campbell Parade, their first-floor, steel-corrugated awnings protecting pedestrians and ground level shop-fronts from the harsher elements. Inside these buildings were dilapidated dormitories or units serviced by ancient plumbing, faulty electrical work, rising damp, leaking roofs and rattling window frames. Upon entering the ground floors of these buildings, extravagant floral carpets ran the length of hallways connected to terrazzo steps lined with marble coping. These musty hallways received little sunlight and were always dark and dingy. Once upstairs and inside your apartment, natural light filtered its way through either the beachfront windows or the back door, which led to the fire stairs. There was little backyard to enjoy and what there was to enjoy was dwarfed by more towering red brick walls from adjoining buildings. In these oceanfront buildings, unemployed locals maintained their sanity by watching the world pass by their front windows. These windows provided an omni-present vantage point, where you could sit and be entertained by the whole beach scene. It was also a great spot to check the surf from. Neglected welfare had a place and a right to be there. Vagabonds, villains and heroes all walked shoulder to shoulder on the same streets.

"I think Manly and the Roosters are playing at Brookvale," replied Dan. "Should be a good one!"

"Ripper! Go the Roosters!" Fitz yelled. He was an Eastern Suburbs Roosters supporter through and through. As a teenager he was a formidable halfback and probably would have played football professionally, but his first acid episode steered him in another direction.

The rain had engulfed the Icebergs Club and was now steadily moving up the hill towards them. Heavy raindrops splattered any bald dirt patches that the council sprinklers hadn't reached.

"We're outta here!" yelled Porky.

The lads hurried across Campbell Parade, dodging in and out of cars. As they safely arrived at Ken-san's glass-plated security door, a loud thunder clap echoed across the beach. Ken-san had become a certified Japanese local, who had arrived in Oz several years before, hoping there was more to life than a chopstick-minded culture. In visiting Bondi and meeting the boys, he soon decided to stay and assume his destiny. Australia had everything to offer. A $10,000 fake marriage, citizenship, some fair-dinkum mates, consistent surf, social security, sausage sangas with sauce and, last but not least, he'd stumbled across the Aussie ritual of bearing the bong. What a rush for the boy from Osaka! He was riding high on his new Aussie identity and fitted in like he was true blue. The boys believed he was really an Australian trapped in a Jap's body. Such was his inclination towards his newfound culture that he became a better scammer than half the beach. For that kinda shit, he was accepted and held in high regard.

Ken-san lived opposite the Hill, in an old 1930s block on the second floor. The tiled entranceway sat between Fat Mamma's Deli and the bakery and was pretty decrepit. Despite its lack of care, the building had an intercom installed during the Hotel Astra days, so late-night pissed idiots couldn't crash out or urinate in the corridor leading up to the stairs. Dan pressed Kenny's buzzer.

"Harro?" was the reply from the Japanese man, his face crumpling up in curiosity around his slanty eyes.

"Yeah, Kenny. It's me and the boys. We wanna watch the footy with ya." Dan's authorative tone of voice was telling him rather than asking.

"Ohh, ya? Who wit chu?" Ken-san was battle worn and weary from previous experiences.

Dan knew not to mention his cousin, as Alex wasn't popular with Kenny. "Me, Porky and Fitz, bruddas."

"OK." Pressing the buzzer, he told them to "come up".

As they entered the beachfront building, the rain started to bucket down. The door closed behind them as the rainwater washed down chip cartons, ciggy butts and anything else that stood in the torrent's way. The gutter trash manoeuvred itself around car tyres and increased in speed as it neared the storm drain. The heavens had just made the street sweeper's job a lot easier.

As the boys approached the stairs, the pouring rain was so loud, they could hear it cascading on the second-floor roof. There was a large hole in the guttering and a water fountain was spouting against the back of the building as it cascaded to the concrete below.

"Sounds like Niagara!"

"The storm water's goin' to change the banks ..." a surf minded Porky commented. Whenever there was a torrential downpour, the storm water drain deposited large volumes of water into the surf. Usually, this produced better sandbanks, which in turn spelt better shaped waves. "It's going to be gushing out that fucking stink hole!"

"Should rip a channel through that fucked closeout bank at second."

"Second" was short for "second ramp". Second ramp had the privilege to be positioned beside the beach's stormwater drain, halfway between the southern corner and the middle of the beach. The opening was legendary with local surfers, as it provided a river-like set up. Every time the rains came down, the stinky pipe would start churning out its polluted water across the sand and down to the water's edge. Heading out to sea, the current would form a rip, which would erode closeout sandbanks, changing their dynamics for the better. Everything that washed down from the street was ejected through pipes that were big enough to walk inside if you dared. In times of no rain, the river settled and formed a lake on the sand bed between the promenade and the shoreline. As days passed and the sun shone, it became septic and sometimes little kids would play in and around it, unaware of the many diseases on offer. It might have been a toxic eyesore for international visitors, but for local surfers, its purpose was important. Over the years, the stormwater pipe had become an integral part of the Bondi surfing environment. It helped produce some of the best right-hand barrels ever seen at Bondi. In the mid 80s, a local Gothic artist named "Droogie" graffitied the pipe to outline its prominence. As a mark of respect to local surfers, he sprayed the legendary Tracks magazine cartoon figure of Captain Goodvibes on the boardwalk wall, incorporating the stormwater drains into the iconic character's snout.

The boys commenced climbing the stairs and Fitzy couldn't help but mention that an old girlfriend lived on the same floor as Kenny.

"You still fucked up about her?" Porks could smell a chink in Fitzy's armour.

"As if. Ya faggot. It was her loss!" retorted Fitz, as another thunder clap exploded so loudly it echoed throughout the enclosed grey stairwell.

"I heard she burnt you good, Romeo," heckled Porky. "Heard you were stirrin' some guy's porridge for a month before you found out."

"Yeah, she loved a bit of Uncle Toby's." Fitz was well drilled when it came to women. His blond curls and tight physique had charmed many. He knew the score, even if this one still tugged a little on his heart strings. You win some, you lose some.

"You see, I'm lucky, Fitz, because a fat cunt like me doesn't get much action and when I do it's usually an ugly, fat bushy anyway, so I don't have to deal with that lovey-dovey kinda shit anyway."

"Yeah, well, that's right, you don't have a clue, ya fat shit, because the only two relationships you have to deal with is the one with your hand and the other with either a gooey fucken' Mars Bar or a greasy packet of chips." Fitz turned his head and grinned at Porks, who was using the dark wooden handrail to lessen his fat load on his feet. "That chick's ancient history, Porks. Had her chance and blew it!"

Dan knew Fitz's ex-girl all too well. She was hot and often horny. Unbeknown to Fitz, she had recently seduced Dan for a threesome with her flatmate after a party at the Icebergs. "You can take the girl out of the cheap underwear, but you can't take the cheap underwear out of the girl." Dan wasn't going to say anymore.

Fitz smiled, "I'd like to sniff her panties again sometime."

"What?"

"Well, I mean, if she'd be up for it."

As they reached the second floor landing, Ken-san half-opened his door and peered out. Another loud clap of thunder rang through the stairwell and the boys were happy to be in from the cold.

"Sounds like we just made it, Kenny!"

"Fucken' rucky Dan, gonna piss down. How you guys? Today you surping?" Ken-san stood 5'7" in his doorway smiling at the boys with a mouthful of fucked-up teeth. He had learnt a lot from his Aussie mates and loved being a surf bum in Oz. It was something he could never be back home where work ethic was what your life and reputation depended on. His flat was his sanctum for his two main passions: going surfing and getting high. Living in close proximity to the beach meant he could don his wetsuit, wax up and smoke himself silly before venturing down to the surf. By emulating his Bondi surfing buddies, he had perfected the art of being a dole bludging, drug taking high priest. All over the white plastered walls of his lounge room were posters and cut-out photos from numerous surfing magazines. Add to that

24

a couple of High Times posters and his walls were suitably decorated for a hardcore surf flat.

"Nah, Kenny, haven't gone for a surf today. Surf's too onshore and I was too hungover anyway," replied Dan. "Swell's coming up though and might be good tomorrow if it turns offshore."

Kenny stood aside from his doorway, which opened into his lounge room, and ushered the boys inside. Rain was pelting against the windows, which were quite large, extending along almost the whole side of the building. They brightened up the place considerably, as it was a back unit with no direct sunlight.

"I surfed early and the waves were sick! There was no wind before the southerly blew up and only a couple of guys out! I was wondering where you blokes were ... suppose you had to get your beauty sleeps in."

Porks put his hand on Ken's shoulder and looked him in the eye, as if he had something important to say. "No partying for me, mate—when I know the surf's gonna be good in the morning!"

Kenny nodded in agreement. "Who wants to go out on a Saturday night anyway? Too many fuckwits out on the piss, all chasing and hassling each other for the same pussy."

"What, Porks? The pussy that you get naught from?"

"No, Fitz. Pork's bery smart ..." interrupted Kenny. He turned to Fitz, who was making himself comfy on a black leather bean-bag. "When surp gud better stay home, not go out. You alway bery smart, Porky."

Porks and Ken-san had become good mates since Kenny's arrival a few years earlier. The previous year had brought them even closer, when it was Porky's cousin that Kenny married to stay in the country. Anything to avoid being sent home to a country with fuck-all dope and very limited surf.

"I know, Ken-san, I can be very smart when I want," replied Porky.

"Then why you not ruse more weight?" joked Kenny boy, as he sneered slyly and patted Porky's round gut. "You more fat dan Buddha."

Porky lunged at his Japanese in-law. "Fuck you, Ken-san, ya slanty eyed pillow biter!" In a friendly exchange, both mates started wrestling each other as family members do and it wasn't long till they were on the living room floor laughing.

Dan quickly interjected. "C'mon, guys, enough fuckin' around! Footy's gonna start and we don't wanna miss the kick-off."

Porky had Kenny pinned under his fat.

"Get off me!" yelled an exasperated Kenny. Porky slowly released his grip and they stood up, silently eyeing each other as though both still thought the other might try and get in one last surprise attack.

"Tora tora tora! Sit down and shut up, Porks!" said Dan, who was already seated on Ken's beige leather lounge. He had found the TV's remote control under the wooden coffee table and was in the process of changing over to Channel 9, when Alex nonchalantly appeared from around the stairwell corner, slipped through the open doorway and into Kenny's sight. "What he doing 'ere?" asked a surprised Kenny.

"It's alright, Kenny. He's not goin' to cause any trouble," said Dan.

"Buushitt. He alway cause fuckin' shit, mate!" Kenny gave Alex an evil samurai stare. They had never really got on. There was a slight pause as Ken-san took centre stage. The boys liked him but they all thought he was a little crazy.

"Don't start shit 'ere, mate. OK?" said Kenny, as he reluctantly let Alex remain inside.

"No worries, Kenny boy. I'll behave, mate." Alex paused for a second, looking towards Dan for support. It was not forthcoming, so he continued, "Promise, mate, scout's honour." Alex showed Kenny his palm, acknowledging the scout's sign for pledging allegiance. "I'll even put in for the mull." He was trying to be as unassuming as possible.

Kenny closed the door behind him.

Ken-san motioned with a wave of his hand for Alex to sit down. The room could seat half a dozen comfortably. Seating arrangements comprised a leather beige lounge backing onto the wall beneath the window, an additional chair that was part of the set, a well worn bean-bag and enough carpet to accommodate two more. Alex sat straight in the chair that conspicuously displayed the rising sun flag on the headrest. "Not dere, iriot." Kenny was locking horns again with Alex. "Dat's my spot!" Alex somehow knew it was Kenny's chair, but that's the kind of reason why they never got on.

"Sorry, Ken. I didn't realise you were sitting there." It was obvious it was Kenny's proud seat. Central to the mull bowl on the coffee table, it was the best seat in the house, with a Japanese flag acting like a coat of arms on top of it. Flanked by the bean-bag and well-worn lounge, it was a place where he could easily monitor his guests' assembly.

Kenny was in no mood to deal with the Maroubra menace. Alex quickly moved his butt onto the floor and in doing so accidentally knocked over the bong, which had been hidden by one of the thick pine legs of the coffee table. Some of it spilt on Pork's black tracksuit pants, but the majority managed to empty over the fluffy carpet.

"Now you've done it. Look what you've done, you imbecile!" Porks wanted to make sure he wasn't blamed for the misdemeanour. Alex jumped up immediately, regretting his mistake.

"Dat's it!" Kenny yelled stressing. "Getta fuck outta here, mate!" His blood level immediately rose to boiling. It was difficult for him to say "fuck" so quickly, so he had sprayed dribble and thick phlegm in trying.

"C'mon, Kenny, Alex is cool!" interjected Dan. Dan jumped between the pair to maintain order. He would usually bag his cousin for such a fuck-up, but this instance needed some diplomacy. "It was an accident, mate. He couldn't see the bong because it was behind the leg of the table." Ken-san started taking short deep breaths. "Truly, Kenny. He didn't mean it. The table was in the way."

"He fuckin' have no respect," said Kenny, as he wiped his mucus off his mouth and chin. "Last time, he piss in da kitchen sink, mate. No fucking good, mate!"

"I'm truly sorry, Kenny boy. I'm sorry!" appealed Alex, as he immediately fetched a rag in the kitchen to clean up the bong spill before it started stinking.

"Always twouble," said Kenny, as bong-spill stench started to waft from the stain. Alex rinsed the kitchen wetex adding some detergent to help disguise the smell. "Don't you piss in dere, now!"

"Calm down, Kenny," said Fitz. "Let's all just watch some footy. C'mon, mate, it's those fuckin' shitty Eagles against the mighty Roosters." He paused for a second and winked at Kenny. "Jesus, anyone would think you guys fought against each other in the war."

"Yeah, guys, let's just watch some football," added Dan. "Hey?" he raised his voice as if to get everyone's attention. "Let's just sit down and have a few billies, OK? Kenny, is that alright?" It was attention Kenny acknowledged. "C'mon, mate, the footy's about to start."

"Okay, but no twouble from him." Ken-san's lip had managed

27

to stop quivering.

"Of course not, mate. We all go for the Roosters, right? So we're all going to watch them win today, right, Kenny?" Dan had an uncanny knack of cooling down heated confrontations. Doing time on the private school debating team served him well on the street, where a quick-witted tongue kept him out of a lot of trouble.

The clean up was a combined effort. As Alex cleaned the stained blue shaggy carpet, Fitz sprayed the patch with some sweet smelling deodorant that he'd grabbed from the bathroom and Porks cleaned the bong filling it with fresh cold tap water. The kitchen adjoined the lounge room and a small hallway led to the bathroom and bedroom. The same lounge room window ran along the entire kitchen bench and Porks smiled at a neighbour staring through the outside downpour from an opposing block of flats. The unit facing him was built layer upon layer of red brick. It had turned a darker shade from being saturated by the swirling rain squalls hurling through the shaft-like space between both buildings.

Porks filled the bong with clean water and then wiped the glass chamber with a tea towel, "Keeps raining like this and they might call the game off."

Everyone sat down and Ken-san turned the channel over to the footy. It had just started and the score was nil-all.

"Did you have that bet with Trotter?" Porky asked Dan.

"Yeah, I've got twenty on it." Trotter was a true blue Bondi lad, except he barracked for the maroon and white.

"Doesn't batting for the other side mean you must be gay? So someone told me anyway." Trotter was an open target and Fitz was just putting his two bob in.

"That rhymes, you must be a poet." said Alex.

"Yes, a gay poet! How commendable!" added Dan.

"Shut the fuck up!" retorted Fitz.

"Wish I had twenty on with the gaylord—candy from a baby," said a confident Porky.

"Who's got some durrie for the mix?" said Fitz. "I can see Kenny's only got those filthy Indo cigarettes."

"Yeah, I got no pwoper ones." Kenny was inclined to puff on the odd fag, but he preferred the clove cigarettes from Asia which weren't compatible to mixing with weed.

"I got one," remarked Alex, as he reached inside his coat and grabbed a ciggy out of its packet. He threw it over on the table in front of Kenny. Ken-san didn't look up, as if to imply that Alex would have to do a lot more to impress him.

"Not too much baccy now, Kenny," said Dan. Unlike the rest of the room, Dan didn't smoke tailored cigarettes and hated them with a passion. He loved his bongs, but with only a small amount of tobacco. This way the weed would be the dominant taste and he could deal with it. He would near puke if he was ever to smoke a real cigarette.

The wind blew against the windows and made a whirring noise as it found miniature gaps in the framework. The torrential rain splashed against the window panes as if someone was throwing a bucket of water over them. It was a deluge.

Ken-san did a good job mulling up and Dan smiled to acknowledge his approval. The game had got under way in appalling conditions, so the action was slow and clumsy. Each side had already dropped the ball in the first five minutes. Kenny packed his cone till it was overflowing and like a real trouper lunged it as hard as he could. He put down the bong on the table in front of him and leaned back snuggling into his chair. In the mulling etiquette rule book, Porky was next to pack a cone as he had cleaned the bong.

"I love it when it storms like this," said Dan. He remembered back to when he was a kid and the security of his family's home on a cold, dark, stormy night. He stared out the window for a second, his mind lost in childhood memories. Cartoons, home cooked dinners, daydreams, innocence and order.

"Get fucked!" bellowed Alex. "Did you see that bullshit?"

"What's up, Alex? I wasn't watching ..."

"You missed it, Dan. The ref fuckin' didn't see Manly knock-on and now they're in our 20!" Alex was starting to sound edgy, like any footy head does when the opposition gets near their line.

"And they've got a heapa tackles up their fuckin' sleeves." Fitzy was also sounding nervous. "Shit!"

Alex had lit up a ciggy and blew a big cloud of smoke out of his tar-soaked lungs in front of the TV. The smoke was so thick it partially obscured the screen.

"Dumbshit! That was smart, ya moron. Use a fog machine next time." Alex just smiled at Porky's ridicule.

"Iriot." Ken-san knew all too well.

Alex started apologising only to Ken-san, as Porks slightly startled him by yelling, "Oh no! Shit, are they fuckin' in?" He looked at everyone in the room and for a split second, no one uttered a sound. It was like they were all in disbelief.

"What? Manly scored?" asked a cringing Dan. "Will you guys stop fucking around? I missed that!"

"No way. Where's the replay?"

Manly had their star five-eight charge onto the ball only 10 metres out from the try line and the ref was trying to see, under the pile of bodies, whether he had got it down over the line. They watched eagerly as the ref seemed to take eternity to reach his decision. The man in the middle conferred with his touch judges. The replay was inconclusive. It took a while but he finally awarded the try.

"Buushit!!" screamed Kenny, with the boys in chorus behind him.

"Fuckin' rip off! How did he miss that blatant knock-on back on half-way?" argued Porky. "Gees, Horrie looks ropeable. Bet he gets up 'em behind the sticks."

"So he should, Porks. That defence was wearin' frocks." Fitz was by no means impressed. "Hurry up, someone, and pack me one!" he paused then thought he'd receive a better response if he used some manners. "Please. I fuckin' need it after that!"

"Hurry up and finish smokin' your bong," said Dan to Porks. "We all need one after that!"

"Yeah, OK, don't get your knickers in a knot," he quipped. He promptly lit his bong and pulled it. He gestured, "Here you go— take the thing off me", with a bob of his head as he exhaled. The bong was a classic "Agung" glass beauty. It was sometimes hard to inhale all of the smoke, because the chamber was a foot and a half long. The stem was aluminium, sealed air tight at its point of entry into the glass shaft by a rubber seal. The cone did the bong justice, being a thick brass piece of work, commonly called a party cone, because of its larger size.

The footy continued and the room remained rowdy. Ken-san had become more relaxed and his guests enjoyed smoking his weed. The bong did a couple of rounds till the mull bowl was empty. It wasn't long till the room's searching eyes started glancing at the bowl. Porky lit up a ciggy and Dan broke the desperate silence to organise a cash donation for weed. Ten dollars from Alex and ten dollars from his own pocket had Kenny cheerfully weighing up a generous gram for them. Chucking their purchase into the bowl, Dan soon chopped it up and had things in swing again. After pulling the first bong, he offered the next to Kenny, to which the smiling Jap cheerfully obliged. It had now become a serious smoke fest.

"Shit, man, Gilly's been knocked out." The boys watched on as one of their Rooster mates lay motionless on the paddock.

"Fuck, hope he's OK."

"Looks like he's got claret all over his face and they're calling for a stretcher."

"Looks nasty."

"As the injured player is assisted from the field, we hope it's nothing too serious," said Rex the TV commentator.

"Yeah, looks like he's got a gash on his forehead and the poor bloke's in gaga land," commented his offsider.

"Lucky the bloke got married last week, because it's looking fairly ugly at the moment," quipped Rex. Being an avid Manly supporter, he couldn't help but throw that in. His game call was generally fair, unless his beloved Sea Eagles were playing.

As the half-time siren sounded, they were all well and truly stoned. The storm had subsided a little, though cracks of distant thunder and flashes of lightning were still occasional. Unfortunately, the Roosters couldn't get over the line during the first half, so the score was still six-nil.

"Well, that ref has to be dropped next week," implored Fitz. "Just too many mistakes." There was no way any of the boys were blaming their team for being behind on the scoreboard.

"Where the fuck did he get his badge?" asked Porky. "In a Cornflakes packet?" It was an old joke, but appropriate.

The intercom next to the door buzzed loudly. A very stoned squinting Kenny dragged himself out of his throne to answer it. "Who dat?" he drooled.

"Me, Kenny—Brendan."

"Oh OK, come up," he said, as he cleared his throat. He sounded and looked as if he were on heroin. His slanty slits resembled Keith Richards or Kurt Cobain on a bad day. He pressed the buzzer and left the door slightly ajar for Brendan to enter without knocking.

The room was in half-time mode and the boys made the most of it, by using the bathroom and making cuppas. "Can I pack meself another?" asked Porks.

"Ya." There was a slight pause, as if Kenny was reassessing his answer. "Pack me first."

"No worries, Kenny boy!" Porks thumbed a cone for his earnest, Asian, bong-pulling mate. As Kenny inhaled, the door opened and a wet, barefoot Brendan entered the smoke-filled room. He probably would have been totally drenched except for a waterproof hooded jacket he was wearing.

"Hi, guys," he said as he greeted the room by nodding at each of his stoned friends. "Not baggin' youse or nuthin', but you can smell that shit downstairs." He paused for a second and examined the bodies lounged around in their zombie state. "Fuck, I'm stoned already and I just walked in." The boys all acknowledged him without a word passing their lips. He continued wondering what he had to say to get a response, "Fuckin' been rainin' cats and dogs out there." He sat down on the floor next to Alex who was sipping his cuppa. The hood of the jacket was still covering his head and he resembled a Gothic abbot.

"You look like Jesus of Nazareth walkin' in here barefoot with that thing on yer fuckin' head," commented Alex.

"Having no shoes seems a blessing when meeting a bloke with no feet!" Brendan was quick. He had a tongue as sharp as a steak knife.

"Hang jacket up, pwease, Brendan."

"No worries, Kenny. He who hangs jacket is well-hung," said his ever polite red-freckled friend. "I'll just put it in the bathroom for ya." He headed past the kitchen and went into the loo, hanging the coat over the shower curtain railing. Being waterproof, it was still nice and dry inside. However, the exterior droplets, thanks to gravity, started dripping into the bath. Just to speed things up he gave it a couple of whacks with the coat hanger, which would normally be used to hang up Kenny's wet steamer. Brendan was now sporting his blue checkered flanno from Woolworths— $12.95's worth of wholesome warmth. It was only wet around the bottom edges, from a brief exposure to the elements, when he bent over to pick up a soaked five dollar note on the pavement.

As he joined his lively bunch of mates in the lounge room, the half-time commercials were on. He knew the zombie room would be watching the game, but as a mere formality, he asked, "You guys watching the Roosters?"

"Fuckin' Sea Eagles are leading six-nil."

"What, Porks?" Brendan had heard right, but this question was one of denial.

"Fucken ref's on their side," commented Fitz.

"He missed heaps of Manly's fuck-ups," joined Alex.

"That'd be right. Ah well, bet Trotter'd be happy." Brendan knew their mate Trotter was a die-hard Eagles fan. Why? No-one knew the reason. Perhaps, it was the rebel within fed-up by being surrounded by so many Rooster supporters, or maybe he was a closet.

"Yeah, he'd love to be here to rub it in," said Dan. "He's probably at home rootin' his seagull doll and wearing his Manly jersey that Bobby Fulton signed."

"With Ray Brannigan's undies on his head ..."

"And with a big grin on his face, 'cause Dan bet him twenty on the game," Fitz added.

"It's only half-time guys, as if we aren't gonna come back."

"Fuck yeah, Porks. We'll stick it up 'em in the second half!" bellowed Brendan. Brendan loved the Roosters as much as everyone else in the room. He was a Bondi boy through and through. His step-dad used to be the head of the Bondi coppers and he had lived with his family at North Bondi all his life. Like Dan, he had been blooded on a coolite in front of the surf club at North and progressed onto a fibreglass around the age of 11. The beach was an escape from a big dad with a heavy hand. He ripped in the surf and was as hardcore as they come. Being blessed with red hair and freckles, this 'Bluey' was streetwise and a straight shooter. No-one could get away with any shit when Brendan was around. The girls loved him for it and what he was lacking in looks he made up for with unorthodox charisma and blunt charm.

"C'mon, Captain Horrie. Get the boys revved up!" shouted Fitzy as the second half kicked off.

"Hit 'em!" cried Brendan.

The boys watched the second half unfold. Again, there was a lot of dropped ball because of the wet conditions. The sloppy play had the boys cringing in their mull bowl. It was exasperating football to watch and many chances went begging. Both teams made hard work of scoring, until a magic ball by the Roosters' second rower, "Fletch", put the fullback over under the goalposts. The room exploded in jubilation.

"About fuckin' time!" yelled Dan. "C'mon, Easts!"

"You fuckin' beaudy." Ken-san cheered and packed himself another bong in celebration.

"Can I get some on ticker, Kenny?" asked Brendan.

"What about the tenner you owe me?" Porks was broke and had lent Brendan ten bucks the week before.

"I told ya I'd fix ya on me dole day, so stop fuckin' hasslin' me," was Brendan's swift reply. Brendan's philosophy was simple: he'd rather be retired and hanging on the beach from the age of 20 to 40 rather than from 60 to 80—although, he was definitely keen to have a go at being a pensioner all his life. He didn't want to miss enjoying his younger years and believed in the

Buddhist art of amusing yourself with little. He could be called a modern day Dharma bum, complete with his own metaphysical ashram inside his head. He hated conformity and only needed the bare essentials to get him through life. His prized possessions could be classified as a surfboard and a backpack with a toothbrush (that he only used once every two days because he claimed brushing once a day eroded your enamel), a six pack of beer, preferably VB, can of baked beans, jar of Vegemite, a good book on metaphysics (preferably Aldous Huxley, George Orwell, Timothy Leary or Alan Watts), a packet of tailor-mades, a cake of wax and a couple of tabs of acid could be counted as his only real needs. He felt sympathy for those trapped working for some fat prick who didn't even know what a good barrel felt like. He knew that certain people were always destined to live and work, most of their lives, to the beat of business. He could never comprehend being choked up in a high-rise office in the middle of William Street. He was a free wheeler—a gypsy, but well grounded. He travelled the coast a lot and connected well with the north-coast folk. His daily grind centred on having loads of fun as cheaply as possible, a distant cry from those holed up in a tall slab of concrete, making coffee and making someone else shitloads of money. Brendan had done his schooling at Dover Heights Public. He was knowledgeable and knew that the world would be a boring place if everyone was the same. He was an enlightened human being, though most Westerners saw him as a degenerate. It was obvious from the merry twinkle in his eyes that he was closer to the truth than most folk. From an early age, Brendan was passionate about life: life without work.

Being from the East, Kenny related easily to Brendan's simple way of life. It was like an East meets West kind of thing and there would be no problem giving him some credit. "How much you want?" asked Kenny.

"Just a twenty please, Ken-san."

"No worries, Bwendan." Kenny got up and went to the kitchen to grab some foil. The Roosters had kicked the goal to make the score level: so the room wasn't as tense. The storm had eased, though the wind had increased and grey clouds were now scudding overhead. As Kenny made up a deal for Brendan, a yelling match between two females became loudly audible through the front door. The neighbours had made their way out their front door and onto the floor's landing, their angry exchange echoing throughout the stairwell. It was such a catfight that it became a distraction from the TV and captured the room's attention.

"That's those fuckin' freaks from next door!" commented Porks.

"They aren't freaks, Porks," Fitz paused, "They're fashion designers," his tone impersonating a snobby bitch.

"Bloody good looking ones if I do say." Dan and the boys agreed that good looking eye candy was the only thing worthwhile that had accompanied the new cosmo scene to the area.

"Don't sound too beautiful at the moment," was all Brendan had to say as he sniggered at their slanging match.

"Yeah, well, it sounds like a lesbian tiff to me."

"As if, Fitzy. If they were real lesos, they woulda thrown each other down the stairs by now," said Dan.

"If one of them got thrown down the stairs, it'd snap 'em!" said Alex.

"Wouldn't mind snappin' one of 'em ... Kama Sutra style, that is," said Fitz with a cheeky grin.

"Fuckin' yeah," swore Alex. "Her karma can eat my hot dogma with mustard."

"And onions," joined Porks.

"Hey, Fitz, you know me uncle Rob, aye?" Dan's uncle won a World Junior title in the 60s and was a source of information when it came to Bondi's surfing history.

"Yeah ... what about him?"

"Me uncle used to tell me about these heavy fights between the surfie chicks and the rocker chicks. They used to hang at different milk bars in Roscoe Street during the 60s. A 'rockers' milk bar and a 'surfie' one. Anyway, he told me that the chicks used ta blue better than the blokes."

"Weary?"

"Yes, really, Kenny boy ... and he told me about a biker mole named Vickie, who was supposed to be the grouse."

"I heard a story about her. Even the blokes were scared of her."

"Darn right they were, Porks! Then there was this blonde surfie chick named Barbie. Both of them had a fight for half an hour in Roscoe Street, right near me uncle's original surf shop, right near where the old Kings Picture Theatre was. Anyway, they were into one another, ripping out hair and punching into each other until the blonde chick got Vickie in a headlock and rammed her into a telegraph pole and knocked her straight out. Then Barbie had the rep and everyone didn't bother fucking with her again!"

"Well, fuck me." Alex was impressed.

"Fuck them wingeing, blow-in, yuppies from next door," shouted Porks. "Wish Barbie was 'ere to tell 'em to shut-up, so we can watch the second half!"

"Who cares? Let them pull each other's hair out," gagged Dan.

Kenny agreed with Dan and insisted the boys ignore the fracas and watch the game. The argument was obviously an everyday occurrence, as far as he was concerned. "All da time, mate," was all the light he was willing to shed on it.

The catfight soon stopped and the game continued. Each of the boys verbally put in 110%, urging the Roosters to glory.

"Smash him!" and "Rip his head off!" were indicative of the language used, to encourage their team in defence.

During offence, the language was more like: "Pass the ball, you stupid spastic!" or "How could they drop the ball with the try line wide open?" It just didn't seem like it was going to be the Roosters' day. The wet conditions were playing havoc with any efforts to go forward. The occupants of the room probably would have been satisfied with a draw, considering the conditions and the constant pressure Manly was forcing upon their team.

The attack comprised of big forwards going forwards one off the ruck—pretty drab kind of stuff—until with only five minutes to go, the Sea Eagles put a string of passes together and their winger scored in the corner. The room sat in sombre disbelief.

Ken-san let out a tremendous roar, "Fuck dat!" Then, once again, buried his head into his mull bowl and lit another cone.

"Game's over," said Dan regrettably.

"How long to go?" asked a diehard Fitzy.

Pork was quick to answer. "About five. Gonna be a miracle to win from here."

"Not over, till the fat lady sings, mate." Brendan's Zen words were dismissed by the room's negativity. Everyone's hopes were fading fast.

"Well, if they can get outta this one, I'll shout a pizza with my winnings off Trotter." Dan had placed his customary twenty dollar bet with Trot the day before on the Hill. He had now, for some obscure stoned reason, committed himself to feeding the boys, if the Roosters could miraculously pull this one out of the bag. It was like he was trying to do a deal with God. Maybe God would let his team win in order for him to feed his mates. He knew there was something in the Bible about miracles, so he thought maybe he was half a chance. He then had an uncomfortable stoned flip-side thought about the wager. What if God wanted him to lose in order to feed Trotter and his little daughter? Surely, they were more important than his THC brain soaked mates. In his marijuana induced, spaced out mind, Dan now believed God would want Manly to win for the sake of Trotter's family.

"You're only saying that now, because you know we're not going to win," argued Fitzy.

"I could go some pizza." Pork's stomach was sending direct signals to his brain.

"Extra pepperoni," added Alex.

"Shut up, you guys!" Ken-san was keen to get on with watching the last dying minutes of the game. He clung on to a slight glimmer of Brendan's hope.

With the bog conditions, it wasn't surprising Manly's conversion kick was short of the goal posts. At 10–6, the game looked over. Kenny and Brendan's faith was hingeing on the seemingly impossible.

The clock ticked and the bong was flying around the room as though it was commiserating the loss already. You could also put it down to the stress of a nail-biting finish. The play was slow and in the torrential rain Manly had Easts pinned down in their 20. Things looked hopeless.

"Only a minute to go," said Fitz feeling like he was the bearer of bad news.

"We've got one more crack at 'em," shouted Porks.

"C'mon, Woosters!" yelled Kenny.

The game was down to its dying seconds. The Roosters were in their 20 and the only chance was to swing it wide. The room sat in silence as the ball started its way out the backline. The rain was now bucketing again. As Captain Horrie was passed the ball, his obvious option was to continue it wide. However, seeing inside support, out of the corner of his eye, his instinct was telling him something different. For most of the game, he had sensed someone on the inside of him and out of total frustration that player finally screamed: "All day!" at him. Horrie swivelled and changed direction, connecting with his inside man—his perfectly timed pass putting the junior player through a gap as big as Sydney Heads. It was on! The pint-sized speed machine was away. As the Rooster sped over halfway, with only the fullback to beat, the boys were well and truly out of their seats. Side-stepping the fullback, the kid put it down under the posts with 12 seconds left on the clock. The hero was new to the team. Only last year, he was playing in the local Jersey-Flegg competition. As his team mates made the long haul to congratulate him, the rain started to ease again, just like the tension in Ken-san's lounge room. The boys were in jubilation. As the extra two points were added you could hear the room's occupants hooting from North Bondi. There was a scene of post-victory celebrations, as the room danced with each other and sang praise for their local club. "Roosters, Roosters!" was sung in chorus as Ken-san packed cones at random for everyone.

As the pandemonium subsided, the boys caught Rex's last bit of commentary, which rang something like, "Oh Jesus ... That is so unbearingly gut-wrenching that I think I'll have to go home and beat my wife."

"Way to go, Rex!"

"Dan's shout for pizza!" yelled Porky, as he licked his lips.

The boys were all stoked. In their eyes, Dan had gambled on Trotter paying for their feed and pulled it off. Dan thanked God, as if his mass-feeding deal had just been honoured. The boys were thinking he had provided, but his head suddenly found itself in a moral dilemma. Wasn't it really God paying for the meal? Should he admit the deal to the boys? Not that it ever mattered to the boys who was going to pay, because a free feed to the boys was a free feed. For a split second, Dan felt he had deceived someone. He wanted to stop thinking shit, so he grabbed the bong off Ken-san and packed himself a motherfucker of a cone.

"Can we get a Supreme with extra pepperoni please, Dan?" Alex seemed slightly agitated but, for some obscure reason, was extra polite in trying to persuade his cousin.

"No fuckin' anchovies," yelled a cheerful Fitzy.

"Or Owives," said Ken-san.

Dan was lucky he had it covered until he collected the bet. As he wrenched his cone, every topping under the sun was getting thrown at him. "Yeah, yeah," he coughed, as he exhaled his oversized cone, adding: "We should get a large Coke, too."

His brain kept trying to complicate things and posed another offbeat question: "Why would God want to feed a bunch of yahoos before his mate's family anyway?" Dan again wondered whether he was in some kind of dilemma. He perished the thought and pointing to Alex said: "You can run downstairs and order it from Mario." Dan's words started echoing in Alex's ears. Alex hadn't told anyone, but he had dropped half a tab of acid just after half-time. He nodded at Dan and knew there was an adventure in store.

By the time the boys had decided on what pizza they wanted, Alex was really coming to life.

"You know what kind of pizza, Alex?" Dan asked as he slipped him the money.

Alex wasn't sure, so he said the first stupid thing which came to mind: "A pizza with heroin on it. Heh heh ..." Alex simply smiled, thinking he was funny. He had been tripping a million times before and took it all in his stride. He once swallowed five trips at once and wound up in Callan Park for a couple of months.

Porky joined the comedy: "Get 'em to throw a coupla eckys on as well, please, Alex."

"I need cigawette for mix," said Ken-san. "Alex wuns aweady pinish."

"I'm goin' ta bolt down and get some," said Brendan. "I'll give ya a couple outta mine." Brendan had a tab at the deli downstairs. It was a common practice amongst a lot of locals and small business. Most proprietors were witness to the boys growing up in the area, so most of the time they knew who to trust. The bill was usually sorted when dole day came around and the fortnightly payment cemented the credit relationship.

On that note, Brendan got up from the floor, did the top button of his flanno up and bailed out the door. He strolled down the stairs heading for the deli on the Campbell Parade front. The acid was starting to kick in for Alex, as he tried to follow Brendan down the stairwell.

"Don't be long, Alex!" was the last thing that echoed in his ears as he commenced his descent. He started seeing flashes in front of his eyes and kept tasting the strychnine. He could hear murmurs from behind doors. Even though tripping was a regular occurrence for Alex, he occasionally got rushes of paranoia. His mind started to focus on the trip unfolding. The terrazzo stairs commenced flickering, as if the quartz within had begun its own celestial dance. Some old, frail, retired dude briefly opened his door as Alex passed his landing. He took one look at Alex and closed his door. Alex had caught a quick glance and thought the bloke was someone who owed him money.

"Hey, fuck you, pal. Open ya door!" Alex was way off the mark. His mind had just broken free from its chains and was beginning to load and compile data in a very different way. He banged a couple of times at the veteran's door but became distracted by a loud crash in the street below. His curious mind followed the noise downstairs, out the security door and onto the footpath. The inclement weather had caused a bus to collide into a parked Ferrari. The owner came running out of the Lamrock Cafe, yelling obscenities in some Euro language. Brendan was watching from the deli's steps.

"Teach 'im for parking so close to the bus stop," he said to Alex.

Alex turned around with a big acid smile on his face. He was only in his mid twenties, but his go-hard attitude to life was already appearing on his face as small crow's feet were starting their path from the corners of his eyes.

"Silly wog," was all Alex could manage. Being a modern day experimentalist, Brendan was no stranger to the acid either and he started to detect that Alex wasn't quite himself.

"You OK, Alex?" Brendan knew Alex was fairly loose, but he was still one of the boys and caring about him was part of his duty. "Mario's is 'round the corner," Brendan added, to see if he was coherent. "I think the boys are hungry."

"Yeah, no worries, mate." Alex had managed to sound half together.

"The boys are hungry, mate," Brendan repeated as he watched Alex become drawn into the scene of the accident like an ant to honey. The little Aussie bus driver had veered to miss a Pommy backpacker and over-corrected slamming the bus into the rear of some Gucci-wearing wog's pride and joy. Heated words were being exchanged and Alex felt it was his patriotic obligation to step in and help the Aussie battler. Alex was now focused on the big wog raising his hands and screaming obscenities in the driver's face. Adorned with gold, the self-proclaimed Adonis never saw what was brewing on the footpath next to the deli. Another two of his mates marched over from the Lamrock Café as the early dinner crowd stared in curiosity. The trio were carrying on like good sorts yelling abuse at the cowering driver. Enraged by their behaviour, Alex's big frame walked slowly towards them unnoticed. Brendan clicked on what was going on and was content in watching it unfold. Another one of the boys, Jean-Pierre, was walking past and asked Brendan: "What's happening, bra?"

"Dan's meathead cousin from the 'Bra is about to entertain us. That's what's happening," explained Brendan.

The wogs were absorbed in their Ferrari-mourning ritual and didn't see Alex looming up behind them. In a sudden movement, Alex grabbed the biggest wog by his long Banderas' curls and flung him onto the road. Before anyone knew what was going on, Alex had punched him senseless.

"That was great!" Pierre said to Brendan.

The second and third about-to-be victims were caught off guard and were quite stunned at how quick and savage the attack on their friend had been. The short bus driver was a local named Brucey. He let out a "bravo", but Alex didn't need any cheer squad. A feeling of apprehension grew heavy on the two Ferrari boys. Alex was now staring at both of them. He took a deep breath and then hissed as he exhaled slowly. His body had become a fighting machine and he would soon be coming for them.

"Look how scared those fuckin' blow-ins are now!" commented Brendan. By now there was quite a scene watching the sequence of events. Traffic was starting to bank up behind the bus and some drivers were getting out of their cars to see what was going down. The pavement was filling up with onlookers passing by. Alex was oblivious to all of them. The café diners watched from their seats as Alex put the boot in one last time. The crack of Mr. Gucci's ribs was clearly heard by all.

"Go Alex!" yelled Pierre.

Brendan knew Alex had the fight covered, so all he did was watch. Pierre couldn't help himself. "I'm jumpin' in for some fuckin' fun." Pierre ran over to the Ferrari and started kicking in the passenger door. Alex was now running after the other two tough guys. They split up and Alex kept chasing the one who thought the brightly lit, newly opened, Lamrock Café looked a safe place to run. Maybe he thought his girlfriend might step in and save him.

Wrong! Alex was beyond reasoning and he now had a taste for blood. The poor bloke never had a chance. As the guy reached the café's steps, Alex grabbed him from behind and pulled him to the ground, where he gave him a beating he would never forget. Pierre had run across Campbell Parade after the other hero and caught up with him on the Hill. The guy pleaded, but there was no compassion. Pierre told him: "You cunts want to fuckin' come round 'ere causin' trouble!" Pierre was a prolific steroid-taking bouncer who loved a fight. The wog was in total terror and had every reason to be. Brendan could hear Pierre from across the road punching portholes into him. With one last punch to the guy's already disfigured face, Pierre issued a brutal warning: "And don'cha ever fuckin' come back 'ere again!" He looked over the street and, through the drizzle, saw Alex throw the other dude through the glass doors of the café. The shattered glass decorated most of the diners inside. One lucky table had been served an Italian dish.

The sirens were finally audible. The police, as usual, were going to be too late. Alex smiled reassuringly at the café's terrified patrons, then heard Jean-Pierre running across the Parade yelling his name. "Alex! C'mon, brudda, let's get outta here. The cops are comin'." By now, Alex was really high from the acid and it was hard for him to grasp what exactly was happening. His instinct told him to run, but he was enjoying the terrified attention he was getting. As Pierre caught up to him, he led Alex down Lamrock Avenue and into Bondi's backstreets. They had avoided the heat for the moment. Jean-Pierre knew they should get out of the 'hood for a while, so he tried to clean themselves up a bit using someone's front garden hose and then hailed a cab. They got in and Johnny said to the driver: "Kings Cross, please, mate."

On the Run

The taxi driver was some wog who didn't speak much English. He had on a clean white shirt with a big gold chain hanging around his neck complementing his big gold earring. To the deranged passengers, who occupied the backseat, he was a goldmine ready to pillage. His black hair was slicked back, like an Italian Godfather. Like a suspension bridge between two pine forests, his facial hair was connected to the shag pile on his chest, by a stretch of thick, hairy carpet. He turned his head a couple of times to catch a quick glance of what he'd just picked up. Alex and Pierre were chuckling to themselves, occasionally bursting into laughter from the buzz you get from escaping the law.

The driving was erratic—foot on the gas, foot off the gas—an old trick to click over the meter more quickly. The boys were either oblivious to it or didn't care. A cop car sped past them in the opposite direction with its siren sounding and Alex watched in amusement as the lights flashed decorative patterns all over the darkened glass doors of the Hakoah Club. The taxi made its way up to the top of Glenayr Avenue and turned left onto Old South Head Road. As they headed through the lights at Penkivil Street, heading toward Bondi Junction, the mayhem they had caused was now way behind them.

Pierre knew Alex was dialling on some kind of substance, so he asked: "What you on, brudda?"

"Some orange juice me dad gave me," was his off-beat answer. It was so not funny and Pierre knew instantly poor Alex was lost in limbo. Pierre stared at his friend's comic expression. Alex's eyes were bulging and he was wearing a smile like a Cheshire Cat. Pierre was studying him and thought: "Maybe, being really bent was a better place for Alex after all." Embracing the moment of attention, Alex began sniggering; all the while keeping his smile intact, which now seemed to be driving his trip. His grin soon changed into a laugh, with its distinctly gawky tone instantly annoying the driver. Unfortunately for the driver, it was going to get a lot worse before it got any better. He peered into the mirror, observing his passengers. They were adrift and he knew they were trouble. He wanted to tell Alex to "shut the fuck up", but settled on stewing about it. The driver was a little indignant after getting mugged a week before by a couple of larrikins he thought looked just like them. As Alex reached new heights of manic laughter, a foam ball appeared from somewhere in the back of his throat and was calling for a quick exit. Alex was just doing what came naturally when he sprayed the back of the front seat with spit. The driver wasn't spared either with droplets reaching the back of his hairy neck. Upon witnessing his mate's effort, Pierre was in hysterics. Alex just kept on laughing and spraying anything in the back seat worthy of spraying.

"Hey, fuck! What you do, mate?" At first, the taxi driver thought it was something like a mist bottle or a water pistol. But, when he turned around and saw the foam protruding from the side of Alex's mouth, he clued straight on. Alex caught his glance and smiled at him like a lunatic. It was as if he was totally oblivious to the incident. His trip had taken on a loopy innocence.

The driver pulled over to the kerb and ordered the boys to get out. Both of them couldn't stop laughing. They didn't mean to show the cabbie any contempt, but that was exactly how he saw it.

"You dickheads, mate!" he screamed at them. He stuck his head between the headrests and yelled again: "Get out or I kills you!"

At that moment, Alex suddenly changed. It was as if the word "kill" activated a different computer chip in his head. The laughing petered out and Alex withdrew his smile. His face quickly distorted in shape. A brutal frown similar to the crazed killers in the Texas Chainsaw Massacre took over. The cabby's psyche immediately registered that something was amiss. His subconscious mind tried to warn his conscious ego, but it wasn't quite quick enough.

"You Aussies fucken' troublemake ..." slipped past his lips, but the driver didn't finish his sentence. Alex had sent a blinding left uppercut to the cabby's furry overhanging chin. It put the guy's teeth through his bottom lip and his head put a huge dent in the roof. Blood automatically fanned over the taxi. The white shirt of the cabby now resembled a St George supporter's. He slumped in the front seat of the car and Alex stuck his head over for a better look. The shiny gold neck chain stood out like dog's balls as it shimmered from the glow of a nearby streetlight. Alex ripped it from the guy's neck as Pierre fleeced the front seat for any worthwhile cash. He uncovered about $50 in small notes from the brown leather change pocket hanging from the handbrake lever. It had been a slow arvo shift.

It was soon apparent to Pierre that they had stopped at a busy intersection in Bondi Junction and that time was of the essence again.

"Let's bolt!" he said, as a car behind beeped its horn. Alex stumbled out of the taxi, following Pierre's lead. Alex loved danger. He was smiling like a kid at the Royal Easter Show.

The pair strode off down Edgecliff Road heading for one of Pierre's drug dealing mates' houses, where they could sort out some shit. The rain had stopped from earlier that afternoon, though the streets were still wet and shiny. They snuck down a back lane to avoid detection, as both were splattered in blood and looking fairly suss. Alex was just happy to be there and tagging along. It seemed he was oblivious to what was unfolding (or just didn't care) and was more interested in stomping in puddles of water. Pierre was afraid Alex might try talking to someone, so he told him not to.

There were cops in numbers heading to the area. The boys' night hadn't even kicked off, but they had certainly left their mark. One could almost sense their night was going to be a good one. As the boys drew closer to the dealer's terrace house, Pierre slowed in motion and used street bushes to hide and observe if there were any suspected signs of them being followed. No strangers in the shadows, no curtains being peered through, no silhouetted body frames lurking in cars and no cop paddy wagons circling the block. It all indicated that it was fairly safe to proceed with the house call.

On ringing the dealer's doorbell, a scantily clad 6'2" blonde opened the door. Pierre's drug buddy, Raúl, had a short circuit camera mounted above their heads that was connected through to a separate monitor inside his lounge room, so he could watch and know who was at the door. It was only a small screen and it easily fitted into the bottom cupboard of his TV unit. He wouldn't have to leave the couch, if he didn't want to see them. It was one of his little power trips common amongst dealers. It was seen by many criminals as a worthwhile investment—an investment that had saved Raúl's arse several times from the stiff arm of the law.

The blonde gave them the once over, then checked the street to see if anyone was nosing. "Come in, guys. Kinda dark out there."

"Think they call it night-time," said Pierre, jokingly with a cheesy grin. She recognised Pierre, but didn't know Alex. She knew that both were only small time, compared to the wicket she was already on. She was fairly new on the scene, but she was already feeling cooped up with having to hang out with "the boss" all the time. The boys were young punks running amok and she was down with the cockiness of it all. She was a typical crack-whore, who really didn't know what she wanted. In her thinking, hanging around guys with money was going to help her find her Nirvana. Hanging out with a drug dealer kept her close to her source of pleasure and in her wild world that's all that mattered. The blonde was feeling horny and when she looked at the boys, she got a tingle from their rugged appearance.

"Been spraying each other with a tomato sauce bottle, have we?" she mused, "Looks like you've been causing trouble somewhere, aye?"

It was a statement as much as it was a question. Pierre didn't respond, but Alex got out: "Heaps of fun, darlin'!"

She used her finger, as if to summon them. Her eyes connected with Pierre's and he felt her petting. "Raúl's this way." They entered into the narrow Victorian hallway, where a Brett Whiteley self-portrait hung lopsided. Pierre couldn't help but right it so it looked level. Alex stared up at the stucco mouldings on the ceiling and thought he was in some angelic house of reverence. To him it resembled the artwork of Michelangelo. The old-style intricate plaster design danced for him and cherubs floated in harmony with the choir inside his head.

"Come in, guys," said Raúl from his comfortable leather lounge. He didn't know Alex, but he trusted Pierre's judgement. He was watching some home porno and as they entered the living room, he didn't even look up. "Check out this booty, boys."

The word "booty" distracted Alex from his heavenly hallucination. His eyes descended from above and focused on some chick getting nailed by two black cocks on the widescreen box in front of him. "Now, she's a real angel! Wow, that's good shit, man." He smiled at Raúl, as if in agreement that it was worthy entertainment. "She's fuckin' hot!"

"I know that chick." Pierre moved nearer to the telly for a closer inspection.

"I wanna know her ..." Alex had his mouth open and his tongue was licking his lips.

Raúl took his eyes off the TV set and cast a glance at the standing duo. Pierre stood smaller than Alex, about 5'9" in height, but was puffed up from the amount of steroid gym work he was into. He lived in a unit above the Bondi Road Gym, so it was convenient to train during the day, before going to work at night. Alex stood like a modern day version of the John Steinbeck character, Lennie. He was big, simple, fearsome if provoked, but ironically gentle in a lot of ways.

"Looks like you guys need a fucking wash." The bright chandelier lights fully exposed their harsh, untidy appearance. Their blood-splattered clothes were evidence better disposed of.

Pierre caught a glance of himself in a gold-rimmed, elaborately framed mirror above the cedar mantel of the room's old-tiled fireplace. He had a long tear on the arm of his dark blue Quiksilver jacket. There was also a small scratch on his neck. Both were courtesy of the terrified wog that he had punched out earlier at Bondi. There was criminal evidence all over him. "Yeah, you could say that, mate. Alex is due for his weekly soaking!"

Raúl looked up and gave Alex the once over. A half-crazed, tripping nut-case running from the law was his first impression. He was good at identification. His description was made easy by the splashes of red claret all over Alex's attire. Not only had splotches of blood decorated his clothes, but bits had found their way into his nostrils and ears and coagulated. Some of the dried blood had been thick enough to gel in parts of his shoulder length brown hair. It gave him a punkish resemblance, like someone who had wandered off the set of "Clockwork Orange". Raúl tried to clear his throat and rub his jowl, as he studied the situation. He had to be judicial by nature. It was all part of his profession. It was his business to identify with everyone who came within his circle. One loose cannon could blow a porthole in his operations. Raúl had known Pierre a long time and liked to think that he wouldn't bring anybody around who was a threat.

"Hope you guys made sure no one was following you?"

"C'mon, Raúl. Nothin' looked suss. I'm not that stupid; you know me better than that." Pierre looked at his South American mate for confirmation that what he had just said was acceptable.

"I suppose nothing looked suss out there, except you guys."

"Any billies?" asked Pierre politely.

Raúl pulled the teak mull bowl out from under the couch and lobbed it on the glass coffee table in front of him. "Here you go, mate. Punch one of these."

"Nice buds?"

"A mate of mine has just started growing this shit under lights. It's fucking the crypt."

Pierre didn't want to dirty his mate's lounge with his damp butt, so his eyes searched the room for an appropriate place to park it.

"Better if you sit on the floor, bra." It was covered with Balinese sea grass matting over polished floorboards. "And

47

what's ya buddy's name? Looks like he's been in the wars."

"This is Alex, Dan's cousin." Pierre sat in a semi lotus position and took off his wet soiled jacket.

"I'll take that," said the curvy blonde. She turned to Alex, who was still standing and taking the lounge room scene in. She tugged at his K-Mart hooded top. "And yours too, big boy."

"Put them straight in a plastic bag, darling. We'll burn 'em later. Don't want any evidence of the boys getting their kicks now."

"Burn 'em? I nearly got locked up for stealing that jacket."

"Yeah, burn 'em. Get rid of any evidence."

"Oh, okay then ... better to be safe than sorry, I s'pose."

"Now you're thinking. Anyway, I've got some nice gear you can choose from in the garage."

"Alright. Sounds good ..."

"How did you get in such a state?"

"Alex has been in fine form, bra! He's been causing a bit of havoc, stickin' up for the boys down the beach and sendin' blokes home who deserved it." Raúl gave Alex the once over. "He only belts blokes who deserve it," reassured Pierre.

"Yeah, well, before he sits down, he can jump in the shower," implored Raúl. "We can't have ya leavin' some kind of evidence on my new satin pillows, now. You know what I mean? You never quite know when you're going to be paid a visit."

"No probs, champion!" Pierre wrenched the cone with fervor, as though his life depended on it. He sucked all the smoke out of the chamber. Exhaling, he responded to the mix of cannabis and tobacco with a satisfying sigh.

"Looks like you needed it."

"Fucken oath! And I promise ya that I checked the street outside before I knocked and it was all totally cool." The cone's effect gradually swamped his senses. He placed his palms on the matting behind him and leaned backwards to feel more comfortable. It was the new, potent, sticky-icky poison, named Hydro. It was still in its infancy and not quite perfected, but it rocked all those who dared indulge. "Fuck, that's good shit!" He rolled his head once and tried to crack the vertebrae in his thick neck.

"Alex? Would you like one before your wash?"

"Yes, thanks." Alex's tone was the euphony of a gentle giant. He wasn't all there. His childish grin got even wider as Raúl packed the cone and passed it to him. Sometimes he was coherent and other times he was off with the pixies. "Smells excellent, man," he said with a chuckle.

Alex smoked his cone and looked his newly-acquainted South American friend in the eye when thanking him. Alex observed Raúl's deep brown eyes. There was nothing too shallow about Raúl. He was a thinker who thought through every move he made. He possessed a cool, calm composure. His white designer shirt complemented his clean olive complexion. Raúl's grace gave the impression to Alex that he was some kind of descendant from royalty. Alex was now studying what he thought were princely features. "You sure look like royalty, Mr Rawool."

Raúl was wearing a gold Rolex and matching gold neck chain. Alex noticed Raúl's long narrow sculpted nose, then panned further to appreciate his combed straight black hair, clean-shaven face with trimmed goatee and immaculate white teeth. To Alex it all befitted a mighty Inca king.

"Why, thank you, Mr Alex."

Raúl let them have a shower in his marble bathroom upstairs. Alex went first.

"Make sure you make good use of the shampoo!"

After showering, both lads stuffed their stained threads into the plastic garbo bag already containing their jackets. They made their way downstairs wearing matching yellow towels to find Raúl talking on the phone. It was obvious that he was occupied and the leggy blonde led them out into the back garden to the storage shed. The backyard was more like a prison courtyard with high walls. A couple of pot plants broke the brick and concrete monotony. The night sky was awash with dark clouds. The inclement weather had ceased and the moon was trying to peek its head through any gaps in the evening canopy.

"It's fuckin' freezing out here!"

"Nice night for a toga party ..."

"If you're a fuckin' Eskimo!"

The blonde opened the storage room door and ushered them in. "Welcome to the change room, boys." Her eyes wandered over their muscular bodies. "Raúl said for you guys to pick out a couple of fever outfits to hit the town in."

Raúl had plenty of varied threads to choose from as his storeroom was full of hot garments. He had recently done 'a shifty' with a retail clothing chain store company who needed an insurance job on their warehouse. Turned out they shifted the merchandise before they burnt the joint down. The storeroom was stacked with boxes and resembled a jumble sale. After searching high and low Pierre donned a crème Ralph Lauren long-sleeve shirt with some nice black corduroy threads and Gucci belt. His Converse sneakers looked a little out of place, so he asked Raúl if he could borrow some shiny black shoes.

Raúl sent his girlfriend upstairs to fetch Pierre's request.

"You'll also need a jacket with that outfit." Raúl pointed to a box at the bottom of a pile. Pierre dug deep and found a black leather jacket—completing his slick appearance. Pierre was more than happy with his look.

"You're a fucking legend, Raúl. We owe you big time!"

Alex had more of a department store mentality and opted for a pair of Levi jeans and a blue Country Road sweater. He affixed the gold chain, robbed from the cabbie, around his neck and nodded to Raúl, confirming his satisfaction.

"Fashion has always said a lot about the person who steps into it," commented Raúl.

They all headed back into the living room. The blonde went upstairs and brought back down the plastic bag for Raúl to burn. A sparkle appeared in Raúl's eyes. He had an affinity with fire, which started as a boy with a box of matches. He always watched the flames in amazement. Maybe Raúl's ancestors delighted in burning virgins at the stake.

One night, when he was still small time, his yearning for the smell of burnt flesh got the better of him. He was partying down Bondi with Cookie and Cookie's youngest brother, Hiddy—short for "Hideous Creature". They were at a mate's pad in Sir Thomas Mitchell Road and were extremely pissed. Hiddy was showing off, as usual, sticking Tom Thumb firecrackers down the eye of his dick and lighting them with his ciggy. Standing there naked with gunpowder on his knob, he revealed a troubled side of human nature. He was a man with no shame and loved showing his cock to anybody who'd bother looking. As each cracker exploded, he would roar into his heinous laugh. As the boys drank on and got more rowdy, their thirst for longnecks had taken the count well into double figures. As things progressively got messy, a game of rumble ensued and ended up with Cookie pinning his naked bare bottomed brother down on the floor. Cunningly, Raúl managed to spray a handy can of "Glen 20" all over Hiddy's shagpile chest. Breaking free, he leaped to his feet and stumbled backwards, peering in disbelief at the thick coat of foam below his chin. Not finished yet, Raúl aimed the can towards him and flicking a lighter flame, pushed down on the aerosol button. A stream of toxic fluid shot a three metre fireball towards the naked target and exploded on impact with Hiddy's toxic soaked chest blowing him backwards against the wall. The bizarre sight of the flaming "Toxic Avenger" initially stunned the perpetrators. Raúl and Cookie were not only astonished, but amazed that the flame covered the distance and hit the target. Within a split second, they were rolling on the floor laughing so hysterically, they couldn't even help put out the flames. Hiddy eventually managed to extinguish himself by rolling on the carpet. At St Vincent's, where he was treated for minor burns, the staff couldn't help but laugh when administering relief to his naughty bits—including the eye of his dick—especially when the joker went into detail about his ordeal.

Raúl agreed to his mate's requests and carried the plastic bag with the evidence out to his back garden and disposed of them joyfully. He took the grill plate off his Weber BBQ and emptied the contents. He enjoyed dousing the gear with petrol and striking a match. The initial combustion sent a wall of flame so high it almost touched the rafters of the first floor patio. The pyromaniac smiled gleefully as the flames engulfed the fabric.

His girl told him, "Don't burn the house down, honey." After all, she knew he was good at burning things down. "Just make sure you fire me up later, honey." Her comment could have meant a number of things.

He strolled back inside to the lounge room, rubbing his hands, just as Alex was examining one of several Pro Hart paintings adorning the walls and getting lost in the colourful oil somewhere. Pierre was adjusting his collar in the mirror mounted above the fireplace. Next to it was an expensive mahogany sideboard, which was cluttered with bottles of grog and bar utensils.

"Lend me a little extra cash and I'll work it off for ya?" Pierre was always straight to the point. Raúl and Pierre had been mates since high school and had fought many a battle together. They had made a pact when they were young to always watch each other's back.

It wasn't the first time Raúl had been asked this question by his old school mate. He took a wad of fifties out of his brown leather wallet and flicked through the new notes as he counted, "Here's a coupla hundred."

"And a couple of grams of coke too, please, brother?" Pierre was very fond of nose candy. He believed it was a great drug to combat alcohol and tiredness when talking to ladies. Like most operators, he used it to seduce ladies and it had got him laid on most occasions.

"Fuck, you're pushin' it," answered Raúl. His girl suddenly appeared in the room, as if the word "coke" meant something to her. "Suppose you want some too?" Raúl was now referring to his blonde princess in waiting. Pierre could see the drug habit in her. She was 22 and still quite cute and innocent. However, her sudden appearance hinted that it wouldn't be long till Raúl was moving on and she'd be propped up against some wall, working the streets in Darlo.

Raúl slipped out of the living room into the hallway and headed up the narrow terrace stairs towards his bedroom. Alex peeked down the hallway and saw Raúl ascending into what he believed to be Heaven. The cherubs were enticing Raúl to come up.

"Michelangelo," uttered Alex, "your angels are calling you."

Pierre had been into Raúl for cash and drugs many times before but always managed to square up at some time. Raúl wasn't going to start denying his good friend now. His girl took the opportunity to pet some more with Pierre, who kept showing her his ever present attitude. She thought her cute looks and sweet talk could impress Pierre. He knew there would be a hundred of her type out on the town and the last thing he was going to do was show his mate's girl any added attention. He knew, underneath it all, she was just an attention-seeking drug moll, who was on a campaign to tag any "bigger better deal" that was available. Being so attractive, she probably had about 3 to 4 years till her use-by date was up.

Alex interrupted the conversation she was having with Pierre. "You got any sharps?" He wanted to bang some of the coke. As much as he wasn't a full blown drug addict, he definitely fell into the user category.

"I'm sure she does, Alex," commented Pierre. He smiled at her and she blushed slightly, as if she was a little embarrassed about being an intravenous drug taker. It was as if she still cared some, about what she had fallen into.

"I've got a couple of clean ones." The cute blonde was stoked she had someone to share a taste in the spoon with. Her boyfriend never injected, though he didn't pass judgement on it, because drug users made him rich. However, he didn't like his girl doing it regularly, so she would try to hide it from him. She was such a good looking accessory to him, so he would usually turn a blind eye.

He would say to her, "Keep doing that shit like that and you're goin' to end up a hag by 25 and no-one will want ya ..." For her, dealing with the consequences didn't even enter her mind. She was living like so many bad habit dependents—for herself, right here, right now—with the attitude of "fuck everyone and everything else". As long as she could latch onto a rich fucker and spit a kid out before she got too old, she'd be apples for the rest of her life, or so she thought. It was a selfish opinion on life that she kept to herself. After all, she'd be stupid to let that cat out of the bag, especially to a supplier.

"What was your name, darlin'?" asked Alex. He obviously felt he now had a deeper connection with her. The acid was still alive and well in his system and he was going with the flow.

"Donna," she replied.

Pierre kept noticing her twitching every 30 seconds. "Raúl had his hands full with this one," he thought.

"Do ya wanna, Donna?" came out of Alex's mouth like he had remembered an old school nursery rhyme. He thought he was funny and let his dorky laugh fill the room. Donna already knew he wasn't the full quid and left the room heading for the spoon drawer in the kitchen. Alex soon downgraded his laugh to a broad smile and looked over at Pierre. Pierre couldn't help but smile back at his freaky mate.

"Fuck, man, you're making me feel like I'm on that shit," pronounced Pierre. "My fatty tissue is startin' to kick in just lookin' at ya!" Pierre laughed, but Alex didn't understand. After years of acid abuse, the LSD supposedly gets stored in some of your fatty cells. When you lose weight and your body starts living on your fat reserves, chances are you are going to start tripping or at least experience bouts of heightened awareness. Pierre felt like he was having flashbacks just standing in the same room as his mate. "Looking at you, that shit would bring a dead dog back to life."

"More like a dead elephant!" Alex mused. "... a real big, old dead one!"

Raúl's footsteps on the old wooden staircase had Alex's ears pricked. "Party time," he said as he dropped his head into his neck, like a little kid sometimes does when something exciting is brewing. Alex's eyes looked as big as golf balls.

"This stuff is fucking killer!" Raúl boasted about his merchandise. "Sit down with Pierre, Alex, and I'll clean the mirror." He picked his regular coke mirror up off the polished sideboard and started wiping it with a tissue. Donna yelled out to

Raúl from the kitchen. Raúl couldn't hear her and started walking towards the kitchen asking, "What, Baby?"

He emerged soon after and told Alex to "go in and join her".

"Sure, Raúl. Thanks heaps, aye, mate!" Alex waltzed in to the kitchen for his shootup with the devil woman.

"We've got the room to ourselves, mate," said Pierre to Raúl.

Raúl rolled his eyes and joked, "Who are those kooks anyway?"

"Fucked if I know," laughed Pierre.

It was down to business in both rooms.

Donna had most of her room's requirements ready by the time Alex had strolled in. The black and white tiles on the floor didn't really look very straight in his head but being the tripper that he was, he was down with it.

He looked on the sink and saw two spoons and two fits filled with 40 mL of water. Donna dropped a healthy amount in each spoon and then slid Alex's along the laminex top in front of him. He picked his fit-up and carefully squirted the water into his silverware. There was no way he was going to let his trip fuck up this procedure. It was another override of his drugged senses. It was if his body knew that when doing this kinda shit you don't fuck around—a secondary defence mechanism for any junkie who doesn't want to blow his taste.

He started mixing the contents of the spoon with the water, continually staring into the abyss. There was a whole world in there for him to explore. As he watched the coke dissolve, his mind sank deep into its turbulence. His mind started reminding him of the situation at hand. The fright of thinking he was falling into the mental equivalent of a black hole made him snap out of it.

"You alright, man?" Donna was a little concerned. "Don't spill it."

"No worries," he answered, "I'll be sweet." He was a bit vague, but back on track.

Pierre and Raúl were indulging in their own way. Raúl spilled out a small mound onto the shiny, metallic surface. He picked out a razor blade from a miscellaneous items box on the table and commenced cutting their own white lines. The pair chit-chatted about current shit going down in the 'hood and Pierre got onto describing the fight they had earlier at the beach. Raúl had figured just by looking at Alex that the boy could go. He rolled a crisp fifty dollar note and cleared the back of his throat, swallowing the mucus. His nostril had a wide opening, which he believed was part of his South American breeding—a convenience that he took advantage of more than enough. He held the rolled note tight and snorted a line.

"Shit, that's good," he exclaimed as his lifted his head back and sniffed hard, making sure it got as far in as possible. On occasions, he had trouble with his sinuses, from excessive snorting. "That's better," he said as he passed the mirror and note over to Pierre.

Meanwhile in the kitchen, Donna was slapping her arm. She then grabbed it and pumped the vein. A nice little blue lump popped up through her smooth, suntanned skin. She loved sun baking and used Raúl's upstairs' back verandah to soak up the sun. No-one could see in, so she mostly baked nude. If you looked close enough, like a lot of guys probably did, you would notice that she had no white bikini lines anywhere. The girl focused in on the usual point of entry in her arm. Alex's veins were bulging already, so he didn't have to do much, but still squeezed and pumped his arm, just out of habit. Donna hated needles when she was young and that still registered somewhat. "Ow!" She ignored the prick and navigated the needle into her chemical highway. She drew back the syringe and watched the blood get sucked out of her vein and into the water chamber. She was pleased with herself that she'd hit 'spot X' first time. What a relief that she didn't have to keep jabbing. She hated missing. Miss long enough and you're fit goes blunt and it hurts twice as bad.

Raúl watched as Pierre snorted a massive rail. Lifting his head up and back, with the note still well lodged into position, he inhaled, encouraging the powder to drop down the back of his throat. He then wiped and tasted a bit from the mound or what was left from it. He made sure he rubbed it on his teeth and gums to experience the pleasant numbness associated with the stimulant. He grinned and composed himself with the note still sticking out his nose.

"Pass the billy, bra." Raúl reached under the table and brought out the bowl and chalice. He handed them over the table and Pierre wasted no time in packing himself up.

Donna slowly injected the contents of the fix into her blood vessel. Within a few moments, an overwhelming rush filled her senses. "Yeah," was her affirmation that the gear was working.

Alex got a bit messy, missing a couple of times till he hit the jackpot. He drove the shit into his veins, all the time bursting with excitement.

"Good, aye?" Donna was instantly drawing deep breaths as she coped with the rush.

"Awesome." answered Alex, who couldn't help but start to move his feet to the stereo music coming from their next door neighbour's. It was loud enough that you could clearly hear the break beat base through the kitchen wall. Alex grabbed Donna and twirled her round like she was his dance partner. He then drew her face to face with him and she rose to the occasion. Dancing was one of her passions, even if it was with a lunatic. She cut loose with a few moves of her own whilst Alex was flowing with his own routine. He tried to jump up on the sideboard as if it was a podium, but slipped in the process. He head butted the side of the bench and went down like a bag of shit.

"What was that?" Pierre was referring to the thud Alex had made when hitting the tiles.

Alex jumped up quickly, as if nothing had happened, though possibly a little sore and embarrassed. Somehow, too many drugs saying too many things at once didn't help his calculations whilst in motion.

Pierre and Raúl finished what was on the plate before checking the noise in the kitchen. Upon further investigation, all was sweet except a small bump on the top of Alex's head.

"I hit it on the fucking sink, but I'm sweet ... no worries."

"Great technique, big boy." His new, leggy, drug buddy was impressed. "Kinda like a cross between rugby league and hip hop!" she chuckled.

"You want to get going, Alex, before you wreck the joint?" asked Pierre. "You done, fucking around with your spoons and shit?"

"Yeah" was all he managed to concern himself with saying. His smile was the only consistent thing about him.

The boys thanked Raúl for his major hospitality. Pierre told him that he'd ring him in a couple of days and visit. "I'll surprise you with a present, brudda."

"Scotch always goes down well."

"Consider it done, brudda. One of my exes is working the bottle shop at the back of the Bondi, so I'm onto the five-fingered discount!"

Raúl saw them to the door, with his bird lurking behind. "Don't do anything I wouldn't. And try and make it home in one piece ..." were his parting words.

It was getting late and the Cross was waiting for them. It was a gloomy night and the clouds were still hovering overhead. In some parts, the streets were still shiny from the moisture. The street lights shone bright and cast dark shadows in corners and backlanes where they couldn't reach. The boys headed away from their earlier scene at Bondi Junction, down Edgecliff Road towards Double Bay. They were clean and well dressed, apart from the sweat that had started pouring from their underarms. It was pure crystal.

The walk to Double Bay shops was a good distance from Raúl's residence. They would have jumped into a taxi, but all seemed occupied. Passing Cooper Park, Alex felt eyes peering at them behind its dark, mysterious curtain. It lacked lighting and the woods were pitch black. If you wanted to, your imagination could take you anywhere. Alex kept peering in, telling Pierre there was scary shit happening in there. "Could be anything in there, Pierre!"

Pierre definitely wasn't scared of what might lie behind the dark curtain. "Yeah, the Lord of His Ring is gonna come fuckin' outta there and punch you in the date!"

Alex looked at Pierre. He was still trying to register what Pierre had said. "Really?" he was puzzled. He had never read any Tolkien, so the comment went straight over his head. Pierre was no great academic, but his grandmother had read the Hobbit books to him at bedtime, when he was a child. The imagery of dark woods and misty mountains had stimulated his passion for adventure, but he didn't believe in goblins or the fairy godmother, even if one of his favourite TV shows had been "Bewitched" (mainly because he had a crush on Samantha).

Pierre strode on like an intrepid trouper, straight and defiant, whilst Alex seemed to be walking on a layer of compressed air. Passing the archery range, Alex started looking down at the world of the pavement. There were intermittent puddles caught in the low spots of uneven, warped sections of concrete. Over the years, trees aligning the road had grown and their roots had buckled parts of the pavement. His heightened awareness was by no means goofy when it came to negotiating anything he already stored knowledge about. As he trudged on, his walk became more and more aesthetic. It was as though the disfigured footpath and his mind were one.

Both continued forwards, Pierre taking the liberty of searching for the next cab, as Alex was preoccupied with his trip. It was Sunday night and the weather, being inclement, meant there

wasn't much chance of hailing a vacant taxi till they reached the
main road. New South Head Road was an arterial link between
the city and Eastern Suburbs and there was always a chance—
rain, hail or shine—to catch a cab. Out of bored lunacy and a little
frustration, Pierre started singing; "Once, twice, three times a
cabbie ..." Then, pausing for a split second as he mimicked
holding a microphone to his lips, "and you'll always be a cabbie
to me!"

Alex didn't know what the fuck a crooning Pierre was on
about, but he didn't care. He looked up and smiled again, like a
psycho. They were both fully off-guts and loving it.

They were high rollin' down through the streets surrounded by
the majestic mansions of the suburb they'd nicknamed "Double
Pay". Basically, this area's illustrious shopping centre sold you
the same old shit, only with some wanker's name on it, to make it
more expensive. If you weren't wearing tweed and driving the
latest sports car, you were never going to get the model girl in this
neighbourhood.

On reaching New South Head Road, the pair were desperate
for a taxi. Several cabs had passed them by—obviously wise old
cabbies sensing something was amiss. Observing Alex in their
rear vision, giving them the finger, confirmed they had made the
right decision.

"I'm fuckin' over walking," said Pierre. They had just
completed a two-kilometre trek from Bondi Junction down into
the heart of Double Bay's shops. Being Sunday night, the shops
were all closed and, except for an occasional pulse of traffic, the
place resembled a ghost town. Designer shops with neon lights
lined the deserted strip.

"You'll have to come back tomorrow if you want to buy
something." It was hard for Pierre not to be sarcastic. There would
always be people born on opposite sides of the track. "Look in
that window, bra. The socks only cost 49 bucks!" Alex wanted to
put his fist through the window and grab some joggers that
appealed to him, but Pierre persuaded him not to.

"Don't think of doin' shit like that mate ... Come over here. I
got somethin' for ya." Pierre held the bag of coke in the air
motioning with his eyes that it was feeding time for their nostrils
again. Pierre ducked into a dimly lit alcove and stuck his finger
into the bag. He shoved his index finger under Alex's nostrils and
told him to "sniff". Every last crystal disappeared. Alex was a
natural vacuum. Pierre followed suit, except his crude finger's

worth was a little bigger. He was a glutton for the shit!

It wasn't long till they were hopping in an RSL Taxi. It was an older style Kingswood and the customary smell of taxi leather filled the cabin.

"Where to, mate?" The driver was a white Australian.

"At last, a fucken Aussie," said Pierre. "You and us guys, we're a dying breed, mate." Pierre wanted to look the guy in the eye whilst talking, but the driver wasn't up to it. "Us white Aussies are at the bottom of the pile these days! What fuckin' happened? It's the fuckin' politicians, don't ya reckon, mate?"

"Where to, mate?" asked the driver again.

"The Cross, driver," replied Alex. In his state, he didn't care to know much about politics or for that matter white Aussies. The one and only important thing that had sunk into his skull was that they were heading to Kings Cross and the thought of bar girls and partying stimulated his excitement receptors. He stared across the street at a police paddy wagon. A young woman constable caught his dorky eyes and thought he was cute. She smiled at him. Pierre caught on to what he was doing and leant over to check her out. She teased the boys by sucking on one of her fingers as the cab departed. The girl in uniform gave Pierre half a stiffy.

"Anyway, mate. Don't ya reckon?" Pierre wasn't finished. He was searching for an answer that would support his political white Aussie male opinion.

"Yeah, mate, for sure. Don't like politics." The cabbie wasn't too interested in the conversation, but his profession required, all too often, a bit of diplomacy. After all, the job was full of danger. You would probably never know if you picked up a couple of crazy motherfuckers till it was too late. His gut feeling was already giving him a careful signal regarding his new passengers.

"You got all these cunts coming here from God knows where and wanting to all hang together. Then, they want to put shit on us blokes for puttin' up with 'em in the first place." Pierre had the driver's ears pricked. He was starting to like what he was hearing. At times, he too had felt victimised in his own country by migrants and nodded his head in agreement.

"I mean, I don't mind immigration, just as long as those cunts appreciate it. I've got plenty of wog mates and they're half decent blokes!"

"They can cook good spaghetti!"

"Thanks, Alex, but I'm trying to have a sensible conversation with me mate, the driver, OK?"

"OK, but they make good garlic bread, too."

"Yeah, Alex, whatever. I like eating at No Names, too. So, where were we, driver?"

"Politicians."

"Yeah, those bludging bastards."

"I know what you're on about, matey! It's all the pooftas and lesbians in the government to blame." The driver held an opinion similar to Pierre's.

"Exactly! Changing the fucking laws for all the soft cocks," continued Pierre. "Politically correct shit never did any good for me! Those self serving pricks have a divide-and-conquer theory happening."

"Yeah and what's that?" asked the driver, who was now sucked in to the topic.

"They want to throw a bunch of foreigners and pooftas in here to undermine what our fucken families already did for this country!" Pierre was passionate about his heritage. "Who asked them to come here and start putting shit on us because we're different from them?"

"I agree, mate. My grandfather fought on the Kokoda with all the other Diggers to keep the Japs outta this place," said the driver. "We'd all be speaking Japanese, if our grandfathers didn't stop 'em."

"One got through, mate," added Alex. "His name's Ken-san and he's got some fuckin' sick buds!"

Pierre ignored Alex's comment and had plenty more to say. "Yeah, well, I've had plenty of crew telling me that judges have picked them up from 'the wall' heaps of times, which proves this country's gettin' run by fuckin' pooftas and lesbian bitches."

Alex interjected again, "I know a bloke that got sucked off by a priest."

"There ya go. There's another fuckin' rort—fuckin' religion!" fired off Pierre. He started tapping the driver on the shoulder. "You religious, mate?"

"Nah, mate," came the quick reply. They were stopped at traffic lights near Rushcutters Bay and the driver knew it wouldn't be long till they vacated the cab. Pierre muttered some disgruntled shit to himself as he looked out the window. After thinking about the religious question for a sec, the driver hoped a bit of humour would keep the situation under wraps. "Oh, I'm religiously down the pub Fridays and Saturdays."

"Me too!" Alex was smiling away. His big head was sort of

bobbing to some imaginary beat. He peered out into Rushcutters Park and was enjoying the twinkling of the boat lights as they rocked gently in the harbour. They were moored to their million dollar marinas, waiting for their millionaire owners to come down and play. At a younger age, he always had fun in a mate's tinnie on Rose Bay and his imagination was wandering. He visualised in technicolour the splendour of captaining one of these luxury yachts. The thought of becoming an ancient mariner at the helm had him gazing into the bay. Fitted with a customary hook and eye patch, he would wreak havoc on Sydney Harbour with his trusty parrot on his shoulder. Alex was really enjoying his trip.

"Drop us up the Kardomah, please, mate." Pierre was looking forward to a bit of fun in the popular Sunday night bar.

"No probs." The driver had been wise enough not to get on the wrong side of this pair. Although he agreed with a lot that was said, he knew both boys were volatile. It would have been hard not to pick up on the strange vibe. He was accustomed to this sort of thing and had become very tactful in his job. The week prior, he was threatened after dropping a ride off at La Perouse. A big Islander had put a knife to his throat and thieved his takings. It was only 40 bucks, but the incident would remain in his head forever. The instinct of knowing which fare you could trust was the key to his job. After all, the city was filled with crazy motherfuckers and it was a bit of a lottery who your next passenger might be. He knew all too well that occasionally cab drivers got murdered.

Pierre liked the driver and paid the fare. "Be careful, bra. Don't pick up any crazed killers, now." The driver looked into Pierre's eyes and saw demons. He thanked the boys and sped off into the busy heart of the flickering neon lit strip of the Cross.

*

Moose was a northside punk rocker who worked the door at various establishments including the Kardomah Café on Sunday nights. He was a biggish bloke—six foot two—with a good-sized frame. His prized Docs never left his feet. He was your typical romper stomper, who was blooded on the Sex Pistols. He first became familiar with Bondi in the early 80s after he met Alex's cousin Dan at a World War 24 gig behind the Newport Beach Surf Club. Dan took an instant liking to the Moose and was instrumental in introducing the big guy to a lot of the boys in Scum Valley. Dan surfed a lot around the Newport area in the

early 80s. It was a time when he was sponsored by Fitzy at Hot
Buttered and therefore became good mates with some of the
Newport Plus crew, who Moose hung out with. Dan enjoyed
getting out of the hustle and bustle of Bondi, to hang with a
different crew and enjoy some quality surf. He was stoked to be
accepted by such a fine surfing tribe. The gig was shut down that
day because the lead singer, Bird, had a few rude words to say to
the whole world, including a paddy wagon and highway patrol
car. Later that arvo, Moose travelled south over the bridge with
Dan for some nightlife entertainment and from that day on
decided to stay. The harshness of inner city living was appealing
to him and he loved a bit of masochism!

Pierre stood at the top of the entrance looking down the flight
of stairs to the front door. The doorway was a big semi-circular
archway built of sandstone with a big brown door constructed of
solid wood. The nightclub had been an old 1800s basement, built
of sandstone foundations. It was appropriate for such a faintly lit
seedy venue. It was around 11 o'clock and there was a small
queue waiting for Moose's instructions. Moose was busy talking
to the door bitch, who was new to the job. Pierre started ambling
down the stairs with Alex close behind.

"Moosey!" The big fellow knew the voice and swung around
to greet Pierre. "Talking to the pretty ladies again, are we?"
Moose smiled and gave Pierre, then Alex, a brotherly handshake.
All three were young punks at heart and well bonded. Previously,
Pierre had lived with Moose in Francis Street, Bondi, and both
had done a heap of scamming together.

Not one to miss much, Moose asked, "And my, how bug-eyed
you guys look."

"Yeah, been havin' some fun with Alex. He's totally off his
head," Pierre turned to Alex. "Aren't ya, mate?"

Alex just smiled at both of them, in his delirium, and let out
another snigger. The door bitch raised her eyebrows, uncertain of
who Moose's mates were. These guys looked dangerous and she
figured if Moose knew them, at least they were on her side.

"You guys look as though you're up for a big one?" she asked.

"Always, princess. What about yourself?" Pierre liked how
glamorous she looked.

"I'm working," was her quick response.

Moose cut in. "You fellas heard who won the football?"

Someone in the lineup shouted out, "Go the Roosters!"

"Not that game," said Moose. "The one up Waverley Oval?"

Alex's brain seemed to only comprehend violence and football. His acid brain flicked through its footy files. "Bondi United against the Paddo Colts," came out, automatically. He knew who had played, but didn't know who'd won.

"That's the one!"

"Paddo won," came a voice descending the stairs. It was Cookie, accompanied by his second youngest brother, Matty. Matty played fullback for Bondi United and had played in the local derby that afternoon. Matty was only small in size—about five foot six—but had the heart of a lion.

"Hardaker scored the winning fucking try!" added young Matty, who displayed a few customary bruises from giving his usual 110%.

"Yeah, but we belted them in the biffo," said a proud Cookie, as he gave Moose and the boys some skin. Winning the biff was almost as good as winning the game. Moose sported a broad smile in his buddies' company. The door bitch was familiarising herself with Moose's friends. It was part of her job. Call it flirting or whatever, but she was keen to be getting her share later that night.

Moose waived them the 10 buck cover charge and told the boys to "go in and fuckin' enjoy yourselves". They entered through the gothic doorway and blended with the crowd in the light-starved cellar-like room. The club was fairly crowded and the queue outside was getting longer, backing up the stairs and out onto Bayswater Road. An international pommy DJ had drawn in the masses and, as the boys finished their first beers, he started his set with some funky house beats. Alex's legs couldn't keep still and he became drawn to the dance floor. He pushed through the crowd and positioned himself right in front of the DJ. He started doing fancy hand-jive moves, all the time in total sync with the music. He pirouetted a couple of times without, miraculously, colliding with anyone. It was obvious his air shoes had followed him onto the dance floor. They were like two small hovercrafts on his feet. One could have mistakenly thought he was in total control of what he was doing. Pierre was heading back to the bar after a quick visit to the white line cubicle. He couldn't help but notice Alex jiving on the floor. His big bopping head with his clown-like smile signalled he was having a ball. He wasn't causing any grief, but Pierre couldn't help but wonder what was going to happen next. Alex seemed to have several young chickies interested, because he had it all flowing with no ego involved. However, as he started taking it to another level, the wheels

63

started to fall off. His face crunch impersonations of Billy Idol, followed by his over the top Prince guitar solos, had a few dudes in hysterics, but the DJ was scratching his head instead of the vinyl. Everyone within striking distance was getting a little concerned about where Alex's routine was headed.

Cookie had been way down the back talking to one of the regular bar staff, Deb, and had missed the beginning of Alex's dance routine. She had fixed him up with a few drinks for the boys and he walked through the crowd looking for Pierre to give him his beer. She was a well-rounded figure with a heart of gold. Punk ran through her veins, though she was a harlot for any night scene with thumping beats. Like Moose, her Doc Martens never left her feet and were made for stomping!

"Here ya go, mate!" Cookie yelled, as he nudged Pierre in the back. "Deb sends her love, bra." Cookie had once dated Pierre's sis, Vanessa, and they had become good buddies. Pierre was a few years younger than Cookie and had slept on Cookie's couch plenty of times.

Out of courtesy, Pierre gave his hood rat brother the bag of woof and told him, "Don't have too much!" The bag was already half gone. Cookie's eyes lit up. He thanked Pierre and scurried off to the toilet. Pierre was feeling unreal as he sauntered through the crowd, talking to any girl who showed attitude. His good looks and confidence meant he generally picked up. His policy of "the bigger the challenge, the better the prize" was in full effect.

Coco was a short Argentinian, who had hot salsa genes. He was the Bondi dance master. He lived in Sir Thomas Mitchell Road with his mum, who adored him. He had a lucrative small time business operating out of his bedroom, dealing and scamming right under her nose. He paid her rent, which made her turn a blind eye to anything shifty operating within the unit. Like any mum, she could make a million excuses why Coco did what he did. The units they lived in were only a couple of blocks from the Hill. For these reasons, he was regularly surfing the left hand shore break in the southern corner with various accomplices. He surfed small fat double-enders, similar to the boards Joey Engel used to surf, and they were usually single fins. His Latino blood had him primed for dance floors all over the city. He had jumped on the club merry-go-round from an early age and never looked like getting off. From the Metropolis in North Sydney to any party, anywhere over town, he was always there, partying in all the clubs with the best and worst.

He walked past the line on the door, winked at Moose, who was busy stressing at some bloke, and waltzed in. The dungeon-like room was full of party people. He gave the room and its contents the once over and headed for the bar.

"Coco!" came a yell from a dark shadow in a dark corner. It was another party animal, Danzig. He was wearing black torn shreds, so all Coco could make out was his pale skin in patches. "What the fuck are you doin' here, ya Mexican!"

Coco couldn't mistake Danzig's punk tone. "Amigos," he replied, "How is my punk rock friend?"

"Very gooood, amigo." Danzig's Spanish accent sucked. Not that he gave a fuck. He didn't give a fuck about a lot of things. He was a crazy punk who always wore a smile. It was a mischievous kind of smile—partially sadistic, similar to the ultra violent lead actor, Alex, in "A Clockwork Orange". He was by no means violent, though, being way more of a lover than a fighter. He wore black leather, black denim, studs and silver—another adrenaline junkie, who thrived on the inner city streets.

Coco wanted drugs. "I wanna get higher. Can you get me on?"

Danzig was already off-guts. He didn't hesitate to shove an eccy in his mate's mouth. "Eat this, motherfucker."

Coco's eyes bulged for a split second, as he swallowed the pill dry. He hoped what he was tasting was MDMA. He grabbed for Danzig's drink to wash it down.

"There ya go, mate!" yelled Danzig, "Get that into ya!"

"Thanks mate ... needed a heart starter."

Pierre was walking to the bar with some chick that was going to buy him a drink, when he noticed the sprightly pair. "They let blokes like you in 'ere?" was his sarcastic way of greeting them. He wanted to catch up and talk awhile with his mates, so he told the bird to "buy a couple more drinks and get 'em off Deb". Cookie came out of the bathroom feeling great. Raúl always had the good South American connections. If the boys got it from Raúl they knew they were being looked after. Pierre spotted Cookie's head cruising in the crowd and waved him over.

"Hello, fellas," Cookie said as he greeted his Bondi brothers. He secretly slipped what was left in the bag to Pierre. "Thanks, matey," he whispered, as if to keep things quiet.

Coco wasn't one to miss much. "Thanks for what?" he enquired.

Pierre smirked and flashed the bag. He then invited Danzig

and Coco into the dunny for a line with him. He told Cookie to "wait for the glamour with the drinks and they'd be back soon".

"Which glamour?"

"The one talking to Deb at the bar over there!"

"Righto, mate!" said Cookie, as the three little piggies ventured off through the crowded room towards the loo.

The trio opened the men's dunny door to a rancid smell. Someone had actually shit themselves. Pierre shouted "Fuck that!" and proceeded into the ladies lavatory. The boys followed with most chicks not bothering to raise an eyebrow.

"Hi, Coco, how are you guys?" It was Anna. She was a party bitch from Newtown. She loved getting it on with the boys. "Meet my friend, Sophie." Sophie was a fine young specimen and horny as hell. She was wearing a white, frilly layered skirt and a skimpy, tight black and white striped top that emphasised her medium cleavage and exposed her midriff.

"Well, hello, boys." The 19 year old sounded like a porn princess, probably because she had already starred in two cheap videos shot in some cheap Surry Hills studio.

"You're shit hot, bitch," said Pierre with all the confidence in the world. She ate it up. She could take mouthfuls of his confidence and still want more. His forward tone of voice had instantly created a wet patch in Sophie's panties, which needed tending to. Anna could see the boy's interest weighing towards Sophie's great tits. Even though she was quite cute, she was jealous and needed to interject to shift the focus. "What have you got for me today, Pierre?"

"Nothin'," he answered, as he scooped the next available cubicle and disappeared inside.

"Where's he going?" asked Anna. "I want some." She couldn't help but look a little desperate to the boys.

"Yeah, wait your turn, bitch," said Danzig, who wasn't shy in letting any chick know.

Anna growled at Danzig and discontentedly told him, "I'll be waiting out here."

Coco and Danzig followed Pierre inside and closed the door behind them. Pierre already had some cocaine hanging out of his nostrils when he presented Coco a note to roll. He then finished racking four lines on the cistern. Each boy had their go whilst chicks chatted about girlie shit on the other side of the door.

"Where's mine?" came with Anna banging on the door.

"You guys bail," said Pierre with something in mind.

"I'm stayin'," said Coco.

"Fuck off!" Pierre didn't feel like he wanted to share too much with Coco. He pushed him out and said, "Come in, Anna."

The boys left Pierre to his coke slut and Coco hinted to Sophie to join him. She had other things on her mind and slipped into the cubicle behind Anna.

Cookie was talking to Pierre's drink lady friend, when the two lads returned. He had the gift of the gab going and she was impressed. Cookie loved his ciggies and he was sucking them back with a vengeance. He was a typical rugged alcoholic who had plenty of stories. His mannerisms were a bit unorthodox, as he described things, but the girl was liking it. Full of intrigue, thanks to the coke, Cookie never let the truth get in the way of a good story.

"Where's Pierre?' he asked.

"A little busy," replied Coco.

"Caught up with a couple of buddies." Danzig loved his sarcasm. He was a cynic, or a realist, as he saw it in today's climate. He was highly intelligent, though you wouldn't have thought so, looking at him. He was in his early 20s and had already learnt so much from his sage—the street.

The nightclub became even more crowded and Alex finally wandered off the floor and found the boys.

"You want a drink, Alex?"

He smiled at Cookie's hospitality.

"Here ya are. Drink Pierre's. He's taking long enough!"

The place started to rock, with the DJ belting out some rhythmic breaks. In such a short time, Cookie had talked Pierre's drink girl into going home with him. She didn't like Pierre's arrogance much anyway. He told the boys he was bailing and the girl told the boys to tell Pierre that he "missed out".

After a quick skull of his newly acquired drink, Alex was up for round two on the dance floor. Feeling in the groove, he couldn't keep his feet from moving. Coco was keen for a perve and a chance to show off his moves, so he followed Alex's big frame, which was parting the crowd like the Red Sea.

Flanked by Anna and Sophie, Pierre found Danzig. He didn't even bother asking after his glamour girl with the drinks.

"Some chick bailed with Cookie and said you missed out," said Danzig. The two girls were grabbing Pierre like wild vixens. It was obvious every square inch of the cubicle had been used.

"Where's big Alex? I want him to meet the girls!" asked

Pierre.

"On the floor with Coco," replied Danzig.

The boys, with Anna and Sophie in tow, headed towards the dance floor for a better look. They were all bopping with the crowd. Some new crazed house chicks in their typical black outfits with white socks and black school shoes were cutting moves next to the dance floor. Hood rats socialised in the nooks and crannies and all types were leaning on the many sandstone pillars holding the ceiling up. Adjacent to the dance floor on a split level sat aged rockers and their wenches in cubicles of leather. The place was jumping and patrons everywhere were starting to peak—none more than big Alex, whose narcotics and alcohol mixture kept coming in waves of energy. Coco was carving up the small dance floor space he had to operate in and Alex was trying to emulate him. He managed to capture the attention of most of the joint as he proceeded to do the worm on the floor in front of the DJ. Jumping impetuously upright from the legendary dance move, he got a heavy head rush and almost passed out for a second. In a split second of half unconsciousness, he managed to fall towards the DJ's decks and mixer. The boys watched in awe as the big cumbersome lad fell backwards like a stone cold Lurch. Coco tried in vain to grab him as he fell and the horrified look of the DJ was worth bottling as the music system broke his fall. As the Pommie's world of decks and records came crashing down around him, the pasty weed's headphones became entangled and he went down like a bag of spuds. He fell onto Alex, who awakened and started hugging him in fits of senseless lunacy. Pierre and Danzig cracked up, as Coco leant forward and offered Alex his hand. People who saw it were either laughing or dumbfounded. People who didn't see it were wondering why the music had suddenly stopped. Moose was on the scene in no time with some other big bouncer. Pierre and Danzig moved in to watch Alex let fly if he had to, but Moose knew better and called security off. The skinny, pale, pissweak DJ got up swearing at Alex and telling Moose in his Manchester accent that he should, "Do fucking something and counter this act of fucking terrorism!"

Moose wasn't prepared to hear any shit from the DJ. He was rubbing his smirking face in disbelief of yet another classic stunt by his boofy mate Alex.

"Well aren't you gonna fucken' throw the bastard outta here?" the DJ asked.

"Listen here, pommy. This ain't your fuckin' town," was his

swift reply.

"Do somethin'! This cunt's just fucked everything!"

"Whatta ya expect, geezer? He's as full as a Pommy's complaint box. Ha!" said Moose, as he totally dismissed the East End wonder.

He was solid with the boys, no matter what went down. He knew punks fucked up and shit happened—he was one of them. They were all brothers watching each other's back in the big wide world. They were all out of the same mould.

"Encore, encore!" yelled the boys.

Moose helped Alex up with Coco and, with his usual brotherly, smart-arse grin, commented "Flash dance, bra!"

Another day

It was a glary morning and Dan and Cookie were hanging on the Hill checking the surf. Dan came prepared and had worn his wraparound terminator sunnies to shield the bright sun that had just popped its head over the green pastures of the North Bondi Golf Course. Cookie forgot to wear his and had to settle with a squint that would have put a Chinaman to shame. They chose to sit amidst the shade of the tall pine trees and surrounding shrubs to filter any blinding rays that would hinder them watching the surf. The pines were slowly dying from all the detergent pumped into the sea beyond the golf course. Each time the wind blew nor-east, it served up a tasty menu of city waste.

Since early childhood, Dan marvelled at the sight of the enormous brown patch, known as "the murk", which provided a chocolate backdrop for two mermaids reclining elegantly on top of a very large rock. The mermaids, "Lynette" and "Jan", were modelled off two local swimming champions and made instant world headline news mainly due to the fact that both were topless at a time when nudity was unacceptable. They became Bondi icons until a severe storm condemned them to a watery grave.

A winter low pressure system had just dropped a load of snow on the Aussie Alps and was heading out into the Tasman, generating a solid six-foot swell. It was welcome nourishment for the local surfing community. On this day, the surf was serving up plenty of options. Three breaks held the Terminator and Harry Who's interest: the right-hander, behind the southern reef, the left shorie, in the southern corner and the right bank, down at Third Ramp. It was their big decision of the morning. The wind was sou-west, off the mountains, which was common in winter. The crisp offshore breeze had swept any foreign matter miles out to sea and the bay looked splendid, almost pristine. Stacked swell lines stretched back to the horizon, blending into a dark blue ocean, like regimented lines of an Eastern Block military parade. Emerald waves pitched their watery caverns in the transparent green shallows and washed up and over the brilliant white sands. Seagulls frolicked around the tide mark and went about their breakfast duties, as joggers huffed by. Local members, wearing only their Speedos, swam laps in the chilly water of the Icebergs pool. Occasionally, waves of white-water would roll in and hit the pool's oceanside wall, sending spray high into the air. All the time, the sun glistened on the water, shining its magic over the whole setting.

It was evident to the boys that, every minute the tide moved in, the waves at Third Ramp were improving. High tide was only a couple of hours away, so the shallow sandbank on the inside was filling up quickly. As usual, the rip was motoring out through a deep channel, causing water to draw up the face and turn the waves into well shaped wedges. Fitzy and the Coleman brothers were positioned in the rip, picking off slabs of ocean and getting barrelled. They were using the rip like a chairlift, letting it drag them out the back and into the take-off position. The surf in the southern corner, behind the reef, was also looking brilliant, thanks to the backwash from the baths. The waves were rebounding off the baths' wall and hitting the incoming swells, making them stand up and throw like a judo master. The two surf trojans, Sloth and Andy, were dominating the peak, taking the best set waves on offer. Their smooth styles complemented each other as they raced across the inviting sections, throwing spray high over the back of the wave, every time they jammed off the top. Riding over the perilously shallow cunje on the inside shelf, they were free-falling into hollow, sucky bowls and getting tubed more often than not. Once past the reef, they would glide stylishly out into the channel, arms raised above their heads, assuming a classic 60s stylish pose.

Coco, Porks and Corro seemed happy surfing the solid left-hand shore-break with a bunch of keen grommets. Reforming waves from the outside bank were pushing through to the shore-break and feeding the frenzy. These waves would roll over a deep gutter mustering volume and power to finally stand up and pitch again as they reached the shallows. It was hard for Dan and Cookie to know where to look, with surfers dotted from North to South. It was a good day to be surfing anywhere along the beach. Only one area was void of wetsuit-clad waxheads. A solitary set of flags, posted smack bang in front of the Bondi Surf Club, designated the spot where any hardcore lunatics should swim. A lone body-surfer braved the chilly 15-degree water temp. Keeping him company, sitting on a surf rescue ski, the head lifeguard, Laurie, was catching a few waves of his own. From the Baths down South to the kiddies' pool up North, surfers had the reign of the beach. It was a day local surfers longed for. It was a day many would've sold their souls for, if they weren't already mortgaged.

It was a day that made being on the dole worth it. It was a day that saw ninety percent of Bondi's surfing workforce take a sickie.

As the boys looked over the beach, the offshore breeze was mustering strength and trying to blow right through them. The cold air, flowing down off the Blue Mountains, had plummetted temperatures, out Penrith way, to below zero during the night. To combat the cold, Dan and Cookie were glad to be wearing their latest woollen jumpers, bought at Vinnies in Hall Street. Dan wore a high-neck skivvy under his jumper for extra insulation and resembled an Austrian ski instructor on the prowl in an après-ski bar. He liked skiing and had a plastic bag full of winter gear tucked under his bed for trips to Thredbo. Most surfers in the water wore nothing less than full length steamer wetsuits. Those who didn't risked blue balls. Any human part not covered resembled a half frozen prime cut. Losing circulation was a common sacrifice to surf good winter swells. The biggest challenge to the system was always the shock of entering the icy water. Once this hurdle was cleared, the ensuing numbness usually blocked any further signals reaching the brain. Some preferred to dive straight in, dealing with the shock as quickly as possible, whilst others paddled out with their head held high, like a periscope, trying to keep their hair dry, delaying the inevitable ice cream headache for as long as they could.

Surfers were getting slotted, regularly emerging from the barrel like human projectiles being shot out of a cannon. On the left shorie, Coco was in his element. He was surfing a classic, red, 7'2" Lightning Bolt that he had borrowed, instead of his regular six-foot, single fin, double-ender. Being goofy, he was on his forehand, pulling through some nice cylinders, using the extra length of board to his advantage. He had grabbed the board from Wade, who owned the popular Gabby's Health Café, down south on Campbell Parade. They were good mates. Wade was a few years older and a competent chef. Most locals would head to his well being café, famished after a marathon surf session, to munch and slurp on healthy cakes, pastries and banana smoothies. It pumped the tunes out and also served the mega breakfast. It was a casual hang. Upon entering the wide open doorway, you strutted past your typical plastic tables and chairs on one side, with elevated dining benches and stools on the other. At the counter, Wade's upbeat face greeted everyone, with the usual "What'll ya have, mate?" An aromatic waft filled your nostrils, as you contemplated the daily specials listed on the blackboard. Once seated, you looked straight out onto the street, making it a good spot to socialise with the many passers-by. After filling your belly and acquiring a rock of hash for dessert, you were rolling out the door, ready for a session, followed by your next surf—or nanna nap, depending on how stoned you got.

Coco had borrowed the Lopez board six months earlier and being the slack arse that he was "Gerry" wasn't comin' back anytime soon. This red, pintailed boomerang had been on a long, wide arc, since it left Wade's hands and was now stuck in a monkey trap. As he pulled under each curtain, you could see his lemur-like silhouette threading the eye of the tube. The Binky Bill of the session was Corro, aka Starman, who was also in his element, occasionally dropping in on Coco and anyone he felt like burning. He sat furthest out from the pack, his blonde moustache and goatee harbouring shiny ocean droplets between the stubble. His red and yellow board and matching panelled wetsuit gave the impression of a comic book super hero. Sitting, waiting for set waves, he was always overflowing with a burning desire to be the best. Just like Steele, like Crumbles and good old Joey Engel, he displayed a lust for surfing that lifted him into the elite level. Free surfing at Bondi had always been dominated by a local rat pack and the 80s was no different. It amounted to one big competition. Every man and his bitch pushed each other so hard, it just kept raising the stakes. Starman was relaxed and enjoying his morning surf. He was generally top of the pecking order, except when older, respected crew were about. Even then, he was still cheeky and would try and paddle on the inside of pretty much everyone, except maybe Col Sutho. Casual as ever, he would take off late, purposely looking back at whoever was inside him, before fading them into oblivion. He didn't care. Surfing was always about having as much fun as you could and, so, dropping in and taking waves off your mates was all part of it. It was something to be expected and not taken too personally. You knew the guys you shouldn't and couldn't hassle. Sometimes, egos clashed and blood was spilt, but that was normal for any beach. It kept a social order that connected the whole 'hood. The left shorie at South Bondi was always a test of your resilience. When it was pumping, the cream of Bondi engaged in a frenzied pursuit of pure fun.

"I'm headin' to get me board and hit the left shorie!" The Cookie Monster had awoken. The early morning stink bud session was wearing off.

"Good call, brudda! You can clear the water for me."

"Thought you were going to surf Third Ramp?"

"Yeah, I was, but uh ... well, someone's gotta help Starman drop in on everybody."

Starman always carried on a bit, but good surfers generally hassled in the water. That's how they got good! You weren't out there to catch slim pickings. Everyone had an appetite. Some were just hungrier than others and some, like Corro, were just plain starving. His sacrifice to quit the tour epitomised the "fuck that" Bondi attitude. He wasn't the first Bondi surfer to shy away from the surfing spotlight. Such a famous beach had a strong underground and to many surfers this provided all the stimulation and enjoyment they needed. The street culture of Bondi was a world unto itself. Sacrificing a surfing career to stay at home oozed disregard and the rebel in Corro burned bright.

"Meet you out there in five."

As the Terminator and squinty Chinaman turned to split, a familiar voice crossing Campbell Parade yelled out, "Why aren't you lovebirds out there already?"

It was Alex, sporting a black eye and a ripper cut on his forehead. He was smiling, as usual, even though it looked to pain him somewhat.

Looking dishevelled, it was obvious Alex had been in the wars again.

"Looks like you've been wrestling with your boyfriend again!" said Cookie.

"How 'bout I knock your other front tooth out, so you can learn to gummy suck!"

"You sound a little bummed out, bra—musta been on the bottom copping it hard, right?"

"You okay, cuz? Everything sweet?"

"Fuckin' course it is."

"Be fuckin' somethin' different, if he wasn't."

"Last time I saw you, I was waiting for me pizza a week ago at Ken-san's place. What the fuck happened, brudda?" Alex squinted, as the sun was still bright. It seemed he couldn't deal with that question right now, as it was a long story. "Thought you could've come back at least and celebrated the Roosters' win with us!" Alex's disappearing act was common, but Dan was understandably concerned, wondering how long his cousin could keep moonwalking on the edge. He was pleased to see his cousin alive and kickin' after every inner city mission. This frontline had helped mould all the boardriders' characters at some stage. All were doing their own tour of duty and you had to repeatedly keep one eye out for possible danger. If you didn't, you were susceptible to the many pitfalls the big city lights attracted.

"That twenty bucks sure went a long way."

"Your best mate Kenny's livid."

"Well, he can eat shit for pizza, the slanty-eyed cunt!"

"Anyway, good to see you made it back to the valley in one piece mate, even though you look a bit beat up."

"Yeah, always good to be back in the land of the living." He scratched the top of his head. His bung eye was constantly being harassed by a spasmodic, twitching muscle under the socket.

"You been AWOL a few days now, big fella. Have some fun, did we?"

"Got tangled up in the city with a bunch of fucking pimps and prostitutes." Alex had refrained from giving the boys the ritual handshake, as his knuckles were sore and swollen. "Got a bit fucked up, heh heh." He had taken more drugs in a week than a Callum Park lunatic and was unsteady. Occasionally, his head drooped back into his shoulders. One could tell some of his inside lights had been turned off and Dan only hoped a shutdown didn't occur whilst he was in a vulnerable situation.

"Hope you haven't been smoking heroin with your lady boy friends again." A vision of Alex waking up with a sore bum, in a seedy, banged up, inner city terrace, sauntered through his mind. "Was a bit fucking worried about you, cuz, but I knew you could handle yourself, big fella. Boys told me about your wog-smashing effort across the road and I should commend you on such a fine display of brutality." Dan wasn't a huge fan of violence, but when it came to sticking up for his beach and mates, he was all for it. "And the Kardomah effort had everyone down the 'Bergs in stitches. Moose was impressed and gave everyone the rundown!"

"We've all heard about you fuckin' up the Pommy DJ and ruining his life," added Cookie. "I was spewing I left early and missed that shit! Lucky I got laid."

"That story has done the rounds and all your Maroubra mates have raised you to legend status. Someone's gonna write a book about you one day and I'll be able to brag that you're me relative!"

"Yeah, well, I suppose some cunt's got nothing fucking better to do with their time than to talk about other cunts!" He winced from his sore head. "Fuckin' grapevine!"

"Don't be like that. It's somethin' to be proud of. Aye, Alex? Big colonial boy like you, letting those wogs and pommies know. Fuckin' legendary Eureka Stockade material, mate!"

"Yeah, you're a modern day Les Norton!"

In retrospect, the gentle giant squirmed somewhat. For a split second, he wrestled with an idea that popped into his head from some far-reaching place that actually harboured sensible thought. Had he possibly made a total fool of himself? A split second later, it fell out of his head. He lost that caring, responsible, out-of-character consideration and smirked—because that's what he did well. He was a smirker. No matter what was thrown at him, he seemed to always produce a self-satisfying grin at the end of it. His smirk was contagious and the boys joined in. There might have been a lunatic jumping in and out of his head, but he was a comfortable visitor. He shrugged his shoulders. "It was nothin'."

"That shit on yer face ain't from those Oxford Street fairies you been hangin' out with?"

He leaned back on one of the parked cars, looked wryly at Cookie and started a verbal defence. "Nah, mate, fairies tend to open ya up in other parts ... and blokes like you are usually droppin' messy fuck ... fuckin' facials on 'em ... glitter fuckin' ones. Actually, I've seen fairy dust on yer arse many a time. Maybe it started when your tooth fell out of your fuckin' head and the tooth fairy fucked ya! Ha ha!"

"You're just fuckin' jealous," replied Cookie.

"How'd you know, fairy fucker? You're the poofta who went and seen Gary Glitter, when you were a grommet!"

Cookie couldn't better that, off the top of his head, so he went with it. "Well, me elder sister dragged me along and I got me first pash, so it weren't that bad."

"So, it wasn't the tooth fairy who broke ya in, after all."

Dan changed the conversation. "What really happened to ya, cuz?"

"What, these little pissy scratches on me melon? Well, just a bit of a rumble with some Islanders and copped a couple."

"Looks sore."

76

Being fond of the biff, Alex was never one to elaborate. He had been in enough blues that he would minimise most of his savage encounters. They just seemed natural to him. The bruising and cuts on his face—from what seemed some sort of metal chain—were wounds that would heal soon enough—and if they left a scar: "so fuckin' what!"

The incident occurred a couple of nights earlier. He had just arrived back in Bondi from his week-long city adventure and was 'round at a mate's flat chilling out. The pad was on the 2nd floor of the legendary Britannic Mansions, next to the Biltmore Hotel, on Campbell Parade. The front room overlooked the whole beach. It was a popular hang amongst the boardriders, because you could see the surf from each unit. The units were situated above one of the many pizzerias which dotted Campbell Parade—called Nino's. Before all the trendy cafés blew in, Papa Giovanni's and Nino's were popular Italian haunts for the community. Italians were wogs, but the majority had earned their respect after migrating to Oz after the War and part of the reason Aussies warmed to them was because of their food.

The Britannic units were a surfing clubhouse with crew leaving their boards there so they didn't have to lug them from wherever they lived. Having a unit or even a garage close to the beach was always popular for the surfing fraternity. From the mid 70s, the six units of the Britannic Mansions were patronised by local surfers and everyone knew each other. Surfers constantly moved in and out and even ricocheted between units. They were grotty and cockroach infested, but it was cheap rent and it was right on the beach. The dark and dingy Mansions were Bondi's surfing central, until they were gutted in the wave of new development in the late 90s.

Wade, who ran Gabby's Café, and his staunch mate, Brucey, rented the particular art deco damaged apartment Alex had visited the night of the attack. Wade was a medium sized, thick-set guy, who had straight, shoulder length brown hair that hung over his face like a sheepdog. He was a thinker, but like so many surfers back then, not academically inclined. There seemed to be a bit of Zorba the Greek in him, because he had olive skin and sported a ripper tan in summer, over his solid physique. He loved to party and the bit of wog in him mimicked flamenco and salsa steps way before they ever became popular. He was a regular at the Cauldron, Kardomah and any other club that was pumping. Sure, he had some kind of Euro blood in him, but he was first and foremost an Aussie larrikin. He had a harem of girls and was always dressed smartly for any occasion. The guy could make anything look good—even a kaftan. He took pride in his café's food and brought some of the first vegetarian cuisine to the beach. Before Gabby's, it was only milk bars, such as Vallis' or Bates', with their hamburgers and milkshakes, catering for surfers. There was one exception: The Flying Pieman, on the corner of Curlewis and the strip, which sold state-of-the-art meat pies with dead horse and, as an extra culinary delicacy, served indigestion that kept repeating itself afterwards, so you could spew the contents back up in your mouth during your next surf and either spit or swallow. Standard good Aussie tucker!

Wade cooked up spinach pies, veggie pattie burgers, muesli apple crumble, assorted wholesome soups, energy shakes and his hash cake was a specialty. It was so potent that he could have easily forgotten that he had lent his prized 7'2" Lopez to Coco. A chef by trade, he had all the boys eating well, by promoting healthy food and his five-buck breakfast filled the place up every morning.

His flatmate, Brucey, was a short, stocky bloke, with a good sense of humour—a smaller version of Wade. However, there was no Euro blood in this boy. He was 100% blue-blooded Aussie, his sun-bleached hair hanging and curling around like he'd just come out of a Tasmanian devil spin. Had a bit of a snoz on him, which always seemed like it needed to be blown. From a young age, he worked out the best way to avoid a nose bleed was to keep his snotty nose out of trouble. Being an observer, he made it his business to know the ropes and made sure he was shying away from the slippery ones greased up from all the Bondi grime. He held his cards tight against his chest and usually thought twice before making any moves. It was intelligent philosophy, because blatant behaviour was confronting and usually met its match pretty quickly in the scum of the Valley.

That fateful evening that led to Alex's beauty bumps, Wade, Brucey and Alex sat in the front room minding their own business, when there was a loud banging at the door. Brucey went to answer it and another local mate, named Damian, charged in screaming, "Quick, shut the door. They're fuckin' comin'!"

As a slightly confused, stoned, little Brucey started shutting the big brown, old, paint flaking, wooden door, three huge Maoris pushed through the entrance and smacked him aside, yelling, "Where is the cunt? We'll kill 'im!"

The design of the unit was very unusual. It was unorthodox and its crazy old floor plan was surely an experiment in its 1908 architectural design. It had a central hallway, which connected a series of bedrooms and a kitchen. Damian knew the joint backwards and was so quick in hiding that no one knew which nook or cranny he had taken refuge in. When Wade and Alex appeared from the front bedroom to check out the commotion, one of the Maoris started belting Alex with some bicycle handle bars. Everyone half-pie shit themselves and ducked for cover. Alex rolled under another swing, then connected with a punch of his own. But, before he could continue his assault, another 250-pound tattooed warrior crash tackled him across the room. He covered up and thought it best he lie motionless on the floor. Another put the boot in for good measure, before they realised the white boy they wanted wasn't in the room. The blood-thirsty posse headed back to the hallway and continued searching for their main target.

Being maze-like played into the boy's favour. Towards the back of the unit, the narrow hallway forked with a kitchen on one side, leading into a back bedroom, and on the right, a little storage alcove that doubled as a bedroom, where Brucey had slipped into and hid. As he crouched behind the door in nervous anticipation, it burst open and Damian yelled, "Quick, mate, and close the fucking door this time!"

Brucey was classically headstrong for a stumpy bloke and this time 'round was not pleased about being pestered again. He immediately arced up, as he was sick of copping shit that he knew nothing about. "Fuck ya! I'm sick of this shit. Get the fuck out of here. This is my hiding spot!"

A split second later, there was a repeat of what happened at the front door. The three incensed Maoris came barrelling on through, hot on Damian's scent. A fat, tattooed, hand, planted firmly in Brucey's face, pushed him aside, whilst they lunged at Damian, who managed to jump through a narrow interior window and into the pitch black of the back bedroom. The three stressed coconuts thought he had escaped out the rear window of the building and down the fire stairs into the darkness of the night. Lucky for Damian, they were all fooled by the placement of the internal window. The plan of the unit had saved him. Regarding his exit strategy as a disadvantage, all three islanders back-tracked and ran single file out the front door to pursue him around the back alleyway.

Wade closed the front door and quickly bolted it. Damian did the same to the back door and sarcastically blurted, "Thanks for coming, ya black cunts, and next time try not to shit yerselves!"

As the boys met in the hallway, they were all in a state of shock. It all happened so quickly. After a few "Fucks" and "Shits", they couldn't help but start laughing at the scene that had just gone down. It was a nervous laugh, but a deserving one. Damian told them that the havoc was all because he had accidentally spat on their tow-truck tyre.

"You mean, they were fucken' tow truck drivers?"

"Yep. Heavy, Botany ones, at that."

"Well, that's just fuckin' great. You'll have to bring them over again sometime, Dames."

"Make sure they bring their shiny metal chains with 'em, aye?"

"What if they come back?" asked Brucey.

"No probs." Alex emerged from the front room, loaded-and-cocked pistol in hand, "I'll have to show them my little persuader."

There were no hard feelings towards Damian. Shit happens. Brucey grabbed an ice pack from the kitchen fridge for Alex's battered scone and Wade headed back to the front room to mull up and help calm any lingering tension.

Afterwards, to pick things up a little, they all decided to head to Selinas, at the Coogee Bay Hotel, to check out The Angels and Radiators. Alex's head was throbbing to the beat of the music, but the pain was nothing a few Jack Daniels couldn't cure.

Dan continued his caring conversation with his cuz, "Nice scratch, big fella." The morning sun had a few beads of sweat running from Alex's hairline and into the wound. "You're lucky: it doesn't look as though it needs any stitches."

Alex kept grinding his teeth; combined after-effects from a hit to the head and any residual toxins ingested during his week-long city indulgence. "Yeah, well, I'm more worried about my fuckin' dick. It's feelin' kinda … a bit of pressure, when I fuckin' piss." As he spoke, mashed spit managed to creep out from the sides of his mouth.

"Teach ya to go hangin' with whores, brudda. Hope you didn't end up at the Taxi Club, gettin' sucked off by a trannie."

80

"That mightn't be all that bad, Glitter Boy. I heard they suck dick like a bubbler in the desert and I'm sure a fruitcake like you wouldn't pass it up, if you were pissed enough."

"Yeah, well, I suppose lips have no gender, aye, Alex?"

"True, Cookie. But, assholes don't either and I think you prefer them anyway." Alex might have been slow at times, but he had the edge in this bagging session. "You got a spare ciggy, bra?" he continued.

"What am I, a ciggy caddy?" quipped Cookie. Alex jostled his arm, so he pulled out his Winfield Blue packet and gave his big goofy mate a durrie.

A good set swept into the bay and Starman dropped into the pit and disappeared behind the curtain for a few seconds. It was enough to put to rest any further "Tales of Alex" and get them on their way.

"Okay, we're going surfin', brudda, so we'll have to catch ya later." Dan was now keen to get in the water. "You can watch us drop in on Starman."

"Cool, cuz. I'll just hang here and watch ya get a couple."

"Okay, Alex. Don't go fightin' too many fairies, mate. See ya soon, bro," said Cookie.

"Leave me a coupla durries, mate?"

Cookie knew Alex had seen his near-full packet, so not to begrudge his mate, he heeded to the command—with a sly huff, just to continue the heckle.

On that note, the boys headed home to grab their boards and join the Starman and Coco Show on the left-shorie.

The day turned out to be pretty epic, the beach becoming a tapestry of sunshine, great waves and of local mates surfing their brains out.

Later that afternoon, some tired, but not done-with yet, board riders gathered on the Hill. They were watching the late session and sucking on a few VB coldies. The crew in the surfing line-up were mainly workers, the few who had actually gone to work that day. The sou-wester had shifted west and blown hard all day, knocking the top off the marching swells. As the strip's tall buildings cast their late arvo shadows across the beach, they were taking advantage of the day's last rays. Most of the lads were burned-out, but still cruising on auto-pilot. As long as there was signs of beer or chicks, their motors kept running.

Brendan's freckled nose was peeling and Cookie's eyebrows

81

were crusty, like two Doyle's oysters on a rock-salt bed. Horse had hit up all present for some drinking money and had strolled down to the Bondi Hotel bottle shop and brought back a case. At a discounted price, of course, thanks to Pierre's ex, who also happened to be Horse's ex—*and* some of the crew.

Horse was a staunch local personality who was well respected. He was a gifted natural-footer, who had done his fair share of time in the water. Being a big-hearted kind of guy who loved the drink, he was very popular with most of the local alcoholic surfers. Because of this, he carried a VB baby-gut around with him. But, anyone who dared bag him usually came off second best—a victim of Horse's lightning fast wit. Porky's gut was normally a much bigger and easier target.

"Anyone hittin' the Diggers Club, tonight?" asked Horse. Only a few of the boys heard him, as most were engrossed in their own conversations. They were generally talking about how insane the day's surfing had been.

Someone in the midst of the crowd had his ears pricked and replied, "Fucken oath, bra. There's a filthy bikini fashion show or somethin'. So there's gonna be heaps of chicks!"

"A bikini show?" asked Cookie.

"Sounds like G-bangers everywhere, dude," yelled an excited Fitz. His forehead vein was awakening, as always, drawn to the excitement of sex, drugs, music and surf—the four cardinal points of his immoral compass.

Horse took another swig of his beer. "Why do ya think I'm goin', ya morons?" All radar was now being tuned into the bikini conversation. Airwaves that mentioned tits, legs or arse took preference in the boardrider's handbook.

"First I've heard of it, but count me in." There was no way Brendan was going to be left out. "I wanna show off me new Rudolph the Reindeer look!"

"Sweet! I'm going, too!" exclaimed Fitzy, sporting his customary Colonel Sanders smile. The lad was in heaven. For the Colonel, as for a lot of the boys, Bondi was heaven—a blessing in the rigours of a supply-and-demand world. This evoked an almost Zen state of mind, which some mistakenly attributed to drugs. "What a sick day, aye?" said the ever positive Colonel, as he meditated on the day's beauty. After a slight pause, he continued, "Surf, beer and pussy. What more could you want?" His vein had started to pump, "FUCK, I LOVE BONDI! YEAH!!"

It was sure to be a good night for the boys. The Diggers Club always turned it on. Situated halfway along Campbell Parade, The Diggers was an institution intimately tied to the local community. The staff dressed in the standard black and white uniform and all were born-and-bred in the area. Overlooking the beach made it a centrally located watering hole. On the ground floor, it had a swimming pool and steam room, which were really popular on Mondays, when most crew needed to detox. The carpet flooring was a 60s floral design and there were poker machine addicts roaming over it everywhere. You couldn't escape it, because it rolled down each set of stairs connecting each level like the Blob. It was even in the lift. Like most RSLs, many a local pension or dole cheque was spent in hope of five Incas filling the middle frame. The drinking hole provided all the comforts for a community to indulge in, including Bingo, meat tray raffles, darts, entertainment stage and a rooftop for barbecues. If you didn't win a meat tray, or were too pissed to cook at home, there was an affordable bistro, serving steak sangas and roasts all under ten bucks.

"Cool, Colonel. I'll pick you up around eight," said Cookie. "And we can get a bit sideways before we go!"

"Sounds good to me. Yeeeew!"

The Diggers turned out to be a good night for the boys, with bikini clad vixens strutting their stuff in front of their eager eyes. The beer was, as usual, nice and cold and the crowd got understandably more vocal as the night wore on. It was all appeasement for their young virile senses. Dan had met an ex-girlfriend early in the night and told the boys he was "taking her home for a good thrashing". Looked like she was up for it, by the way she was grabbing his dick. Unfortunately, the late night shift were so legless, by the time the girls finished parading, they were unable to hold a coherent conversation and struck-out in that department.

Across the room, their Porsche-driving, Rolex-wearing, Edgecliff blow-in competition ended up with the booty. These upper class, gentrified lads were always odds-on to win the girlie stakes that night. Like Kingston Town at Randwick, they were never going to be beaten.

"Fucken yuppie kooks," commented Brendan, as he glanced sideways at their table. A tinge of jealousy might have been detected amidst the insult.

83

Horse didn't care. He was drunkenly adamant when he gave his opinion, "Who gives a fuck, anyway, you tosser." He half snarled, then continued, "Can't you tell?"

"Tell what?"

"Those guys might have all the money in the world, but guess what?" Horse's question had the delirious attention of the table. Rudy and the rest of his reindeers said nothing, as their eyes asked the "What, Horse?" question for them.

"Well, ain't it fucking obvious?"

"Wot, geezer?

"Haaa. They might have all the money in the world, but they can't fucking surf!"

The table started giggling. At that time of night, it didn't take much.

"Yeah, well, I suppose everyone surfs these days, but not everyone's a surfer," added Brendan, cynically.

The money was generally going to win-over the women, especially on this occasion, when the only competition was a table of sloppy, chauvinistic, pissed idiots.

"Hey, why do chicks stare at guy's arses?" Brendan's nose had become a glowing red snoz. Santa's sleigh would've been heading to Mars.

"Why?" asked the Colonel, with an inebriated head wobble.

"To see how big their wallets are!" The table sniggered. They were happy drunks at home at their local.

Across the room, another local friend, named Getz, had just put his last borrowed redback through the card machines. It was obvious he was maggotted, as he steered towards the boys' table. Getz was from Hun stock and one might have thought he had Bach or Beethoven ringing in his head as he crossed the floor. The stylish paralytic waltz was evidence that his controls were on auto-pilot. He had a classic sway happening, with his hands in his pocket, as he careened one way and then the other. Six foot in stature, with a grin like a Messerschmitt pilot tailing a Spitfire, he arrived at the table, letting out his customary "Whoooooa!!!!!" followed by, "Who'll get me a fucking beer?"

"No-one on this table, Getz!" Horse, like the rest of the table, had heard it a million times before. "Get a job, ya Kransky-eatin' Sauerkraut!"

"Fuck off, Horse, ya fat cunt. As if I wouldn't buy you one!"

"Hasn't anyone fuckin' told you?" threw in Cookie.

"Wot, Kookie?"

"The German army's kaput, shit-face!"

"Oh, really?"

"Yeah, ask any Jew you want."

"Dover Heights and Vaucluse are full of the fuckers!"

"Then let me drown me sorrows and buy me a beer."

Towering ominously over the table, Getz would've looked more appropriately dressed in an SS overcoat than his chequered flanno and faded blue jeans.

"'Cause you lost the war or because the Eastern Suburbs is full of Jews?"

"Fucken both!"

"Well, you get nought, because we're all broke!"

"Well, you pricks may as well be wearing skull caps, yerselves then!"

He thought about his chances and whether it was worth having another go at extracting some coin from the table, before deciding it was easier to open an account elsewhere.

He settled with a final, cheeky reply, "Wunderbar! You guys are cunts!"

He gathered his thoughts and, with one hand still in his pocket, headed towards the bar to ask the same grovelling beer question to some other patron, who might just buy him a beer to get his camel breath out of their face. As he stumbled past the Porsche-driving yuppie table, he received some dissatisfied looks, as if his appearance was more suitable to a Matthew Talbot home. As usual, it was untidy, but that was to be expected from the boof-headed Kraut, especially after a night on scabbed piss money. His shirt was hanging out and his pants looked as if the arse had fallen out of them. But, as always, he was comfortable.

Never one to hold back, he popped the question, "What the fuck are you cunts lookin' at?"

They felt like saying something in response, but knew better. It was the end of a rowdy night and there were a lot of drunk locals in the room and they knew Getz was one of them.

Getz usually wore no undies, so the hand in his pocket was rubbing on his dick. It gave him an idea to counter the contempt shown by the Edgecliff boys. "What are ya shittin' yerselves for?" In saying that, he pulled his side pockets inside out, unzipped his fly and lobbed his long uncircumcised pride and joy out. He walked closer towards them, his manhood swinging from side to side like a giant pendulum. "Do ya like me lazy elephant, guys? He's really friendly." Gasps were heard from the table, "Hey, girls, do you want to stroke his trunk? He doesn't bite. I swear. He lets me pat him all the time." Once again, Krusty the Clown had exposed himself to an audience of kids. Bordering on disgust and horror, they hastily stood up and bee-lined for the exit. Getz arched his eyebrows, quite at home with his old fella hanging out. "Sure you don't wanna give him a kiss goodbye?"

"Put a bit of mustard on that kransky and you might tempt 'em, bra," yelled a local observer, from the bar. Showing all his class, Getz spat on the empty table relinquished after his circus act. Slowly, he turned his fat neck towards other patrons, like a satellite dish pans to pick up a signal. His beer antennae again commenced to search the room for a suitable wavelength to plug into.

The night for the boys was coming to an end. As last drinks were called, the bar-full of local drunks was proof that it was a cherished venue. The boys had been applying themselves to the surfing rulebook. Every beach had their own book of rules, based on their own accepted code of beach ethics. The Bondi boardriders' interpretation of what was morally acceptable was contrary to most universal law. Their rule states that, "He who ends up the most fucked up, wins". They were all in contention. Horse, Fitzy and Brendan entered the bright lights of the lift with a couple of fellow drunken comrades, Rick and Larni. Rick and Larni were fellow boardriders, familiar with the rules. As they stumbled out of the lift and into the ground floor lobby, it was muck up time, as usual. As the rulebook states, "Messiness corrupts. Absolute messiness absolutely corrupts".

All were carrying-on amongst themselves, making sure they jokingly told the bouncer where to go, as they entered a well-lit Campbell Parade. Getz was staggering metres in front of them, totally out of it, with a big smile on his face and hands still in his pockets. He lived only a couple of blocks away, behind the school in Glasgow Avenue. His dad was Austrian and his mum was Lithuanian and they had worked hard for their brown brick haven—your typical Bondi semi. Not caring too much for school, Getz was street wise and artful at getting through the day with naught in his pocket. He shared the house with his mum, as his dad lived elsewhere. She was a big woman, who ruled the house with an unsympathetic iron fist. "Ah, don't tell to me fuckin' bullshit!" She was a hard lady and, although she was often short of affection, she loved her son dearly. The Nazi regime had obviously put a lot of shit on her back in the home country. Her demeanour and accent was so heavy, the boys would be scared shitless when popping around, especially when they were up to no good. If she found them in the kitchen she'd rip into Getz with, "Ah, so you been feeding za kids again, huh?" If they were stoned, on top of that she would add, "Ah, look, your eyes, huh, smoking da marijuana, ya, you fucking drug addicts!" On many occasions, poor Getz' mates copped the brunt of her Nazi oppression. She was a sweet lady if you weren't involving yourself in her son's aberrations. She was even nicer if you agreed with her that all Jews were fucked and her son was in need of some discipline. Getz loved her dearly, but the only way he could deal with her constant harassment was to bag her—to his mates— mocking her mannerisms, drama and accent. He would make faces behind her back, trying to make them laugh. When they were stoned and especially if they were tripping, it was impossible not to bust out into fits of laughter. Incensed, she would commence slapping their heads, until they'd flee to the safety of the street. Getz' behaviour was nothing short of sadistic. He didn't worry about copping any of his mum's shit. He was used to it. He had a lot of his dad in him and didn't let her bother him. He'd just walk off with her raving and ranting, because that was just how it was in Getz' house. And if there was a girl hanging around. she wasn't spared either. "Ah! So, always fuckin' da molls!" was her normal response, as she gave the girl the stink eye. "Why you not fuck at your own mother's house?" By this time, most girls were either ducking for cover or heading for the door. "Get out, you molls!" wasn't required, but she wasn't going to let the opportunity pass.

After the Diggers night out, Getz was planning to wobble straight home to his beloved pillow that he had nicknamed "Elle—he knew there was salami and cheese in the fridge and he needed to soak up some of the drink.

"Getz, ya Gaylord." A voice yelled from behind, as he staggered further along the strip, "Whaddya doin'?" yelled a stirring Rick.

"Fuck you!" came back at 100 miles an hour. Getz was past comprehension and couldn't quite make out who it was or what they'd said, but he knew how to answer any question referring to him as a "Gaylord".

"Getz, ya rude cunt!" Horse was old school and keen to sort out any disrespect shown, even if it was only in fun and games.

"Sieg Heil to you too, Getz." said the Colonel.

"Yeah, Getz, ya pillow biter. Fuck you, too." continued Rick.

Getz raised his voice to another level. "Fuck off and leave me sweet 'Elle' alone!!"

"She's the only chick you'll be rootin' tonight," added Brendan.

"Fuck off, beetroot nose!" Brendan could only smile at the comeback. He was actually amazed that Getz could focus on anything as small as his nose.

"Looking for a bit, Getsie?" continued Horse. It was obvious that Getz was walking on thin ice with the boys and a rumble was on the cards—one of those rumbles where you're not supposed to want to hurt your mate but, really, you do.

"You guys are cunts," retorted Getz. "Probably copping large dick in ..." he hesitated, as he became aware that the boys' pistons had commenced chasing him. "Yer bum!" The pissed rumble was on!

Although he had a bit of a head start, it wasn't long till the lads had him pinned on the ground. As it was, he was lucky to make it to the corner of Wairoa Avenue, only a few metres away. The alcohol racing through everyone's body had them sucking in deep breaths.

"Pants him!" yelled Horse, as Getz tried in vain to break free. The boys didn't need any more encouragement and proceeded to not only pants him, but take every piece of clothing off his body.

"Guys ... guys ... c'mon, guys ... leave us alone!" The big Kraut had turned into a hopeless, drunken sook, pleading to no avail for the boys to stop. After they undressed him, they couldn't help but cork the big, naked, white bummed bear several times in the thigh and arms for good measure. Rick and Horse shoved his clothes into a large blue Good Samaritan bin close by, while Larni, Brendan and Fitzy kept him under a tight hold.

"Let us go, ya pooftas!"

Soon enough, the boys left Getz alone on the sidewalk to assess his naked situation. It was simple. The boys had just stripped him, and left him there, as the rulebook allows. He stood up tall and proud, with cock in hand, ready again to look the world right in the eye.

"Where's me clothes? Ya cunts," he whined. "You guys are fucked!" was the last thing the boys heard, as they headed south for a late night pizza at Nino's.

Getz looked around, though his eyes weren't focusing too well. He was trying to gather brain cells, in order to comprehend what actually went down. A couple of passing cars tooted their horns and he gave one the finger and showed his backside to the other. A couple of chicks walking his way strategically changed over to the other side of the road to avoid him. He was messy as usual and loving it. No-one in the world gave less of a fuck about anything. People could not help but admire how shameless he was. He spotted the clothes bin and his survival instinct overrode the haze from the alcohol, as he was starting to feel the cold and he wanted to retrieve his favourite flanno. It was the most obvious place the boys would've hidden his threads. He walked over to it and started climbing the metal frame. His dick slapped the cold steel, surprisingly giving him half a hard-on. As he clambered on top, he peered into the depository hole of the Samaritan bin, hoping to see his clothes, but it was too dark. He then leaned over into the abyss to feel for them. He grabbed at some clothing, but overbalanced, his upper body lurching, then falling and getting wedged in the narrow opening.

It was just at this time that a police paddy wagon was leaving the station in Wairoa Avenue. As it approached the clothes bin at the end of the street, all the two constables could see was Getz's bare, white arse in the air.

"Looks like we've got a real live one here," commented the constable driving.

The police pulled over and approached the bin. Getz's arse was shimmering in the streetlight. Both coppers grabbed a leg and awkwardly tried to yank the German nudist back down to earth.

"Ahhhh ... What's goin' on?" On the way down, he managed to fart in their faces. "Cop that, ya cunts!" thinking they were anyone else but the law. The loud breaking of wind made it hard for the coppers to keep a straight face.

"Go easy," was all he could manage, as they threw him in the back of the cage-like wagon.

In the back of the van, the cold steel bench gave him a rude awakening. It was like the numbness of the alcohol had been expelled and replaced by the icy night chill. He started shivering, as the coppers drove off, in the opposite direction of the station.

Another day

Getz was trying to ask the constables where they were taking him, but the law thought it was a good idea to ignore him and give him some time in the back to think about things. After a few laps of the beach, Getz was half frozen. His teeth were chattering so loud that it sounded like there was something amiss in the wagon's engine. It was 12.30am and his mum had been asleep for quite some time, when the two bemused coppers knocked on her front door. It took some time for her to hear them over her earth-moving snoring. When she finally reached the door, she was in a state and adamant she wasn't going to open it to no-one.

"Vhy you here for?" she asked in her heavy Gestapo accent.

"We have your son, lady, in the back of the paddy wagon."

"Ah, so he been a bad boy! Alvays trouble."

"We've just brought him home, so he doesn't hurt himself, Mrs. Getz." Being familiar with local families, with pisshead boardriders for sons, was part of their communal responsibility.

"Vhy, vhat he do?"

"It's just he's very drunk."

"Everyone drunk. I don't cares!"

"Well, he's also got no clothes on, lady."

"Yes, we found him on the street in the nude, Mrs Getz."

She finished with, "Take da bludger and teach him lesson. I not vant him ... Go avay!" There was a moment's silence. The coppers were expecting some kind of compassion, but had only received a mother's scorn.

"Okay, Mrs Getz. We'll look after him and drop him off in the morning."

"Yes, he has to sveep da house. I live in clean house. I not live in Stalag, you know."

With the nod of the head, the coppers hightailed it back to the wagon. They were no match for Getz' mum. She was tough and rough, but in saying that, always thought she was doing the right thing by her beloved son.

"Okay, Getz. We're taking you to the Bondi Hilton for the night."

His teeth were still chattering, but he managed to spit out, "Thank God for that." The holocaust had been averted.

As the driver revved the engine, ready to pull out from the kerb, he muttered to his partner, "Think we just saved him from World War 3."

90

Jab Jab

It was a hot summer morning. Dan was cruising down south to check if he had made the team for the upcoming Australian Surfing Teams' Titles. He was glad to get out of his tiny Hall Street unit. Before 9am in summer, it seemed to turn into a hot pizza oven and in winter, it stayed cold all day like a VB on ice. Every year, a team was picked to represent Bondi—the names posted on the local surf shop window. Dan had been busy during the year, following the national surfing tour, as well as heading to Hawaii and Japan for the international trials. His competitive surfing had been on a roll. He had won a national Pro/Am contest earlier in the year and had won the local R.B.S. (Rude Boys Surfing) Open Boardriders' Championship, beating the best Bondi had to offer. He was stoked with his surfing achievements, though came up short of being proud. Pride had never sat comfortably with him. It had taken him till his late 20s to gain some wind in his surfing sails and to feel like he was actually learning something about the competitive psyche. He saw his success as much a stroke of luck as anything, knowing all too well there were thousands of surfers of his ability and it had just been a good year for him. It was kinda like he was thankful that it was his turn to have a bit of the spotlight shine his way.

As he wandered across Campbell Parade to get a better view of the beach, the Norfolk Pines on the Hill stood majestic in their morning glory. He could see a couple of surfers checking the bay from the boardriders' hut further south. The town was slowly awakening to the beat of its own drum. Being a Sunday, the beat was more of a slight tap rather than a loud thump. The mynah birds were competing with the seagulls at the overflowing garbage bins, behaviour far too indecent for the pigeons, who chose to scavenge the parklands. Pizza crusts and hamburger buns rated highly on their inner city diet, but hot fish and chips were their favourite. If you ever sat down on the grass with some take-away from a local shop, you were always mobbed within seconds. They could smell a chip from a mile away and fought ruthlessly between themselves for every morsel. They symbolised the insatiable lust for winning the prize, for rising above and the need for being on top of the pile. The essence of capitalist exploitation—and here it was in the nature of the seagulls of Bondi Beach. He pondered how winning was an instinct traced back long ago to the competition of hunting for food in order to survive. He wrestled with the idea of how confused this instinct had become and how greed for that last piece of fish was going to eventually fuck the whole world up. He looked around him at his Bondi home and was happy his soul was exactly where it wanted to be.

Dan was only wearing his Quik boardies, compliments of a sponsorship he picked up after his Pro/Am win. They were torn on one leg—compliments of another sponsorship, dished out by a few mates during a rumble on the Hill. Local surf star, Crumbles, had negotiated the Quiksilver deal for him after Dan had beaten him in a local Mambo contest. Dan was to receive a couple of clothes packs a year and since fluoro was in vogue, he stuck out like dog's balls every time he donned his prized apparel. At this point in time, surf clothes were still in their fetus stage. They had yet to be born into their illustrious mainstream, every man and his dog market. Surfers actually enjoyed the individuality and definition that surfing gear gave them. Surfers were still looked down upon as dropouts for their lack of enthusiasm towards work, but it was a characteristic that never bothered Dan or the rest of the beach. The "deadbeat" label had been worn for decades by their hippy surfing forefathers like a proud medallion around their necks. An integral part of the surfie wardrobe was the durable pair of rubber thongs—always advisable to avoid broken glass, uneven footpaths, bindiis, used syringes or any other sharp foreign matter that might catch you off guard, as your roaming eyes checked scantily-clad sun-baking girls and anything else attracting attention.

Being school holidays, there were a few grommets that had gone for the early surf who were skating the footpaths. Flowing golden, untidy locks flapped in the breeze and hung over their eyes, as if to hide them till their developing minds were ready to be emancipated into the adult world. These kids were in the middle of their beach apprenticeships. The longer their sun bleached hair, the more they resembled their older beach heroes. Rebels with a cause, to be someone, build a reputation and make a name on the streets of Bondi, they were into pushing their limits, trying tricks and showing off to the world.

One almost ran over Dan's foot. "Take it easy," was a phrase that entered the culprit's ear and passed out the other.

Young girls watched from the newly-cut green grass of the

park. For them, a torn dress and smudged makeup made them cool—hot tramps out to prove their own agenda to the world. Being holidays, the place was busy with young live-wires plugged into the colourful, raw beach circuit. The leaders of the skate pack blazed out in front and exercised a cocky confidence—their youthful folly a breath of fresh air to Dan. Refreshing to watch and a reminder of a similar past, not so long ago, when horizons seemed boundless, when time seemed to idle in first gear and when the thought of what was going to happen tomorrow seemed an eternity away. How they were told to cherish the moment but how they couldn't wait to grow up. Little did they realise that, upon reflection, at some stage in their future, they would surely think of how fleeting their youth had been. Their destiny was to be the beach's next surfing generation. Bearing all the inherent traits and qualities of their elders, they were the next link to the beach's cultural community, its historical existence. Just as natural as the tides lapping Bondi's sandy shores and rhythmically undulating to the pull of the moon, these grommets were born into a harmony with the local surfing spirit and ready to etch their names into Bondi history. For a long time already, Mother Nature had been calling them to her shores. It was written in the stars that they should value their surfing lifestyle and that the rest of society could go to hell. They didn't give a stuff. All that mattered now was surfing and finding their identity at their beach.

*

Walking the streets on that delightful Sunday morning was the Fat Lady singing in her high pitched melody, her long, dark hair pitched way down over her large, round waist, covering the back of her sequinned purple dress. Her heavy, black eyeliner and thick green make-up imposed a look similar to a 17th Century Harlem witch. The loss of her children in a car crash had been too much for her sweet mind, drenching her senses in anguish. Her magical belief that her singing bridged the gap between her physical world and her children's spirits was the only thing that kept her alive and partially sane. Her singing was interrupted by the clinking of the Waverley Council recycle truck picking up the many bottles left on the kerb from the numerous eateries that lined the strip. The boys who lived above in the Britannic Mansions dreaded this weekly ritual. It was still only 8am and most folk living above

Campbell Parade, who were trying to sleep in, were now trying to block out the excessive noise by pulling pillows over their ears. The only people known to have slept through the starting and stopping of the diesel engine, followed by the inevitable clinking and crashing of glass, were the smackies. Numb to the world, these specimens of the living dead usually holed up in the Biltmore Hotel, located next to the Mansions, mainly because it was cheap and a convenient, short distance to the inner city, where they generally scored. The shady Biltmore, with its many dormitory-styled rooms, was notorious for rapes, murders, overdoses, rip-offs and done deals.

Scouring the parklands, picking up rubbish on their long spiky pokers, were other council workers, dressed in khaki greens. As they tended to their cleaning duties, cars with boards on top passed through the southern promenade turnstiles and randomly parked facing the beach. The waves were small, but if you were keen it was worth getting wet. If you weren't up to getting wet, it was always a good place to socialise and catch up with some gossip. There was the usual left shorie in the southern corner and Third Ramp had a small right happening. Being a nor-east wind-swell, most of the surf was pushing past the southern-facing headlands, destined to reach Bronte, Tama and Mackenzies. These beaches faced east and captured plenty of swell during summer. A couple of tourist buses had pulled up, down middle of the beach in front of the surf club, and well dressed Japanese tourists filed onto the white sand. They were in stark contrast to the relaxed, bronzed Aussie swimmers parading in Speedos. They happily displayed their arsenal of well-mannered Eastern rituals, including lots of bowing and nodding. "Happy conformists," Dan thought. As the gadget-clad Nips posed in groups to take pictures with their latest Nikon or Olympus cameras, Dan wondered if his Jap mate Ken-san had once been a passenger on one of those buses and never bothered to get back on.

After checking the headlands for any whitewater that could help determine the surf size and conditions around the southern point, Dan decided to cross back over Campbell Parade and ask one of the garbos from over Bronte way for a surf report.

"G'day, Wayno. Anything worthwhile 'round the corner?"

"Hello, Danno. Keen for a paddle, are we? Gonna be a hot one. A little wave at Tama, but the flags'd be up by now."

Wayno was a tanned, muscular, sweating garbo on the move.

He and an accomplice were lifting crates full of green, brown and red bottles and emptying them into the back of the orange Council truck. He was a fully fledged Bronte local, with his parents owning the fish shop over there at the beach. He loved the competition between the beaches and carried the rivalry into most things he did. "I love waking you Bondi cunts up!" he cheered as he discarded another noisy crate and jogged onwards to the next pile. "I'll make sure we rev the truck as we pass the Britannic!"

Dan shook his head, laughed and continued on his merry way. As he was passing Wade's café, Cookie was walking out with a banana smoothie in one hand, attempting to light a durrie with the other. Preoccupied with igniting his nicotine stick, Cookie literally bumped into him.

"Oh, fuck ... sorry mate." His sly grin pulled his lips back just far enough for a ray of sunshine to enter his missing ivory gap and reach the back of his throat like the South Head lighthouse penetrating the Sydney Heads in the dark of night. He took the unlit ciggy out of its crusty oral corner that it was destined to call home for about 5 minutes depending on how hard he'd drag on it. "Watcha up to, Dan?"

"Wiping smoothie off me; banana, if I guess right!"

"Yeah, banana always goes well with a ciggy."

"Ciggy and a smoothie, aye? See ya trying to balance ya diet these days."

"Yeah, you know how it is, Dan; already had a few leafies for breakfast and had to settle me rumbleguts. You know how it is."

"Sprinklin' leafies on our Weetbix, are we?"

"Yeah, sure, of course, every mornin'. I eat half a leafy Weetbix and then top-shelf the rest! You know how it is. Gotta keep my bum cheeks happy!"

"Well, no wonder yer got fucken rumbleguts with half a stoned Weetie up yer arse."

"Yeah, well ..." His stoned mind started issuing out perplexed signals. It wasn't quite the way he wanted the conversation to head. The day was hotting up and a few beads of perspiration showed themselves from the safety of Cookie's receding hairline.

Dan decided to go on the attack. "Suppose you learnt that kinda shit at that Gary Glitter concert, aye?"

"Fuck you! Will you stop bringing that fuckin' concert up? I told you I'd rather forget about shit like that!" It had taken no time for Dan to get Cookie on the back foot.

"Yeah, well, I'd want to forget about being gang-banged with a packet of Weetbix by a bunch of fairies, too!"

"Ha ha ... funny funny ..." Cookie suddenly took a turn for the worse. Seemed like the leafies were churning whatever was sitting in his guts. Looking a paler shade of green, he took a deep breath, hunched over and did his best to have a spew. Dan looked on and had a laugh at his mate's expense. Saliva and mucus hung out of his nose and mouth like a trapeze artist suspended in mid air before dropping to the ground. But he was short of having a really good heave. On coming good, Cookie cleared his throat and spat a black oyster that would've stopped a semi trailer at eighty clicks onto the pavement. Taking a sip of his smoothie, he commented, "Fuck, I need to light me ciggy."

"Yeah, mate," continued Dan, trying to sympathise. "There's nothin' worse than rumbleguts in da morning after a session and it's even worse if ya mate's laughin' at ya. Get that ciggy into ya and you'll be sweet." Cookie raised the ciggy towards his lips, as if his life depended on it. But just as he went to put it in his mouth, he coughed and followed through with a dry reach. Dan kept talking as if nothing was happening, "Though, come to think of it, acid guts are pretty bad. Felt fucked last week after a night on those Superman trips." He patted his bent over mate on the back. "Musta had heaps of strychnine in 'em!"

Cookie looked up through glazed, red eyes and tried to speak coherently, as if his reputation was on the line. "Yeah ..." He cleared his throat again. " ... Heard they're as good as the Green Beavers." He wiped some spit away from his mouth, using the back of the hand that he had his still unlit ciggy in. Never one to lose sight of a down-but-not-out comeback, he continued, "Didya leap tall buildings, wearing yer tight-arsed cape?"

Dan decided to hammer his wounded mate, yet again, "How'd ya know? You've been talking to Gary again ... haven't ya?"

Cookie slurped on his smoothie, to soothe his throat. "Yes, and Gazza sends his love." Cookie heaved a bit, then spat again. "So, Superfreak, where ya headed?"

"Down to the surf shop to see who made the team ... and callin' me Superfreak is a compliment, brudda. Rick James rules with the ladies!" Cookie finally paused from the conversation and managed to light his ciggy. He then managed to say coherently, "Okay, Rick, or Mr Kent, or whoever you want to fuckin' be, let's cruise down and check out who you're gonna be surfin' with!"

"That's if I fuckin' make the team. Just hope I can scrape in somewhere behind you, yer Weetbix kid!"

"Whatta ya talkin' about? You won the boardriders. You gotta be in there!"

"I'll be stoked if we're both in there."

"Reckon Bondi's a good chance this year."

Cookie slurped and dragged on his lungbuster as the lads kept walking. There were a few yuppies eating brekkie at the trendy Lamrock Café. Some gold-wearing fat cat and his good looking accessory were getting squishy over a latte. It was obvious she wasn't there for the conversation, by how accustomed she was to all the bling she was wearing. She was adorned with diamond clusters so in place they looked set and soldered into her olive skin. The boys used to think of how good a fuck they could give "the accessory". Being horny young blokes, their minds wouldn't have disappointed Freud's theory that 90% of thought is devoted to sex—thoughts of how they could woo her away and how she so desperately needed to be hammered properly. After all, how could this old, fat fuck, way past his prime, be able to satisfy this young maiden, except in the generosity stakes? Viagra wasn't on the market, back then. The boys clearly understood the situation. The bigger, better deal had been operating, for both males and females, since time began. Instinct had driven the human race in its pursuit of a better life and this simple truth was evident in the pretentious, consumer society engulfing them. If being a dole-bludging surfer gave you anything, it was plenty of spare time to discuss and bullshit on about what was happening in the world. Most surfers had done the maths and opted to drop out of the race. Why had the world got itself in such a hurry? Why did your parents want to buy you the game of Monopoly when you were a kid? Marketing wealth and glamour had been used to entice and bait us all. And Dan couldn't understand the point of advertising. He believed it was just being used to make us feel inadequate, to make us feel unhappy with what we had or who we were. Dan and Cookie didn't care much for shopping, unless it was for a new board or a rock of hash. How simple it was, but how complicated it had become. The boys took the power of the accessory's glance and gave none of it back.

They turned into Lamrock Avenue and crossed the road to the little surf shop, along from Mario's pizza joint.

"Hope Rad has put the team up." Stirling Radford was the man of the moment. "Stirl", to his close friends, made an impression, opening a small surf shop opposite the Lamrock Café a few years before. His family was filthy rich and happy to get him kick-started, by sponsoring him with cash to open it. His uncle was Bernard Cooper, one of the richest men in Australia and if you gave or took a billion here or there, you could say they were bordering on Aussie royalty. Burt Radford was Bernard's younger brother and Stirling's dad. He had been instrumental in supporting his elder brother continue their father's dominance in banking. From an early age, Stirling was always destined for corporate boardrooms and the family were all excited that he had started his training as an entrepreneur at Bondi, even if it was around a bunch of beach bums.

"Somethin's in the window."

As they got closer, it was obvious Radford had posted the team. The boys started checking the list. Crumbles, Steele, Boofhead, Dobbo, BP, brothers Phil and Bob and, lo and behold, Radford himself! No Cookie and no Dan!

"You're kidding. Where's our fuckin' names?" Cookie was wide-eyed and fuming. He had every right to be feeling ripped off. He might have loved his piss and been a hardened bong-sucking knockabout, but he had been doing aerials before anyone knew what they were. He was a consistent place getter on the national circuit, a natural talent and considered one of the best surfers at the beach. He slurped one last mouthful of his smoothie and threw the dregs over the finger-marked window.

All Dan could do was sigh and utter, "Fuck, who knows what's goin' on, bra?"

This was always going to happen—it was just a matter of when. There was always going to be controversy in Stirling's road to the top. He was always bound to tread on someone's toes and it was better that Dan got used to it sooner rather than later—for the road to the corporate world wasn't paved with good intentions. The Radfords' business manual stated that he should only regard loyalties and associations useful if he was directly benefiting from them. Dan and Cookie didn't quite fit the criteria that the guy had in mind. As far as he was concerned, they were pictured as bong-head losers, who had obviously said no to him too many times and were too hard to rein-in to his future plans. It was now fairly obvious to the boys that there was a powerbroker in town. Things were a-changing. It was now clear to them that the power of trying to control the beach revolved around the point of sale at Stirl's surf shop and the boardriders had become an extension of that.

Cookie started going off like a loaded 303. "I tell you who fucken knows—that fucken, yuppie cunt!" He looked at Dan for solidarity, not that it was really needed. Cookie knew this was an injustice and Dan was probably just as pissed off. "I'll smash the cunt!"

"I had a feeling this was going to happen, Cookie. This guy has never really been one of us, mate. Just look who he's connected to."

"He'll be connected to my fist, if he don't give me a fuckin' explanation!"

"Mate, he's a pure capitalist. Good luck to him. I mean, we were probably stupid to think any different. It runs in his family. It's just the way the world's fucking heading, mate!"

"What the fuck?"

"This is how they operate, mate. It's all about sales and we have never licked this guy's bum enough or bought enough stuff." Dan raised his eyebrows and scratched the top of his head. Their recalcitrance had sealed their fate. "We don't count, mate."

"Don't go comparing him to licking my Gary, now."

"I'm sure Gazza's bum tastes heaps better, mate."

It was fair enough that another salesman had set up shop in an enterprising beach landscape. After all, Bondi was part of a democracy, though, at different times, you could have called it downright anarchy. Stirling's arrival was just another sign that the new, affluent migration to the beach was well underway. Globalisation was setting up shop. All over the planet, culture and local loyalties were being forcibly replaced with a hollow religion called global consumerism. It was just a disguised new form of colonisation.

Stirling had kinda got in under the radar. He'd gone to school with a few of the boys, who allowed him to slip in the backdoor. Some were awake to the breach, but the astute Stirling had studied the book on *How to Win Friends and Influence People* and put its tactics to good use. He used a local, named Sonny Webster, who hailed from a large surfing family, to start a partnership, when opening the shop. This gave him credibility and it didn't take long for him to spread his sweet talk over the beach, like jam over buttered toast, with a dob of cream on top. After cementing himself in, he dislodged his foot, long enough, to boot Webster out of the business. The young mogul's rise was quick. Now that he wielded absolute power over the boardriders, he alone could decide which of the big surf brands were sold in Bondi. His timing was impeccable. Surfing was about to explode onto the world market and he was the only surf shop at the World-famous beach. Surfing wasn't just a good business to be in, you looked great doing it. A few sponsorships here and there and the next thing you know, the best surfers on the beach are eating out of your hand. It had got to a point where the team was being selected behind closed doors. Why even run a local club, if you don't respect the final ratings? It may as well have been called Rad's Boardriders. It was obvious this kid had the Midas touch and was going places. But, with these tactics, it wouldn't be long before he would have a run-in with someone. Business is business and you can't please everyone.

"Shifty cunt! Whatcha expect from fuckin' blow-ins."

"Nah, mate. Someone else has had a hand in this," Dan continued, scratching down his side levers, probing his earhole and scoping its inner lobes for any loose wax.

"Wot? You think this fuckwit didn't pick it?"

"Sure, he had a say in it, but ..."

"But, what?" Cookie wanted answers quick and was so incensed, he clenched his fist and shaped up, as if to put his pumped, freckled, red knuckles straight through the glass window. He settled on spitting a giant, green golly on the door handle, as a welcoming gift and asked again, "But what, Dan? Fuckin' what?"

"But, what?? Well, he probably picked this team with your mate, Gary, when he was 'alf choccas, up him."

Cookie's rage was stopped in an instant, as if some Calvin Klein sex bomb had started fondling his balls and sucking his cock. He had been startled by the lack of immediate annoyance the situation had cast over his mate. He was down with discarding the disappointment and thought it better to join in the comedy relief.

"Well, fuck me, then. Shoulda known he was conferring with the Fairy God, then, aye ..."

"Aye," replied a smug Dan.

"The selection process is flawed."

"Whaddya mean, Dan?"

"He shoulda been fully choccas up your mate, Gary, when they agreed on it!"

"Fuck these rich cunts. Let's check the surf and forget about it!"

"Good call, Cookie."

Dan thought he had a loyal affiliation with Raddy, so being left out touched a raw nerve. He was instrumental in developing the young entrepreneur's credibility. He had worked tirelessly behind the scenes, doing a lot of hard yards for the club. He wrote newsletters, organised contests and updated score sheets for Radford to distribute to club members. He had always been passionate about beach culture, so he would've done it whether Radford was around or not. It came naturally for the born-and-bred Bondi boy. But, now he was feeling a little used, to say the least. But, he was managing to hide it. Steele and Crumbles were assured positions on the team, since they were already recognised on the world stage. But, after them, it was a lottery.

Growing up in a working class family, Dan had a unique perspective on how Bondi was changing. Real estate values were on the way up. Property prices were rising like a solid ground swell. He knew the majority of the locals could never compete with all the money getting pumped into the joint. Newcomers were starting to turn up left, right and centre, thinking that, because they owned a joint in the 'hood, they had to be a local. Dan and the boys knew that you earned respect and it wasn't for sale. All the townsfolk would have been happy for things to stay as they were, but there was something sinister happening that would change the beach forever. A real estate boom was underway and God help any poor local who missed hopping aboard the gravy train. It was now more important that your place of residence was a commodity. It was the start of a nationwide initiative to rob coastal communities of their character and replace them with investment opportunities for the rich and famous.

Maybe Dan and the boys should've played Monopoly more when they were kids. The closing of the local Astra Hotel was a landmark decision that signalled the decline of Bondi's golden era. The opening of the Lamrock Café, with its fancy neon sign, was indicative of things to come.

The beach had always been fed excitement from the fallout of Kings Cross and the city. Everyone had to grapple with high density living, every day. In this dog-eat-dog world, the boys found security in their local beach community. As a crew, they could keep a lookout for each other. Street credibility amongst the crew was valued way more than money. Anyone could make money or be born into it. But, it was a person's reputation that counted. Money mattered to get you through, but to most of the boys, those who had lots of it were the enemy, living in the surrounding hills looking down on them. You could have all the money in the world, but if you didn't have street-cred, you were nothing. In this environment, your daily exploits were the measuring stick of who you were. For beneath the valley of terracotta roofs stood a maze of grand proportion. Under this canopy lay the depth of Bondi's soul and character. The beach was way richer than Double Bay or Vaucluse ever hoped to be. There was something happening there 24/7, three hundred and sixty-five days a year. The creativity and spontaneity of living in the fast lane was a magnet to anyone who enjoyed the ripping off flesh and sinew to get to the heart of what was going down.

The Bondi community always tried to stick together when faced with a crisis. But, the latest battles were being lost because of shady deals. Nothing was going to save this town—as the boys knew it—once the money started pouring in. Rents and rates were soon to soar and displace locals surviving on a basic wage or the pension. Stirling and the like were waiting in the wings. The changing of the guard had already begun.

As Dan sat on the grassy hill, with a forlorn Cookie, both just seemed to be content to let the sunny day absorb them. That was until a voice descended on them from behind. "That yuppy fuck's burnt you once again." It was Horse, with his usual punk head on—fast sunnies wrapped around a Sid Vicious haircut. The water was so glary, you could barely distinguish the small sets rolling into the bay.

A now-dejected Dan managed to spit out, "You get that", only because Horse was such a good mate. Otherwise, he couldn't be bothered even wasting his breath on a reply.

Horse was always a straight shooter, who understood the order of things. He was smart in his calculations, always neutral and calling it for what it was. "Well, I'd be having a word to him, if I was you guys."

"What? So he gets the satisfaction of knowing he has pull at the beach these days? Fuck dat!"

"Nah, mate. So you can tell the drop kick he hasn't got everyone fooled down here."

"Good point, Horse." Cookie knew the new upstart cum best

mate had started to divide the beach. "He'll get his, one day. Anyway, I got more important things to do. I'm going to grovel with the grommets on the shorie. Dan should be the one who's pissed off. He won the boardriders!"

"I'm heading to Mackenzie's, if you wanna head round there with us." Horse had already got the rundown of how good the surf was 'round the corner.

"Yeah, Wayno said there was a little wave at Tammas, but the flags'd be up by now."

"Mackenzie's got a few and I'm out there to get me hair wet."

"Needs it."

"That'll do me. See you after, Danny boy."

"No worries, guys, and thanks for your support on this one."

"As if I'd see it any other way, champ. You know me, just telling it how it is."

"Later."

Sitting alone on the hill Dan let his emotions swish around and rise to the surface. His exclusion had started to become an issue ricocheting around in his brain and a churning in his guts. The initial sense of letting the situation go had given way for a reckoning of the ledger. Enough was enough and it was time someone told this blow-in yuppie he was treading on toes that had been standing on these sands long before he ever graced Bondi's shores.

"Suppose your wondering what you've gotta fucken' do to make the team," came a voice from thin air. It was another mate of Dan's, Pottsie, who was returning from checking Mackenzie,s and Tama. He was a taller, older guy with the odd scar who looked a little big for the BMX he was riding. He was more at home on a Kwacka 1100 with full leathers on but he liked being a versatile character. Letting cops chase him at 220 km down O'Sullivan Road along the Royal Sydney Golf course at Rose Bay was what he called fun. With Jekyll and Hyde looks, olive muscular features and his passion for living on the edge, he'd already been inducted into the street club of "on the edge" living long ago. Dan used to think he would look right at home with a parrot on his shoulder and a patch over his eye. "The boys just told me you got left out of the surf league team."

"Yeah, I don't know what happened, mate. Bit disappointed."

"Of course you are, mate ... you've done the hard yards; it's only fair you should be surfing."

"Thanks, Pottsie."

"Well, don't let that little skinny prick get you down. I'd be having a word with him."

Dan swivelled his arse around and looked directly into Pottsie's aviator Ray Ban sunnies. "Yeah, suppose your right."

"Fucken oath I am. He'll be down from his castle soon enough ... make sure you let him know."

"OK, boss. Thanks, mate."

Instead of seeming upset around incoming mates Dan decided to desert the hill and head towards Bluey's van parked near the southern boom gates where he positioned himself on one of the empty council wood-slatted seats.

He sat there for 10 minutes watching the surf and motioning his hand in the air to a few mates who tooted and drove by. The left shorie wasn't doing much. Some grommets were inspiring him by pulling into some squeaky little barrels. He sat watching the morning activities of the surf and sand. He tried to let his mind drift.

"Big Frank" was running the soft sand and Dan could see the night before dripping off him. Frank was a wheeler and dealer who was a few years older. He had been mates with Dan's dad who, like Frank, was a professional gambler. Frank was a younger generation punter who knew the value of a good horseman. Dan's dad had jumped out of the school window at 14 and been on racetracks ever since. He was part of the old school. He had vast amounts of horse and track knowledge and unless the information spoken was going to take his odds in the next race he was usually willing to impart his homework with those who knew his worth. Frank was an elder and Dan respected him for that. Order at the beach was important to Dan. There was and always had been a surfing community hierarchy and that was something troubling him with his latest dilemma.

Call it coincidence, fate, timing or something in the sub-conscious, or then again it could have just been opening time at the guy's shop, but Radford amazingly turned up to check the surf only a few metres away, oblivious to Dan's stewing. Dan had caught him out of the corner of his eye heading down towards him. He was unaware of Dan, though he was going to know soon enough. Impeachment was soon to be the order of the day and Dan wasn't going to hold back. He kept walking, ignorant of Dan, venturing independently into his snare until he was almost on top of him.

"Ohh, hi, Dan, didn't see you there ..." He was a little surprised though he had his unctuous ring of confidence going which wasn't too smart a move considering his tall thin frame and Dan's boxing background. Dan let it ride for a second and Radford continued, still unsure about Dan's lack of interest. "Why aren't you out there?"

Dan stood up and faced him before bluntly asking, "Why'd ya leave me out?"

"What are you talking about?" Stirling flicked his hair back and scratched the back of his head with a look of he "didn't know what Dan was talking about".

"Don't shit me, pal. You know well and proper what I'm on about."

"Excuse me?" Stirling squinted for a second as if he was remembering what this all might be about. "Oh, you don't mean the surf league team, do ya?"

"Oh no, I mean for the team lining up to suck your cock next—it's a long line, I heard." Dan couldn't help throwing that in. Stirling for a moment didn't know how to reply. "Of course I mean the surf team!"

"No one left you out, mate. We all decided on it."

"You and who? The guys in the cock sucking line in front of me? You're fucking kidding, aren't you?"

Radford crossed his skinny arms like he was now in a business meeting and warranted some attention. Dan was surely going to give him what he asked as long as he asked nice enough. "I don't kid anyone, mate. Team's picked. Better luck next year."

"So that's the thanks I get for helping a wanker like you." Dan was simmering but still in control.

"Fuck off, Dan. You're overreacting a bit, don't you think?"

"Overreacting? What? You think it's fair to put yourself and mates in a team and leave out someone who has earned the right to be in it?"

Stirling looked at him not knowing where the conversation was going. He clutched at his misplaced authority and continued, "Everyone decided that ..."

"Don't give me that shit. You're the one callin' the shots!" interrupted Dan. "Do you think I was born yesterday? I gave you my blood, sweat and tears in helping you with this club. Is this the kinda thanks you give me for being a loyal mate?"

"You're delusional. This club is not about you. Who are you anyway?"

"Don't you go asking who I am, you blow in. My grandfather built this promenade so you and your yuppie mates could fuckin' park your four-wheel drives to sit in 'em and look good. You're lucky we even let blokes like you down here." Dan was close to letting him know who he was. "I won the open boardriders— where did you finish?"

"Settle down, you bong smoking loser." Radford had started trudging down the dim-lit alleyway that had a brick wall at the end of it. He was so misguided by his lack of judgement he pushed his forefinger into Dan's breastbone and tried to turn the offence around. "Guys like you need to have a good look in the mirror!"

That was enough for Dan to show him what the brick wall at the end of the alley looked like in the form of his clenched fist. An automatic double left jab put Radford over the prom and firmly on his arse. A trickle of his blue blood spilled from his nose and onto the pavement. There it joined the other countless stains and became lost which signified his worth when it came to the street.

"Who the fuck do you think you are, you blow-in cunt!" yelled Dan. "Fuck off back to Bellevue Hill and look in your own mirror ... your gonna need it to wipe your royal fucking blood off your fuckin' baby face!"

The fallen mogul clutched at his face in disbelief that someone had actually dared throw a punch at him. "Dan, how long have I known you?" he whimpered.

"Not long enough." Dan had reacted on the lack of respect. Rulebook states that anyone who sticks their finger in your breastbone is fair game. How dare a young, rich punk come into Bondi and ignore the rules. From that point on Dan severed all ties with Radford's shop and club. It hurt Dan to think he would be neglecting the boys but he knew somewhere further down the track he'd somehow be able to make amends. A feud had started and the subsequent ripples would provide the backdrop for the next decade to come—one in which battles would be won and lost and only one man would be left standing.

Go West

The fortnightly dole cheque had helped the community of Bondi. During the 70s and 80s the government's welfare scheme had sincerely tried to address the problem of providing security to those who most needed it. In any capitalist society there were always going to be people beyond the reach of insurance, whether too poor, handicapped in some way or just too inept in being able to save for that rainy day. The Aussie government seriously had the welfare of the people at heart with state pensions financed from taxation, standardised retirement ages, Medicare, unemployment benefits, subsidies to farmers and restricted labour markets. The Good Samaritan was trying to eliminate risk and blanket-cover the country with a cradle-to-grave assurance that everyone would be looked after. However this gave rise for people to game the system. It inclined some people to take advantage of the handouts which played perfectly into the pockets of anyone opting to drop out of society's work agenda. The dole enabled Dan and the boys to tune in to their wavelength and turn their backs on the "hard grind". A hard grind that was always in favour of the rich getting richer and the boys simply weren't into it.

A benefit equivalent to a small wage was all that was needed to give them the freedom to hang at the beach and go surfing every day. It was like a gift from heaven cast down into their bank accounts twice a month. All hail the "Dole God"! When combined with pulling off a few scams like selling a bit of mull or having a bit of part-time work it became a half-decent wage to live on. They felt like they were the "chosen few" who decided to think for themselves and use the system that wanted to tell them what to think and buy. Every day dawned as a holiday to be shared with plenty of other holiday makers.

Most of Bondi's surfers had evolved from free-spirited rebellious roots and many of their ancestors had been convicts. They were just flying the same anti-conformist flag and counting themselves lucky that they were getting paid to do it. Saved them robbing banks though a few still had a go at that anyway. On any given day a tour of Bondi could observe the wild generic mavericks enjoying the hedonistic lifestyle of the Aussie beach culture. After all, larrikin behaviour was the epitome of Aussie life. Part of a misfit religion full of boardshort- and bikini-wearing devotees who perceived the world as too complicated or too controlling. In their scripture a sunny beach day with friends and a few good waves took preference over everything else the world had to offer.

"Bludgers" was a word that might have seemed fitting but Dan believed his surfing life was justified. His dislike for the crony capitalist regime where the rich got rich by exploiting workers meant that his frugal existence was actually part of an earth-saving revolution. He personified how one could be so happy with little as long as social relationships and reverence for "mother nature", and her oceans, were in order.

"If we stick together and keep it simple, none of us will get stuck," were the words of his wise resourceful grandmother. Her philosophy rang true in Dan's ears and he missed her dearly. He had fond memories of family occasions at his grandparents' weatherboard house in William Street, North Bondi. It had a white picket fence and two bushy trees either side of the gate that invited you to come right in. Pop kept the house with a new coat of paint so it always looked respectable and mowed the large backyard lawn every couple of weeks. The kitchen and dining room was the hub of social activity as kin randomly visited and enjoyed a chat whilst Nan poured cuppas and cut portions of Madeira cake. The back, worn, wooded, framed steps led down to Pop's old shed. He had a life of interesting times hoarded in there. From shearing clippers to old leg irons to old sporting memorabilia to a cupboard of nuts and bolts and tools of all sorts. His little transistor was always tuned to the cricket or the footy as he sat back in his old recliner and sipped his beer. His home brew was a fine drop—so good he was into it most mornings around 11am and fair enough: he had earned it. Done the hard yards with his wife and five kids. Seen them through life with all he could give surviving a depression and World war. He was patriotic and very proud of all of his kids as they were all hard honest workers. In days gone by he had worked between odd jobs in Sydney's eastern suburbs and the family's dairy farm on Oxley Island near Taree but he was always a "bushy" at heart.

Leanne was Dan's mum and she was the eldest, growing up in a disciplined homestead with lots of chores and the added responsibility of making sure her younger siblings towed the line in the list of duties. Up in the dark at 5.30am, quick wash making sure you cleaned behind your ears, then down the back paddock to the milking barn, few buckets under a few udders, squirt squirt, running late for school so ride the horse back to the homestead to get ready for school etc etc. Her three sisters and one brother were all close with her even though she was the one giving the orders. Dan's Uncle Paul was the only son who had played footy for Easts first grade in the early 70s and the family was so proud of his achievement. Dan used to go to the old Sportsground near Moore Park every home game when his uncle played and watch him play dummy-half, feeding the ball to such greats as Artie Beetson, Kevin Junee, Johnny Brass, Mark Harris and the like. His mum would take a picnic basket and they'd sit on the hill and watch all three grades.

In Dan's eyes his grandfather was an icon and his hero, an old "snowy-haired" legend. The Leyland brothers had nothing on Dan's Pop. He used to pick up a black snake and whipcrack the backbone out of it, pull his teeth out and make funny faces, take Dan to the beach with his mates and drop them off while he went and had a few at the local RSL, snore louder than a car on the starting grid at Bathurst and cook up the best weekly "leftovers" from Nan's fridge. He used to think Dan and his surfing buddies were good kids. They weren't criminal delinquents and they treated him with respect. And why wouldn't they show a digger like him respect? Old Aussie folk like Dan's grandparents were the "salt of the earth". When Dan thought of his Pop looking down at him from his big beer shed in the sky he would reason with him that he wasn't part of the workforce because his pension cheque had turned up 40 years early and he wasn't going to send it back. Dan also didn't want to take a job position away from someone who deserved it more but he used to save that excuse for when his grandma was taking her turn to check on him.

In the August of 89 Stirling had decided to vacate his small, cluttered surf shop in Lamrock Avenue. He had teamed up with ex-Bronte pro surfer Smithy who was now a rep for Billabong in NSW. It was smart symmetry—business acumen which made perfect sense: the young upstart teaming up with the just retired pro-surfer, respected by most, who was in a position to supply the partnership with all the surfing credibility needed. Both were on the move and the encroaching 5 × 3 square metres of floorspace next to Mario's pizzeria left no imagination for expansion. It was only logical to move operations. However, into new premises tucked away in a newly opened arcade off the Campbell Parade strip seemed a bit obscure. It was only 100 metres down the road towards Wade's cafe and it was much bigger floorspace but it was out of eyesight from the main drag. It seemed appropriate to want to spend a heap on refurbishing a new shell interior as the young Radford had just made his first million turning an old North Bondi semi on the ocean into a state of the art mansion, selling it to some mining baron. It had been a deal made in heaven hooking up with his cousin Hamish and therefore using his Uncle Bernard's pot of gold to fund the project. This real estate venture initiated an avalanche of investment and immediately started Bondi rents and rates on the rise.

What Stirling and Smithy had overlooked was what they were leaving behind: the grubby fingerprinted front window pasted with surf stickers, the uneven boardracks, the texta-marked change room curtains, the wetsuit-strewn cracked tiled floor, the weird and wonderful walls of newspaper clippings and photos that had been cartoon characterised to personify local identities, a graffitied counter full of dust and a lonely uneven stool. This shop had been a trademark of the local hardcore surfing scene, the dirt and grime of underground existence. Like so many surf retailers of the time they seemed caught up in the professional, glossy sports act surfing had got itself tangled up in. The surfing street sub-culture was being sold out by the surfing companies who were coming of age with the pro scene; it was starting to glitter, it was going shiny, like a used car salesman's reassuring smile. It seemed aligned with the real estate boom, and anyone in the take-off zone at the right time was to be riding high on the rolling tsunami of economic success. Sporting all the major labels behind the dynamic duo, the sky was the limit—they were in a great position to make a killing. The era of boutique surf shops was being born.

But what about the future for Dan and the boys? How was it to affect the local beach community or for that matter the rest of the surfing culture on the planet? Surely they didn't want an incoming tide of new avant-garde bodies buying into their beaches and crowding up their lineup. Dreams of avarice were about to invade their world and change it forever and unfortunately, but not surprisingly, the Bondi boys weren't even figured into the new corporate equation. Their beach community and surfing lifestyle would soon be under a full attack. Missing the wave, becoming misplaced in the choppy waters and eventually downright submerged would be described as just plain "bad luck". The "working class" wasn't the image the developers had in mind when promoting the "new" Bondi. Community values were to be tipped upside down. Corporate capitalism at its finest.

During this time Dan had flown to WA to compete in the winter leg of the APSA contests. Four comps spanning five weeks had a flock of national contestants roaming the coastline in search of cash and a good time. Lock your daughters up: the APSA circus was in town. Testosterone was pumping as young men surfed for fame, fortune and the hearts of starry-eyed senoritas.

Dan's good mate Darky picked him up from the airport with his customary ear-to-ear grin. His ivories were pearl white in contrast to his dark skin. Somewhere in his chromosomes lay a dark gene from Burmese origin courtesy of a great-grandfather. His parents were white in contrast though his dad sported a ripper suntan. Their progeny of three boys and one girl were all happy, intelligent and well-mannered, the legacy of caring parents. Living near Triggs Beach had accounted for Darky's interest in surfing. Like Dan it had become his main passion in life. Dan had known his mate for only a bit over a year but their lifestyles being synonymous meant their friendship was rock solid.

"How was yer flight?"

"Boring except for the Ansett ladies. They rule!"

"Women in uniform, mate."

"So respectable."

They threw Dan's large, bulky silver boardbag containing his quiver of four boards onto the roof-racks of Darky's classic olive-green Holden. After completing the formalities of tightening the old multicoloured ocky straps and chucking Dan's duffle bag in the gaping boot both lads smiled at each other and embraced in a hug of mateship. They were both excited to catch up and continue from where they had left off the previous year.

"No hugging me down the beach, now," whipped Darky. "Don't need any of your Oxford Street antics tarnishing my clean reputation, now."

"I'll save the tonguey for in front of the judges."

"Nice."

Driving towards the coast through the city of Perth with the windows down engaged a certain feeling of anticipation. "Stinging for a wave?" asked Darky, knowing by the smell of his mate that he needed a wash. "You're as off as a wog's lunch."

"Compliments will get you everywhere. Wait till you smell my farts."

"That airline food will do that to ya."

"Builds character."

"Don't follow through, now, unless you're wearin' your nappies."

"Knew you'd have a few spare." Nothing had changed, taken off where they had left off as though it was just yesterday. Dan propped his shoulder up and had a whiff of the stench that was brewing under his armpit. "Yuk, I'm definitely keen to hit the water though, bra." Dan did like to keep himself pretty fresh and acceptable. "Need to clean the cobwebs."

"Must be pretty groggy spiders." Darky tweaked his nose back quickly a couple of times as though Dan's body odour was singeing his nostril hairs. "Speaking of 'groggy', keen to char the dotch?"

"Does the Pope shit in the woods?"

Darky was commenting about their usual ritual before surfing. To 'char the dotch' meant to burn the cigarette so as to dry out the tobacco before mixing it with the marijuana. For adamant non-smokers like Dan and Darky, roasting the ciggy helped soften and dry the moist tobacco taste that left an unpleasant nicotine flavour in one's mouth after inhaling bong smoke. The boys believed it helped burn off many of the carcinogens also.

"Got some wicked buds, bra." Darky had many ace connections who grew pot for a living. His personal stash was always the kryptonite. Like connoisseurs of fine wine they always sought weed high in THC so as to comatose the senses. They, like many, believed if you're going to get stoned you may as well do a good job of it.

"I bought over a rock of hash so it looks like we're havin' a cocktail."

"You fucken legend, Dan!" Good hash was rare in W.A.—a delicacy one may say, though back in Bondi it was coming out of everyone's ears. We could all thank Mr Saxon and many other smaller importers for that. Dan rubbed shoulders with all who worked within the trade. Illegal importation was nothing new to him. The hash trade had thrived during the 80s in the Eastern suburbs of Sydney. It not only provided a highly regarded product amongst pot smokers but it had helped farmers in Afghanistan and India. Dan had even brought some back in his brash younger years. Sponsoring surfers on exotic surfing holidays to bring a bit back was common practice. It was a dare that was eagerly pounced on by Dan and many of his mates. The risks seemed minimal and rarely entered their willing, bulletproof minds. The free holiday, perfect waves and couple of grand on return was an invitation hard to refuse. Dan liked to think he was helping some poor bloke feed his family to help balance and justify any wrongdoing in the eyes of the Australian criminal system. He, like many, also used to think how hypocritical the government was in letting alcohol and cigarettes flood the market. Surely the millions dying of cancer and liver disease caused by these kinds of legal drugs were proof that their consequences were just as bad if not worse than someone puffing on a joint. To think the police were ruining kids' lives and careers by black-banning them and giving them criminal records for smoking a bit of pot was just ludicrous.

Bringing hash back in your guts added to the seemingly foolproof plan though other methods included specially made shoes and jackets. The financiers loved fat blokes because they could swallow more. Scrawny, skinny guys usually had to wear shoes as well to make it worthwhile.

Dan was liked because in his fit 65-kg frame he always managed to swallow close to a kilo. His record was 864 grams. That's more than seven quarter-pounders, a feat for any welterweight. The hardest thing about the work was the preparation of the hash balls prior to swallowing them. Each ball of hash putty was rolled into a 4-gram weight, about the same size and shape as half a cigarette. It was then wrapped twice in small sheets of plastic, each time heat-sealed over the flame of a candle. A condom was then pulled tight over the small black nugget and knotted to form the perfect seal. Rumour was they looked exactly like the local black guys' dicks but Dan wasn't about to go verifying whether it was true or not.

The swallow was always commenced about 8 hours prior to departure and washed down with some aqua bottled water. A technique of tilting the head back and arcing the neck as the cylindrical ball was dropped into the back of the throat usually gave it easy passage into the awaiting oesophagus.

After reaching Darky's beach house the boys unloaded the car and upon opening the front door Dan's senses were filled with an aroma that led him into a field full of flowers.

113

"Don't mind the smell. My girl Robin likes air freshener."

"Faggot."

Darky ushered Dan through the immaculately clean lounge room and into his temporary bedroom off a small hallway. Dan immediately was impressed with the upkeep of his joint.

"Geez, brudda, always been a pleasure walking into a place that's clean and tidy." Dan was a Virgo and believed he was a bit feminine when it came to cleanliness. Unlike a lot of his mates he was very conscientious that he lived in clean conditions, benders excluded, of course.

"Yeah, well, having two clean freaks living here makes it easy."

"Well, now there's three."

"Great! You can start in the bathroom. I took a big dump before I left and the rim needs a good licking."

"Better leave that one for your girl, mate."

"That'd be right. Been here 5 minutes and your already baggin' me girl."

"I'm sure she wears your ring of confidence well, bra."

"OK, Dan, enough said. Unpack your shit and I'll meet you at the mull bowl in the loungeroom. Make sure you bring a rock of 'Gibraltar' after all your insults and maybe I'll tell me girl so she can spit in your dinner."

"OK, boss."

As Dan unpacked his clothes he could hear the "snip snip" of the scissors already hard at work. He pulled his steamer wetsuit out with his rashee and threw them on the bed's new floral linen in anticipation of getting his hair wet after the bong session. The warm afternoon sun was beaming through a high elongated window and streaming down over the bed. That morning he'd seen the sunrise appear from the horizon of the Pacific Ocean. He was now four thousand kilometres away across the other side of the continent and he would soon see it set over the Indian Ocean. "Four thousand kms in one day ain't too bad," he thought to himself.

Darky was hunched over his dining table busy chopping his buds in his hand carved wooden Bali bowl with the intent of getting stoned quickly. He'd been busy doing shit all day in town and was starting to get withdrawals. "Hey, Dan, you waitin' till Xmas to get that rock out here?"

"Hold your horses. I'm coming, mate," was Dan's instant

reply. He grabbed the rock and headed towards the "snipping" as if it were bleeps on his radar. Darky was seated with his back to Dan. As he entered the loungeroom Darky was absorbed in the chopping ritual and none the wiser. Wanting to give his WA mate a little surprise he crept up from behind and extended his arms out and in front of Darky's tilted head. The kilo slab of fresh putty towered high above in the grip of Dan's hands almost depicting the dramatic scene of Moses when he raised the 10 Commandments into the violent sky. He promptly released it and it freefell onto the cheap laminex surface in front of his mate. It landed with a thud and almost knocked the Bali bowl off the table. Darky's stunned head remained staring downwards, his eyes fixated on the red cellophane that it had been wrapped in back in India. It thinly hugged the contours of the sleek boulder and his face grimaced then contoured into one of almost disbelief.

"Well, fuck me!" was all Darky could let out as he sat motionless as if time had ceased to continue. The hash gave off an aromatic waft like some exotic Eucharist and Darky sniffed long and hard, lifting his head and then slowly exhaling. It was like a state of spiritual reverence had illuminated the room. The large black specimen sat there like an effigy of a cross-legged yogi, its presence captivating and full of meaning. Its direct meaning being that they were going to be two very popular stoned puppies for the duration of the five-week surfing leg of the WA tour.

*

Smithy and Sterling had made a specific date that they would close the little Lamrock shop. Mario the Italian Pizza Chef from next door had originally sub-leased the space because he didn't need to use it for stock and imperishable produce. Dan, like the majority of Bondi, was well aware of Stirling's intentions to move out of the small shop and had asked Mario to save the new lease for him. He had always dreamed of opening a surf shop and thought it was a great opportunity to pounce. Dan was still guilty that there hadn't been a local boardriders comp since he had pulled stumps, going underground a year or so prior, and couldn't wait to get a new shop and boardriders off the ground.

Dan's dad, Ted, who had passed away a few years earlier, used to always encourage him to open a shop and do something with his life besides just surfing. Better that than think your son might turn out to be a failure. Expectations in his dad's world were totally different to his. They revolved around following what Dan thought was Dinosaur protocol. You were either a winner or a loser. Success was determined by what society labelled you as and if you weren't ambitious there was something wrong with you.

Ted loved Dan dearly giving him a good education and providing lots of opportunities to help him broaden his horizons. However, he could never express himself through tenderness which is what Dan yearned for from his father. To Ted being gentle was a sign of weakness, the real reason being that his mother had died in the "Great Depression" when he was still a baby and it's hard to give something you've never received. His dad was rarely at home being a travelling salesman so he'd grown up in a fairly disciplined, almost Victorian-like, environment, cared for by relatives or his stepmother. Kids should be seen and not heard. It was this childhood background which caused him to jump out of his boarding school window as a young teenager, when his dad was fighting in New Guinea, and start a new life on racetracks around NSW.

The generation gap was like a gaping chasm between Dan and his dad Ted. There was a lot of changes happening on the planet and Dan was growing up in a different world. The "beat" and "hippy" generations of the 50s and 60s had severed arteries between what was once considered normal conservative behaviour. They had altered the way of thinking of millions of kids' minds and laid a foundation for the state of things to be questioned. And rightly so—younger people wanted change and believed they had a right to be heard. Whether this movement was deliberate or not, it touched the rebel within most of the world's younger generation. It basically plotted old against new and drew many battle lines between adults and their kids. For this reason Dan loved his father but was shit-scared of him and surfing became an escape. It was a way of getting out of the house and down amongst the waves with a couple of mates. As long as he had a shooter under his arm he couldn't give a fuck.

If Dan was to open a surf shop it was for the totally opposite reasons than what his dad had hoped for. He just wanted to seize the opportunity to live his dream at the beach and capitalise on the fun in doing so. He didn't really care if he made any money just as long as he could pay the bills and keep the dream alive. Dan truly believed in the fellowship amongst his Bondi surfing buddies. He now had a chance to try and take some control back and put it in the hands of his local boardriding mates who seemed to be getting ignored. Radford already had his team of elite sponsored surfers and believed he had the beach sewn up. He was too busy sitting on his throne to pay attention to any of the beach's common folk. The beach wanted a core club again to hold contests and provide social events for all. His ignorance of this fact would ultimately test his character. He was sitting pretty and didn't think he had to care about any unrest. It was this smug attitude that obscured him from seeing the dark clouds drifting towards him on the stormy horizon.

Dan wanted to kick-start a new boardriders through his surf shop that would provide club contests again and help nurture the young talent in the area. He knew he had the capabilities and he was looking forward to getting his teeth stuck into it. He wanted to emulate the surfing ethic from past Bondi boardrider clubs. For the calibre of surfing during the 60s, 70s and 80s at Bondi Beach was strong. The culture thrived and Bondi's professional surfers were amongst the best in the world and had flown the Bondi flag with pride. These surfers had competed all around the world and each time they returned home they brought back vast amounts of surfing knowledge and shared it with the beach. These teachings were then filtered down through the beach's hierarchy till it reached the grommets. This nourishment was the core of the beach's high surf energy. To know and surf with these guys was a privilege the boys had inherited. Their stories conjured up raw images of surfing huge waves in Hawaii and other exotic parts of the globe. The kind of stuff grommets dream of.

In the order of things the locals who had made it to pro status were seen as modern day gladiators. They were heroes held in the highest regard. They had done the hard yards. They had paid their dues. They were all breaking new ground thanks to their predecessors and in turn were creating a vacuum that the next surfer in waiting could push through. It was a natural progression, one that every grommet aspired to and this was what Dan had in mind when considering his bold new venture. He wanted this orderly structure to take shape again. He believed every surfer—especially the grommets—deserved a leg-up to becoming better surfers. They were entitled to be brought together again as a club lending each other support and having a good time whilst doing it.

Although the odds were stacked against him, taking on Radford
and his money was a challenge too good for Dan to refuse.

*

The famous WA Triggs carpark was packed with cars and bodies.
It was the "King of the Point" APSA contest which was worth
double points and the highlight of the WA leg. Crew from all
around Oz were participating and enjoying the hyped atmosphere.
It was a beautiful sunny day with a crisp winter offshore.
Colourful surfboards and wetsuits decorated with sponsor logos
were laid out everywhere, cars were blaring different music from
"heavy metal" to "UK punk", girls were parading in their
seductive best whilst surfers washed their eyes with the passing
glamour, hot dog stalls yelled out "Get your doggies!" and Mr
Whippy served grommets ice-cream with a lavish crust of
chocolate on top. The contest's PA was filling the air calling on
contestants to collect their coloured shirts for their next heats. The
bass would sometimes reverb and everyone would clutch their
ears and pull distorted faces as if they had just been subjected to
some kind of deliberate torture. Photographers clicked away on
top of the hill next to the judges' stand all hoping to get the next
cover shot for whatever mag they worked for. The whole car park
scene overlooked the beach where a competitors' tent emblazoned
with sponsor banners was set up for official duties. In the water,
between the contest flags, was the surfing arena where guys
displayed their repertoire and hoped it was enough to get the
judges' nod. The surfing was radical even though the swell was
only small with 3-foot sets. Surfers were warming up on peaks
further south and showing great talent. It resembled feeding time
at the zoo—surf animals committed and sharpening their skills for
a bite at the contest carcass on offer.

Day one saw Darky perform well, drawing blood on his rivals
by winning his first and second round heats. He had a hunger to do
well at his home break and he was putting his local knowledge of
the break to good use. It was like he was wearing a magnet as he
snared each set wave and vigourously tore it apart. By contrast Dan
enjoyed casually free-surfing and checking the day's progressive
results. He was seeded into the third round due to his higher ranking
in the national ratings and didn't have to surf until later that
afternoon. Being seeded usually worked to a surfer's advantage;

however the pressure of expectation sometimes played against them especially if they encountered an unseeded surfer who was gaining momentum through the earlier rounds and clearly on a roll. But the majority of the time it worked in a top-ranked surfer's favour. Less fatigued and more experienced surfers generally depicted a daunting task for guys coming from the back. There were only 16 seeded spots the surfing tour had to offer and like the Aussie cricket team of that era it was harder to get knocked out than it was to earn a berth. You only needed to win your first heat to make the quarter finals and be assured of some good points whereas an unseeded surfer would have to gruel out a few rounds before being pitted against the elite.

So many guys ripped and some were destined to a bit of fame and some were destined to self-destruct before achieving their full potential. Like the majority of sporting heroes, fame was fleeting and after their career's worth had expired they would ultimately be thrown onto the surf-star scrapheap with all the others. There their egos would have to squirm and adjust to being just another ex-competitor as new blood etched their own names into the surf media. Replacements were in their hundreds, all hungry for their five minutes in the spotlight. The surfing media entertained the fact that they had the power to expose surfers and enhance their careers. They also had the power to ignore them and refrain from giving a surfer the exposure he dearly needed to make a name for himself. Such was the might of the surfing media and the sponsors who paid for the advertising and ultimately paid for the editor and photographer's wages. Just like how main stream media with corporate banks behind them make and break politicians, they are the real dictators—they are the major players in a plutocracy.

"Ready for your heat?" Darky was just arriving back at the car as Dan was donning his contest rashee.

Dan replied with a little impish smile. He was ready to do battle and was summoning up all his confidence. He was going to annihilate anyone who was to get in his way of winning. It was like he had joined the marines and this was just another mission to fly up the Mekong Delta and commit genocide. He was psyched; it was now up to him to produce the goods, "I haven't come four thousand kms for nothing."

His heat was never in doubt and he surfed with the grace and finesse that had seen him catapulted into the top rankings the year before. He made his way back to Darky's green Kingswood dodging the circus that was still in full swing. A few mates acknowledged his performance with a comment and a wink and Dan was feeling like it was another day at the office. There were another couple of heats scheduled before the contest could be wrapped up for the day and the crowd had started becoming a bit rowdy with the addition of alcohol.

"Well done," said Darky as he patted his mate on the back. "I doubt I could wipe the smile off your face with a cricket bat." Dan was happy with his effort and was relieved to have gotten over this first heat hurdle.

"Time to get outta here and 'char the dotch', I think, brudda."

"No arguments from me on that one."

*

Stirling was busy back in the arcade with his manager Daisy who was overlooking a couple of carpenters knocking up a few cupboards and board racks for the new showroom.

"Should have the shop open within about 3 weeks, Stirl," she said as she fluttered her false black eyelashes. They matched the colour of her hair which was long and flowing. She had a bit of Indian in her so her skin was a lovely olive texture and her slim features were elegant like a gazelle. Her long fingers and legs were bordering on Naomi Campbell-like, and her smile was quite enchanting. She would have looked right at home coming out of a Bedouin tent with scantily clad veils hanging off her sexy bits.

"Yes, Daise ... and start making some real money."

She smiled, flirting with the thought of how cosy it felt to be next to a man with money and power. She didn't have to say anything—her thoughts were signalling her submissive nature. She knew Radford was the man holding the cookie jar and that if she played her cards right it wouldn't be long till she'd be tasting those chocolate chips.

Fitzy had been working for Stirling for just over a couple of years now in his little shoebox in Lamrock Ave. Being such a well-worn local, and good surfer to boot, it had been strategic planning to employ Fitz. Fitzy had been a well-respected footy player for Bondi United and likeable character growing up in North Bondi. In general his drug and alcohol binges weren't detrimental to his reputation as he was generally enjoying the excess with any number of the boys.

"You want me to start that stocktake today?" he asked as he walked into Stirling's new premises.

"Better do it soon. Won't be long till we're moving in here."

"And give that little shop a mop. It's long overdue." Daisy couldn't help herself. She didn't like the fact that Fitzy was Fitzy. Something about him being abrupt and hard to put shit on.

"What do ya think, you're my boss or something?" fired back a "no holds barred" Fitz.

"Just do it. The way you keep that shop is a disgrace!"

"Shouldn't you be in the dunny with your mouth over one of those "blow me" holes, baby? After all, your lips gotta be good for somethin' when they start movin'."

Daisy soured. "You filthy piece of shit!"

Stirling had to jump in before a full slanging match erupted. "That's enough!"

"Oh my God, you apologise to me right now. How dare you talk about me like that in front of Stirling!"

'Yeah, whatever, black mama ...."

"OK, that's enough, Fitz. Daisy's on the team now, mate, and she'll be supervising what's happening from now."

"What?"

"So I suggest you get along with her." Stirling didn't want to upset either of them or favour one more than the other. They were both assets and he'd have to assess the situation a bit more as time went by.

"Apologise, you foul mouthed creep!"

"Or what?" Fitzy obviously didn't give a rat's arse.

"Fitz, please just say sorry. Daisy didn't mean to stir you up."

"Well, she did, and if she's gonna think she can start shit then she better think again. This is my beach, wench; don't forget it!"

Stirling was caught between a rock and a hard place. The phone started ringing which gave him an escape route. "You guys sort it out and keep your voices down; this might be my dad. I'll deal with this later." And with that he picked up the receiver and turned his back on the delicate, tense situation. Both Daisy and Fitzy growled at each other before Fitzy put his smoking gun in its holster and headed back to the shoebox.

"Scum like you won't be here much longer," said Daisy under her breath. A new battle line had been drawn inside Stirling's empire, its stark definition reverbing the "well to do" and "whatever" attitudes that were at loggerheads throughout the

121

beach.

*

Darky and Dan were relaxing at home listening to Darky's "Huxton Creepers" tape like a couple of stoned zombies moulded into the comfy leather couch when there was an unexpected knock at the door. They looked at each other through their red slits for eyes to see who was to make the effort to get up and answer it.

"Do something," Darky muttered so Dan grabbed the mull bowl off the dining table and slipped the incriminating evidence under the lounge while Darky sprayed some air freshener and headed towards the front door. "Hide the bong, too ... quick," he whispered.

Dan grasped the challis off the coffee table, stashing it behind the lounge and making sure it was sturdy and upright so it didn't spill. Darky waited till Dan was seated again before he asked, "Who is it?"

"Detective Sergeant Davis," came a deep voice from outside.

Darky and Dan shit themselves. There was no peephole for Darky to look through so he glanced back at Dan and motioned for him to disappear. A host of sketchy thoughts ran through the boys' paranoid brains. Dan rushed back to his bedroom as Darky slowly opened the door.

"Ha haaaa, got you!"

"You little fucker, Sammy! You had me fucking going, you little black prick!" It was Darky's aboriginal mate Sammy from Geraldton.

"Who is it?" yelled Dan knowing by Darky's reaction that it was a hoax.

"Sambo," answered Darky ushering the long curly haired lout inside and closing the door. "Situation's under control. He's just come round to shine our shoes and sing 'Mammy'."

"Fuck you, brudda. Look who's calling the pot black," retorted Sammy. "How come your parents are whiteys but you're a black cunt like me?"

"He's gotta point there, Darky," added Dan.

"You guys have heard of the last Mohican, haven't ya?" asked Sammy. "Well, Darky, you're the last fuckin' 'Black and White Minstrel' ... haaaa ..."

"No one's asking you anything, Sammy, so tell us what you

want and make it quick." Darky was a bit jaded by being stirred from his arvo chillout session but the drug business never usually hung trading hours on the door.

"Heard you guys have some of the black putty and I'd like to get some."

"Looks like you're made of the shit," exclaimed Dan. "Can't you just fart and produce some?"

"How much you want?"

"How much for an ounce?"

"Four hundred."

"Done."

"Sweet. Sit down while we get back to normal." Darky pointed to one of the dining chairs for Sammy to sit in and promptly collapsed back into his lounge. Dan went about his business and disappeared into his temporary bedroom. He emerged from his office with a golf ball, 28 grams to be exact, of hashish which he had weighed up earlier on his little green "Deering" scales in anticipation of his next customer. He bowled it overarm at Sammy who caught it like Rod Marsh, out to his right side with one hand.

"Good catch," said Dan. "Can see you've played a few games in India."

"India?"

"Yeah the street kids use rock hard hash to play cricket if they can't afford cricket balls."

"What?" Sammy's broad face cringed, doubting Dan's ramble. "So what do they use for a cricket bat?"

"Babies' arms."

"Haaa ... you're fuckin' off the air!"

Dan's answer had been spontaneous but his split watermelon smile said it sat well enough with his demented drug-induced state.

Darky had a bit of a snigger going. "Dead one's, of course."

"Wrapped in plastic."

"Whoooa! If that's what this shit does to ya after a few cones I ..." Sammy seemed lost for words for a second.

"You what?"

"Well, I suppose I can't wait to punch a few, then!"

"OK, Sammy, try one of these before you fuck off and go walkabout." Darky pulled out the Bali bowl and passed it to Sammy. As if called into action Dan guided his hand blindly behind the couch in search of the bong.

"You'll need this I suppose," said Dan, passing it over.

"Yeah, well, I wasn't going to use a baby arm, unless I was going to play cricket that is."

"Same size, though."

Sammy grinned and shook his head and started packing his cone. "I always thought babies' arms were used to describe the size of my cock."

"Just because we offered you a bong doesn't give you the right to start telling us about your fantasies now."

"Yes, Sammy, everyone knows you only pack a half-sucked twistie in your nappy."

"For a coupla white stoned cunts you sure can talk some shit."

"Years of practice."

"And Sammy, who you calling a white cunt?"

"Mate, what am I supposed to call a black and white hermaphrodite like you?"

"Wow, that's a big word."

"Anyway, who gives a fuck about black or white? Just flick me a fuckin' light so I can turn a shader pale of yellow like you cunts!"

"Mate, now you're calling us Chinamen, are ya?"

"For fuck's sake man, what's with all this colour shit?"

Darky threw him a blue "Bic" lighter and Sammy commenced his ritual.

"That's right, Sambo. Doesn't matter what colour you are."

"Or how many baby arms you've wrapped in plastic."

Sammy gurgled and sucked the hash smoke through the chamber. He exhaled blowing smoke rings until he had emptied his smoky lungs, again breathing deeply, then slouching as the spin took effect. A calm silence entered the room helping vacate the heckling session between the lads.

Dan sauntered through his brain and thought about colours, "Yeah it doesn't matter what colour we are. It's all just ink."

"Deep man," quipped Sammy. "Can I call you 'Rainbow'?"

Dazed and Confused

Dan borrowed Darky's landline and rang Mario's pizza shop. Back in Perth the APSA West Oz leg was coming to a close and Dan wanted to know what was going on back in Bondi.

"Hello, Mario's pizzeria," said the curly moustached Italian.

"Hi, Mario. It's Dan."

"Hi, Dan. What can I get you?"

"Mate, I'm in WA. Remember?"

"Oh, of course, my friend, but I don't do long distance deliveries."

"Ha ha, funny, Mario ... Stirling given you a date for when he's moving out?"

"He does."

"Wow, that's great news. When is it?"

"In a coupla weeks. Do you still want to take the new lease?"

"Yes, mate, but don't tell anyone. I want it to be a secret."

"Oh OK. Why you want secret again?"

"It's a surprise. I don't want the boys to know back in Bondi. Please don't say anything to anyone."

"Sure, Dan."

"Promise?"

"I promise, Dan. You count on me."

"Cool, Mario. I'll make sure I buy a pizza every day from you when I open."

"Maybe you get sick of the smell of my pizza, mate ... I not eat pizza for 10 years now, you know. I dream of cabanossi every night—drives me crazy."

"Really, Mario? You sound like a few girls I know ... Anyway, this is my friend's phone so I gotta go and I will see you next week and we can work out the business then, mate."

"OK, Dan. You be a good boy and see you then."

"Thanks, Mario. Bye."

Dan hung up the receiver with a grin from ear to ear. The ball was now rolling. If Stirling wanted to up-grade his surf shop Dan thought it appropriate to jump into the shell he was to leave behind. It was a small shop with little outlay and minimal risk which suited Dan's budget down to the ground. There was little time to lose so Dan booked his ticket home for the next day. He and Darky had enjoyed the few hazy weeks that had proved very advantageous. They'd scored great waves and sold the whole kilo of hash, keeping everyone happy in doing so. Dan had managed to make a small earn but the boys had smoked most of the profits. A couple of 9ths and 5th placings between them had increased their ratings and Dan had enjoyed a few romances along the way. All in all there were no complaints and their friendship had evolved to a new level. These days were to become pleasant memories to reminisce on in years to come. Mates for life, solid as a rock.

"Thanks, Darky, miss you already," said Dan as he hugged his mate before heading into the domestic terminal to check in for his flight home.

"You be alright lugging all that shit inside?"

"Piece of cake. Been banging around the world long enough now that a big boardbag ain't gonna worry me. After all, I'm going back a kilo lighter."

"Look after yourself and good luck with your new enterprise back home."

"You the man, mate. Thanks for everything." Dan knew how lucky he was to have a friend in the "west" like Darky. "Oh, and by the way, try and keep a lid on my shop, please, brudda. Gotta deal with a few things before it opens and I don't want word on the street."

"Secret's safe with me," said Darky as he zipped his lip and saluted. "Been a pleasure, Dan. Watch those Oxford fairies, now."

"I'll keep them wet for ya, big fella."

"Later ..." and on that note WA was over for another year.

Back in Bondi Dan had moved out of Hall Street and was staying at his mum's first floor unit in Roscoe Street whilst he organised himself in preparation for his new venture. He had seen Mario and arranged to pick the key up in less than a week so he had been busy ringing around arranging some finance and ordering stock.

His former sponsor TF, the founder of Hot Buttered Surfboards, was keen to support Dan's new shop and like several other companies thought it was a golden opportunity to get a foot in to the Bondi market. TF had a long association with Dan and had shaped his boards for his rookie Hawaiian year in 84. It had been an eventful initiation for the young Bondi lad, surfing mountains and meeting an amazing crew from around the world who had all converged upon the "Mecca" of the surfing world to prove their worth. The main constants were his trustworthy HB Fitzy boards, epic surf and some chronic "Maui Wowie" stink buds that were sprinkled with "gold top" dust to really evoke his cosmic consciousness. On a shoe-string budget he was doing what some people would call 'tough', but living in his bomb of a hire car on Sunset Point suited him just fine. He was safe staying in front of Mike Willis' house who had befriended him the minute he arrived on the North Shore. Mike was an amazing person, full of life and character. He shaped specialised boards for Hawaii and had a strong local following. This is where Dan had met a young Liam, JBG, Junior, Jason Majors and Mike's twin brother Milton. He embraced his new mates and new hobo lifestyle. Daily life was simple, and free of rent, and there was no planning involved as his course was the one of least resistance. He was learning the ropes from his close Bondi mate Steele who was still shooting for a world title. Pagey formed the trilogy and each day they'd cruise around in Steele's big old rusted Cadillac and surf wherever was firing. When it was flat they'd keep fit by skating down "Pupukae Hill" behind Foodlands. Gordinho's house was way up near the top and he'd become good mates with the boys. After a session of yoga and a game of small court tennis at his joint, they'd pick up their skaters and weave a trail of concrete lines for a couple of kms.

Dan soon became familiar with tons of whitewater crashing down around him. On smaller days "Backdoor" and "Rocky Point" had been a spiritual trip on his small 5'10" square-tail rip stick where he experienced the heightened thrill of surfing totally on the edge. His boards were so responsive they felt like a knife through soft butter. His psychedelic surfing sessions had unearthed a primeval instinct of survival, graced with a purpose of being a living piece of art. With a sharp coral reef beneath the swathe of his board his trance-like concentration arrested his fear and held his lines high and dry. Mushrooms had unlocked the doors of his perception and his new realm was sublime—the burst of spray on his back upon exiting each barrel a sure sign of being one with himself, as well as his surroundings and his place in the universe.

"Dan, are you going to be on that phone all day? I'm expecting a call."

"Sorry, mum. Just one more quick call and I'm going down the beach for a surf."

127

He promptly rang Cookie and arranged that they meet at the hut on "the hill" and get wet.

Parking across from the Rasa Malaysian restaurant at south, half way up the hill, he clambered out of his 2-door, 3-speed, metallic blue Torana eager to check the surf. Dan never thought too much about cars and was happy for them to get him from A to B but he had a soft spot for his XR-1 Torana. Steele's elder brother, Steve, had sold it to him a couple of years earlier for $1400 and it had never missed a beat. Dan had never bothered with roof racks and would always recline his passenger seat to accommodate transporting his surfboard. It was only a 4-cylinder but it sure packed a punch and was especially responsive to Dan's double shuffle.

Glancing through the tall pines as he walked alongside the white wooden fence down towards the hut he could see the common winter September westerly blowing spray high off the back of the 4-foot groundswell as they neared closer to the shore.

Cookie and Porks were sitting on the bench in the hut watching the surf waiting for him. The westerly wind had discarded Sydney's smog far and wide and the blue arvo sky showed no indication of any fallout of carbon let alone any hole in it. Big Ads was drip-drying, hanging around the lads in a long-armed spring suit. He was a local grommet contender who had a chip on his shoulder the size of the Opera House. He had obviously been in the water for hours and his feet and hands resembled wrinkled old bits which were a common occurrence for most groms who never wanted to get out of the surf due to their dedication. Ads was by no means a reflection of his name and was small in stature. He was a freckled little Aussie battler who lacked a formal education but made up for it with heart. He was your classic weathered grommet blooded in the back streets of Bondi and reared by his single mother who was a cleaner. She worked hard for her young son and their ground floor flat's proximity only a few doors down Lamrock Avenue meant that while she was at work he was jigging school and gaining his education from the beach. Living in Bondi he grew up fast, ciggies at nine, tequila at ten and bongs by eleven. By twelve he was a deadset seasoned veteran.

"Look who's comin'—it's fuckin' Dan," said Ads through chattering teeth. "Where you been, mate? Fuckin' been offshore all day!"

Dan dismissed the little shit. "Hi, Porks," he nodded his head, "Cookster."

"How was WA?"

"Yeah, fun. Caught up with Darky and a few of the lads."

"Any surf?"

"Uck, yeah. Margs was sick, got some hell slabs at Kalbarri. Never surfed that joint before—shit, it sure packs a punch."

"Shit, aye."

"Yeah, you woulda loved it on your forehand, Cookie. Mega pits!"

"Cookie's too lazy to fuckin' walk round to Tama for a surf let alone fly over there!"

"Who asked you, Ads? And ain't it time you fucked off home?"

"Fuck off, cunt."

"I think Playschool's about to start and you sure could use a lesson in how to talk to your elders," fired Porks.

"Go and have a shower, Ads, before you catch pneumonia," added Dan. The boys were used to Ads's perverse use of language and understood his lack of education had retarded his vocab. They accepted him as the cheeky kid that he was, and sympathised with his single-parent upbringing which saw a lack of discipline contribute to the brutish mannerism he conducted. He was only 14 but was up to anything anyone wanted to throw at him.

'What does that mean, you prick?" he snapped.

"What?"

"Pewnomia. Are you saying I'm gonna shit meself?"

"Dan means go home and have a hot shower, you little fuck, before you catch a cold or I'll slap you across the back of the head." Cookie cared but knew there was no use being nice to the kid when he had already got his back up.

"Touch me and I'll get me Uncle John onto ya." John was his elder sister's Maori boyfriend.

"Yeah, Ads, see ya, mate," was Cookie's dismissive reply.

"You guys are fucked!" and with that he picked up his board and trotted off home.

Some kids are just dark on the world and of course circumstances vary. With Ads one could only hope they broke the mould after he was born but then again, as Dan's grandma used to say, "If we were all the same, the world would surely be a boring place."

As Ads trudged up the hill and across the road Dan couldn't help notice a large silver unmarked transport truck across the road unloading bubble-wrapped surfboards. The driver named Pete and one of Stirling's young, new workers named Bob were taking the new stock two at a time and disappearing into the arcade. Fitzy had been given one last chance after he showed no backing down from Daisy and Stirling had hired young Bob to train up if he was to show Fitzy the door. After all, Stirling believed he needed "yes" men around him and couldn't deal with anyone insubordinate.

Bob was obviously helping in getting ready Stirling's new shop for its grand opening. Occasionally Daisy dragged herself away from the mundane tasks of polishing counters and vacuuming new carpet and out into the street to have a sticky-beak at anyone who was interested in what was going on inside. The arcade was quite spacious with an open courtyard and a first floor but no shops had actually opened yet except a Spanish restaurant downstairs on the opposite side to Stirling's. A few diners from the Lamrock Café engaged glances with her which gave her an opportunity to show her excitement and stretch her grin into a wide warm smile.

"Looks like Radford's got it all happening in there," commented Dan. "Must be ready to open soon."

"Why would you give a fuck?" blurted Porks.

"Well, I suppose I don't but then again I have my own plan to gain back what's ours."

"And what would that be?"

"Let you know soon enough."

"Well, it would want to be a pretty good plan. That guy's got the beach by the balls."

"Yeah, Dan, Pork's right. And I just read his uncle got voted richest man in Australia."

"Bullshit! Kerry Packer or Murdoch is!"

"And of course his Bondi surf team are reigning champs from last year," continued Porks.

"But half his team are blow-ins who don't even surf here," argued Dan.

"Look!" Cookie pointed to a guy who was ripping behind the reef on a solid right hander. "There goes one right now."

Dan focused and immediately knew the surfer's style, "That's Fred Gerhach from California. What's he doing surfing here?"

"One of Stirling's new recruits." With the absence of club contests Stirling's 'Rude Boys Surfing' team was running a bit low on depth so he was importing pros from all over. "And he's signed up Johnny Shindig from Hawaii who's livin' with one of his mates over at Clovelly."

"Good to see he's nurturing local talent." Dan's sarcasm was hiding his true disappointment but he kept it all under wraps knowing that he would be soon challenging Stirling in more ways than one.

"Well, he's sponsored 'Big Ads'."

"Well, I suppose he's scared of big John," said Dan with a wink.

"Ads's been washing his car."

"And been giving him blow jobs."

Dan refrained from laughing, "Knew there was a catch somewhere. He don't go sponsoring locals unless they are doing somethin' for him."

"Or making him look good."

All of a sudden the boys were interrupted by a couple of scallywags behind them.

"I thought I booked this hut this arvo ... What the fuck are you blokes doing here?" It was Getz with a mop on his head and Horse punked up behind him. They were silhouetted by the arvo sun glaring out from Lamrock Ave so it was hard to identify them except for their outlines.

"You got a ciggy?" asked Cookie who was never backward at coming forward.

"Nah, but if you want to go to the deli for us I'll buy a pack." Horse was ready to trade.

"You're on. Pack of Winnie Blues?"

"And a Mars bar and a can of Coke too. Gotta stick to my healthy diet," replied Horse. Dan shook his head and laughed. "What? Haven't you read the latest fitness section in *Cosmo*, Dan? Fuck, mate, you gotta keep up with what's happening in life, mate, otherwise you'll fall behind!"

"I'm sure that healthy diet's on the same page that they're pushing that artificial sweetener shit that kills ya," replied Dan. "Kinda ironic, don't you think?"

"Who needs that crap? And you know I don't read mags unless it's the surfing bible, and a Coke will kill anything in ya guts. Anyway, if it's good enough for Johnny Rotten it's good enough for me!" If there was one band in the world that Horse idolised it was the "Sex Pistols".

"I didn't say anything," remarked Dan. "Just making a point. If you wanna eat sugar then you should try saccharine. It's been killing old ladies for years."

Cookie kept things rolling, "If you wanna go all the way I'll get a rock of heroin for ya as well. That'll kill ya with a smile on yer face."

"Think I'll pass on that one today, Cookie. Still kinda pinned from the brown sugar I sprinkled on my Rice Bubbles this mornin'."

"Well, Rager just walked past with his frizzy haired ho and I'm sure he's just got back from Cabramatta." Rager was a local pin cushion though he sold anything he could get his hands on. At the time the Vietnamese connection was selling loads of smack on the street in Cabramatta and a lot of junkies were travelling the extra distance on the train because it was that pure. Rager's name epitomised his lifestyle and even though he was continually on it he was a funny bloke and a gem of a guy. He loved the boys and was part of the Bondi furniture.

Cookie took a redback off Horse, traded spots on the bench and headed across the road to Fat Mama's deli.

"Make sure you come back!"

"Yeah don't do an Alex ..." added Porks.

"What's been happening, guys?" asked a curious Dan as he swivelled and got a better look at the lads. "Besides that sheepdog hairdo you're spruikin', Getz, any gossip?" Dan was keen to find out the latest.

"Bowlarama," commented Porks

"Not half as reekin' as your 'rude boy' haircut, Dan. How many guys pin you down and rape you before they got the lawnmower out?"

"Yeah, Vanilla Ice."

Dan's "flat top" with long blond dyed fringe was way worth an avalanche of criticism.

"Don't get jealous, now," was a common reply for Dan or any of the boys to use when one had nothing else up their sleeve. After all 'Vanilla Ice' could take the bagging session anywhere. "So what's been happening ... anything new on the scene?" he added to avert a massacre.

"The Hordern 'House' parties have been cranking," replied

Getz to Dan's relief. The bad hair bagging had been stopped for the moment.

A new underground dance party movement had come to Sydney town and was gaining momentum. "Ten thousand lunatics on ecstasy dancing the night away to all the new 'House' music that's been flooding in from the UK."

"It's nothing on the Clash or the Pistols," said Horse

"Room for both," commented Porks.

"Mando's got some great mixed tapes over in his shop if you wanna check it out," added Getz.

"What kinda music?"

"Oh, there's heaps, like 'Beats International'—their track 'Dub be Good to Me' fucken rocks!"

'Sick, Getz. Sounds happening," replied an excited Dan.

"Shit, yeah. There's heaps like 'C & C Music Factory', 'Black Box', Guru Josh, Technotronic—shit, bra, there's so many ... and you just can't stop dancing. A mate told me the Pommies have brought it here but he said it all started in 'the States'."

"Yeah, that makes sense. I mean, how good is the 'Jungle Brothers', dude, 'I'll House you'!" threw in Porks. "And 'De La Soul'. Some sick beats!"

"Yeah untz untz untz—really deep stuff, man." Horse was compelled to throw in his continual dissatisfaction. "You guys are fucken bonkers!"

"Horse, if you saw some of the sick chicks that've been nailing there you'd have a 'woody' straight away. They are the filth!" If the argument was to swing Getz way he was using the right tactics. Bondi boys constantly had a competition going on about who could pull the hottest chicks. Some of the boys went for quality when others went for quantity—after all, you've got to slay a few dragons to get to the princesses.

"You've sold me," pitched in Dan.

"Never hard to sell you, Dan, when there's sexy bitches involved." Getz gave Dan a high five.

"Mustard's his middle name," joked Porks.

"You know it, so when's the next one?" Dan was eager to check anything new on the clubbing scene.

"Next week, brudda. There's been a crew from Bondi going sick on the 'Es'. Man, it's bigger than Dallas!"

"No-one's bigger than JR," commented Horse.

"I had one of those eccys last week and ended up having an

intimate relationship with my hand for five hours."

"Don't go tellin' that to everyone, Porks. Shit, I think you're overdue for a girlfriend before crew start talkin', brudda."

"Everything starts with an 'E' except most of the words in the fucken dictionary, you morons!" Obviously the concept of love drugs had yet to grow on Horse. Getz would have to use a different type of candy to persuade the big guy.

"What is that eccy shit anyways?" Dan was curious about this new drug doing the rounds. "Is it like the acid or something?"

"It's this stuff called MDMA, bra, and it's like you want to hump every chick in the joint and they want to hump you back."

"No way! Where can I get some?"

"'T's all there, bra, 'in da house', or you can get 'em from the fags in Oxford Street. They're the ones bringing the shit in."

"Hope they're not bringing it in up their bum."

"Ha, doesn't smell like it, but some of them top shelf it."

"What's that?" asked Porks.

"Instead of swallowing it they shove it up their arse and reckon it feels great when their boyfriend punches their donut."

"Oh, my God!" Horse was shocked.

"How can a guy prefer eatin' donuts over muffins?"

"Don't talk shit, Porks. You eat both ..."

"Donuts don't deserve to be demoralised like that!" continued Horse.

"Mate, the poofs are running the whole scene, bra. They organise the parties and they sell the drugs and if you don't worry about 'em who cares? All the more chicks for us!" Getz was not gay but he definitely wasn't scared to indulge in the trimmings on offer at their parties. "Gay guys are no drama, mate, as long as you tell them straight."

"Tell them what?" asked Cookie.

"To stay away from yer bum ..."

"Mate, some of them are nice blokes!"

"Yeah, Getz, when you've got yer dick in their mouth."

"I don't give a fuck about poofs," said Dan. "If they start any shit I'll just knock 'em out! I'm with you, Getz. Bring on the 'House' chickies!"

"Me too. As long as there's horny chicks partying, I'm in." Porks was happy with what he envisioned could possibly be a prelude to his first delirious orgy.

"Rule number one: No poofters!" Horse was adamant. One of

his cousins in Queensland had been molested by a rock spider when they were kids and he had never forgiven them. "Joe Strummer would shoot every one of them."

"I heard he liked a bit of quiche ..."

"Not as much as you, you blasphemin' piece of shit!" said Horse as he simultaneously leaned around Dan and gave Porks a dead arm.

Porky let out a painful cry, clutching his corked triceps followed by a mandatory come back, "Fuck you!"

"That's right, squeal like a pig, boy!" continued Horse "And next time you say 'Shit!' like that I'm gonna tar and feather you and tie you to a pole up the Darlo wall." "The Wall" was situated near St Vincent's Hospital in Darlinghurst. It was a very high wall standing several metres tall and had been built by convicts during the 1800s of sandstone blocks. It was now one of the perimeter walls of East Sydney Tech. The notorious gay hang, where young boys waited to prostitute themselves to the passing trade, was a sight for sore eyes. Not somewhere you'd want your kids to have to walk by on their way to school or for that matter any time of day. Customers generally picked these desperate kids up in cars committing lewd acts whilst driving through "the Cross" then dropping them back with a mouthful. Alex and a few mates named TK and Johnny, aka JC, used to go up there with baseball bats and practise their swinging.

A week later Dan pulled up in his Torana outside his temporary residence at his mum's place. Her flat was at the back end of Roscoe Street which was only for one-way traffic and a few blocks from the beach. It suited her as it was a quiet street and she had a few older lady friends who lived in the same three-storey brown brick tenement. The view from the unit's north-facing balconies overlooked Rose Bay taking in the greenery of the Royal Sydney Golf Course where, as a punk, Dan illegally used to go looking for golf balls then sell them down at the Woollahra course. Kids weren't allowed into the private elite club grounds but that only added to the excitement of searching the bushes and hiding from the regular players. Getting chased was all part of the fun. One day an old bloke fell over after chasing them after having what looked like a seizure. Dan and his mates never actually found out what happened to him—they just kept running and never looked back.

Like so many times before Dan had forgotten his house key

and had to use the intercom to get his mum to let him in from the side entrance. "Hello?"

"Yeah, mum, it's me."

"Lost your key, have you?" she asked as she pushed the button on the intercom to let him in.

"Not yet. Just forgot 'em again."

Upstairs his mum had cooked his favourite, spaghetti bolognaise. Leanne was a classic old-school mum who doted over Dan and his younger sister. There was nothing that fazed her when it came to household chores and she felt a wholeness in keeping a neat and tidy house. Her responsibility was to care in any way possible to guarantee the family nest was what it should be: a haven where her children could bask in her love and support. Dan's dad had disappeared through tragic circumstances a few years before and that had made her even more determined to make up for his loss. Sure, she was their mum but she wore the pants that her husband had left behind and expected that her terms be respected when her children were back at home. The family roof was a safety net that had broken Dan's fall on many occasions. The generation gap might have been wide but Dan knew the rules and understood they were in place for a reason. It was home, the conductor that earthed him when he needed it most. He loved his mum dearly.

"Do you want some more parmesan cheese, darling?"

"No thanks, Mum. Tastes just great as it is. When's Jen getting back from New Caledonia?" Dan's sister was working for Club Med and he hadn't seen her for quite some time.

"Not sure, but I'm expecting a call this week."

"Great."

"She's doing very well over there, you know."

"Happy to hear that, Mum. She might come home with a French man."

"Well, she does love croissants." She was very proud of Jenny who was a conscientious girl who worked hard. "And I'm very excited about your new venture down the beach."

"You haven't said anything to anyone, have you?"

"Of course not. Your secret is safe with me."

"Well, it's just I don't want that Stirling kook to get wind of it till I'm actually open."

"I know and I think that's a good idea. You never know how a kid with all that money behind him is going to react."

"That's right, Mum. The boys just told me his Uncle Bernard was voted the richest bloke in Australia."

"I thought Packer was?"

"So did I."

"Well, he'd have to be close behind him, I suppose, so all I can say is be extra careful if you are going to set up in opposition to a powerful family like his."

"Fuck him."

"Dan, watch your tongue. I don't care what you say when you're down with your mates but you're at home with your mother now."

"Sorry, Mum ... but he just shits me the way he's come to our beach and taken over."

"Well, these things happen, darling."

"Yeah, I know. Suppose I'm just hurt that I spent so much time helping him with the club and that. I was just stupid, I suppose."

"People are like that especially when they have money behind them. Look at your father. He'd go out on a limb to help people and his trust in people ended up killing him, so just let that be a lesson to you about helping people before you know their intentions."

"I love you, Mum."

"Well, if you love me make sure you make your bed in the morning ... and how long till you open your new shop because I can't fit my car in the garage because of all the stock building up in there."

"Sorry, Mum. About another week or so and I should have it all cleared for you."

"Thank you, Daniel. Because you know I don't like leaving the car outside—this is Bondi, you know."

"Yes, Mum. I think I should know—we've only lived in Bondi all our lives."

"And if you could water my pot plants on the balcony ..."

"No probs."

"And please don't try and grow your pot out there this year. I don't want to have to fib to my friends that it's a tomato plant anymore."

"OK, Mum. Don't want you getting thrown in jail for cultivation, now."

"Thanks, darling. Do you want some ice cream?" Dan's mum loved to spoil him and feed him up, especially when he was home, because as she used to say, "Heaven knows what he eats, that's if he eats at all, when he's living down that beach with all those boys." Sure, Dan was a fit fine specimen as his surfing, boxing and all night dancing sessions at inner city night clubs countered the drug binges, but his mum always thought he was a little light on weight.

"Yes, please, that'd be great."

'With chocolate sauce?"

"Sure, Mum. You're the best!"

The big day had arrived and Dan was to collect the key and sign the lease agreement for his new shop venture. He was feeling excited that his boyhood dream was coming to fruition and he had great expectations. He finally felt some kind of justice was about to take place and his allegiance to his fellow boardriders was to be honoured. It was as if, in economic terms, the story between David and Goliath was about to commence but in this analogy it was a long shot whether Dan would ever be able to slay this plutocrat. He was to meet Mario at 12 midday at the pizzeria to do the deal and would start moving stock in immediately, much to his mum's relief. Having a trade as a tiler was the only thing Dan, who was now 28, had ever accomplished in the business world, though he was a paperboy on Old South Head Road when he was 11. During his tiling apprenticeship he had even failed his last year at Randwick tech because of his low attendance record. Quoting jobs was the closest thing he had been to a boardroom so it was understandable that he would make mistakes with his new surf shop. He knew it would be a learning curve but hoped he would quickly get a grip on things so nothing too disastrous would go down. Opening in a recession was a factor he didn't even account for, mainly because he never paid attention to his commerce class at school so he didn't comprehend what a recession was. Unbeknown to Dan, lacking in business expertise and prowess would cost him before he even put the key in the shop door.

Dan didn't ever want to feel malevolent towards Radford; if anything he wanted a truce. He obviously disagreed on what had transpired since Richie Rich walked into town, but his faith in mankind helped him believe that all wasn't lost and the two of them could work things out. It was this chink in his armour which made him pay dearly. Unfortunately for Dan he seemed to have let the benevolence that he'd inherited from his old man bubble to the top. He stupidly approached Stirling in his arcade shop to try and offer an olive branch a couple of hours prior to opening.

"Hi, Stirling, any chance of a word with you?" Daisy was at the back of the shop helping a customer. She nearly fell over in hearing Dan's voice. She knew of the bad blood between them and wondered why on earth Dan would ever bother walking through Stirling's front door.

"OK, Dan, let's go outside," replied an inquisitive Radford as he came around from the counter to join him. For whatever reason Dan was there, Stirling wanted to keep it confidential.

Outside was empty except for a couple of pigeons scavenging some of last night's tapas on the ground. Dan looked Stirling firmly in the eye and commenced, "You know I want what's best for this beach and I think we should try and get along." Stirling stood in his recently-fitted doorway, like a prince in the entranceway to his sparkling palace, and nodded his head. Dan's bold attempt to disperse any animosity had caught Radford off guard and he wasn't prepared to say too much. "I was happy to help you before with the club and you've got to realise I only lost control because I felt you used me and then pushed me into a corner."

"No worries, mate. I understand there have been differences in opinion between us."

"Of course there has and that's why I'm here, and I feel bad about whackin' ya but you did push your finger into me chest, mate."

"All water under the bridge mate." Radford found it hard to look Dan in the eye. He didn't want to seem cagey so he thought it best to seem content and just see where the conversation was going and what Dan actually had to say. The more Dan tried to talk sense and patch up their shortcomings the more Stirling saw it as building up to some kind of confession.

"OK, Dan, you don't need to continue, mate. It's all in the past."

"Sweet, Stirl. I just wanted to make sure that both of us understood that holding grudges ain't worth it." And with that Dan and Radford shook hands. "Now that's out of the way I want to tell you something that I think we can both help each other with." Dan was about to foolishly let the cat out of the bag.

"Sure. I'm all ears, mate."

"I'm opening a new surf shop."

Radford's heart missed a beat but he was never going to show any disorder. "Cool. I'm happy for you, mate," was his controlled reply, a complete contrast to the buffalo stampede that was happening within. He was more than shocked but less than dumbfounded as he knew he had to play this one out till he could get a handle on what further information Dan might impart.

"Yeah. I'm not doing it to tread on your toes and I know this beach is big enough for us both to run a shop." Dan felt an easing inside about his disclosure—it was like he thought things were going to be in harmony at last. "You see, I will be stocking completely different brands than you and if a customer walks into my shop and wants, say, some Quik boardies I'll send 'em down to you and if someone wants a HB hooded you can do the same and send 'em to me. We can work together, mate. There's heaps of trade and we can both earn a quid. Whaddya reckon?"

"For sure, Dan. Sounds great. I look forward to it."

"Really? I was hoping you would. Thanks, Stirling. You're a lot cooler than I ever thought." Dan put his hand out again and Radford shook it for the second time. "You know, I've always wanted to open a surf shop, mate, and I know my dad would be so proud of me right now if he was still around."

"For sure, mate."

"Just like yours is, right?"

"Right."

For Dan it made perfect sense that they could co-exist and he believed being honest with Radford would bring out the best in him. What an imbecile he was! How wrong could he have gotten it? How stupid can one man be? Dan was about to find out more quickly than anyone could have thought possible.

Bob showed up just as the conversation had ended, a bit surprised to say the least that both lads were talking to each other.

"Hi, Dan. Hi, Stirl."

"Hi, Bob," replied Dan.

"How's things?"

"All good, mate. Stirling and I were just discussing a future friendship that involves both of us helping each other out."

"Wow! Sounds interesting."

"I'm sure Stirling will fill you in. He's a pretty cool boss and you're lucky you're working for him." Dan was feeling great and full of compliments. To him things had worked out just fine. Everyone was going to achieve what they wanted and the beach was no longer to suffer any disunity. "I've gotta make tracks, heh. Gotta heap of shit I've gotta organise. Thanks, Stirling, for your time, mate, and I'm stoked we've worked things out."

"No probs, mate."

"Talk soon." And off Dan jogged with a feeling of satisfaction that he'd been open with his former foe and resolved their differences. He just hadn't realised that the only thing he'd really opened was his arse and it was about to be fucked hard!

Dan was sitting on Mario's doorstep at 11.55am in anticipation of having the deal signed, sealed and delivered. As planned Mario turned up at 12 midday. It was commonplace to open for lunch. Dan was so keen about things he shouted at Mario from several metres away. "G'day, Mario!" he stood up and moved forward to shake his hand. Mario avoided eye contact and brushed past him with keys in hand to open his large glass sliding door. "Hey, Mario, what's up mate? What are you doing?" There was something wrong. Mario turned the lock and started to pull the door open. "Hey, Mario, don't you say hi to your new neighbour?" he paused for a second, smelling a rat, but his head was too upbeat to let anything deflate him, yet! "Mario? Hello?"

Dan grabbed his shoulder and tried to swing him around but the Italian defiantly shrugged Dan's hand away and stepped up into his shop. Dan was suddenly dumbfounded—a stream of panic shot through his body as if his whole world had started to crash down upon him. "Please, mate, tell me what's happening. I've got all this stock coming in the next few days."

Mario finally had a quick glance at the state of desperation the boy was in. "Sorry, the deal's over." A sinister element coated the heavy Italian accent.

"Whaddya mean? You can't be serious? We've agreed on everything already." Anxiety gripped Dan like a hand squeezing a squash ball. "What's happening, Mario? Don't kid me around."

"Sorry, I busy. Please go."

"Why are you doing this to me?"

Little did Dan know that the cheating Italian had received an impromptu blank cheque from Radford to keep Dan out of the picture "at all costs" after they'd had their "man to man". Dan felt defeated and understandably couldn't believe what was unfolding.

"Go away ... I not want to talk to you no mores." And with that the wog closed the door shut on Dan's deflated figure. He stood in front of the pizzeria for a minute and didn't know really how to react. So many emotions and only one stupid brain to access the situation. Stress plus had him pacing and slapping his throbbing forehead. Dan pulled it together after a minute or two and started to question what must have transpired. Surely a mandate was involved from someone who obviously didn't want him around. It wasn't rocket science. "Stirling!" he thought. "How could I have been such a fool!" He clenched his teeth and wanted to scream at the top of his lungs but a voice inside stopped him from doing so. The voice calmed his volatility and whispered for him to head home so he could think things through and regroup. Could it have been his dad or even granddad or both looking over him? He hurriedly jumped in his Torana which was parked in the back lane, smoked the wheels and sped off.

Closing his bedroom door behind him and locking out the world he lay down on his bed and gazed at the white painted ceiling. Sinking into depression he started thinking about a lot of negative things that had occurred through his life. He knew he had been blessed in many ways and there were many people on the planet who were having to deal with a lot more suffering but he still felt disturbed, almost perplexed, so almost unconsciously began to ride his emotions and let them take their course. He questioned his position in the shape of things and wondered if he was just trying to wedge a square into a round hole. He went further into his mind and asked why people had to suffer at all? Surely there was enough on the planet for everyone and couldn't fathom the greed that had engulfed it. He reasoned that it was the same that it ever was, but sunk deeper, concerning himself with why mankind hadn't woken up to his art of woe. Why did good intentions seem unorthodox and unpopular? Why was Wall Street winning? Why was mother earth dying? Why had all this shit forced his father to take his own life? Why? Why? Why? Why? Fucken why?

He lay there for what seemed ages but could have only been a few minutes. It was as if his mind had dismissed time as just another dimension, another burden attached to his physical being.

There was a soft knocking on his door. "Daniel? You OK, dear?"

He was now stuck between his own rock and hard place. It was obviously his mum, who, through being his mum, knew something was wrong. Was he to pull his manhood pigskin on or was he going to turn to jelly in the arms of the only person who really cared? The rulebook states that "boys don't cry" and as much as he wanted to let his tears fall he quickly composed his thoughts and replied, "Yes, Mum, all good."

"Can I come in, dear?"

Clasping his face he rubbed his temples and sat up to disperse his depth of despair. "Sure."

The door opened slowly and his mum reservedly stuck her head in before emerging. She observed a poignant figure sitting on his doona and knew there was a job at hand to discard his sorrow. Her hesitation made him prop his head up and look at her. Her unconditional vow to be there for him emanated an undeniable angel-like presence. Her grace had somehow backslammed his negativity and she moved forwards and embraced him. His look turned infantile as she held his head close to her bosom. She knew her boy was in a weathered frame of mind and he needed her strength and parental sage-like perspicuity.

"OK. What happened?"

Dan felt a bit better immediately. Sometimes when you're down all you need is someone to care. His spirit was partly resurrected within an instant. Enough to at least start to engage in conversation. "Shop's been pulled out from under me, Mum."

"OK. So ..." She was cut short.

"Shit, Mum. I've got everything on the line here ..."

"What do you mean, 'everything', darling?"

"Man, I've got stock ordered, gear already sitting in yer garage—this is my reputation, Mum ... it's teetering on the brink of ... shit! What are the boys, the suppliers, what are they all going to think of me? I'm so stupid. I was getting a lot of the stock on credit and I've already paid deposits ... what am I going to do, Mum? It's a fucking mess!"

"OK, so let's work it out."

"How am I gonna pull this off, Mum? Once everyone hears about this I'm fucked!"

"No, you're not ..."

"Yes, I am. They're gonna all laugh at me. I'm such a dumbshit!"

"OK, enough of this. We will find a solution. Remember that's what you're always saying to me."

"What?"

"No problems, only solutions—remember?"

"Geez, Mum, I sure need a solution right now and fast!"

"OK, Daniel, let's go through the options."

Dan hadn't even cleared the debris from his mind to think clearly that he even had any. "Options?"

"There's always options, dear, and don't think there ever isn't any. That's what killed your father."

"OK, mum, suppose you're right." Dan was starting to emerge from his depression and there was a crack between the storm clouds. "You think I can save my arse?"

"Smart boy like you, no problems. I'm sure we can work something out."

"Seriously? I've hardly got any money."

"Don't need money when you've got two heads like ours. Let's just take it a step at a time, aye?"

"You reckon?"

"Of course. What about we check out another shop?"

"Another shop? Doesn't that take lots of cash and time, Mum? I haven't got time on my side, I've ordered stuff and it's on its way."

"Slow down. I'm sure we don't need lots of time to get this sorted. We can keep anything being delivered downstairs with the other boxes until we work this out."

"But how we gonna do it, mum? Cheap shops are hard to come by in Bondi and all the stuff is just gonna be sitting here!"

"Doesn't matter if it takes a bit longer and costs a bit more."

"A lot more."

"Doesn't matter. Let's just go and see what's available. Things happen for a reason and it could work out much better."

"You really think so?"

"I know so." Dan's mum was adamant and could feel things slightly swinging her way. "Look how passionate you are about this and how committed you are to your destiny." She looked down at her son's fazed face but now saw he had started thinking about options. "Daniel, you will open a surf shop and you will make it one of the best surf shops around. I promise you. Your Uncle Rob had one of the best surf shops ever in Bondi ... can't you see—it's in your blood."

"You think you're right, mum?"

"I know I am, and if someone knows the surf business it's you, Dan. I'm going to back you on this one and if we have to borrow some money, so be it! You can pay me back and I know you will." Dan had no assets so if he were to apply for a loan he would have to use his mum's bricks and mortar as collateral.

144

"You for real, Mum?" Strong rays of sunshine were now bursting through the veil of cloud that had been thinned considerably.

"You'd better believe it, bucko!"

"Mum?"

"Yes, dear?"

"I love you."

"Love you too, mate."

His blue skies were back and he had one last thing to say, "And thanks for everything, for putting up with me for 28 years."

"Wouldn't have had it any other way."

Dan wasted no time: kissed his mum goodbye then headed down the beach to check his options.

Photo: Bill Morris

Photo: Dan Webber

Photo: Peter Maguire

Photo: John Webber

Photo: John Webber

Photo: John Webber

Photo: Geoff Peters

Photo: Deb Morris

Photo: Deb Morris

150

The Surf Shop

Dan headed straight for the many real estate agents that were spotted all over Bondi. Being closely-built made Bondi the most highly populated suburb in Australia and by the late 80s it was full of dilapidated units mainly erected pre world war 2 or during the two decades after. A compact mass of bricks and mortar shaped it into a real estate agent's rental dream. During the 60s, 70s and 80s renting was a huge part of living in this coastal residential district for the working class who inhabited its shores. A lot of the units were dodgy, cockroach-infested holes in the wall but it suited the likes of the boys down to the ground. Cheap rents and lots of sharing meant they didn't have to fork out too much of their pay packets or dole each week. When the sharemarket crashed in the late 80s and negative gearing started it created a big shift in investment towards real estate. Buyers were moving in and rentals were on the decline. Most of Dan's mates were living week to week and never thought much about how in a matter of years they would be priced out of their own local market. None of them ever believed they would have to leave their home and move on.

After checking a couple of smaller real estates in Curlewis Street and having no luck Dan decided it would be a good idea to seek some help from an older friend named Greta who managed 'Ray White' in Hall Street. Greta was an ally, a sweet older lady with a monumental nose, round midriff and eye for shrewd accounting which Dan believed were definite Jewish trademarks. Dan didn't know why she had taken a liking to him but she'd always tried to help him when it came to many things, especially renting. He gathered that she was just a sweet Jewish lady. She had helped him find a way to wipe his numerous parking fines when he lived in the units opposite her offices on the corner of Jaques Avenue. She obviously had good friends in council. Grey uniformed traffic cops had been bringing joy to locals for years down Bondi way and at one stage Dan had racked up about 10 fines in 6 months just by parking outside his residence.

The first thing she mentioned was a discontinued cafe lease just opposite 'the hill' on the corner of Lamrock and Campbell Parade. Dan had only been back a couple of weeks from WA and hadn't really paid much attention to the newly closed business—either that, or was too stoned to notice.

"It's been closed a few weeks and I'm sure whoever holds the lease will want to get some money out of it and probably sign over the lease."

"You reckon?" Dan couldn't believe his ears. His mother had mentioned that everything happens for a reason. "Oh, this is great news." Dan couldn't believe how quick such an appealing option had landed in his lap. He now felt that there was a chance of getting things back in order. "How much do you think he will want for it?"

"Depends on how long the lease has left on it. The lease might be almost up and you could then deal directly with the agent."

"Do you know who that is?"

"Look, Dan, I've been so busy with all our work here that it's none of my business." She paused to pass an instruction onto one of her workers in her nasal monotone voice. She swivelled back around to Dan and never one to miss a beat continued, "But in saying that I'd like to have that property on my books. It's probably the best location on the beach." Greta had so much work on her desk that she had recently hired an extra helper to get through it all.

"Yeah, you're right as always, Greta." A big smile came over her face. "And it's a great spot for me. It's right across from 'the hill' and central to everything."

"That's right, and it has a bus stop straight out front to catch all your passing trade coming down from Bondi Junction and the city."

"Wow, I can't believe this." Dan's head was slightly spinning from the sudden change of fortune that was upon him. "Greta, this could turn out better than ever."

"Well, getta move on, then. You'd better see if there's a phone number in the window or find out who lets it before someone else thinks it's a good idea to open some kind of business there and beats you to it."

"You're a legend, Greta. Thanks heaps."

"Off you go and good luck to you."

"Thanks again." And with that he was out of there and in his Torana before she could shuffle back to her desk and give her weary weighted legs a rest.

His hands were trembling as his nervous system threw out mixed signals. "Yes!" he said to himself as he pulled away from the kerb and headed towards Bates corner. He indicated right and sped into Campbell Parade like his reputation depended on it. A couple of mates waved at him but he didn't see them for his task at hand blinkered pretty much anything that wasn't straight in front of his sights. He illegally parked across the street from the Lamrock corner encroaching into the allocated area of the 322 bus stop terminus. Briefly he glanced across at the terracotta coloured facade that encircled the large glass shopfront. Door closed and no sign of life. He jumped out his door, checked if the road was clear then bolted over to the shell of a shop. As he reached the kerb he felt this was meant to be and no matter what it took he would be in this shop within a week. He took a few steps forwards, used his hand as a visor to block the glare and peered inside. He could see it was in fairly good condition and comprised a medium-sized front room that funnelled into a narrow back room. It was perfect and what's more it had a small hand-written "for lease" sign on the wooden slatted floor that had fallen from its original position in the window. It was just visible to the naked eye so Dan ran up to "Parade Music" and borrowed a pen and paper from his mate Mando to write down the private phone number.

Dan stood back a couple of metres from the big glass pane. It was way bigger than Mario's little square box and on the main strip visible from the whole beach. "Hell," Dan thought, "you can even see it from Ben Buckler!" An undeniably majestic feeling overwhelmed Dan. "And it looks as though you're going to be able to watch the surf from the comfort of the showroom floor." He shed a winsome grin as his confidence grew and tipped his lopsided emotional scales back in his favour.

"Doesn't matter what has happened, I will work towards what has to be done to live my dream," he uttered under his breath, as if to reassure himself, as his grin broke into a fully fledged smile.

"Time to get to work," he thought and as he skipped across to his loyal waiting Torana he started singing to the AC/DC Black album, "I'm back, smack, whack, yes, I'm back with a hack!"

Unbelievably it was a complete 360 degree turn from where he was earlier that day. He had now begun to believe that with his mum and shop suppliers' support he would prevail. Perseverance furthers and nothing was going to stop him. Excitement had reared its cheerful head once more. It was kinda the same feeling he experienced when he was a kid and knew he was about to embark on his way to Luna Park. There was a lot of fun to be had behind those big pearly whites!

As he opened the car door to jump in, 'H' man was enjoying

the afternoon rays in his prime south Bondi, 322 and 365, bus
shed. He pondered on how he would be able to watch 'Harry'
every afternoon and blow him kisses. Jumping in he slammed the
door behind him and said, "Let's go!" He adjusted his rear view
mirror and looked himself in the steely eye. "Dan, you can do
this!"

As soon as he was in his mum's door he beelined straight for
the blower.

"Darling, how did you go? Any good news yet?"

"I'll let you know as soon as I'm off the phone, darl."

Dan had a mixture of anxiousness, excitement and nervous
jitters as he contemplated talking to whoever picked up the
receiver.

A deep man's voice with a middle eastern accent answered,
"Hello?"

"Hello, sir, my name is Daniel. You actually don't know me
but I got your number out of the window of your cafe down at
Bondi."

"Yes, Daniel."

"Well, I just wondered if you hold an existing lease for that
property and if so whether we could meet and discuss the
possibility of me taking it off your hands."

"I'm sure," the man cleared his throat before continuing. "I'm
sure we can sit down and talk things."

Dan found it hard to hold his back his stirring delight but knew
he had to at least try to not sound too keen. "Wow, that would be
great, sir ..."

"Please call me Abdul."

"Yes, sir, I meant, yes, Abdul."

"Much better." Abdul's voice was very controlled and he was
already rubbing his hands together on the other end of the phone,
anticipating this being a good opportunity to seal this deal and get
the bankrupt shop out of his hair. He had been waiting for an
interested party for a few weeks now so he was glad to receive the
unexpected call. "When would you like to meet me?"

"What would be convenient for you, Abdul?"

"Ahh, let me see. What about, hmmm ... are you busy this
week?"

"I'm sure I can fit in with whatever time suits you, mate."

"How about later in the week," he paused for a moment as if
he was checking his schedule, "say Thursday evening around

6pm? I have a lot of work to get through so I can't make it any earlier." It was a lie but he was playing the game. Both parties were now engaged in the denial of the eager-beaver stakes. Whoever could bluff to the other that they didn't really need the deal to go through, unless it was on their terms, would undoubtedly win. Unfortunately for Dan his inexperience and glowing passion was ripe for Abdul's picking.

"That sounds fine."

"OK. So I live in Five Dock. Are you familiar with Five Dock, Daniel?"

"I actually did my apprenticeship there—was working for an Italian tiler."

"I just had my bathroom renovated. It's a shame I hadn't met you before."

"Well, Abdul, if you ever need a tiler in the future I would be happy to be of assistance."

"You sound a very nice boy, Daniel. How old are you?"

"Twenty-eight."

"Oh, I remember when I was twenty-eight. I had harem and ate baklava till my eyes nearly popping out."

"I love falafel, Abdul." Daniel was happy there was some kind of connection and the guy was actually carrying the conversation further than just business. "Ya Habbibis restaurant in Gould Street is very popular down this way."

"Ah yes, a favourite of mine too. Michael is a good friend of mine. Tell me, Daniel, have you got a pen and paper so I can give you my address?"

Dan's mum was standing across the loungeroom listening intently in on what was transpiring. He motioned to her to get him a pen and paper as quick as possible. "Just getting a pen and paper for you now, mate." His mum was there in flash. 'OK, mate, ready."

"OK, it's unit 5/35 Crescent Street, Five Dock. Do you know the street, Daniel?"

"Ah, I don't think so but I'll just check it in the Gregory's, mate, and is there any chance I can see it quickly before the meeting?"

"Sure. I will tell my friend the real estate to ring you and make time." Abdul was to make sure the real estate agent told Dan nothing about his shop's demise.

'OK." Dan gave Abdul his phone details

"OK," said a smiling Abdul. "Well, I suppose I will see you on Thursday, then."

"You certainly will, Abdul. Thanks for everything."

"My pleasure, so I see you then." And then he hung up.

Dan put the phone down, turned to his mum and clenched his fists in front of him whilst looking up to the divine. "Yes, yes, yes ..." He jumped up and strode over his mum's soft beige carpet and gave her a huge hug. "Mum, it's panning out."

She smiled as she looked over Dan's shoulder staring at the blue and white striped wallpaper across the room. The hug was to last a while as they both felt the love and enjoyed the embrace. The white sheer curtains that adorned the long window and obscured the opposite units from gazing in fluttered but there was hardly any breeze. She saw it as a sign that someone, possibly Dan's dad, was looking over them.

The next day Dan went for a surf in the morning and decided that afternoon to head to the Woolloomooloo Police Boys for a boxing session. He had been wanting to start some fair dinkum training again and after his panic attack and depression the day before he thought that the sooner the better. His mate Shane P and JB were regulars at Woolloomooloo but they also frequented Paddo Police boys and occasionally Ern McQuillan's gym at Newtown. Dan had actually got to know Ern fairly well over the years and done some tiling for him at his house at Canterbury. Dan had no trouble finding it because it was near the racetrack where Dan had worked for his dad a bunch when he was younger.

JB was a versatile welterweight. His "Stray Cats" rocker haircut accentuated his pale high cheekbone face to where it almost seemed drawn. But it was more of a sharp, gritty look. He was a tough cookie. His firm, determined face combined with his taut physique gave the impression he was a no-nonsense man. His straight talk backed that up. He was a fierce fighter who had been brawling since an early age. His parents had arrived from England in the early 70s and landed in Canterbury. They conceived Jason and moved straight to Hall Street and liked Bondi so much they decided to stay. He went to Dover Heights Boys School where over the years he'd fought his way through the school to deserve a place at the top, well at least as far as the schoolyard was concerned. Boxing was in his genes as his uncle was a highly acclaimed fighter back in the UK, which is one of the reasons he had won all his 12 amateur fights, mostly by TKO. He was a gentleman at heart and was very passionate about his surfing which made him a popular figure amongst the boys down the beach.

Shane P was as mad as a meat axe when he got going and his tall frame and long reach made him a good build for the ring. Being in his early 20s he had really filled out into a middleweight over the last couple of years which had added to his power and strength, not to mention his mousy good looks. His blond shoulder length hair and blue eyes made him popular with the ladies. He hadn't really taken to the pro fight scene, only having one fight for a loss, but he was always "at the bit" to do some training. He and Dan had been flatmates back in the day and it was only natural they'd been training together for a few years now. Originally Alex was in there with them belting away but he gradually faded from the gym as he got deeper into drugs and crime.

Being 89 Mike Tyson was on the top of the Heavyweight division and understandably all three lads loved watching him demolish his opposition. They also loved watching Hagler and Sugar Ray and you could find them down the "Rex", "Rats" or "Diggers" glued to the monitor when most big fights were going down.

The three of them trained hard that afternoon with ex-Olympian Bruce Farthing putting them through their routine. Stretching followed by skipping, shadow boxing, footwork and bagwork got the pulse racing and sweat dripping. Every movement displayed tenacious expression and muscles rippling in a personal battle of body and mind. They also did a few rounds against a couple of handy fighters, trading blows with fellow gym co-patriots David Amoa, Sean Frew, Jamie Wright and Steve Dack.

By the end of the session they were buggered and ready for their mandatory spaghetti bolognaise at the original "No Names" which was tucked away down a little laneway off Crown Street. Ducking into the inconspicuous doorway and following the cream washed walls up the ceramic tiled stairwell you could have mistaken the drab eatery as a dormitory food hall except for the inviting smell and big serves of Italian cuisine. It was definitely the cheapest and best pasta in Sydney town at the time. For five bucks you had a bowl slapped in front of you, full to the brim with spaghetti, accompanied with a basket of white crusty bread and as

157

much orange cordial as you could handle. Parmesan cheese was optional and vinegar was on the table which the boys used to soak their bread in then spoon their sauce on top. Some nights the famished line waiting for tables ran back down the stairs and out the door into the laneway. It was worth the wait for many and the queue moved quickly as the speedy service had customers finished within minutes. Behind the open counter were large pots of pasta and sauce being manhandled by big bulky Italian fellows gulping glasses of red wine with lots of steam, heat and sweat swirling around and creating a mass cooking orchestra that was oblivious to the world on the other side of the counter. The waiters and cooks were past no-nonsense and resembled old mafia men who had possibly hit hard times or were doing what they had to so as to get by as illegal aliens escaping persecution from their Sicilian enemies. Their slick black, greying hair and "Papa Giuseppe" twirling moustaches complemented their gangster garb of neat shirts, oversized trousers and requisite braces, white socks and polished black shoes. Therefore the white aprons and notebook in hand didn't quite seem appropriate and didn't they let you know it!

Sometimes they'd look as you as if to say, "You punk arse kid, you wouldn't even know how many guys I've garrotted only to end up here serving a dirty rat like you!" However you could see these guys had been working this underground establishment for years and were probably just doing what came naturally to them, minus the cold blooded killing.

"I've heard you've got a little secret that's been let out of the bag, Danny boy." It was a statement from a curious mate when it left Shane's lips, though one could have mistaken it for a question.

"And what's that, mate?"

"Well, a little birdie told me you're gonna open up a surf shop or something like that."

JB almost choked on his food. Shane gave him a heavy-handed pat on the back and he countered by lifting his head, raising his hands and almost shaping up. JB was one of those guys who shadow-boxed down the street and would shape up to any obstacle that got in his way. He was defensive of people touching him as a lot of boxers are and even though Shane was just trying to help him it was just a reaction. He washed down the burley in his throat with a swig of his cordial and said, "I'm OK" in a croaky voice.

158

"Sorry, mate. Sounded like you were going to kick the bucket," said an apologetic Shane.

JB managed to clear his throat a bit before spitting out, "Is that true what Shane's askin' ya, Dan? You really gonna open a surf shop down Bondi?"

"Well, I think so."

"No way, Dan! That would be bullshit!" JB's excitement was bubbling. "How long have you been keeping this from us?"

Dan paused from his next mouthful and placed his fork back into his bowl. He stared down at the intersecting pasta splashed with sauce and for the first time had a sense of clarity about how close his lifetime dream was in becoming a reality. He had been excited before about things but his feelings couldn't have quite given him access to the certain satisfaction that his progress was charging him at that moment, especially on the eve of possibly his final hurdle. He was opening the cocoon that had kept him restrained and his probation time was drawing to a close. He was soon to be in a position where he was vying for a stake of sovereignty in his hometown and he was now feeling somewhat overwhelmed by the subconscious motives surfacing. For it wasn't just impulsive ambition driving him but also a deeper moral cause. On a personal level he had felt betrayed but his pugnacity was contrived from a broader base. Who was it that he wanted on their knees begging for forgiveness? Was it the bankers who bankrupted his father and drove him over the edge? Was it the wealthy top 5% of the world who wallowed in decadence, all the while letting the millions in Africa watch their newborns die of hunger? Surely we were all tainted with the same brush of sin but how could one make a real difference? He suddenly felt like he was a young crusader who would be flying the flag of liberation. The atmosphere around him was buzzing and he now understood that his conquest was well underway. But amongst this elation lay an adolescent mind complete with a mixture of confidence and insecurity. So it was only natural that one could expect nothing less from him than bravado and despair.

"Ahh, a little while. Still haven't got things totally finalised yet but ..."

"You sneaky devil."

He looked up, then looked both of them in the eye, just to reassure he was ready to let any further information pass his lips. Of course he knew these guys were real friends but he still was a bit hesitant in parting with too much with the Stirling episode still fresh in his mind. He summoned his judgement and thought it OK to continue. "Just been covering my arse. I'm up against some stiff competition, you know."

"Radford's gonna be happy," said Shane. His sarcasm translating into a cheeky smile.

"Who gives a fuck about that guy?" remarked JB. "That guy hasn't given a fuck about any of us blokes ever!" JB was behind Dan 100 percent. "Fuck, Dan, I'm so happy to hear this."

"Well, I've got one last hump to get over. I have to meet this guy in a coupla days to work a deal out for his shop. I don't know exactly how it's gonna pan but I talked to him the other day and seems like he wants to work somethin' out with me."

"You don't know how happy I am hearing this, mate." repeated JB. "Can't stand that Radford with all his money and hanger-onerers. Thinks his shit don't stink."

Dan had passed his contemplative atmospherics and was now tucking into the rest of his dinner. "Pass the bread, please, Shane."

"You only need one piece and you can feed the thousands." Shane's comment was an obvious reference to one of the many miracles Jesus performed in the Bible. Shane's dry wit was awash with funny connotations. "Next thing you'll be walking on water from Ben Buckler to Bronte."

The boys couldn't help having a chuckle.

"So where's the shop gonna open?" JB's voice was filled with anxious curiosity. "Is it down the beachfront?"

"Let you know after tomorrow but if I pull this off I promise that I won't disappoint you."

"Meaning?"

"Well, I'm gonna start the boardriders again ..."

"Bullshit ... no way! You mean, you are going to run club contests again?"

"Yep."

Shane couldn't help himself. "All hail the king!"

The next couple of days seemed to drag on forever. He used this time mostly in his room deciding to navigate away from the beach and any possible confrontation of any sort. He listened to music on his record player enjoying his broad collection. He loved his 70s' stash of rock stars: Hendrix, The Doors, Led Zeppelin, Jethro Tull, The Stones, Supertramp, Joni Mitchell, Pink Floyd, right through to Jeff Beck, John McGlaughlin, Lee Ritenour, then into his 80s' collection of Dire Straits, B52s, Van Halen, Sex Pistols, The Clash, Bob Marley, AC/DC, The Angels, etc, etc. The weather had turned bad and intermittent thunderstorms were drenching Sydney. Blistering southerly wind squalls sometimes pelted rain hard against Dan's bedroom's glass-paned door which opened onto the pebblecreted balcony and he cringed for the homeless down Bondi and hoped they were warm and safe. Larry the "20 cent man" and Napoleon were two of the more well-known hobos of Bondi. Cave Woman was another. There were quite a few of them and the refuge dorm for "down and out" souls was situated down the opposite end of Roscoe Street near the beach. It was close by to "The Chapel by The Sea" where most of them were fed and clothed. Larry was a classic acid case who used to be enrolled in East Sydney tech where he studied the arts. Strolling along Campbell Parade he used to hit everyone up for two bob and most of the lads obliged. You could generally find him on the corner of Hall Street outside Bates' Milkbar. It was close to the newsagent because he'd obviously worked out that's where people usually had change in their pockets. He was, like the others, part of the Bondi long-line of furniture and most of the local folk accepted them and felt good about parting with some change.

Who knows what sent Napoleon over the edge but he was a chronic alcoholic and you could smell his bottle of turps from a mile away. He was always wearing a long overcoat and his long, wild eccentric hair and bohemian boots made him look like a mad Frenchman. He and Larry could regularly be seen hanging out with the rest of the walking casualties outside the chapel near Gould and Roscoe Streets, passing the bottle around and breaking out into fits of laughter. The lunacy included spasmodic screams, crazy rants and the odd yelling match. They rarely got stuck into each other, the exception being Cave Woman who was pretty handy at opening her mates up. Cave Woman got her name because she lived in a sandstone cave on the beach at south. She had a mattress down there and a few home comforts like a table and chair and was constantly trying to drag men back there. With language that would've put a bushy to shame, leatherjacket skin, untidy and overgrown body hair, missing tooth smile and smelly odour, you could be forgiven for not wanting to accept her invitation.

*

"Just a block of wax, please, mate."

"No worries. Two bucks, thanks." Stirling was manning his till and waiting for a couple of his sponsored riders to come in and pick up their new boards. His shop was looking like a million dollars. The boardracks that lined the back of the shop were chokkas with brand-spanking-new product of all lengths, shapes and sizes. They were so new you could still smell the new fibreglass which has always given board shops their authenticity badge. The clothes racks were tidy and rows of clothing adorned the hangers. New posters of Tom Carroll, Occy, Pottz and Kong were framed using teakwood and hanging in places on walls which were artistically designed for them. The shop was aesthetic, something Stirling and Smithy had hoped for and something they should have been proud of. The only question still lingering over it was its location, location, location.

Daisy breezed over feeling Radford's uneasy frame of mind. It had been that way since the whole Dan shemozzle went down. She tried to make some small talk.

"When do you want me to get the boys to move some gear back over to the small shop, boss?"

"Daisy, please don't call me boss ..."

"OK, sexy."

"Well, I don't know about that either until I seduce you one day and take you out on the harbour with my cousin Hamish and his dad."

"Promises, promises." She bit her thumb and fluttered her long fake eyelashes like a pop goddess displaying her fertility. "If this weather clears up that mightn't be a bad idea—might help take your mind off things. I'm sure I could, anyway."

"Always got my mind on my money, honey." It was almost an admission of some kind.

"Well, don't let a punk upset you too much. You're way too good a man to let that worry you."

"Never ... there are too many pleasures in life for me to enjoy. And the punk you are talking about will always be a punk! I'll always be successful and rolling in money and right there lies the difference. You don't have to be Einstein to work that one out."

"He's so jealous of you."

"That's what troubles me."

"Oh really?"

"We'll just have to see if this guy's a spent volcano or if he's just lying dormant."

It was getting late arvo and the electricity grid had been just turned on bringing light to the maze of streets across Rose Bay and upwards over Dover Heights. In September it always got dark around 6pm and with the added dark cloud, inside and out of the cold felt a good place to be. Dan dragged himself up and off his futon that Ken-san had given him and gazed out his glass sliding doors over the suburban matinee of car headlights on their way home to their decorated boxes. For most, it was another day chasing more dollars, to buy more stuff, to try and make life feel complete. Dan recalled a conversation he'd had with Sloth's work partner Andy while waiting for set waves one day behind the reef. The waves were small so there was a long time between swells worth riding. A lot of surfers used this time and space to talk of all sorts of things or contemplate whatever came to mind. It was a unique opportunity away from the hustle and bustle of the landmass.

Looking back towards the beach landscape they were gazing at their beloved rundown units that bordered the strip and Andy had mentioned he was working up at Dover Heights, one of the many affluent suburbs high above on the hill that frowned down upon them.

"Yeah, big difference between the joints up there and what we live in," commented Dan. "Fuck, they've got some wicked houses up there!"

"More like estates." Andy flicked his long blond hair out of his face. "You should see the one I'm workin' on at the moment: 25 bedrooms, ensuites, spas, sauna, gym, big Olympic pool with grounds as big as the Botanical Gardens—you can deadset get lost in the joint!" It was a little exaggerated but Dan got the picture.

"Wish you had the keys so we could plan a party. Imagine how much fun you could have wrecking all that expensive shit?"

"This one's got boats and a garage with Mercs and Ferraris and all kinds of stuff!"

"Bags the Ferrari!"

"It had burn out written all over it! ..."

"The Maori boys would pay you for this information."

"Oh, shit, they probably would, too ... Mate, there's heaps of stuff in that garage."

163

"Fuckin' stuff!" It was just about to turn into a "stuff"-stuffing-the-planet conversation when a little peak popped out of nowhere and Andy swung around and picked off a little right. He managed a couple of small turns till he threw his board up for a closeout reo and hit something in the lip. He recovered to pull the manoeuvre off but the debris had put a crack in the rail. Paddling back out he cursed the hard, plastic face shield before hoiking it towards the beach where it fell in between countless ciggy butts and other crappy stuff lying on a granular bed of ocean white sand.

"What happened?" asked Dan.

"Fuckin' bit o' plastic just dinged me board on the shorie!"

"See, just another piece of fuckin' stuff that's contributing to trashing the planet."

"Well, it sure trashed my fucking rail—put a lovely crack in it."

"Yep, more stuff that's in yer face every day!"

"And in front of me board."

"Yep, there's stuff everywhere."

"Funny, that."

"Retail therapy has a lot to answer for, Andy."

"Yep, suppose it does ... when's it gonna stop?"

"When we're all stuffed, I suppose."

The fact is that Capitalism got its hit in the arm when Eisenhower and his world economists sat down in Bretton Woods as World War 2 was drawing to an end. He declared an economic system to continually drive the US economy and give the World Bank and the IMF global control of loans issued to countries that needed re-building was essential. The bold new world was to be totally based on supply and demand. Their model's main dealers were Wall Street, the Dow Jones, the US FED and any corporate boys that had enough money to buy in and become world players. The world was to sell out its soul for stuff and Andy and Dan, like millions of others, were just expected to keep the big wheels turning.

"Thank fuck for surfing! Thank fuck we have different values to all that other shit."

"Yes, and a new stick under our arm is really our own stuffy salvation."

"Oh, oh ... You're becoming a priest, are you?"

"And thou shalt not catch the next wave before thee."

Dan closed his wooden slatted blinds and headed out to the kitchen to see what his mum was cookin' up. Enough thinking—it was time to eat.

*

Next morning and the weather was still miserable. Stirling woke
up in his parents' palatial home in Bellevue Hill and stared out his
double glazed floor-to-ceiling windows and watched the heavy
raindrops on top of the swimming pool's surface. It was pouring
and he hoped it would clear for an afternoon yachting session with
Hamish. "Damn!" he thought as he knew wet days were no good
for business down at the beach. He really wanted some good
weather to feel out how his new shop was trading. It was early
Spring and he wondered where the birds and the bees were hiding.
    "Why didn't you stay at your new unit down at Bondi,
sweetie?" His mum was curious why he had opted to sleep in the
family mansion the last few nights. "We'll have to start charging
you board."
    "That beach is such a ghost town in this kinda weather, Mum,
so I'd rather be here with you and dad."
    "What time are you heading down there? Have I got time to
cook you some eggs? They're free range, you know ..."
    "Always got time for your cooking, Mum, and that's another
reason why I'm here—there ain't no-one who cooks brekky like
you, Mum."
    "That's very kind of you, darling. Does that mean our
attractive young maid could still learn a thing or two from your
old mother?"
    "Of course, Mum. You're the best!"
    "What about that Lamrock Cafe? I thought they had taken you
away from me. Your father and I ate there last week and the eggs
Benedict were superb. I'd highly recommend it to any of our
guests from overseas."
    "They're good, Mum, but as I said, they'd be hard pressed to
cook it with the love and tenderness you do it with."
    "You're so sweet, Stirling. You do know your father's about to
buy the latest Toyota four wheel drive, and, well ..." She paused
briefly like mothers do when they want to announce something
special. "I might just mention to him that I think you should have
another car besides your outdated BMW, plus you will need
something with a bit of room in it now you're keeping all that new
stock in our storage shed. How else are you going to get it down
to the beach?"

"What am I buying him now?" Radford's towering dad Burt walked into the spacious kitchen from the adjacent hallway full of expensive stuff. It was a house that Dan and the boys would have had a load of fun trashing. Burt stood over 6 feet and his designer bag of fruit indicated his exquisite taste.

"You don't have to buy me anything, Dad. I have got my own money, you know."

"Yes, thanks to your good natured cousin and uncle you did earn a pretty penny from your real estate investment, but your mother's right as usual and you should have another car to help you with stock and the other stuff. My dealer's doing me a great deal and I should be able to knock him down a bit more if I get two."

"Well, maybe you should get one for Dylan for when he comes back from his stint as a Jackeroo." Dylan was Stirling's elder brother of about 5 years who never cared much about surfing, choosing to become a bit of a city cowboy who played polo and hung out with his rich rural mates down Kangaroo Valley way. "Probably should get it delivered to him."

"Oh, don't be silly, Sylvia. He's 500 miles from nowhere on his uncle's property in the south-west of Queensland."

"Can't they drop it off in a helicopter or something?"

"Mum, Uncle Bernard isn't going to lend you one of his helicopters for that kinda stuff."

"That's right, Sylvia. Have you had your pills this morning? Because I think you need some."

"Burt, please!" Mrs Radford loved her pills and wasn't too happy about her husband having a go at her about them. "Don't start on me or I'll bring up how you can't make it past eleven am without a whisky."

Burt adjusted his tie and leered at her.

"Mum can I have some brekky, please?"

"At least someone around here appreciates me. Certainly, dear."

Burt screamed out at the young maid to summon her and then gave her some orders about tea and toast to be brought to his study with the Herald so he could obviously check the latest stock market fluctuations.

"Can't your Uncle Bernard hire one of those military helicopters to take the car to Dylan?" asked Stirling's mum as she pottered around her stainless steel modular kitchen with all the trimmings. Stirling chose to plonk himself at the kitchen's centre console with shiny pots and pans hanging above his head. It had a big, thick wooden chopping board lying flat on it and Stirling enjoyed watching his mum chopping up a meal. It was close to the action and Stirling was hungry. It was a lot less sophisticated than sitting at the dining room table. After all, the large open dining room enjoyed stunning 180-degree views across Rose Bay and around the harbour, as well as up and over the reaches of Dover Heights and Vaucluse, and was reserved for a more formal occasion.

"You can always ask him, mum ... might be a spare helicopter lying around—no harm in trying."

Later that day, Dan drove his Torana over the Pyrmont Bridge, passing the coal loading docks, on his way to his rendezvous with Abdul. He'd swept out a coal ship once to help a mate finish his shift early and always thought of the docker's experience when passing the wharves. A couple of solid Bondi boys, Doogsa and his younger brother Paul, did shift work there for years, unloading the coal ships, then coming home covered in soot, but it a was good wicket. In the late 70s and early 80s the wharfie unions were still strong and saturated with perks. The two brothers were bringing home big pay packets for work ethic that one could say was compromised but no different to a politician's gig with their boys' club, superannuation and corrupt deals. The boys and their co-workers felt entitled to the privileges and rightfully so when making electricity companies millions every day. Unfortunately during the 80s, a crackdown on unions and a new port development at Port Kembla saw a quick end to their easy work and conditions. It was obvious they were picked on and discriminated against as well because that's something that'd never happen in the political arena.

Dan had his Gregory's open on his passenger seat just in case he couldn't find the address. He was trying to imagine what Abdul would look like and thought of him as a fat bald bloke in a kaftan. He flicked through the ID cards in his brain and found a match, concluding that Abdul also had a big nose and customary moustache, a wife who wore an "I Dream of Jeanie"-like costume and a son who drove some kind of "hot rod" with low suspension and 18-inch mag wheels. It was a stereotype depiction but illustrious at the least and feeling quite peckish, he hoped they offered him a kebab or at least a hash pipe when he arrived.

He was now in Five Dock and he was near to the street where

he was going to turn left into. The weather had cleared from the
storms but there were still puddles on the side of the road showing
how heavy the flooding had been in different areas. He pulled up
alongside a bus stop where a bunch of middle-eastern teenagers
were hanging, chatting and enjoying their bit of twisted fun. Dan
was stopped opposite them as he waited for a green light and they
noticed the white boy alone and vulnerable.

"Whooo said ya coulda drive frough our part of town,
Skippy?" one of them screamed.

Dan ignored them as there were about ten of them and he had
more important things to attend. "Where's Alex and the boys
when you need them?" he thought.

"Hey, white boy, you fuckin' deaf or sumpin?"

Dan, with obvious good reason, impatiently waited for the
light to change.

"You fink you are pretty tough, aye, punk boy?" All of a
sudden they were mobile and strutting towards the Torana like
they were starring in a B-grade movie called the "Wild Wogs" or
something. The passenger side door was locked already and Dan
didn't want to move or do anything sudden as this pack would've
moved swiftly into gear.

At last the light changed and the two cars in front of Dan
motioned forwards. Dan couldn't wait to get out of there but
thought, "Fuck it, I'll just let these little pricks get a little
closer", which he did. He let them get close enough so they
could clearly see his middle finger, stepped on the gas and sped
off just in the nick of time to safety. He looked in his rear vision
and saw them all making obscene gestures to him and egging
him to come back.

He cruised a couple of blocks further on, turned left and
slowly checked the letterbox numbers till he saw the only set of
units in the street, guessing that they were where Abdul and his
family resided.

He walked up to the first floor and knocked on the door with a
big brass number 5 on it. It was right on six o'clock. A fat bald
bloke wearing a kaftan with a small fat nose answered the door.
"Two outta three ain't bad," Dan thought to himself. He felt like
asking, "Where's Jeanie?"

"Hello. Well, you must be Daniel."

"Yes, Abdul. How very nice to meet you."

"Oh, the pleasure mine, young boy. Do please come in." Abdul ushered him in using extended hand movements like a waiter in a high class restaurant.

"Thank you." Things were off to a formal but pleasant start.

"Straight through to the balcony, Daniel, please. I never speak business in front my wife." Abdul's wife was out of sight in the kitchen of the trinket-infested unit. "Would you like a coffee?"

"No thanks, mate. Wouldn't be able to sleep."

"Cup of tea?"

"You're too kind, Abdul. Thanks, but no thanks." Dan's gut was now rumbling from the waft of middle eastern flavours floating through the air and sinking into his senses. Mrs Abdul wasn't just cooking in there—she was creating a banquet, a feast for her king. He felt like asking Abdul if there were any kebabs but knew better. He strode across a fine Persian rug towards the already opened terrace door passing a big water pipe. He also refrained from asking if Abdul was going to mull up.

Dan sat down at a mosaic-tiled coffee table on the mosaic-tiled floor and looked out over the ethnic, mosaic community of Five Dock. Most residences were old quarter-acre blocks with vege gardens, fruit trees that had been planted after WW 2 when a lot of these migrants arrived and quail or chicken coups with corrugated tin for roofs that were noticeable in many of the backyards.

"Nice view you have here ..."

"Not as nice as living on the beach, not that I have ever lived there, but it was a great spot to have the cafe."

"Yes, mate. Very nice spot."

"You live down there, Daniel?"

"Yes, pretty much been there all my life. You could call me a third generation Bondi-ite, I suppose."

"So, Daniel, a nice looking young man such as yourself must have some big plans ahead of you to want to take on a shop?" Abdul was heading straight to the point.

"Well, Abdul, I think I might be able to make something of it."

"Well, boy, I looks like I have to head back to Lebanon in the near future; my parents are getting older and my father needs a bit of help."

"Oh, I see. I hope he's OK."

"He's OK, thank you, Daniel, but my boy is thinking about taking the shop on but I told him I wanted to see if someone can give me a reasonable offer. It has got another 3 years on the lease, you know."

"Oh, OK ..."

Both were interrupted by the door of the balcony being flung open. "Hey, Dad, can I borrow some money? We are going in to da Hoyts to see Batman."

"Ahmed, can't you see I'm busy? Go and ask your mother ... and have a shave—you can't go out looking like that."

"Wax your hairy chest, you bald headed wahash!"

"You dare call me a beast! Ahmed, you get outta my sight and I mean it—you have a shave before you go anywhere or you be grounded for a week and I take your keys of your car too!"

"Dad, I had a shave yesterday ..."

"I don't care. You know my rule—my family always look clean, hairy-free. OK?"

"Just because you look like a bowling ball, you old fart. I'm going to see mum."

"Hey, you listen to me, boy. If your sister has to shave herself so do you!"

And with that Ahmed closed the door and disappeared.

"Sorry about that, Daniel. My boy, he get's smart-arse sometimes ... where's were we?"

Dan was kind of stunned. "Umm ... can't remember ... ahh ..."

"Well, anyway, I am a business man, Daniel, and I know how much that Lamrock Cafe earns every week. Do you know how much, Daniel?"

"No, sir."

"Profit alone I thinks they clearing between 10, 20 grand a week that is ... do you know how much that is a year, Daniel?"

"Not really."

"It's a lot of money, Daniel—big money, very big money. You want to earn big money, Daniel?"

"Sure, I suppose."

"You see the shop already, ya?"

"Yes, Abdul, the real estate showed me quickly yesterday."

"Ah, then you know my shop better than the Lamrock!"

All Dan could do was go along with the flow. "Probably, mate."

"Well, my lease is worth 15 grand, Daniel, and it's not nego. Bondi is about to go booming and you will earn that back very quick. I feel very disappoint to ask such low price but my father ..."

oh, I not want to have to talk about how much that make a me sadder."

Daniel knew the bottom line was coming and didn't really know how much anything was worth in the world of leases. He was like a duck out of water. All he knew is that, just like when buying a kilo of hash, he could probably barter a bit. "C'mon, Abdul, I'll offer you eight."

"Twelve."

"Ten and I'll have the cash to you by Monday—that's in three more days." Abdul sat there and contemplated the counter-offer with a look of sophistication. The night air had a chill to it but Abdul's oil was rising to his forehead and turning to beads of sweat just like a bubbling middle-eastern crude oil well. Daniel felt greasy just looking at him. "C'mon, mate ... hard cash."

"By Monday, you say, Daniel?"

"Too right. Can meet me down at the bank at Bondi and we can head straight to a solicitor and finalise everything."

"You drive hard bargain." Abdul was bullshitting his way into getting rid of a headache and making 10 grand on top. "You remind me of old friend who used to sell me da Persian rug." Abdul took a soiled handkerchief out of his pocket and wiped his thick caterpillar brow. Dan thought he might wipe his eyebrows off in the process because they looked so fake it seemed they were stuck on. To his relief they stayed put. Dan wondered how much money Abdul's family could make if they put their unwanted hair to good use and started a mirkin factory.

"OK, Daniel, you have deal, my boy!"

Comings and Goings

The following Monday afternoon Abdul had been paid off and the formalities of transferring the lease had been finalised. Dan's mum had put her signature on a 20-grand bank loan to make it happen. It had cost Dan a substantial bit more to take the beachfront shop but Stirling's prevention tactics, although costly, had possibly provided a bigger opportunity in a better location. It had certainly cast Dan into the spotlight so it was now up to him to show the beach what he had to offer. He put the key into the lock and turned it. He had only briefly seen the inside when the real estate agent hurriedly let him in for a quick peek. He had been only able to check out the two commercial rooms visible from the street and was unaware of the full extent of his prize.

Swinging open the plate glass door he entered his new domain. It was a sudden electrifying transformation. He was fully charged to where his cells were tingling, his body was producing adrenaline and he was soaking it up; however, his buzz was grounded as it all felt part of his destiny.

Like he had said to himself prior, "I'll be in the door within a week!" and so he was. He walked a couple of paces into the empty, front room rotating 360 degrees. "You can fucken see the surf so clearly from here, all the way to north! No way, this is bullshit!" He again felt an incredible rush of ecstasy, an overwhelming blanket of emotion. He held back the tears of joy and thanked the universe for his turn of fate. It was now clear to him that this was a natural chain of events. Here he was at last, 28 years of age and ready to run his own surf shop. For many of those years it had been just a dream and right now at this single moment it was a full-blown reality. "Fuck!" he said. "I don't believe it!" He envisioned the desk in the corner with him sitting behind it on a high stool, music beats pumping, sunnies hugging tight, tab of acid shooting sparks around the room, customers throwing money at him and girls parading in tight-fitting bikinis. His smile resembled a split watermelon and highlighted the stained bong marks around his lips. "Now, that's a surf shop!"

He followed the parquet flooring through to the narrow back room. It gave way for a divide. The upper level was boxed off and Dan thought the enclave would be perfect for a change room. A couple of steps led down to a lower level where the former cafe's kitchen used to pump out food. "Munchies and a beer fridge," he thought to himself. The kitchen was big and open, with a tall white painted ceiling and a few stainless benches and sinks. The burnt red painted concrete floor gave it a commercial feel. The main thoroughfare continued towards a back entrance. Dan investigated further passing a dark bathroom with no windows. Peeking in the door he found the light switch and turned it on. It reminded him of the size of a cell block at Waverley lock-up. It comprised of a basic toilet and shower with hot and cold water which ticked his living requirements. "Going to need that hot water after a surf, especially in Winter."

Moving right along on his virgin tour he exited the building through a large, open, almost gothic-like black metal door which led up and onto a long elevated, flaking, white timber deck. This enclosed deck was in a concealed courtyard and had "Bondi underground" written all over it. It was a shaded shelter, blocked by the tall surrounding buildings from all but a hint of afternoon sunshine. Corrugated iron and opaque plastic sheets unevenly lined the roof and obscured Dan from the view of the back landings of the upstairs apartments. At the end of the extended timber deck there was an adjoining storage room which you stepped down into and immediately Dan claimed it as his new bedroom. The main area of the verandah was enclosed by a three-quarter high stucco plastered wall where the exposed top opening provided ventilation and subjected Dan's new space to the elements. A small encased garden bed that lined the perimeter of the wall was home to a few plants that received just enough daylight to struggle fraily upwards, adding a bit of nature to the dwarfed, inner city beach abode. The artificial world had taken over and greenery almost seemed alien under the heavy structures. It was "Better than nothing", Dan thought.

A big bolted wooden gate gave access to what was waiting outside. He opened it and before him lay an open quarry-tiled courtyard flanked by a bottom unit from a first-floor white apartment block that bordered the back lane. It led him to a narrow side corridor that stretched its way down the back units to the same lane, where a high steel locked gate kept unwanted guests out.

"You mean I get all this?" said Dan to himself. "It's a fucken rabbit warren."

The back lane connected Lamrock Avenue to Sir Thomas Mitchell Street which also ran off the beach and had once enjoyed the notoriety of having the illustrious Astra Hotel on its corner. The lane had a couple of bowlegs in it and was bordered by narrow garages servicing the towering dark brick units that monstered over it and deprived it of lots of sunlight. Before school some of the local school kids would smoke ciggies and pash girls in its dark corners out of sight of anyone who might dob them in. Only locals used the laneway and if you were driving down either street that enclosed it and blinked you could have easily missed it.

Dan's new "rabbit warren" was unique in that you could enter or exit it from either the main drag or the back lane for whatever the circumstance may be. "Attack and defence ... hmmmm, I like it!"

The shop needed a new coat of paint, racks for surfboards and clothing, counter, till, some steel bars for the front showcase window and door, curtains for the change room, a few surf posters, bit of floor sanding and a new coat of varnish and some renovations to fit the stock room adjoining the landing out back including a loft for a bed. He decided on a partitioned stud wall dividing the long back landing so he could make a bit of lounge room and deck it with some furniture next to his bedroom. So over the next week or so, with the help of a few friends and family, the shop was fitted out with the bare necessities and Dan moved stock in, to the relief of his mother who could finally park her car in her garage. It was a very satisfying preparation and he was constantly on a happy high where his stoned mind led him to think that he was sharing the same space with benevolent celestial beings that he envisioned were adorning the stucco plastered walls out back. Good pot and stucco walls always got the imagination firing. Someone was looking over him—he felt it and believed it!

Some of the community thought it was about time a blooded local opened another surf shop. Dan knew that it was in his blood and his new venture was following in his Uncle Bonza's footsteps. The last true-blue Bondi locals to fly the surf shop flag at the beach had been Rob and Victor Ford until they moved to Bondi Junction. But even up there their once respected operations were under attack and coming to a close. They were seen as the old dinosaurs in their final throes, though what was dying with them was an irreplaceable knowledge of surfing's fundamental mechanics. For these guys were the original shapers and test pilots, so to walk into a surf shop and pick their brains when buying a board was gold. A new chain of outlets called Surfing

Perfection was establishing itself around Sydney and the north side, and the rich kid who owned it had money to burn. It was a blatant indication that the surf fashion industry was at the threshold and the old local, laidback surf shop was teetering on the brink of extinction. Dan unconsciously was prolonging the inevitable. It was as if he was the last batsman whose innings was against all odds. He was to be the stubborn tail-ender whose doomed fate was sealed before he started swinging. But that didn't mean he wasn't going to try to hit a few sixes whilst at the crease. Some thought Dan was punching above his weight, having no money and little pull with the bigger surf labels, but he didn't care how anyone saw it—he had always had a plan and was now having a go. This was no stoned stupor; this was his dream and no-one was going to wake him up from it.

"He's got lots of new stuff in there," Big Ads told Stirling. Ads was a turncoat and didn't know who he wanted to back. On one hand there was the rich kid with all the money and prestigious labels behind him and on the other there was the hardcore local with only a small bank account but a fervour that was igniting the past embers of Bondi's beach heritage. "Yeah, he's got skateboards hanging from the walls and a bunch a boards and gear."

"What labels, Ads?" asked Stirling as he took a sip of his takeaway latte from the Lamrock Cafe. He needed it. His dreams had been unsettling of late. Obviously Dan wasn't lying dormant. It was 8.45am and his arcade shop didn't open till 9 but he knew it was a time to be on guard. The battle lines had been drawn and the taking of the beach wasn't the cakewalk any more that he'd become accustomed to. Swords were now drawn and although his financial position would never be threatened he now had to focus on his reputation and how he would have to play the game, now that his royal position was at stake. He knew he was destined to become a corporate mogul somewhere but right now his priority was to disguise his silver spoon upbringing which was kinda feeling like a lead weight around his neck. He didn't quite know how far his arsenal of sponsorships and money could take him any more.

"Pipedream, Pacific Dreams, Richo ... some of them look nice shapes and he's got some Hot Buttered clothing." Stirling was staring at the froth in his coffee cup as "Big Ads" rambled off more information about Dan's new shop. Ads had helped paint the showroom and had been Stirling's eyes and ears to what was transpiring behind the newspaper-clad windows during its transformation. The brat could have been a valuable member to the CIA. Dan's secretive measures whilst preparing and fitting the shop were understandable after Stirling's initial blow of mistrust. Blocking curious eyes from checking out what was going on inside had also been part of the plan to add interest to his new business. He had wanted it to be like opening a present wrapped in newspaper for the whole beach. Dan wasn't completely paranoid though he now knew Radford was ruthless and more than capable of making things tough. His ultimate goal was obviously to take down the threat of Dan's business as quickly as possible.

"How's it looking as a surf shop?"

"Pretty cool. He's got a big mal hanging out the front over the entrance with the shop's logo and 'underground' painted on it." Ads noticed that Radford's staring eyes hadn't left the froth in his latte. "Have you got a bug in your coffee or something?"

Stirling ignored the question as he associated "underground" with where he wanted Dan to be. Six feet under and pushing up daisies.

"OK, Ads, that's enough. Thanks, mate—now fuck off!"

"What about that legrope you promised me?"

Stirling reached behind the counter, grabbed a leggie and threw it at him. Ads spat out "Thanks" and bolted out the door. It was still chilly in the arcade. Being crammed between buildings there was never any direct sun. Ads's footsteps faded in the distance as if they were echoing in a cold school quadrangle.

Up the road Dan sat behind his secondhand counter with a Hendrix guitar solo emanating from the speaker boxes positioned in the high corners of the showroom. The brilliant sun shone through the shop front and Dan watched it sparkling on the bay. Small lines on the ocean that were kept clean by the offshore made their way through the heads. Surfers enjoyed the crisp September morning and Dan was smiling at the refreshing scene outside his front window. Guys were shooting the curl up and down the beach. It was essential nourishment for a surfer's body and soul, ensuring a quenched metabolism. He looked down through his glass counter and tidied up the wax and stickers. His attention to detail had the shop neat and in perspective.

A couple of groms entered for the first time and immediately were in awe.

"Look at that new Ray Barbee deck up there," remarked one.

"Wow, and look ... there's a Bucky Lasek."

One cruised over to the counter with Dan's eyes monitoring his reaction. He didn't appear to notice Dan till he was very close as he was preoccupied checking the skate wheels, trucks and stickers like he had come across a treasure chest. "This shop is awesome," he blurted.

"Why, thanks, grommet," replied Dan even though the grommet had commented with no intention of a response from anyone. It was hard for Dan not to say it with a touch of pride, happy about the grommet's delight.

"How long you been open, mister?"

"Just a few days."

"Thought so, because I never seen all this here before."

"Well, you guys ain't seen nuthin' yet." Dan had their upmost curious antennae tuned in to what was coming next. "If I get my way you will have a skate ramp and bowl down here one day then you'll have a real reason to jig school."

"How'd you know we jig school?" asked one of them. "You been talking to me mum?"

"Ha ... Just put it this way: if you brought your mum down here to buy some of this sick shit then I could possibly talk her into lettin' you join the boardriders too."

"What, mister?"

"I'm going to be starting the Bondi boardriders club next month and we need kids like you to join and make it something special."

"That sounds great."

"But we can't surf that good."

"So what? All the guys in the club will look after you." They were encouraging words that kids like them were stoked to hear and he knew how much the support meant to a couple of young punks. It gave Dan immense satisfaction to help out and see their eyes light up with excitement. "What's your names?"

"I'm Beau!" said the dark haired kid. He was all of 13 years of age with a couple of freckles and a light wafer-like moustache that his mum probably wanted to wax clean for him.

"Cool, I'll call ya Jangles!"

"And I'm Reg," answered the more timid adolescent. His brown hair was cut in a bit of a bowl shape and reminded Dan of a cross between Davy Jones and Ringo Starr. His fresh face sported rosy cheeks and his cute disposition fell somewhere between

Bobby and Cindy Brady. Both were the epitome of young carefree beach kids who had already started their long journey to becoming professional street dwellers. Their wheels were stuck firmly on the tracks of adventure and the beach was a treasure trove of what life had to offer. Like all those who had trudged the beach before them, they too wanted a piece of the action.

At that moment Pottsie and Jason walked into the shop silhouetted by the sun shining behind them. Not only were morning rays beaming into the showroom but an apparent brightness oozed from behind the counter as a result of Dan's wide, unlaboured smile. It seemed to insulate the surf-clad space and symbolise the humility of the venture. A glistening reflection of doing what comes naturally. "G'day, Jas, Mr Potts. What's up?"

"This shop ... that's what's happening!" remarked Jason as a Hendrix guitar solo fissured through the speakers as if they were about to erupt. It was as if the prodigal son had just come home— the shop atmosphere fed Jason acceptance and a feeling of nothing to prove but everything to gain. "When you gonna run the first boardriders contest, Danny?"

The grommets' ears pricked up as their eyes didn't know where or who to look at. The fresh optimism of something new was drenching their senses and they were a bit overwhelmed by it all.

Pottsie was inspecting the board shapes adorning the racks. "Yeah, Dan, when you thinking about having the first comp?" he added as he slid one of the boards out and felt the curvature of its rails.

"Ah, probably another month after I recruit a few more grommets ... gotta spread the word and give 'em a chance to join."

"How do we join, mister?" asked young Beau.

Dan pulled out an exercise book. "Just write down your details in this book and fill out your age and I'll shove you in the cadets by the look of your size."

"Does it cost any money?"

"Yeah, Dan, do we have to throw you any money?" reiterated Jason.

"Nah, guys, first comp is free and then we'll have a meeting and work it out from there. Make sure you tell all your mates, now."

Beau and Reg were swallowing every word. "Really, mister, you really mean the club is for everyone?"

"Uck, yeah!" said Jason. "Doesn't matter, grommies, if you're black, white, big, little or as silly as me—you're in!"

178

"And you don't get anyone more silly than Jas ..." joked Pottsie.

"Except Mr Pottsie," quipped Dan. "But he just pretends he's loopy so people underestimate him."

"He's a wolf in sheep's clothing so watch out, groms, or he'll eat ya for breakfast!" Pottsie was the Fagan when it came to using grommets, those who weren't frightened to go near him. "And who you callin' 'silly Pottsie'? You wanna go a few rounds, do ya?"

"You guys just beware. Pottsie's a professional wax burglar," added Dan.

The comments drew a blank from the man under threat. Anything further said would only unveil the woven riddles of Pottsie's enigmatic life. He was known as the "Mad Man", the parsimonious, streetwise and to the point hustler. He was a survivor and his brain constantly calculated the benefits on offer. He was popped out of a faulty mould that had completely shattered as he hit the ground running. A gifted surfer, a bit older than Dan, who had been blessed with the strange "animal" gene common to the many unconventional surfers of the 60s and 70s.

He cast his stiff smile complete with serpent eyes over the attentive room as if to announce that all was good and everything really meant nothing. Space travelling had come natural to him— a lot of the time he was on his own planet. Hendrix wailed in the background, "Doesn't anybody want to dance with me?"

Ignoring the question, as not to spook the kids, Jason changed the subject. "So you grommets put your name in the book with your details and let your mates know about the new Bondi boardriders club ... OK?"

"That's right, grommets ... let 'em all know that this shop is starting the club contests and has all the surf and skate gear they need."

"OK, mister."

"Don't call me 'mister'. I'm Dan and this is Jason and the weird guy over there is Pottsie. Here's the book, Jangles, and make sure you both write a phone number next to your name and age."

"Please don't go givin' our number to the crazy guy over there."

"Grrrr ..." growled Pottsie exposing his canines and flicking his tongue between them like Hannibal Lecter.

"Nooo, never ... don't need to subject you to any of his madness."

179

"Did you know that bottling up past trauma can lead to inadequate coping strategies in later life?"

"Who told you that?" asked a wide-eyed Dan, amazed that such a clinical fact could come out of a grommet's mouth.

"It's too late for him, kid!" Jason chuckled.

Pottsie's narrowing eyes shot a steely Freddy Krueger look across the showroom that packed deadly finger blades intent on horrifying its targets. They felt the sharp razors as they hit their bull's eyes.

"He's creepy," whispered Reg to try and keep the emerging fear on his breath out of the weirdo guy's earshot.

The comment gave way to initiating a lesson about fearing your elder surfers.

"You still got my axe out back, Dan?" It was in the rulebook that a grommet's senior could scare the shit out of them if the elder felt the need to. "Need to dismember some kids before I get withdrawals."

Adrenaline started pumping through the vessels of Jangles and Reg. Their eyes grew wider in apprehension of whether the "mad man" was serious or not.

"Don't listen to him, grommets. He's full of shit!"

"Sweet meat!" cursed the glaring butcher. "Somebody stop me!"

The grommets were now backing behind the counter, terrified in their young white skins.

Jason cut it all short. "Knock it off, Pottsie. Ya scarin' the shit outta them."

"Is he for real?" managed Jangles.

"Well, he once, unwittingly ate his sister ... no, I'm only joking. Of course he's not serious; he's just bullying you guys."

The grommets breathed a heavy sigh of relief.

"We'd better get going, mister ..."

"What did I just say?"

"Can't remember."

"It's Dan, not 'mister', OK? And you better finish jotting down your names and don't bother leaving a phone number if you don't want to."

"Oh, OK. Thanks heaps, Dan!"

"And if you want to leave the beach alive you can buy me a milkshake from the deli next door." Pottsie was happy to keep stirring. He gave them the once-over again to check if the groms were cashed up Richie Riches. They looked at each other not knowing if he was serious or not. "C'mon, no holding out, you gotta pay your dues!"

Dan jumped in. "Don't listen to him, grommets, and if he ever offers you lollies take as many as you can then kick him in the shins."

Jason laughed and continued, "And if he doesn't offer you any lollies, well, you can kick him in the shins anyway."

The grommets finished writing their names down and promptly headed for the door. They had been frightened and were still trying to get their head around their first rulebook lesson in dealing with intimidation. It might have been the first but it certainly wouldn't be their last.

The day was full of surprises with a steady stream of people flowing in and out of the shop. Some of them buying, some just inquisitive with something new. Dan set the mood by carefully selecting the music tapes in accordance with his head at the time. Joan Armatrading, Neil Young and the new Matt Finish album captured his contemplative moments whilst Midnight Oil, Talking Heads and Dire Straits had his leg shaking and air drums swinging. Around midday Dan was feeling a bit peckish so he asked a willing Porky to keep an eye on things while he slipped out the back for some lunch. Porky thought it a good opportunity to perve at the steady stream of beach girls browsing the bikini racks and jumped at the chance. "Can I tell chicks I own the shop?" was all Dan heard as he disappeared down the steps and into the kitchen.

He made a ham, cheese and tomato toasted sambo and washed it down with an orange juice and a few hash cones of course!

Out on the back terrace the cordoned off lounge room had been decked out with a comfy couch, coffee table and small TV. And lurking in the shadows, of course, a standard Agung glass bong, usually stashed behind the spongy, well worn lounge from unexpected eyes with its close companion, a nice wooden mull bowl. Both were close buddies, kinda like Beavis and Butthead, where one couldn't perform without the other. Their hidden symbiosis gave the room a gratifying or a sinister feel about it, depending on how you felt about it.

Authority was always ensuring the boys' unlawful ceremonies were kept well off the street. Cloaking their mystical rituals only seemed to attract a stigma and heighten them more. These so-called "indecent" practices were only frowned upon because they had been deemed illegal. By who? Dan used to contemplate about "how can one substance like alcohol be legal but other drugs of choice be illegal?" Old school, rigid laws and values had become filled with hypocritical holes and were at loggerheads with alternative thinking especially among the youth. Since the "beat" generation public scrutiny of government restrictions on drugs had been building momentum.

Cocaine had been legal till 1914 and found in a variety of refreshments so why had it been disapproved? Hemp had a thousand uses from quality rope to strong garment fibre but was on the outer because cotton textile companies lobbied governments to ban its widespread production, claiming it was a health risk to society. LSD and other hallucinogenics, under clinical conditions, had been proven to help certain people break through depression and anxiety by discarding their egos and changing a person's grid for the better.

The power of hallucinogenics often appealed to several of the boys and generally gave them two options: Option 1 was a challenge to strip their own egos and discover who was lurking beneath the covers which seemed, for many, a task too stark and extreme to ever even consider. It was a trip that pulled no punches and mirrored one's inner being, with no violins and no sympathy at hand. A brutal insight into what you were. Scary as shit to some but self-revealing to others—an exercise in enlightenment.

Option 2 was to layer the mental journey with alcohol and other drugs so as to circumnavigate the truth and set loose the purity of the experience: indulgence to the highest degree as they partied hard and laughed aloud amongst the angels and demons within. No self-discovery but plenty of comical situations resulting in hysterical laugh-outs!

Heroin had been used to alleviate stress and pain from suffering. Its euphoric effect on one's senses and sharp addictive qualities had an army of followers. Some were drawn to it by its heavy, utopian reputation, others by getting hung up on initial prescriptions by their possibly already addicted doctors. Labelling it illegal had spawned a huge black market where unavailability and expensive prices had turned once civilians into lying, thieving products of a cruel craving in search of their next hit.

"Speed" and other mind-altering accelerants were given to soldiers to help purge their minds into crazed, irresponsible killers. Was that the reason they banned it but thought it a good idea to give it to the military? "Pretty selfish," thought Dan.

Why were drugs like sugar, nicotine, caffeine and alcohol, all harmful stimulants to a person's health, different to the illegal ones? They were all burdensome on humanity with their unique characteristics, and their experimentation would seem justified as "getting high" had been part of man's earthly plight since time began. Whether the motives were to be "enlightenment" and ultimately closer to God or just plain "high" to enjoy the bent experience, Dan believed changing one's mental state was of personal taste and a freedom of choice. The medical system and law agencies had it all wrong. Drugs weren't supposed to be money-making businesses for pharmaceutical companies, the black market and law firms. Addiction was a medical problem and why people were labelled criminals for indulging in their drug of preference was an injustice!

To the authorities Dan's questioning was to become a problem. He stared at his wooden Buddha carving sitting at the bottom of the garden and totally disregarded Porky's impatient cries for relief of his duties. He had brought back the statue from Bali many years ago and the tropical teak wood had dried out and split on the top of Buddha's bald head. The Buddha sat there in his resting place, calm and uncomplaining. Dan smiled thinking about his life's alternative choices and fumbling quest for enlightenment and said, "Well, baldy ... you da man!"

The day marched on and Dan sat like a smug sunglass-clad Cheshire cat behind his sticker-plastered counter enjoying the interaction with friends and customers. He had earlier washed his mouth out with Listerine and chomped on a Coconut Honey Log to disguise his bong breath. His sunnies hadn't left his face and he proudly sported his up-graded flat-top, "Max Headroom cum Vanilla Ice", haircut compliments of Joe the Lebo who had moved in a few doors down, next to Big Ads's "ghetto" block. Joe was a confident, slick, shaker and mover who wore tight black t-shirts, black slacks and shiny black shoes. On his small-framed gym-contoured body he wore a gold necklace and an elegant sapphire single earring. His hair was cut at sharp angles and his speech had that distinct first-generation heavy Lebanese twang to it. The boys thought it sounded quite funny when it over-layered typical Aussie lingo. "Youse knows what I'm a talkin' about, biyatch, don't youse?" His red haired, fair, petite Aussie hip wife was therefore the complete contrast to his sleek Lebanese appearance. Opposites attract and they were a good couple. They were new to the area, involved in the real estate game and were surprisingly down-to-earth and easy to talk to. A hairdressing attribute. Dan loved the special attention they laid on him when snipping his locks at their popular Bondi Junction salon. Joe introduced a white-fringed "vanilla ice" flat top look to Dan which ended up attracting a new nickname for him on the party scene. They gave locals a greatly reduced price which sat well amongst the boys and were frequent party heads entwined in the new wave "house party" scene sweeping Sydney's inner city. To add to his popularity his eccys were top quality, full of MDMA, and got you falling in love with the world and everybody in it. His eccys were made in heaven and often waking up next to a complete stranger was a direct result of them working their magic.

The day was getting on when tall Rager walked into the shop with his signature auburn, paddle-pop mane on top of his shoulders. He was a white Kiwi who loved the white stuff, especially when it was racked up on a mirror or in a spoon. He, like many, had found his niche in Oz through hustling the streets and getting totally off-guts deep inside the inner city drug scene. He downed any drug he could get his hands on in any fashion and was respected for his tolerance levels.

On this particular day he was out for a stroll through Bondi with his heroin girl and suit-styling Western Sydney buddy, George. His girl was living around the corner in Francis Street with a classic local guy of Italian descent named Moz who worked the area supplying almost anything that could tickle one's fancy. They were all out of the same freewheeling mould: motley moths attracted to the light of narcotic selling and taking. Moz was the only one who surfed and had grown up in Bondi where he had been an avid learner of street politics and was therefore well known, though he kept his whereabouts under the radar for all the obvious reasons. He had an extra couple of kilos around the middle and usually somewhere round his house if he could remember where he'd stashed it. You knew when he was coming down by the continuous beads of sweat trickling out from under his unkempt black shoulder-length hair. His oily olive skin seemed to produce toxic perspiration that could have got you high for a week and his bushy dark eyebrows, trimmed moustache and pinned eyeballs harboured many a shady secret. He was a great storyteller especially after a line of the "white dragon", though the truth was always bent to guarantee your full attention as he thumbed and pulled another cone between deep breaths for air and intermittent laughter. His brusqueness with non-locals was admired and a laughing matter amongst the Bondi brotherhood who always supported any irreverence towards the "latte" encroaching crowd. With Moz what you saw was what you got—he was a "Scum Valley" boy through and through!

"Wow, Danny, you've got it all happening in here, sahn! Turn that music up!" signalled Rager as his hand gestured turning up the decibels on an imaginary dial. It was some new "house beats" and his wench Helen started shaking her arse in front of the counter. "See, mate, me girl's stingin' to give you a show!"

Helen was tinselled right up. Her hair was out and about, almost floating, frizzed up, like someone had plugged her in to a power point. She purred and squatted and noticing the attention she squirmed and wriggled her sexy body in her crazy, seductive ways. Her head was moving side to side like a cobra being seduced by her master's flute and her high heels gave her a platform to flirt and gyrate. Thick makeup and long false eyelashes complemented her red lipstick-puckered lips as she moaned and ran her long skinny fingers up over her cupped boobs, tweaking her nipple, much to her and Dan's delight. Her leg-hugging flared blue jeans linked her heels and "grab me as tight as you want and bend me over" midriff. She was a street vixen who could evoke a riot.

"You like, Danny boy?" asked George. He was nicknamed "Hollywood" because he was an entertainer who talked a million miles an hour and told stories that could have ended up on the big screen. He always used a metaphor or a simile and must have had thousands of them stuck in his memory bank ready to part his lips. He looked like a cross between Jimmie Jazz and Jack Kerouac and had "tidy and quick-witted teddy boy" written neatly all over him. "Hey, Danny, last night we were so high we were flying around heaven like horned angels with wings." He paused and always looked everyone intently in the eye as if he was hanging on the mood of your response so as to know what to throw at you next. "Touched God, then told the guy that I'll be back when I'm good and proper ... and you know what he said, Danny?" George leered and broke into a cheeky smile, "He said ... he said, 'George, I already have enough horny angels up here.' I mean, what kinda fuckin' answer was that? I mean all I wanted to do was free the tadpoles ..." George's face contorted into a labourer's who wasn't happy that his boss had made him work 10 minutes past knock-off. "I mean, what a wanker, so I left a little despondent and I can tell you, Danny my boy, fuck him—I won't be inviting him to my next orgy either! Might be downstairs and I don't think he'd be welcome anyway!"

"I'm sure you won't, George. Heard your orgies are more fun than a barrel of monkeys!" was all a coming-down stoner could manage. That was until, out of the blue, a Talking Heads song popped into Dan's weary mind. "Actually, George, I don't think you're really missing much up there."

"Why's that? I mean, he does seem a bit too high and almighty for me."

"Well, Brian Eno reckons that everyone's trying to get into the bar up there but nothing ever happens, so it can't be that good, can it?"

"Well, I've never bumped into him up there. I mean, maybe he ain't got his VIP pass yet—actually he sounds like just another try-hard to me ... I mean, you know, Dan, me and God are 'thick' ... I mean, when you think of it I probably deserved being on the outer ..." He paused and leant closer to Dan as if he was guilty of what was coming next, like it was some kind of confession. "I've been telling a lot of God jokes lately and the big guy probably took offence, though me other mate—you know, the guy from downstairs where the barbie's always on, you know, Dan, Satan ... yeah, the guy with the cape doin' a bad batman impersonation— well, he's probably havin' a bit of a laugh now, don't ya reckon!"

Dan was happily occupied by the three colourful guests spinning around his shop. It was an unexpected free circus that had spilled in off the street and it was pleasurably captivating.

"These surfboards, Danny," said Rager, "I mean do you think you could teach me one day, Dan? Like, if I learn to swim could you show me some of your hot moves?"

"Being able to swim helps," replied a yawning Dan. The effects of the pot were wearing off and he was coming down again.

"Yeah, what about if I wear floaties? I mean, I've got a snorkel too, look," Rager pointed to his big twitching nose, "when I blow it, snot comes out! Ha!"

The amusement under the big top continued till Dan was pretty worn out and the three entertainers realised they had a date with some powder and something that rhymes with moon. They all looked at each other as if some secret sensory button had been hit all at once. Kinda like a "you thinking what I'm thinking?" look.

"See you later, Danny Boy!"

"See yas!"

"Don't want to come with us and throw some money in your arm?"

"Thanks for the offer, but I don't think so. I'm trying to hold off till I'm on my death bed then I'm really going to whack meself!"

"Don't say we didn't ask?"

"I won't! Taa-taa ..."

It was about 6pm when Horse and Trotter entered the shop. Dan was counting the day's takings and just about to close. The day's sunshine had slipped behind the tall promenade buildings and the beach was in shadow. Some North Bondi units, standing tall like soldiers at attention, were the last guards to say goodbye to the "giver of light". Their top windows reflected its last rays like an illustrious circuit of neons.

"Dinner or what, Vanilla?"

"Fuck, Horse, would you stop calling me that ..." Joe's bleach "fringe job" had naturally invited the comment.

"Ice, ice, baby ..." continued Trotter.

"OK, then, how 'bout my shout at the 'Rasa' if you put a sock in it."

"You're on, Mr Moneybags," shot out of Horse's watering mouth.

"Did you know your hair resembles that double-flyer, rounded pin hanging on the rack over there?" Trotter's bagging transmission was set on "keep pummelling" and was almost impossible to contain. "We can call you 'weapon head'."

"Thanks, that'd be nice ..."

"Don't go pointing it at me, now. Wouldn't want it to go off in public!"

The Rasa was a Malaysian/Vietnamese restaurant a few doors up the strip next to Bikini Island and its carrot, minced meat "Pie Tees" were to die for. It wasn't the only great food on offer back then, either. Bondi had a variety of good cheap feeds, not to mention the great tucker on offer from the many cafes and eateries dotted all over the inner city. You had your normal bistros in the pubs and clubs around Bondi, namely the Rats, the Diggers, the Regis and the Bondi Hotel, serving delicious Aussie roasts, burgers and steaks. You had the Golden Horse Chinese next to the Flying Pieman on the corner of Curlewis and Campbell Parade, Home Cooking up across from the Royal Hotel in Bondi Road that was renowned for their huge ten-dollar roasts and the Cubura located next to the old Astra on Campbell Parade served the best Eastern European cuisine in the eastern suburbs. It was a long and deep restaurant with lots of eating cubicles and the char grill was located in the front window tempting diners with flavoursome smells of steak Diane, cevapcici and raznjici. Ya Habbibi's in Gould Street behind the bank was where you got a pipe and a rock of the putty after a mouth-watering Lebanese feast. Its decor resembled a harem with Persian rugs and silk-clothed walls and belly dancers were available on request. El Rancho's, also known as the "hole in the wall", was on the corner of Francis and Campbell Parade. The shop was tiny and seemed carved out of the curved wall under the Thelellen Hotel. There was a well-known local story about a Bondi lad taking his SAS psychotic mate there one day and in broad daylight how the army dude tried to insert his knob in the hot chicken and then promptly proceeded to fuck it in full view of the traffic passing by. The unpredictable nutjob was probably trained in "how to kill someone with a chicken bone from three paces". He was also trained in the art of "wolfing down the chicken", after you've fucked it, of course!

Papa Giovanni's on the main strip which opened up in the 70s and blooded most Bondi locals on a scrumptious taste for Italian Pizza was a very popular, cheap family eatery. Dan used to head there with his mates and their parents after Prosser's swimming training as a kid and loved the Pizza Margherita which boasted the simple ingredients of tomato sauce, cheese and oregano. Its opening was followed a bit later by Ninos which was downstairs on the strip next to the Britannic Mansions where many a local was found after the closing hours of the Astra, Regis and Bondi hotels. Another early morning haunt was the "Devil's Triangle" located between the corners of Boonara Ave and Castlefield Street across from the Royal Hotel in Bondi Road. The trigonometry of a kebab, chicken and pizza shop gave this "Bondi Triangle" its name. It was a popular dingy strip with the majority of late nighters as it offered a variety of mysterious looking foods and stayed open until daylight. It was a place where many drunks were actually lured to by strange forces even though they knew they were at serious risk. A place where you could indulge the starving taste buds in anything from rubber potatoes that actually bounced, disguised crumbed chicken, spinning Shawarmas to 3-day-old, fat-soaked burgers which supposedly helped settle the boozy guts.

Over Randwick way there was the Duke of Gloucester that one of the local lads' parents owned that served a great steak, the Imperial up on Oxford Street, Paddo, served the best chicken snitzel with veges and gravy for five bucks, the Sheaf down Double Bay had a sizzling BBQ out back in the beer garden and was usually where "Black Brenda the mind bender" welcomed you, the 18 Footers also at Double Bay served a nice a la carte menu and was situated on the wharf so it was a romantic spot for dinner with a girl, No Names and Bill & Tony's had Surry Hills covered with the best, cheapest Italian in the whole of Oz and Good Vibrations on the corner of Hall and Glenayre Streets was vegan heaven with an extremely popular dish of cornbread with herb butter prepared in the kitchen by legendary "Maori Pete".

The pie-tees were calling the boys. "I'll meet you up there in five," said Dan. "There'll be a 'Crownie' cold waitin' for ya!"

A couple of weeks later Dan was visiting Moz up in Francis Street. He lived on the first floor of an art deco typical block of Bondi flats and tolerated sharing the two-bedroom premises with Rager's whacky girl, Helen, and his loyal local dog Seven. It was a sparsely furnished unit fitted out with only the bare essentials and a floral 60s carpet flooding into each room. The needle was really damaging Helen's life though her outrageous demeanour buoyed by her girlie makeup, tight waistline and gaunt, though unusually sexy, charisma obscured the undertow of disturbed emotion.

"Hi, Dan," she said whilst waltzing through the unit in high heels and pretty smile. "Nice weather outside. I'm so happy Summer is just around the corner." She was such a jovial soul. It was deadset gaiety against all odds. The only thing that would seem in her favour was a spoonful of heroin but you wouldn't have picked it. Her melancholy was so overlayered she had probably forgotten that it existed, lurking in the depths of her chemistry like a dormant virus in the depths of the earth. "Doesn't that smell give you the shits?" she asked.

Dan didn't quite know what she was talking about. Was it about her perfume, Moz's unwashed underarms, the distinct canine odour or the musky waft of a carpet with mould and fungus from a lack of maintenance over a few decades? "Which smell?" he asked.

"The little doggy one. She keeps doing poo-poo everywhere and I'm just going crazy. I really can't take much more of it, Dan!"

"Moz's dog?"

"No."

"What dog?"

Moz interjected. "The little dog Rager and Helen brought home a coupla weeks ago." His words rang out from the open door of his bedroom as he chopped a few cones. "Do you want a dog for out the back of your shop? 'Cause Helen can't fuckin' train it to do jack shit and I'm not going to clean up after him."

"Oh, fuck!" cried Helen as she tumbled from her heeled platforms whilst trying to avoid the cute little puppy scampering out from her doorway. She went down like a bag of shit and Dan was seriously concerned if her frail toothpicks for bones had possibly snapped from the weight of her shoulder pads and heavy makeup. The pup whizzed past Dan and headed into the lounge room where he propped, twirled, then sniffed, before extending his back pegs and squeezing out another little mess. Helen was on her knees and holding her head as if it was about to alight from her shoulders. "Fuck me!" she groaned. Her modest sized tits were escaping from their respective positions inside her bra and she kind of liked the fact that they wanted to expose themselves. It was as if they were separate entities from the rest of her body, as if they were acting out of their own accord and it sparked in her a sense of pride that they'd used their own initiative in wanting to do so.

Dan offered his hand and helped her up. "Thank you, sweetie. You're such a gentleman. I look at you, Dan, as my younger brother, my little brother who always helps his big sister."

"Why, that's very kind of you Helen. Rager won the lottery when he found you."

"Oh, you make me wet, Danny boy ..."

"What about the dog, Dan? You keen or what?" Moz was hoping this was a fortuitous gift for Dan. After all she was a good looking pup and he knew Dan needed a guard dog for the back of the shop. "She's a King Charles, Blue Heeler cross ... unusual mix but looks like he's gonna be a great dog."

"And she's a good pooer," added Helen.

She was a lucky little bitch. Lucky to have been saved from the evil that was ready to send her to her maker just a few days after she was born. Fortunate that Rager was walking along the same path that her cagey foe had chosen that fateful September day a few weeks prior. Rager and Helen had been pretty fucked up after a hard night on "it" so they decided to venture down South

Bondi way for a shot of sun and some fresh air. It was a bright, beautiful day and Bondi was crowded with the sun worshippers who had been waiting all winter for the warmer springtime weather. You could smell summer in the air: the distinguished whiff of sun, salt and the increase in humidity. They decided to avoid the sand and head wide of the beach up past the Icebergs towards Marks Park at the southern peninsula. As they approached the cliff tops Rager could sense something in his dehydrated numbness that wasn't quite right and began to lengthen stride along the popular, scenic pathway. He squinted and set his sights on a figure close to the craggy precipice who was clutching a bag and looking rather suss. As he moved closer he could see it was an Asian guy about to launch the white chaff bag and its contents over the ledge.

He yelled at the guy, "Hey, what are you doing there, pal?" with his morning-after, hoarse, rasp of a voice. It startled the thin yellow man and he dropped the bag and legged it up the hillside of the park towards Bondi Road. With his girl struggling to keep up and the sweat of last night on his brow, Rager picked up the bag with keen interest of what was moving inside. He opened it, peered inside and was confronted by a little Aussie dog that had cheated death for the first time. The little pup looked up with a cute, innocent beauty that almost brought a tear to Rager's googly eyes. As much a criminal that Rager was he still had a natural, caring connection with what really mattered in life. He was stoked to have saved the little bitch's life and he pondered on how much easier it would have been to eliminate the person who had contemplated such a sadistic act of killing this poor, defenceless animal. "How could anyone possibly consider throwing this little creature from the towering heights of a Bondi cliff?" The thought of pulverising the Asian culprit didn't even toy with his head for the maths behind it was easy—throw the scum off the cliff and save the little mutt instead! Doggie behaviour was not rocket science. A dog was a loyal mate who would always be there for you no matter what, whilst on the flipside of this equation many a human couldn't be trusted. As far as he was concerned the Asian prick who wanted to send her to her grave was a perfect example of the insensitivity of man towards creatures great and small.

As he looked around to see if there was any last sign of the guy he witnessed a young girl in the distance running around the park with her pet black Labrador. He drifted off for a second and saw the loving connection between her and her canine companion as they chased each other and she fell to the ground, succumbing to a lickfest. It touched him and was in stark contrast to what he'd just experienced. It resurrected his faith immediately in human nature and helped him conclude that there was good and bad in everyone and it just depended on which mouth you fed.

Dan looked downwards at the little pup and gave her a couple of short sharp high-pitched whistles. Her ears pricked and she ran over to his leg and affectionately rubbed her cheeks against his ankle. She whimpered a bit and proceeded to lick his thong-clad foot.

"Looks like she likes your toe jam, Dan," said Helen. "And I bet she's not the only bitch that wants to lick you there." She smiled and licked her luscious lips.

Dan didn't hesitate. "I'll take her!" It felt right to him and he knew the pup needed a good home. "And since she's got bluey in her I'll call her 'Ozzie'!"

"Oz dog, the littlest hobo." shouted Moz. "Now accepted into surf shop royalty!"

"She's now my girl," acknowledged Dan.

"I'm jealous," said Helen. "You sure you don't wanna take me instead!"

New Beginnings

Dan was up early; his new shop venture was evolving into somewhat of a natural responsibility, resembling something treasured, like an infant child—fragile, dependent and in need of nurturing. He knew he had to be at the wheel for the shop to blossom. It had already sprouted considerably from its opening and he knew his vigilance was like a surrogate mother nourishing its young, imperative for its continued growth. The custodian was up early and already into a routine to make sure things were right, racks were dusted, floors were mopped, windows cleaned and stock swapped around every day to give that "something new" atmosphere. He revelled in his duties. He was used to riding towards shore on the crest of a wave but now he was also riding high on terra firma. It was the compass he had been longing for, giving him direction towards what he felt was his destiny, a footprint ingrained with hardcore patterns reflecting the proud reality of his life. The shop would be OK as long as he remained focused on providing service and knowledge of what he knew best: the surfing world. Being educated in beach and street ethics was the key for his survival. No tricks, no illusions, no hard sell, just keep it real and promote a good deal.

He was single and enjoying his late 20s. Most of his dating was no more than just incidents. He had a couple of longer term relationships under his belt but most of his sexual encounters had been nothing more than a challenge. His dad had once commented that he'd had more girls as a younger man than Dan had eaten "baked dinners". And Dan had eaten a lot of baked dinners, so he could only surmise that sexual conquests were primarily "notches in his bedhead". Virgins counted for two "notches". For sex and girls had been a puzzle, perplexing to say the least. Through adolescence his church upbringing cast a taboo on the subject. His dad and mum weren't the sex-education types and his peers likened it to a game. A cauldron of misinformation and dirty secretive signals, underlined by puberty and ignited by a hard-on that Ron Jeremy would've been proud of, had him almost in despair when it came to the game of love. It wasn't until he had a few conquests to brag about and his ego had started to take hold of the situation that he felt he had some kind of handle on it. He had been a cute boy and been lucky with attracting the opposite sex. Even a few of his baby sitters who he held in "Goddess" status had affectionately stroked his hair and kissed him. Sex, surfing and the beach had enraptured him from an early age. Surfing and the beach were easy lessons compared with where he stood in the world of lust and love but like most young boys of the 70s he knew as long as he wasn't gay then he was heading in the right direction.

The bay sparkled and the morning sun pierced the beach hamlet to the tune of a new swell corrugated to the dark blue horizon. Distant fairy floss clouds puffed high into the sky and gulls rode the offshore breeze. The right-hander was cranking behind the baths and a company of surfers were indulging in the spoils. As Porky launched into a surge of water that would have enveloped the *Titanic* he raised his arms in defiance of the beast and screamed, "Yeeeewwwww!"

Upon reaching the bottom his morning serving of 6 sugar-coated Weetbix, bacon and eggs, orange juice and toast with jam, helped him plough a powerful bottom turn that shot him across the open face like a cannon. Being a natural footer all he had to do was stand there as the menacing lip threw over him. Again he threw his arms above his head and heroically decided to look back into the bowels of the monster. Eventually the jaws of the beast clamped shut and squatted the casual silhouette on the inside reef.

"Nothin' like a good smashin' especially when it's Porks on the receiving end," said a lean and hungry Cookie. His surfing addiction, like most on the beach, saw him slender, fit with no fat. Being lean and hungry was an advantage—it kept your prowess at an optimum so most benefits couldn't slide by you. Contentment was an illusion and made the next gain so much harder to fathom.

"I'm with ya on that one," replied the local "mad man" Pottsie. Well, he wasn't quite mad but he liked people to think that. It let him get away with the more unusual things he was renowned for. He was good at befriending new comers and offering them accommodation all the time enjoying the spoils of earning a dollar off them as he made them feel at home. Ten percent was a fair commission, after all he was almost acting like a tour agent for these new adventurers. Many were Japs or foreign girls who usually had money to burn. Pottsie wasn't stupid in his selective process. He made money off them across the board but in turn saved them from the many pitfalls lurking beneath the beach's attractive sunshine.

He sat wide-legged in a provocative manner on his BMX, coolly leaning back, arms outstretched firmly squeezing the handlebars. Sporting dark sunnies and inhabiting a soiled leather jacket he looked like the iconic Marlon Brando in his starring role, "The Wild One". The morning was warm but he hadn't dressed for the occasion. He'd deliberately adorned the attire late the night before when he'd decided on a midnight ride to initiate the tab of acid he'd dropped. He had started sweating long ago but he kinda relished the swelter in a masochistic way. Inside the jacket felt like a sauna but he was a strange guy and strange things can be tolerated with no known reason. He was reconciled to his strange condition and smiling about its secrecy.

"Ain't you fucken' hot?" asked Cookie, to which he replied, "I'm mad, bad and dangerous to know!" Typically offbeat!

Both lads were hanging at "the hut" on the hill contemplating their opportune moment for hitting the water. "I reckon he's got a mouthful of reef on that one!" Timing one's surf in the popular valley was all important. Watching the surf wasn't just viewing the spectacle, it was determining where and when you wanted to escape into the surfing arcade.

Big Ads strolled down the grass with his little terrier dog, Lindy. Living just a few houses up Lamrock Avenue and being absent from school most of his life meant it was the same as it ever was. Baptised into the world of apathy where the pertinent question was always, "What's in it for me?" Lindy was his staunch street companion and considered a certified local. Local dogs were all part of the surfing family. Most locals wouldn't think of leaving their canines at home when checking the surf. There were no leads, and dogs roamed free, loyal to their masters. The dog catcher was a bit of a worry and on par with the disregard surfers had for clubbies. Like their minders, the local dog contingent were happy to call the beach their playground. Most of them were smart and stayed well away from the dog catcher but whenever one of them went missing the boys knew all too well to pick their best mate up from the pound the next day.

"Good morning, Ads."

"Who fucken said it was a good morning?" Obviously Ads had woken up on the wrong side of his bed. It was nothing new—he was as unpredictable as the stock market, fluctuating between highs and lows. His lower class shined as bright as the morning sun.

Pottsie sprayed an undertoned laugh like a burst of distant machine gun fire, "May as well just kill yourself, then, aye?"

"Don't fucken get smart with me or I'll get me uncle onya ..."

"Shut the fuck up, Ads. Don't you think we are all tired of you saying that?" joined Cookie, dragging on his ciggy, prizing each inhale like his motor ran on nicotine. He was wise to Ads's mercurial nature. "If you wanna carry on like that go and get big Johnny and we'll tell him how much of a fuckwit you are!"

"Go on, fuckin' get 'im. See if I care."

"See, you don't like people sayin' it to you all the time, do ya?"

"Ads," Pottsie used a calm voice not knowing whether it would cool the cranky kid down. "Why don't you go get your board? There's some pretty sick waves coming through behind the barrier. Porky just got a howler."

"That fat cunt! He should head back to his pen, farmer fuckwit's probably missin' 'im."

"Well, he'll be squealing at you when he comes in and hears you've been into him!" Cookie tried hard to keep a straight face and had just about done a 180-degree turn on his approach to the conversation. It just wasn't worth letting Ads ever get under your skin. He was so screwed up in so many ways that to take him seriously would only drag you into an abyss of woefulness. "And I think he still owes you a beating from sticking his busted board up in the pines that big day coupla years ago."

"Haa ... Funniest thing I've ever seen!" replied Ads. "Fat cunt sprung wings goin' over the falls! Who said pigs didn't fly?"

"At least he had the guts to paddle out, Ads."

"Yeah, well, suppose he was lucky he landed in the trough ... haaaa!"

All the boys had a bit of a chuckle. Taking the piss out of lumps like Porky was all part of the rulebook. Ever since kindergarten any kid with a big gut was fair game. To fit, young specimens there was no excuse. Fat cunts were lazy, slow, clumsy and always lagging behind. They were rotund bodies fit for bed and lounges. Schoolkids have always been searching for that sense of significance, and bullying was all part of growing up, grooming for the big world. No sympathy was given and no slander spared. Fat chicks copped it even worse. "Bush pigs", as they were commonly known, like Captain Goodvibes, really had to be made of steel. A lot of them were cool chicks and good sports, banging around like dunny doors in a southerly, though it was hard for them not to feel victimised. The street was made up of all types and didn't refrain from dishing out disparaging criticism to anyone in the firing line. The resolve you learnt was called the "school of hard knocks" and the way you dealt with it was embracing the person you were meant to be.

"Don't you know the boar was held in high regard in ancient myths?" Space cadet Pottsie, like Cookie, was trying to lighten things up and mocking Ads's lack of education at the same time. "Actually the pig spirit symbolised coarser passions, constantly at war with the conscience." Cookie turned and looked strangely at the "Wild One" cum "Zen Master". After his enlightening words his black BMX bike seemed to have fused and become another part of his anatomy. "True, Cookie," he continued, stupidly raising his eyebrows as a prankster does similar to something Larry, Curly or Moe would have done. "And maybe Ads was born in the year of the pork chop because he certainly carries on like one."

"Ahhh, grasshopper ... I am moved by your words of wisdom," said a squinting Cookie reciting a respectable Asian servant from one of the Orient's many B-Grade movies he'd watched. All Ads could do was shake his head and grimace. Cookie continued "Ahh, Piggsy, why you rook at me rat ray? U not know squirrel who runs up woman's leg doesn't find nuts?"

"Whaaaatt?" stammered Ads. "You guys are the ones who are fuckin' nuts! What's a fucken squirrel got to do with it!" Ads was now totally pissed off with his morning encounter with the two wise men. "You guys are, are," the pause was a sign Ads's head was going to explode, "are fucked!" he screamed.

"Yes, Ads," continued Pottsie in a chilled, balanced tone knowing it would burst one of his vessels somewhere in his brain. "And the pig was known to be the companion of the famous boy, Kintaro." His private school history was blossoming in Ads's face, shining, horrifying the boy, like a precinct's interrogation lamp.

It was becoming all too much for the young punk, "Stop talkin' shit and get a life, you morons! You wouldn't know a pig from your girlfriend you, you ..."

"A little shit like you should be listening to Pottsie," interrupted Cookie. "He actually went to school."

Ads's freckly face had become clammy and his hands were moistening from sheer frustration. His haughtiness was no match for the boys who had defended Porks like true diggers do.

197

"Maybe you should find a pig for a girlfriend," continued Cookie.

"And lose your virginity so you don't keep taking your shit out on the rest of the world!"

"I've dipped me wick, cunt ..."

"Maybe you could find a squirrel ... oh, that's right, you've got Lindy!"

"Fuck you, guys. You think you can just say anything to me ... well, I'm nobody's fool!"

"Well, maybe you can get someone to adopt you." Cookie was quick and found his mark. "Maybe from somewhere on the other side of the planet."

"Grrrrrrr!" Ads was steaming like Vesuvius.

"And did you know homosexuality is condemned in Thai prisons?" added Pottsie just to throw some more triviality into the loony pot of shit. "So they let the prisoners fuck pigs."

"Well, maybe that's where you and fucken Porky belong, you cunts!" Ads was angrily sinking deeper into his despondent pit. He put his best sour head on and finished with, "Lindy's done her shit now so I'm gonna fuck off and fuckin' hope you walk in it."

"Oohh, tushy tushy. Go home and root your squirrel."

"Faaark! C'mon, Lindy, let's go. These blokes are fucked!" And with that profane kid, with the weight of the Opera House on his shoulders, waddled off, then hunched his back and bulldogged across Campbell Parade sticking his fingers up at any car that passed his way.

Dan sat on his stool behind his shop's counter, alert like a sentry, in hope of some worthwhile business walking through the door. Outside the suspended big surf shop Malibu sign slightly swung and creaked as it caught some the periodic gusts of the offshore breeze. It was firmly bolted into the awning to stop any brazen theft. It was a natural precaution, for the streets were as unpredictable as Big Ads's emotions. Two-legged traffic continuously crossed Campbell Parade patronising the bakery and Fat Mama's deli next door to Dan's shop then, hands full, crossed back over to the hill and down to the beach. The 380 bus drivers travelling down from the junction used their compression brakes as they down-shifted the gears to deposit beachgoers outside Dan's door. Occasionally they were tempted to enter and buy something. Girls bought bikinis whilst surfers bought mainly sex wax and accessories. There was no denying Dan's shop was smack, bang in the middle of South Bondi's activity.

Dan could hear the skaters from a mile away with their wheels turning as they rode the rickety pavement. Most would come to an abrupt halt out front dressed in baggy t-shirt, shorts hanging half way down their bum and comfortable bulky shoes. They'd waltz in, some distant, some crazy, some with attitude, others without, but most had the same respect for the amount of skate stock Dan supplied and usually always found something they liked. Anything from Santa Cruz, Dogtown and Airwalk proved to be great sellers and skate stickers walked out as quick as they walked in. Stickers always helped one to align their association with beach culture and make a statement.

On this particular day a local, Brett, walked in and scanned over the stickers on the top glass shelf of the counter.

"No way, gimme that one there," he said as he pointed into the messy array of colourful shapes and sizes.

"Which one?"

"Dude, you mean you can't see the one I'm pointing at? It's the shit."

"Can't see any poo stickers. What are you talking about?"

"Dude, the one that says 'Warning! The surgeon general has determined that skateboarding in any form is hazardous to the health of our society, because it promotes creativity and individuality at a young age. Prolonged use of this unacceptable activity can result in devastating amounts of enjoyment', that one!"

"I couldn't have said it better myself."

"Man, this shop is so cool."

"Fuck off! Are you trying to ask me on a date or get this sticker for nought or both?" They both had a chuckle, "That'll be two bucks, mister."

"Best two bucks I ever spent," and with that Brett the skater disappeared out the door thinking, 'That Dan should have at least charged me five bucks for this piece of inspiration, or kept it himself, because it's the grouse,' and off he went destined to ride the footpaths of Bondi all afternoon or possibly scab a lift to the skate park at Five Dock, with a cracker smile on his melon of course!

A couple of months into the shop's existence and Dan was already in liaison with council and the police to try and get them to build a skate ramp at the southern end of the beach. One of the council workers, Faye, was so impressed with his good energy towards developing activities for the kids of the area that she had officially made him the "youth liaison officer" of Bondi. She was a caring middle-aged lady, very refined and poised. A willing and appropriate candidate interested in building a bridge between council and the local surfers and skaters. She found a rapport with Dan that was to last a few years and help satisfy her belief that the local youth should be factored into Bondi's equation. She wanted more recreational facilities put in place to help prevent delinquency and create entertainment. She was taking the "bull by the horns" and for that Dan really admired her. He now had a role of attending police and council meetings as a voice for the youth of the area, a position of some significance within the municipality.

By the afternoon Dan was sick of hearing the boardriders' accounts of great waves and thrilling rides. He had constrained himself from jumping in the water knowing that it was Saturday and usually the busiest day of the week for customers patronising the shop. He had even refrained from getting stoned, though Cookie and Pottsie had done their best to lure him away from his responsibilities. Around 3 o'clock his angst had got the better of him and it was time to ask one of the lurking grommets, Big Shano, a loyal larger-framed grommet at that, to fill in behind the counter.

Once in the water his desire to get "amongst it" was fullfilled as he jostled and picked off some beauties. "You're paddlin' round like a maniac, Dan ... you been cooped up all day or somethin'? Hogtied to your boyfriend's bed, I suppose ..."

Dan just smiled. "Nah, Horse, I've just been perving and servicing all day and getting paid for it! What are you doin' for a crust again?"

"You mean you've been crackin' a fat watching blokes' arses as they try on boardies and Speedos?"

"Got some good photos and phone numbers for ya if you wanna check 'em out later ..."

"We on for a beer at the 'Diggers' later?"

"Yeah, mate, sounds like a plan." Dan and Horse synchronised strokes towards the pack sitting outside. "Pretty keen for a bistro roast!"

"As long as it's got a ton of gravy on me veges ..."

"You know 'em!"

"Then maybe we head down the beach club?" The Beach Club was the name the Bondi Hotel had given to the old Bondi Tram nightclub. It was mainly different because it now had a DJ playing new dance beats as opposed to the older generic Aussie and international pop chart hits that had plagued the 70s and 80s.

"Yeah, I'm up for a drink off!" Both lads paddled hard as a set wave approached. It looked inevitable it would break in front of them. "Synchronised duck dive, Horse ... yeeeew!"

"Keep away from me, ya poof!"

They were almost hitting rails as they penetrated the ocean and dived deep. Opening his eyes Dan watched the swirling clouds of submerged whitewater as they exploded around him. A glimmer of light from above, between the puffs, showed him the pathway up to oxygen. He angled his board with his back foot towards the exit and surfaced. Horse came up next to him and both shook their heads to rid them of the droplets irrigating towards their eyeballs and wanting in. The next wave stood about six feet tall, a perfect wet specimen of natural grace. To the boys' terror the one surfer you didn't want rocketing towards you across the face of a set wave was awkwardly adjusting his stance after rising to his feet. "Dangerman", as he was known to other locals, was cutting an unpredictable line and making a meal of a worthy face. The boys looked at each other in horror, "Fuck, no!" cried Horse.

From then on in it was as if everything turned into slow motion. Dangerman wobbled rail to rail, as if he was having a fit, and the boys didn't know whether to paddle forwards, stay motionless or back pedal. It was as though the guy was hurtling along a tightrope which was connected to each lad's anatomy. His arms swung like a gorilla's and his pelvic thrust added a comedy to the seriousness of the situation.

"Holy shit, Batman!" screamed Dan as the accident drew closer.

"Bail out, boy Robin!"

As mental as the situation seemed both Dan and Horse pitched their boards and headed deep, praying to King Neptune that he intercept the threat and avert a catastrophe. Wishful thinking as each lad felt a terrible crash, jerking their legropes, a sure signal that the missile had hit both targets and exploded.

" Two birds with one stone," thought Dan as he twisted and turned underneath the wave.

Guys who witnessed it from shore couldn't stop laughing. Most had winced initially on the impact but as usual someone getting hurt was pretty much hilarious. The local ding fixer,

Marcel, was still scratching himself over from his last sanding. He rubbed his hands at the sight of the collision and in anticipation of more business said to himself, "Thank you, 'Dangerman', you are a disaster made in heaven."

A Cross to Bear

Stirling was enjoying lunching at Chiswick Gardens in Woollahra. It was a favourite haunt of the rich and famous. It was decorated with all the trimmings that an upper class traditional English restaurant provides. The majestic, large white house surrounded by beautifully manicured gardens, were a sight to behold. Glass in hand and feeling very relaxed he had been summoned to the luncheon by his dad, Burt, who was wanting to catch up on his latest dealings down at the beach. Committed to meetings in global boardrooms combined with a mixture of secretive scandals and backroom deals had turned this banking mogul into a glutton for greed and excess. On occasions he felt the need to concern himself with his spouse and at this particular lunch wanted to offer some advice, if warranted, to his favourite son and apparent heir. His elder son Dylan showed absolutely no interest in running the family fortune and was more at home in the outback breaking in brumbies. He enjoyed country estate sheilas, as long as they were wearing "Country Road" outfits, could handle their drink and were fond of cowboys with big balls.

"Son," he frostily said as if talking to a subordinate in the company, "your mother tells me that you've been making headway in your surf shop business."

"Yes, dad."

"You don't think you're wasting your time down there at Bondi?" His dad was trying to understand his son's attraction to the many misfits he was exposing himself to. "I mean, what's the attraction amongst all those barefoot deadbeats?" Burt was ready for a decent answer, so he tucked into his popcorn prawns in hope of hearing at length what his son had to say.

"Dad, it's fun! That's the main attraction. I'm just enjoying the beach and I love surfing!"

"OK," Burt said without looking up, devising what he would devour next from his delicate, tasty dish. Waving his knife-holding hand as if to "keep talking" he ordered him to, "Go on and tell me a bit more about your business."

"I'm firmly in control of the surf business in the whole area, Dad, and it's all because of what you have taught me, you know, Dad, all those books you wanted me to read." Stirling looked for some sign of praise but his father was enjoying his mouthful and intent on receiving a complete rundown of his son's state of affairs, similar to what he expected from his corporate managers. "The ones about business, Dad, the corporate ladder ones and that book 'How to Win Friends & Influence People'—wow, I got right into that." His dad could only continue grinding his mouthful. His question hadn't yet been answered and he looked down at his plate as if more interested in his hunger than what his son was saying. "I'm really making progress, I've acquired lots of new friends ..."

"What?" spluttered Burt almost choking on his food. "Business isn't about friends, son. It's about winning and you don't win anything having lots of friends around you. They just make winning more difficult."

Stirling flinched a bit, a little apprehensive about his dad's abrupt, confronting tone.

"How many times do I have to tell you that if you're going to even contemplate running my corporates when you get older that you have to understand that the only people you want as friends are the people who can help you climb the ladder of wealth!"

"But they are, Dad. I have listened to you and they are helping in lots of ways. I mean they're helping expand my reputation and build my wealth."

His dad looked up at him and cracked a smile. His imperious manner had suddenly subsided. Using a lot lighter tone he then asked, "Is that so? So you mean you're using them?"

"Of course, Dad. You think I'm silly enough to let them take a lend of me?"

His dad washed the rest of the prawn mouthful down with a swig of Crown Lager beer. "That's better, son." He let out a long "Ahhh" on savouring the beer and food and then continued, "You might just turn out all right after all."

Burt was the epitome of global enterprise, the master of supply and demand. Like his own father, he was a man never content with the millions accumulating in his vault at the bank. A never ending portfolio, with a motive to rule the masses, fed his lustful appetite of dominance. To a capitalist these seemed almost pure intentions—walking over people in the race for supremacy was competitive, ambitious and praised within the new World order of economics. Wall Street and the Dow Jones, take a bow. To be king at the top of the pile was where aspirations lay, bum wide open, defecating on the masses and anyone coming within arm's length.

An insatiable desire drove the wheels of commerce and Burt fitted the mould like a hand in a skin-tight surgical glove ready to felch the next sucker in his sights.

"So what's on the agenda later this afternoon, Stirling?"

"I'm going to go and check on the shop and then have a surf."

"Your mother told me you acquired a new shop location."

"Yes, Dad. It's looking great and I have this new guy working for me who has a lot of pull in the surf industry. He's an older guy who has a good track record as a surfing pro so he's definitely an asset."

"Don't give him too much power ..."

"Dad, please. I'm not that stupid."

"What's his name?"

"Smithy."

"Don't like him."

"What, dad? You don't even know him."

"Sounds like a commoner."

"Dad, he's an asset, I promise you. He's got pull in the surfing world and he has respect from the locals."

"OK, OK, but I just want to see you perform well down there and show me some indication that you're cultivating the successful blood lines that you've inherited. You do realise we live in a country full of retards?"

Stirling didn't quite know what to say to that, "Go on, Dad ..."

"Well, any country that makes perfect sense to decorate its highways with large fibreglass bananas, sheep and prawns really needs to have a good look at itself." Burt stuffed another load of avocado laced with French dressing and a skerrick of caviar past his citadel of shiny capped teeth and into his open, salivating mouth. He looked over at the waiter who was almost at attention a few metres away. He didn't need anything but was just making sure his personal service officer was on the ball and hinging on what he might want next.

"I've also had to keep my other small shop open due to this local guy who thinks he can muscle in on my business."

His dad's ears pricked. "Interesting."

"Yeah, he's opened a shop on the front strip but it won't take long till he goes broke. He's got absolutely no idea and I heard that he's borrowed money to get started."

Burt stopped masticating for a second and reached for his Crown to wash the remnants of his mouthful down. He pondered on what his son had just said and there seemed an awkward moment of silence for Stirling. He didn't quite know what response his dad was loading from his arsenal. "A bit of competition, would you say, son?"

"Hardly worth mentioning dad. The guy's a loser ..."

"Hold on a second ..."

"Yes, dad?"

"You say he's a local? Does he have a following?"

"Well, you wouldn't call it a following, Dad. He's just got a bunch of young kids tricked into thinking he can give them something, but he's got nothing, Dad. As I said, he's just a drug-addict loser."

"I thought barefooted bums had an affiliation with drugs, and a loyalty to their own kind."

"Dad, he's dealing with inferior clients and his stock is just an assortment of secondhand companies that are floundering against all the big name labels that I do business with."

"Hmmm," Burt pushed himself and his chair back from the table, giving his well rounded gut a bit of space. He picked up the elegantly folded white, cotton napkin and wiped his puffy lips. Stirling waited for his father's pause to end.

"You know, son, it's not smart to underestimate anyone."

"I'm not, Dad. This guy is a definite loser."

"Hang on just a moment and listen carefully." Burt was about to deliver one of his imperious speeches. He cracked his knuckles as if to imply "get ready for what I have to say". "Do you understand the strength of ethics, of loyalty, of magnetism through one's charm when one has nothing to lose? Do you understand the persuasiveness of a likeable maverick's ideology?"

Stirling sat in silence knowing these were questions that were better left for the wicket keeper. For Stirling knew his father could lash into a rage at the drop of a hat, with the fearful flailing frenzy of a taut cable suddenly cut.

"This loser you speak of, don't dismiss his undisciplined appeal, for what I have come to know about surfers is that they are a loutish lot who can find our intentions at odds with their beliefs, so don't take this guy lightly. There is a good chance he's not playing the game of avarice but one of murky morality." He took the last sip of his Crown Lager and continued, "There are two elements in this clash that you have to understand. Our beliefs endow the great capitalistic system that we have the right, by law, to monopolise, where there is a good chance this pleb you are dealing with may only want to embellish community values." He let out an "Ahhhh", a satisfying impulse to a beer worthy of drinking.

"You see, there is a certain danger about this, son, as this kid's motives probably encompass local attitudes and stir discontent towards us, towards what we stand for. Our actions concentrate on dividing and conquering to ensure confusion and an environment suited to taking away from them what is retribution for our hard work." He clicked his fingers and the waiter was there in a flash. He didn't even bother talking to the servile lingerer preferring to just point at the bottle of beer. "You see, in this milieu, that is what the world is all about and don't ever think any different. In our daily life many things are squalid, scandalous or odious. Corrupt systems can only be won through corrupt ideals and careful, cunning planning. It's yours for the taking, young man. Just learn to be insensitive and uncaring, learn to lie and play the game with shrewdness and keep your cards close to your chest. Do you think I became a millionaire through being respectable? Every great empire ever known has been built by dominance, son, and dominance isn't pretty. We owe these people no favours— they are lucky they are not living 200 years ago when foes who got in the way of people like us were eliminated accordingly."

The waiter brought his opened beer over and placed it courteously in front of him and promptly retreated from the table. He used the white napkin to clean a bit of mucus from the side of his mouth and continued, "Is this sinking in, son?"

"Yes, Dad, of course."

"I want you to pretend you're one of them, I want you to win down at that beach and show me that I can trust you with what you will inherit from me. I can't make it any easier for you to understand. I want to see you undermine this guy under the guise of a calculated charade. Your destiny is for you to win. Don't disappoint me, now—we are not in the corporate banking business from being nice guys."

Stirling's head was absorbing his father's advice like a Christian heeds a priest's sermon. "I understand, father," he replied.

His dad's words rang so true when talking about the world and what it had become. He would have to keep cool about Dan's emergence as a contender, all the while plotting to bring about his downfall. He now had a lot riding on the outcome, and a better understanding of the risk involved. His father's endorsement meant the world to him and would ultimately give him the keys to a global fortune. That also meant the world to him, literally.

As he drove home to his parents' Bellevue Hill home in his lavish, new four-wheel drive, his mind was ticking over, reasoning with the lecture he had just been given. However he felt like his body was being tugged in different directions. For on one side he knew his inherent destiny of a comfortable life was stamped and sealed, but on the other side he felt almost an allegiance to his supporters down at the beach. Why was he feeling lousy about using people? Surely they were just using him? His dad, his uncle and many of their associates were examples of winners who took advantage of people and that was quite acceptable and justified in the world of business. But the beach kinda wasn't the business world. It was made up of disparate people dropping in and out of each other's lives. It was a surfing playground with camaraderie and a fabric of mateship weaving it together. It seemed to defy his dad's logic. It was for this reason he felt uneasy. It seemed what he was supposed to walk over had got some kind of hold on him. It was as if he wanted respect from them too but knew his money and upbringing made it hard for him to gain any real kind of credibility on the street. Yes, this is what confused him. The moral of the beach revolved around "who you were", not "what you had". Like the young self-obsessed adolescent that he was, he wanted it all but knew he probably couldn't have it both ways. It seemed he was carrying a cross acknowledged as morality. Or was it a cross of avarice? A decision had to be made on what final path was to be chosen to step off the shaky carpet his mind was currently walking over.

A car beeped behind him as the lights had turned green on the top of Edgecliff Road and he'd missed his cue to accelerate. He hit the pedal and moved forward, though a little hesitancy had also found its way into his driving. His mind was dealing with a creeping malaise. A nagging pain had now started coming and going at intervals. Then abruptly, again, like a wildly swinging pendulum, he felt extremely good about his position in life. He knew he was being groomed to be one of the richest men in Australia. How could he not feel good?

"Yes," he suddenly thought, putting things into a perspective. "That's it ... if I don't take the beach then someone else will."

But soon enough the ambiguity reared its ugly head again as he again felt concern about his responsibilities in dealing with the beach folk. The boardriders had their own loyal rulebook and over time he'd warmed to it. Proving his steel to his father seemed to mean that eventually he'd be selling out on all of them and throwing the rulebook out the window. Was selling his soul for money and power really worth it? Somehow right now, for whatever reason, he wondered why this was all giving him a hard time. He liked the beach but he ultimately knew whatever the outcome of his venture down there, somewhere down the track he would be leaving it all behind.

Eventual desertion was "to be OK". he reasoned. "Conservation wasn't in his family's vocabulary," he tried to conclude. "Tyranny was in his breeding," he acknowledged. The debate was always loaded. He would always be loyal to his father. The beach was just an apprenticeship. "Get over it!"

As he finally seemed to dismiss any morality as a weakness he began to feel resolutely better. Once the caring was replaced by rationale based on family tradition and his dad's teachings, he felt OK. At last he thought, "things were becoming clearer". As assurance he deliberately looked down on the seat beside him to the bank statement and the million dollar balance jumping out of the page and smacking him in the face. Any cross to bear quickly lost significance and wasn't so heavy after all. Any resistance to the bottom line, the bank balance, grew lighter by the millisecond.

The conflict that had plagued his mind dissolved quickly, like a good heroin hit speedily fixes an addict's grief. He now realised there was no unwieldy cross—it had been an illusion. Morality was for the weak. He had been resurrected at last, leaving any suffering below him.

As he thought of his sovereignty over the beach he thought he heard someone yell out to him and say, "Oh Lord, won't you buy me a Mercedes Benz ..." but he quickly realised that it was only the Janis Joplin tape he'd pressed "play" on a few seconds earlier.

The Contest

Bondi's surf wasn't good compared to other Sydney breaks but the locals dealt with their fair share of grovelling whether it be in or out of the water. The pessimists had a field day calling the waves "straight handers" but were just simply told to "fuck off if you don't like it!" Through the years there had been several surfing clubs and Dan's new club was just an extension of the beach's custom. For him it was a natural progression to set something new up after being heavily involved through the 80s with the boardriders and most of the beach's surf contests. There hadn't been a boardrider club contest for a couple of years since he fell out with Stirling and that had created an open window to kick-start something fresh and exciting, a "hardcore" club to emerge from the shadows of urban backstreets and dim-lit laneways. Raw talent had been bubbling beneath a sea of joy for quite some time. These new contenders were the supposed misfits left out of Stirling's elite loop. They now had a welcoming surge to ride, a foundation to begin a long awaited rise. This new direction was a rudder to steer them towards unity and a chance to enjoy surfing under the same Bondi banner.

Dan felt it a privilege to be serving the beach. It was something to do with the brotherhood of man and the innate connection he felt between his surfing mates. Most of the new club members dreamed of becoming respected surfers and he believed they deserved a chance to stamp their names on the prestigious list of Bondi surfing dignitaries. After all, it was only following in the beach's tradition.

Being a loyal "traditionalist" Dan was in awe of his Bondi surfing forefathers and he couldn't be happier doing anything else than keeping with the flow. Bondi's surfing culture was what he lived for; it charged him, it was what had moulded him throughout his life and he couldn't imagine existing in any other way. He had always wanted to be a part of letting the days go by down at the beach. Ever since he was a youngster, when Sloth's elder brothers used to walk him down to North to take him surfing, the waves, sunny days and free-spirited friends were so magnetic that he didn't want to grow up anywhere else. The salt was in his veins and he relied on his regular surfing fix to keep his heart pumping. He loved the open beach atmosphere and the jaunty aperture that he had fallen into after moving to the strip after he'd escaped the constraints of school and living at home with the oldies. It had an organic symbiosis about it and the lifestyle symbolised a kind of purism, the overwhelming sense of making it on your own, the sight of the ocean, the cracking of the breakers, the flight of the gulls, the smell of the stink pipe, the rebel yell of his mates, had all become part of his bodily fluids. It was like being spun around on the "Cha Cha" with its engine whirring and lights flashing with a turbulent bunch of spontaneous young locals. They were living in the gleeful moment with the spice of the world at their waterlogged fingertips. It made a flavoursome entrée into life for all of those upstarts craving the freedom of the big wide world and its main course.

This natural beach backdrop juxtaposed against a city of concrete and its hard lines presented a perfect yin and yang. The crazy, beach city life seemed certainly fractured and even curdled at times but it was as if the flamboyant surfing lifestyle had a licence to deal with it. The twists and turns were something absorbed as you went stumbling along—there wasn't much time for retrospect, the line of scrimmage was forever changing—but again the white sand and surf were the constant salvation that kept the fabric intact.

Dan loved the father of the beach, Bluey Mayes. He was the original. He was the surf and sun worshipper who pioneered soul surfing in Australia from the 1930s as a teenager. Every day as crew would make their way to the hill to see what was up for the day, he'd be parked as usual on the promenade next to the southern tollgates. His vehicle of choice was a ute with his campervan living quarters mounted on the back. It always had pole position, for he was the F1 surfing legend, and you could always find him cruising there, checking the surf with his loyal surf dog by his side. He proudly sported "Hang10" number plates way before personalised plates came into fashion. For obscure reasons he liked wearing stubbies and fairly camp sandals and the boys didn't know whether he was the instigator of 80s surf fashion or it was just following his lead.

His much loved son Brad was also Bondi royalty and had enormous credibility through his pro surfing and underground shaping efforts. When Brad was sauntering up or down the coast on surfing or shaping sojourns, his dad stood proud at the southern tollgates burning the midnight lamp. Bluey's vehicle was

211

always a hub for surfers to congregate and exchange stories. No-one else was ever known to park their vehicle on the prom and stay there at night like Jack did. He was above reproach. Council knew it and so did the rest of the beach. He was regarded by all as the blond surfing king and it was uncanny that he did look a bit like King Neptune. His Viking-like, wise, lined features created a suitable environment for his long, straggly shoulder length hair, droopy moustache and goatee beard. In the water he commanded respect and no-one, and I mean no-one, got in his way!

Bluey and other inspirational local legends, namely Kevin Brennan, Rob Conneeley, Max Bowman, David Spencer, Dennis Lindsay, Scott Dillon, "Magoo", Chris Brock, Noel Ward and many others spearheaded South Bondi boardriders and Windansea board clubs in the 60s. Then came the "pin-up" club "Panache" that was formed in the 70s and had so much surfing talent they were labelled "Too radical for the system". Steve Corrigan (Starman's elder brother), Col Sutho, Bluey's princely son Brad, Bruce Raymond, Ronny Durkin, The Ford brothers, Gary Bostock, Dave Cram, Col "Biafran" and a host of others inspired the next crop of late 70s, early 80s protégés. Steele, Crumbles, Joey Engel, Dion Gatty, Zappa and George Wales were all sucked up in the mushroom cloud these previous clubs left behind and were blown into the stratosphere where their surfing left a trail of destruction. Bondi's surfing was intense and it would seem no-one could ever put a lid on it.

To think that the new club was just another chapter of all this used to blow Dan's mind. With all this and more running through his briny veins he was ready to give it all he had. Surrounded by so many heroes and villains it was easy to be proud of such a great surfing beach. He now found himself again being able to put something back into the beach that had provided him so much joy. It was time for the first contest of the new club—the start of something new that would help bond the younger crew and keep the beach strong.

The initial contest was a fairly organised affair. Dan had been chomping on the bit to get the club going and it was now the time to turn it on for the faithful.

It was held on a Sunday morning and Dan woke up around 6am in his little den at the back of the shop. He snuck in a couple of cones and finished brekkie with knocking on the adjoining bakery's window and asking old grey haired Johnny, the baker, for a couple of apple turnovers with cream. As usual he obliged passing them through the sliding frame and collecting the dosh. A buck a piece was half price, a privilege for a neighbour who had to deal with the constant slamming of dough on breadboards all night.

With the help of a couple of amped mates he started hauling the tent, coloured rashees, blackboard and other necessities across a lonesome Campbell Parade to the hut on the hill. The sun had popped its radiant head over North and it was shaping up to be another hot summer's day. A few keen groms had been waiting on the hill for the boys to materialise and were more than happy to lend a hand in setting up. Some of their fathers who'd brought them down had hung around in anticipation of watching their grommets in action. They too were happy to help with a few mundane tasks, like running over to the newsagent to photocopy judging sheets because Dan, being too stoned, had overlooked doing it the night before. Pulling a contest site together was always an effort and Dan appreciated the many helping hands making light work of it. It showed enthusiasm which was a good sign for the rest of the day. Once the old green tent was up the contest site started drawing even more interest.

The hut on the hill was sacred ground and its wooden roof had saved many a local's melon from many a melanoma. It was a favourite with local dogs cocking their hind leg over its pine treated supports and on this morning little Oz dog kept up the tradition. It also provided an excellent vantage point to judge a heat.

As Dan set up the blackboard he yelled out for any names that hadn't been written down in the book. After a few late entries were scribbled down in their respective divisions he cleaned the board and commenced writing down the first of the cadet heats. Cadets and then grommets would be first in the water as usual, being the keenest. Open competitors generally showed up a little later. The later they appeared the more chance they got laid and had a sizzling story to tell. Saturday night heroics were always a hot topic and bagging sessions were never spared on anybody. A lot of "opens" waltzed down in their reeking fever gear wearing their sunnies like champions who had just a couple of hours earlier been meddling with their darker side in some inner city Kasbah. Some guys still pinging were pulling dance moves around the contest site as tunes pumped out of the portable tape player. Some older surfers had wandered over and were mingling, soaking up the rays and happy to see a boardrider comp after a couple of years in the wilderness. A few of the dads who had hung around were also enjoying the festivity, some of them re-living their childhoods, others just getting acquainted with the scene. They chatted and quietly checked their young kids' heats on the blackboard as if to suggest that they weren't overly interested, even though their apparent aloofness was just a cover, disguising their complete parental attention. Porks' dad even wobbled up from the Icebergs and brought with him a bunch of sausages. Someone bolted home and grabbed a barbie, and someone else bought some bread and tomato sauce, and the next thing the "sausage sangers" were being devoured by the hungry tribe. Cookie manned the tongs asserting his authority, carefully turning the meat cylinders so none of them burnt.

"They taste 'tops', mate," said a skinny grommet. "Me mum usually only lets me eat vegetables and tofu and stuff like that."

Cookie pointed the tongs at him as if to summons his gremlin ears. "Yeah, well, 'uck that. Tell your mum to start cookin' you some carcass or you'll end up looking like Iggy Pop."

"Is he a vegetarian like me mum?"

"Nah, he's an Astral traveller who plays music."

Cookie now had the grommet scratching his head. "So his mum doesn't make him salad sambos on rye for school?"

"Nah."

"Because mine does and everybody bags the shit outta me."

"Nah, grommet, he's more into spoon feeding himself." Cookie raised his eyebrows at the thought of the grommet understanding his comment.

"I ate a pie at school once with a plastic spoon but don't tell me mum, aye."

Cookie attended the grill plate, turning a few more over as Oz dog lurked beneath his bare feet hoping he got sloppy and dropped one. Cookie looked down at her and obliged. "Get that one into yer, Ozzie."

"Is he sick or sumpthin'?"

"Who?"

"The guy eatin' from the spoon, the Iggy guy."

"The sickest bloke in the world, kid!" and wanting to nip it in the bud to focus on perving at bikini wowsers strolling by, Cookie told him to, "Go over and see what Dan's doing, kid. You might have a heat coming up."

"OK, mister, but I hope your travelling mate Iggy eats some

214

meat too, then. He's probably hungry from all the trippin' around and stuff."

"Maybe," chuckled Cookie. "He does like trippin', but then again he's not like Dan's mate Gary."

"Who's Gary?"

It was time for a bit of payback. "A glittering fairy friend of Dan's who eats lots and lots of meat ... he can't get enough. Actually, when you check your heat ask Dan if he's given any of his sausage to Gary lately. OK?"

"OK, mister," replied the grommet, "but I wish Dan could give my mum some of his sausage too. I reckon she needs it."

"Well, she can have some of mine."

"Really?"

"Yeah, grommet. All chicks like me meat."

"OK, I'll go and tell her. She's just over there near the car." The grommet pointed towards an old yellow Vee-Dub parked further up the hill. The kid's yummy mummy was leaning back—her contours matched the curvy car, her cleavage was out like two lost puppies and she was flicking her hair around whilst scouting the scene behind big designer sunglasses.

"Wow! So that's your mum, kid?"

"Yep."

"Well, you'll have to invite me round for some of that home-made cookin' sometime."

"Sure. I'll tell her."

"And kid ..."

"What?"

"There's really no need to tell her anything. It's quite clear she knows there's a sausage fest going on."

"Can't wait till she wakes up and has a sausage fest of her own, mister!"

Cookie didn't want to corrupt this young kid's mind and let it slip through to the keeper.

The waves were getting better with the higher tide and many of the local crew were enjoying free surfing around the contest showing off their individual repertoires and practising for their upcoming heats. It was a merry band of surfers who had been waiting for this. It was their turn—some had paid their dues, others were paying them, some grommets were yet to find out what a "due" was, but they were all revelling in coming together

215

as a boardriders.

"Bondi natives at play on a hot summer's day ..." commented one of the dads.

"Look's like you've got the beach amped, Dan," said Porks. "Must be a hundred blokes here."

"Too right, Porks. Pretty stoked, aye ..." Dan used a megaphone to summon the next heat to pick up their singlets. On occasions he would throw a little marketing spiel in about the shop but who could blame him. "Get the latest Pipedreams, Nev and Southerly Change boards from me new surf shop, guys, and get a real deal from the shop that supports the boardriders!"

Grommets were stoked on the buzz engulfing the hill and the team of mates, old and new, amping on the waves and local fanfare. Older crew were taking it in their stride—a case of "been here, done this"—but of course it was different for the young kids. They were being born into a surfing world full of cultural fascination. Their fragile bones had been in the warm fleshy womb of childhood long enough and they were now savouring the experience of free-falling amongst a wolfpack of older, salty surfing whores. These were the initial steps towards grommet heaven, a time to hang out and make some ground against the onshore headwind of the beach's surfing heroes and villains. A time to try to harpoon some brownie points and start making a name for themselves along the way. A grommet's first local boardriders meant he'd finally been accepted into the guts of the beach, but only as an apprentice. It was like a young surfer's pilgrimage had finally kicked off and most of them only saw the challenging path ahead paved in gold!

"We on for a few billies tonight?" suddenly came through the loud sound system. After Dan's business-like announcements it was some welcomed humour. A startled Dan turned around from the blackboard just in time to catch Trotter putting the loudhailer down and saying "It wasn't me", all the time chuckling with the rest of the crew.

Cookie, never one to miss an opportune moment, picked up the mic, like it was a loose ball, and blurted, "Yeah, Dan's got the filth if anyone's interested." After all, heckling was contagious and once it had started it was harder than a tap with a faulty washer to turn off.

Cat calls and hollers erupted from most of the boardriders as Dan's public reputation was deemed fit for assassination. Cookie wasn't into preservation and Dan was clearly in the spotlight, meaning to bring him down was a regulation in the rulebook. Cookie was still dirty on him from the time Dan had packed him a straight tobacco bong in the back of the bus at Newcastle when they were surfing at the NSW state surfing team titles. Dan had finished the mix earlier and was trying to pretend there was some left. It was just before Cookie's heat and his nicotine delirium and lack of breath saw him unable to paddle out past the four-foot chundering shorie. It cost Bondi the title that year and lay Cookie's reputation in tatters. Not one to hold a grudge, Cookie joined Dan and the boys at the mandatory drinkathon at the "Beaches" Merewether pub that evening with staunch locals Tezza, Mort and Magoo and as usual got maggotted. They also pulled a couple of roots so the trip north was considered well worth it after all. For this was how the boys rolled, the same as it ever was in the rulebook of boardriders of Bondi.

As the morning wore on the grass on the southern hill became the bum capital of the beach. A large crew of surfers and onlookers had ascended down from the Bondi 'hood happy to be part of the scene. It was a significant social event and the boys were enjoying locking horns in some friendly competition, all the while soaking up the positive energy and putting a few moves on any new lady talent showing up. There was plenty of exposure on this summer's day and many eyes watching the motion, in and out of the ocean.

The successful turnout wasn't missed by Stirling's eyes either. Whilst Fitzy manned Stirling's small shoebox in Lamrock Ave, Big Ads couldn't help but reporting every hour about what was happening on the hill. Fitzy ended up telling the mole to "fuck off" because being the non-caring local that he was he couldn't give a shit about shop politics. He was also rapidly deteriorating from a new binge he'd taken on board and didn't want any negative vibes entering his personal trip. For the moment he was content to hang behind his dark sunnies, sell boards and get paid for working down the beach. It gave him a chance to clock up some time in the water, though that was to change soon enough.

"Go and tell that glamour puss Daisy because I don't give a fuck!" was the last thing he had to say for Ads to take a fucking hint and stop bothering him.

Double-parked cars on Campbell Parade hindered traffic as crew leaned in passenger windows discussing the last heat with the driver. If anyone got upset with their local rights the boys just laughed and let the grommets display their book of insults knowing they had all the backup in the world. The boys fully supported the cheeky upstarts. "Why write kooks off when a grommet can do it for ya!" Sound boardrider thinking!

Dan didn't necessarily want to become the patriarch of the Bondi Boardriders club but his experience and current actions had now thrust him forward and into the spotlight as the appropriate candidate. All along he had wanted a united beach, a beach where everyone shared the attributes and in turn created a place of order. Fairness ranked high in his outlook on life. The fallout with Stirling had been a setback but in the scope of things it was possibly the pivot that was required to jolt the boardriders back on track. But Dan wasn't doing any of this in spite of the altercation with Stirling, and if anything he wanted a truce. To Dan it was just a continuance of the forefathers' culture—it was Bondi tradition. Respect the value of your fellow surfer and what he can offer the beach in return. For the Bondi boardriders were solid even if there was a lot of shit going down around them. The local football team, "Bondi United", said it all.

All in all it had been a successful day. Accolades rained down on all involved and the next comp, in a couple of months time, would continue the boardriders roll.

That night at the back of the shop Ozzie was crashed out on her comfy pillow on the floor after a big day at the contest site. She'd hardly eaten any of her can of "My Dog" as she'd stuffed herself full of sausages and snacks at the comp, generosity of her new boardrider family. As much as Dan had become the man at the helm, little Oz dog had made her mark as the club's mascot. As she lay asleep on top of the painted deck, the boys were lighting up, watching a bit of TV under the corrugated iron roof. The stuffy oven had been heated up during the day and the humidity of the night was slowly roasting them.

"Wish it'd fucken rain. Kinda like a sweat box in here, brudda." Eugene was a local Maori lad smoking himself to death with Dan and Trotter. "Can't you buy a fan or are you just spending all of your money on drugs, whores and little boys?"

"Well, do one of your Maori rain dances ..." retorted Dan.

"Yeah, get a few of your mates here and you can do a 'Maori-go-round'!" sneered Trotter.

"That should be no problem, bro. I'm sure they'd like to stomp on your head, Trots, as they ran around the mulberry bush."

"Hang on ..." Trotter was laughing but none the less back pedalling. "Go easy. I was only joking, I know my Hills hoist'd break with only one of them holding on ..."

"So was I, but you'd probably look more handsome with a tattoo of an Adidas footprint on your face, aye." Eugene was smiling all the while as he joked some more and his white immaculate teeth glistened like he was in a Colgate ad.

Eugene had been spending a bit of time with Dan of late, in the surf and in the nightclubs. He was a small time wheeler and dealer who had an eye for making a quick buck. His other Maori mates were a mixture of delinquents and criminals but the Bondi underground scene was full of all types and the Maoris were just another piece of its anatomy. Maoris were generally big blokes but "Euge", as he was known to his mates, was leaner than most. His shoulder-length black straight hair, dark eyes and matching skin, combined with his sleekness, added a refined look to this street hustler. He was streetwise, intelligent with his words and saw the funnier side to most of the silly, ballsy things he was privy to getting involved in. Scams deemed "too risky" he stayed at arm's length of, but he'd still chuckle from a bird's eye view as many of his blatant accomplices took things by the horns.

Some of his friends were happy stealing RX7s or even Porsches from the surrounding affluent suburbs before using them in ATM ram raids. One time he waited up the street in a leafy, tree lined park, whilst one of his big Maori mates targeted a house that he'd been tipped off about. His mate brazenly walked into the grounds, up the pathway and opened the front door, all in broad daylight with the owners still at home. He boldly lifted the keys from the hallway dresser and the guy's wallet then nonchalantly strolled down the stairwell to the basement below where the Porsche was parked. Needless to say he left a large burnout behind him as he cleared the electronic roller door by inches and floored it into the quiet, unsuspecting Vaucluse Street.

"Ah, come on, Euge. I'll have to tell Ads to get his big uncle John onto you, then ..."

"Ha! If you haven't already noticed, little Trott, but Ads's uncle is a Maori too, mate."

"Bwaaaah ..." the boys blurted in tandem.

"OK, Sambo," added Trott.

Eugene arrived in Oz in 78 with his large New Zealand extended family and immediately felt right at home with so many other

The Contest

tattooed Maori folk already residing in Bondi. "This joint's just like Auckland," he used to tell the boys. He took no time in meeting lots of other kids and fitting into Bondi's attractive way of life. Institutions didn't do it for him and after being kicked out of a few schools the only thing he had learned was how to make a lot of new friends along the way. He used to frequent the "hang" at the back of the pavilion with a bunch of other Maori street kids when he was younger. It was dim lit and a place of drunks, derelicts and kids wanting to be bad. It lent itself to obscurity and most surfie grommets knew to avoid ever walking down that way in fear of being mugged. But as much as Eugene was at home with his wayward mates he was also accepted by the twisted surfing fraternity. He had started surfing out of boredom and one of his mates lived in the Bondi Pavilion because his dad was the caretaker. He thought it was cool hanging out with his mate there with its striking old architecture. There was nothing like the old 1920s' intricate facades and internal courtyards back in Auckland and it gave him a sense of living in the nostalgia of a former Aussie beach culture, back when attitudes towards surf bathing changed from a restricted and dangerous activity to that of a national pastime. It also gave him an opportunity to leave his board next to the beach and go surfing whenever he felt like it with little fuss. He wasn't violent—his temperament was jovial and modest— but he never backed down from a stoush and that gave him credibility up and down the beach. His "cool as" father and elder sisters had brought him up well, teaching him manners and how to respect his fellow man. He conducted himself with what you could describe as a comic discipline, witty and sharp to remark when it was called for.

Trott was a space monkey—well, that was his nickname, anyway. He actually was thought of as a bit of a ladies' man with his blond boyish looks and Lithuanian suave charisma. He had a cheeky smile which seemed to lure girls in. He had an elder brother named Spotter who was a well-respected surfer. As much as he had created a slipstream for Trott to slide through, Trott constantly felt he was always walking in his brother's shadow. None the less Trott was an achiever and his goofy style saw him inside the barrel on the left shorie more often than not. He excelled at screen printing and on the whole was very creative. He was the young surfing, guitar-playing, womanising rebel who never walked the line. There was always the good-looking personality hindering his morality. The female gender was fair game whether it meant breaking another heart or telling another lie. His good blond looks were an attribute to him for the present but on the flipside they were obscurely a lead weight around his neck depriving him of ethics and maturity. But at 25 years of age virtuosity wasn't about to become a big part of his repertoire, and after all the game of love is just a game. All's fair in love and war!

After the bong had done a few rounds the boys were slouching and sweating like three caged stoned primates. Scratching, plucking undies out and around cracks, picking nostrils, cracking neck vertebrae, cleaning fingernails, grinding teeth and every couple of minutes changing posture like a game of lounge "Twister" to try and find that perfect comatose position that seemed to keep avoiding them all.

"Anybody home?" accompanied a loud knocking at the back wooden gate. Oz dog opened one eye and started a repressed, under her breath growl, as if to cordon off the area until her master gave an order. The "Bluey" in her was acting in accordance to her duty.

All the boys could do was look at one another as if to say, "You answer it."

"Well, either of you guys gonna open the door or are you gonna fantasise that I'm gonna open it?" Dan wasn't even considering moving off the couch.

"Let us in! It's Getz!"

"Woof!" Ozzie snapped.

"It's OK, Oz dog." Dan was happy with her alertness. "Good girl."

Ozzie shut her watchful eye and went back to dreaming she was in sausage heaven.

"Yeah, coming," said Trott as he summoned his body off the couch.

Lifting the latch and opening the door Trott was greeted with Getz and bodhisattva Brendan, smiling at him as if to agree with his stoned appearance. A couple of lights from the upstairs apartment balconies reflected a twinkle off Getz's big front ivories.

"Well, don't just smile at me. You're giving me the creeps." Trott turned his back on the two and headed back to his sweat-stained pillow on the lounge. "Anyone'd think you'd found a new bum to rummage."

Trott had made the mistake of putting ammunition on the table in front of a couple of lads who engaged in guerilla tactics, whenever and wherever possible. Upon entering Brendan lobbed

221

his dick out and swung it around a few times, like Jesse James probably used to do with his gun, before charging at Trott. "Here you go, then. Get some of this into ya!"

'Shit!" yelled Trott. "You got probleeeeemmmmsss!"

Getz just dropped his pants and gave everyone a full view of his moon, much to Dan and Euge's amusement, then started backing up around the coffee table to an already traumatised Trotter.

"Get away, you filthy fuckers!"

"You've changed, Trott," said Brendan standing aside and zipping his fly back up. "You were never this shy!"

Getz wasn't finished with his passionate backside show. He manoeuvred around the coffee table and sat in Trott's lap and commenced wiggling his hairy Kraut bum over Trott's thinly boardshort-covered manhood, gleaming in his misspent youth. Trott screamed, "Whhaaaatttt! ahhhhh! Help me! Get off me, you faggot!"

Getz managed to stay on Trott's lap like a rodeo rider bucking for a high score. He stayed put, much to Trott's dismay, long enough to finish with a loud, bass fart that sounded like he'd followed through and shit himself.

"Haaaaaaa haaaaa ... haaaaa haaaaaaa ..." the room erupted as Trotter finally managed to push the hefty German outta his doggy position and onto the floor. Oz dog flew over to his bare arse and nipped it for good measure which was the icing on the cake.

"Woof woof!" Ozzie barked at the reckless lunacy. "Growl growl, snarl snarl." She wasn't quite sure what she was supposed to be doing. She looked at Dan for guidance and saw a clown, hysterical and of no help at all. She barked even louder which only added to the madness of the moment.

"It's not funny!" Trott was livid. "Look at me pants, ya cunt. Yer shit yerself!"

Tears of laughter continued to cascade down the contours of everyone's face in the room. Trotter leapt up and bolted for the dunny to clean up.

"Noooooo ..." he cried as he ran out of sight.

Dan, Brendan and Euge couldn't say anything. It was a laugh out that wasn't to end any time soon. Getz just lay on his side—his exposed, bitten, hairy bum seemed to be pointing at everyone as if it wanted to get to know them, just hanging there, an effigy of Getz's better side, displaying his public contempt. As he writhed around on the floor in fits of his own laughter it was as if the head had no idea what the bum was doing.

The shower pipes rattled from the brasco as Trott squealed some more as he tried to wash his shorts clean from the toxic poo. "I'm gonna kill you, Getz!" he shouted making the boys squirm even harder.

Ozzy had already had enough and was done with barking at what she'd gathered as quirky human humour. She resumed her place in the corner and sighed. She laid her head down on her paws and was relegated to listening to a bunch of jolly good fellows. "Ah," she thought as she tried to drift off, "I'm one lucky dog."

Dick and Fart Jokes

"Caviar dear?"

"Mum ..."

"Yes, dear?"

"I don't like it."

"But it's always fresh, Stirling ..." she looked at her princely son in despair as if eating fresh caviar was a family culinary tradition that shouldn't be frowned upon. "It's not the pasteurised kind, you know. Your father always buys the best."

"It smells ... but hey, mum, thanks."

"My pleasure, darling."

"You know I like fish, but stinky little black sperm at 10.30 in the morning, I think I'd rather pass."

"Rubbish! It's an acquired taste, dear, and it tastes good at any time." Her blue blood wasn't too shabby and over the years had managed to refine itself to enjoy all the spoils of the filthy rich. At times she wrestled with the "wife of a wealthy aristocrat" syndrome but it really hadn't been too hard to come to terms with it. Those age-old mega-wealth symptoms at her disposal were pretty hard to take. The mansion on the hill, the Porsche parked in the basement with the rest of the quiver, the fleet of leisure cruisers and sailing boats moored just off Rose Bay in front of the Royal Motor Yacht club, the country estates, the family private jet, the best table in the house at the finest restaurants and clubs around Australia and of course the credit card limit of a few hundred thousand a day, had all taken a bit of getting used to but in the end had twisted her arm enough to win her over. But then again there had to be a lot on offer to make up for the flip side of the deal, where her man's rarely at home as power and money take preference.

"I suppose it's too sophisticated for your adolescent liking, then. One can only hope that as you grow older you can appreciate the more expensive things in life."

"No, mum, I know it's an acquired taste. I only meant that I'd much rather a ham, cheese, tomato toasted or something else, that's all."

She looked him over, perturbed at his response. The young maid entered, her black soft shoes stepping easy over the recently polished marble floor. The sealed white stone highlighted the dark

granite bench tops and dark stained mahogany cupboards. She
dusted and frolicked around the large adjoining dining area before
she noticed Mrs Radford's empty glass.

"Another glass of champagne Mrs Radford?"

"Please," came the dignified reply. She loaded up another
portion of her pet caviar, using none other than her "mother of
pearl" spoon that had been especially made for her to avoid
tainting the roe.

"Where's Dad?"

"Don't ask me about your father."

"OK, then," Stirling swivelled on his kitchen stool and
directed his next question to the apron-wearing servant. "Any
eggs Benedict?"

His mother giggled. "Oh, that always reminds me of the Pope,
darling. Don't you want me to make it for you?"

"Sure, Mum, but you just relax and enjoy your champers.
After all, how is our hired help going to learn if we don't give
them a chance to cook my favourite."

"Suppose you're right, dear."

"Yes, Stirling, I'm happy to cook for you," replied the timid
maid making sure eye-contact was met. She had been working for
the family for a year or so now and had fitted in just nicely. Burt
had hired her on the condition that she was to keep her distance
and not to fraternise with anyone under his roof, but unbeknown
to all Stirling was knocking her up on the sly. She thought he
fitted in just nicely as well.

She was a pretty girl about 25 years old with a diffident
manner about her, but that was quite normal, being so young and
in awe of the money, power and stinking rich reputation that the
Radford family was known for. She wasn't tall, had cute dimples,
big jugs and an arched bum that Stirling thought was worthy
enough to rest his beer on. "Quite an extraordinary shape," he
would think to himself when he had her clothes off. She was
pleasant enough and enjoyed her time with the boss's son. It was
hard not to be coy about it—she was young and "love making"
was something she embraced. Stirling also pleasured in the
fragrance of the act and found their secrecy to be exciting,
attractive and erotic.

"What's on your agenda today, darling? It looks so wonderful
out there." The morning shone bright outside the glass-panelled
room and Stirling's mum was enjoying the view out over the

Royal Sydney Golf course and the harbourside suburbs. She had found comfort at sitting at the kitchen table, sipping her champers and admiring the lives of the eastern suburbs townsfolk diligently going about their duties. The small cars heading up and down Old South Head Road, and the many other interconnecting streets, the ferries and cats motoring up and down the harbour, all seemed to intrigue her as she looked at them as turning the wheels that made them rich.

"Gonna head down the beach and do a bit of work, then have a surf."

"Sounds like a great plan." She took another sip of her bubbly brew as the maid prepared the yolk, butter, lemon, vinegar, salt and pepper to make the Benedict sauce. The Manly ferry was heading back up the harbour towards Circular Quay and the many sailboats on the harbour were taking advantage of light winds and blue skies.

"How is your shop going, dear?"

"All good, Mum."

"How's the new location?"

"OK. Can't complain. Sure is a much bigger floor space and I can display everything so it looks much better."

'Yes, well, that little shop was just too small."

'Yes, Mum, but I've kept it."

"Oh, really?"

"It's better that way at the moment, just till the new shop becomes more established."

"I'm sure it is, darling. Do you need any money?"

"Mum, thank you, but I've got plenty of my own."

"Oh, that's right. Sorry, I almost forgot. You were very smart in joining together with your cousin Hamish on that real estate project."

The maid whipped the ingredients and Stirling sniffed hard inviting the aroma of the Benedict's sauce to fill his senses. "Oh, I love that smell!"

At that exact time the poor young maid accidently blurted out a loud fart which reverbed in her undies, like the bass at a Metallica concert. Mrs Radford looked up in shock, staring at the back of the maid's skirt. It was as if she was expecting, by the sound of it, for something to materialise.

"Don't know about that smell, though," quipped Stirling as he looked out the window catching the ferry just before it disappeared out of view around Point Piper. "Geez, the Manly ferry's bloody loud this morning," he added.

The maid blushed, her face redder than a ripe tomato. "I'm so sorry, Mrs Radford. My stomach has been ill of late."

"Oh, child, please excuse yourself next time and leave the room."

"Yes, Mrs Radford." She looked over at Stirling who was holding his nose.

"Lucky you didn't light it with a match, probably would have scarred mum for life!" He looked her in the eye with a "I'm now gonna have to smash you twice as hard later for doing that" look.

"Stirling that's enough."

"OK, Mum. Just trying to lighten things up. Haa, get it? Lighten things up!"

His mum was clearly not amused but as he met again with the young maid's big brown eyes she managed a shy smile that could have been interpreted as a cheeky, silent snigger.

Back down at the beach the boys were on the hill again checking the waves. Across the road on the corner of Lamrock and Campbell Parade Dan's surf shop door was wide open for business. Dan sat behind the counter hiding his stoned eyes behind his sunnies whilst cranking some Midnight Oil. The pointscore for the first boardrider contest was in the window of the shop and he'd been taking names down for a couple of weeks for the next comp coming up in February. Steele entered the shop sporting his "Rainbow Rock" T-shirt. It was a company he had started with his mate Hawaiian veteran Johnny Orr. It was a psychedelic consciousness trip empowering nature and all who enjoyed alternative lifestyles. For Steele had been leading the alternative surfing trip throughout the 80s. Unlike the 70s, the 80s was a decade where pro surfing had wanted to "straighten up" the image of surfing. Sponsors wanted squeaky-clean surfers for their marketing strategies to capitalise on the million dollar expansion into mainstream global markets. Surfing's "cool potential" of mastering the balancing of a board on a moving slope of water had captured the imagination of the planet. By the end of the 80s surfing was firmly in the sights of the masses and whether they could or couldn't surf didn't enter into the equation. Surfing's broad base of followers were changing and all that seemed to matter was that they wore surf clothes and looked part of the developing trend.

There had been some hard lessons learnt for Steele through the

80s. But he'd kept stoic on his path of approaching his surfing from outside the square. He had become weary early on in his career of the so-called extravagant life of a pro surfer jetting around the world, and instead of wanting to be labelled and thrust in a framework of the pro surfer persona grata, he opted to develop his character individually. He also sought out his spirituality and that kinda went against the grain of his young, upstart competitive ego but he was trying to find a balance between the lines. Somewhere amongst the many victories he had achieved and the ever-present new challenges that he constantly bestowed upon himself, he was pushing the boundaries of his own perceptions. Like the search for new equipment when everyone else was powering on the thruster program is a good example. To Simon's credit the "thruster" was an incredible innovation which changed the face of surfing, but again this was just the reason why Steele believed in his own experimentation. He was also looking at it from a different perspective trying to discover something unique, new and refreshing. A lot of people misunderstood his plight, but the one thing nobody could argue with is that he did it "his way". A lot of the time it was too weird for the ASP to handle and many of the established members who ran world surfing dismissed him as a lost cadet out of the rejected hippy era. It did hamper his surfing career and probably cost him the men's open world title but Steele was the last person to regret any of it. For this, he had to be admired—most of Bondi had accepted Steele for who he was a long time ago, and dug him for the person he was.

Steele had briefly talked with Dan before his annual December trip to Hawaii and made it known he was happy to lead the new club as Captain reasoning that it was the only club holding club contests for everyone at the beach. He believed any club that was worth any salt had to do that. Like Dan, he had been part of Stirling's club but was dissatisfied by the lack of nurturing towards young grommets at the beach. Sure, RBS was the elite club having national surf league titles and such under its belt but Steele was on the same train track as Dan, feeling morally obligated to provide a platform for the beach's young kids to improve. Winning wasn't everything and rather than just ignore them he seized the opportunity to put something back into the beach that had given him so much.

"Here he is, the 'Billabong 50 thousand dollar man' himself!" Dan was referring to the contest Steele had just won a couple of weeks earlier at Sunset Beach, Hawaii. These two had been mates since early teenage years frequenting Luna Park, the George Street movie theatres and of course mucking around Bondi in general as young kids do. Like any beach, surfing and skating as a local pack with all the other subterranean grommets of their childhood days forged lifetime friendships. Steele had left the beach early, breaking into the pro ranks at the ripe age of 17. He was always referred to as the "blond bombshell" from Bondi and the beach followed his early career intently as he broke new ground, winning world contests in his stride as his tenacious "take no prisoners" attitude rocketed him into the heights of surfing fame. One could only imagine the sudden rush for a young kid from urban Bondi as he etched his name in surfing history and took the surfing world in his palm. Since those early days he had been runner-up on the world tour 4 times and his main sponsor, Gotcha, had ridden on his back to become a multi-million dollar company. Things had changed over the decade and Martin Potter was now the focus of Gotcha as he was the new kid on the block and his aerial surfing had just clinched the 89 world title. Even though Steele had just resurrected his career in a monumental way, he was unfortunately destined, in the next few years, for the surf star scrapheap as new blood appeared and took his spotlight. It was sad to think that it was becoming common practice for these surf companies to use surfing heroes in their lust to be successful, only to discard them without a percentage or, in a lot of circumstances, without as much as a parting gift.

"Mate, we are all so proud of you. You killed it over there, brudda! And all the groms still can't believe you are going to be the Captain of our club." Dan was sincere in his praise. "To win the Billabong and make the 16, mate ... who woulda thought!"

"Yeah, well, it's just an honour to come home to Bondi and get to surf with everyone again," he replied humbly. Steele's smile resembled the clown's pleasurable expression above the gates of Luna Park where they used to visit to enjoy riding the roller coaster of youth. He obviously was still buzzing from the Hawaiian win which was the first event he'd ever won in the Sandwich Islands. Not only had it restored his confidence but it saw him clinch 3000 vital points to leapfrog him back into the Top 16 after a year in the trials wilderness. For it was a mammoth achievement as his barrel riding, through tight sections at 8 feet Sunset, had let him slide back into the elite club, a conquest

229

accomplished by only four other surfers in the pro history of the sport. It was as if he was that youngster entering the fun park once again and was back, but this time he was re-entering the exclusive club of the ASP tour. He deserved it. It was all supposed to happen. The cosmos had finally rewarded him for all his spontaneity, all his creativity, all his trials of greatness, and he had been saluted by the universe for his troubles. Dan recognised it, for Dan had been on tour with him on many occasions. Seen the guts of the guy, exposed, fragile, clinging on, but all the time moving forwards. It was now a time to rejoice but it was also time to embrace the next chapter in a significant man's life. A rolling stone gathers no moss and Steele had been rolling since he was seized and hoisted into the surfing limelight in his teenage years.

"The second comp's up next month, right?"

"Sure is."

"Not too late for me to get into a heat, is it?" he asked.

"Mate, it's only for guys who can actually surf ..."

"Yeah, well, I've gotta comp in Santa Cruz early March. So what date you looking at?"

"About the third week in Feb so should be no probs."

"Looking forward to taking you out!"

"In your dreams!"

"Same as it ever was."

Steele angled his way round the counter and upon signalling the signature bear hug actually caught Dan off-guard and wrestled with him till he had him in a headlock. Dan had been seated on his loyal counter stool so it had been easy for Steele to come over the top of him and gain the advantage.

"Get off me, you beefeater!" Dan was used to wrestling with Steele. It had all started years earlier after one of their first early surfs together back at Joey Engle's place above Tamarama. Needless to say the game never finished until the ever competitor, Steele, won, though Joe used to give him a better run for his money than Dan.

"OK, calm down. I'm not gonna pull any of my 'Brown rice' moves on ya today, ya haole!"

Dan's sunnies hit the floor and smashed. "Yeah, good on you, Mr North Shore ..." They were only 20 dollar cheapies and Dan really couldn't give a fuck about them. He was just so stoked to see his old surfing mate and on such exciting terms. Dan now looked like he was having a bad hair day—there was "vanilla" sticking up everywhere. It looked like Steele was ready to release his grip on Dan until he unexpectedly pushed Dan's face down near his arse and farted.

"Thanks for that!" said Dan sarcastically as Steele freed him from his constraint.

"So good to see you, mate!"

"Are you talking on behalf of your arse?"

"Nice perfume, aye?"

"You fuckin' stink. That's exactly how Neil's lentil arse from the 'Young Ones' would smell, you fuckin' tofu muncher!"

Steele was the opposite to a salad dodger and had been on a vegan kick for a couple of years, though Dan knew he snuck in a bit of carcass here and there on the sly.

"Neil's a legend!"

"I suppose you do resemble a long suffering paranoid hippie!"

"Gotta love the 'Young Ones', mate. Any sitcoms who have Madness, Motorhead and the Damned playing live have to be good!"

"Fuck, yeah. The boys watch it religiously! Horse models himself off Vyvyan."

"Be great to sit down with you all and have a laugh."

"Mate the boys'd be stoked!"

"Fuck, it's good to be home, mate."

"As long as you don't fart in my face again it's good to have you back home, bra. You know everyone in Bondi was hooting after they heard you won the contest over there. JB, Cookie, Porks, Trott and the boys, we all had a big night that night. I think we went to the Cross first and then ended up at the Hordern pissin' on trough boy and melting on the good. Mate, you should see these Hordern Dance parties—oh my God, it's 10,000 lunatics raving mad and going for broke." Dan's mouth was motoring. "The boys are so keen to take you to the next one. I think it's in a couple of weeks and Grace Jones is gonna be there or something. Mate, the girls, whoooo ... they call them 'house chicks' and they wear short tight, black dresses and these cute white socks with black flat heels. There is thousands of 'em. Mate, they are the bomb, a bit pasty but once you're on the MDMA you turn into a man made for lurve."

"Mate, stop thinking you're a porn star. What's with the Casanova accent? Can't you say 'love' properly?"

"Yeah, but it sounds poofy. Gotta say it like a woggy porn

addict, luuurrrrvvee!"

"Oh, OK ... you haven't been using one of those penis extenders, have ya?"

"Been meaning to borrow yours!"

"Ha haaa, size does matter, you know!"

"I don't have any problems there!"

"See, I knew you were using one of them!"

"Bwahhhhhh ..." the boys sprayed. It was good times and dick and fart jokes were always funny. Dan used to think he'd like to write a book full of 'em!

"So sounds like we're gonna be bustin' some dance moves," continued Steele.

"Yep, so I hope you've got your dance shoe quiver at the ready because we gonna be shreddin' across the dance party floor of lurve!"

"Mate, don't you know me? I've got a cupboard full of 'em."

"That'd be right, you fucken' centipede!"

"Better not play 'this little piggy goes to market', then!"

"Too fucken right!"

Subliminal

That next day a few of the boys were smoking a few billies at a mate's second floor unit in Curlewis Street. He was out for the day but they'd grabbed his keys and were putting his bong to good use. It was a Saturday morning and the beach was already scorching and crowded with thousands of beachgoers. There wasn't much else to do as the surf was flat. The boys weren't really interested in suntans unless they were on the opposite sex. Every day on the sands of Bondi the rubbing of oil onto smooth skin was commonplace so there was no real urgency in the blistering heat to bolt down and lube up any chicks. That could always wait till tomorrow.

"Stoked Steele's joined the club, Dan," said an excited Porks.

"Yeah, well, I reckon the next comp is gonna have twice as many people turn up."

"For sure," commented JB. "Steele has been my hero since I was a kid."

"Yeah, mine too," added Porks. "After Captain Goodvibes," he said with a smirk.

"After Lash Clone." The game had begun ...

"After Bunker Spreckles."

"After Paul Hogan."

"After Strop."

"After Delvene."

"After Abigail."

"After Joe Hasham."

"After Alf Sutcliffe."

"Who the fuck's Alf Sutcliffe?" asked JB.

"Some fag."

"After Gary Glitter, then," giggled Cookie.

"I'd thought you'd say that, ya poof."

"Thought I'd say it before you did, ya jealous cunt."

"After ummm ..." Porky missed a beat.

"Keep it going, you idiot!"

"After Linda Lovelace!"

"After John Holmes."

"After Bob Hawke."

"After Bob Hope."

'After Bob Barrett."

"After two bob."

"After two boobs."

"After Elle."

"Elle? Now your talkin', Dan."

"Yeah, I heard she was in yer shop trying on a bikini or two."

"Briefly, before a hundred grommets found out and were trying to perve under the change room curtain at her."

"Did you ask her out back?"

"Big Shano was lookin' after the joint for me.

"Knowin' Big Shano, I'm sure his eyes undressed her a few times."

"Well, did he ask her for ya, Dan? I mean, I hope he maintained your high standards."

"Did he get to sniff her undies?"

"Whooooooa! What ... are you guys out of your fuckin' heads?"

"Yeah ... pretty much."

"Whaddya think my shop is? Some hardcore, perverted bastion full of twisted misfits?"

"Yeah ... pretty much."

"Yeah, well, that's what happens when you leave grommets behind the counter whilst you're out and about up to no good." Cookie couldn't help but continue. "Scaring glamours and shit, no wonder your shop's becoming 'grommet central', bra ... you better watch it or they'll be calling you a dirty old man!"

"Too late, Cookie," said JB. "He's the new sugar daddy on the block."

"Go easy, guys." Dan tried to defend himself.

"Someone's gotta sell them 20 dollar foilies, I suppose," added Cookie.

Dan's stomach wasn't about to digest that one. "You guys are gonna get me in trouble talking shit like that."

"Ohh ... can I play my violin for you?"

"Yeah, well, whaddya reckon? Just because I gotta board club running outta my shop doesn't mean I've gotta take the weight of the beach on me shoulders just because I sell a bit of dakka!"

"Suppose they may as well buy it off you than some respectable citizen."

"That's right, Cookie. At least I sell them a full gram."

"Whaddya fuckin' mean by that, Peter Pan?"

Being the blooming surf shop owner had its setbacks—every

move, every word was now open to public scrutiny. Dan was happy to take a swing but sometimes he just had to let the ball go through to the keeper and hope it didn't hit the stumps. "Ah whatever ... at least I get to fuck Tinkerbelle."

"Yeah, well, you blew it with Elle. She won't be waltzing into 'grommet central' any time soon lookin' to blow you!"

Dan offered no reply and thought packing another cone was a better option. He thought that when it came down to it he could pretty much cop all the shit the boys hurled at him and anyone else for that matter. You could label it a "Tall Poppy Syndrome" when referring to others' taunts and insults but it was definitely only a joking, deluded "Tall Pot-Smoking Syndrome" when it was laced with herb in a smoky fog-filled room with the boys. The attention also meant Dan and the boardriders were now more than ever considered contenders. He was revving the engine and smokin' the wheels of traditional virtue and both honoured and blessed in doing so. The spotlight on the shop showed interest from many and placed a target on his ever-changing skin. There was a bounty on his head but Dan didn't care and would do what he had to do—promote the man in the street and a fair go for all and try and sell them a foil while he was at it. He was evolving like a sub-species and his shop was doing the same. Any resistance, expected or unexpected, signalled the challenge he'd been waiting for and the hardcore crew associating with his cause were happy to be turning into urban soldiers of fortune. It was really becoming a lot of fun for all, except maybe those in opposition.

The boys' rebellious righteousness was striking a chord with all those in the underground. Tagged explicitly notorious, the cavalry of the indigenous Bondi tribe were now on a mission not to give ground in the surf and on the streets.

The boys lounged about as pot smokers do—someone made cuppas for those who wanted to wet their whistle, a loaf of bread and last night's left over pizza got demolished compliments of munchie madness. Time cruised slowly as it was a hot day with no chance of a surf. With a million people visiting the beach it was just best to stay put and keep puffing away. Dan probably should have been at the shop but he had a smokin' hot young girl named Kathy in there who was attracting a lot of customers. He figured he'd head there after lunch and grab a bite to eat from the fish and chip shop on the way.

There was a knock at the door and as JB was still up, after

235

pillaging the contents of their friend's fridge, he went to answer it.

"Who's there?"

"It's me, Jas: Brad!"

Jason promptly opened it and gave his hoodrat brudda a "hello brudda shaka" handshake. Mikey B filed in behind him and received the same warm greeting. Brad was the bass player for the band "Stiff Arm" who were the hardcore local beach band at the time. Trott was the grungy vocalist and lead guitarist while Mikey B played drums. Brad was a legend. His bass lines brought the dead back to life. He was a gritty goofyfooter who loved surfing MacKenzies Bay when it was on. It was only natural as he was living with another underground musician, Lucius, in Kenneth Street just above his beloved left-hander. Of course he also loved the guts outta the left shorie at Bondi, but he had an uncanny knack of scoring sand-dredging pits at Mackenzies before the crew turned up. He was always keeping a beat and he had "funky shit" stamped all over him. From his boofy wig, to his oversized trousers, to his droopy socks and airwalk shoes, he personified sloppy, punk, be-bop, grungy metal, if that's possible! He loved street surfing and was stoked Dan had all the latest skate decks on display as it saved him from travelling to the different corners of Sydney to find them.

All the boys acknowledged the newcomers.

"Sit down and we'll pack you up," said Cookie who was designated packer.

Dan was pretty stoned and instead of pulling his next cone passed the loaded billy to Mikey.

"Thanks, Dan." He was a polite kid. "Big Ads's having a barbie in a coupla weeks. You gonna go?" He was excited that the band would be playing there and he could smash some pigskin. The boys used to think he was the coolest cat at the beach. He'd been surfing the beach for years with his elder brother, Brendan, and both were rock solid. Their parents had migrated from India so the boys were of a dark complexion and very hard to find in nightclubs, although their white shiny teeth and eyes usually gave them away. But it was all cool because their legendary dad was always there beside them, partying like there was no tomorrow, and his warm, cheeky grin never left his face. He was comfortably in his late 40s and obviously still having too much fun. His excess party factor had him slip right into the boys' wavelength and they loved him for it.

Mikey B had a sensual timidness, softly spoken, almost feminine quality about him, but he was by no means a poof. He was very handsome, some thought he was destined for Bollywood, and well mannered, although he busted out of his shell when under the influence and hanging with the bruddas. He was small-framed but he sure could jam a cutback. He had the fluidity of a gracious stylemaster and when he laid the board on its rail he found speed and lines that flowed all the way to the beach.

"Well, you gonna go, Dan?" he repeated.

"Suppose, as long as Cookie's not there," came Dan's sulky reply.

"What's up, Peter Pan? You wanna have a little cry?" replied Cookie. "Have a little cry into the mull bowl, ya pussy!"

"Should be a coupla nice wenches at Ads's," interjected JB to fob off the lovers' tiff.

Dan was quick to leave it all behind and commented, "I reckon, Jas." And he was even quicker to snatch the bowl off Cookie.

"Hey, I'm packin'!"

Dan ignored Cookie and continued. "I hope that sick bitch who's been hangin' out with Getz gets her sweet ass there." He'd been sussing this chick for a while and the contest to pork her first was well and truly on.

"Is Getz doin' her or what?" Porks had asked what everyone in the room was wondering. It was a general question but no-one knew the answer.

Dan twirled his eyebrows and broke the silence. "He'd be braggin' about it if he did and I haven't heard shit so I'm calling he's gettin' nought." He was very adamant about what he'd said. He definitely didn't want to think dirty, big Getz's kransky had been there before him.

"Must be doin' the sauerkraut's head in 'cause she's fuckin' gorgeous." Cookie was drawing on direct signals from his personal hormones.

"I getta fat just thinkin' about her," were Porky's words of wisdom. He'd opened himself up and had to cop sweet the onslaught.

"Well, you better go to the dunny, then, and have a tug," hurled Brad.

"Don't forget to take your tweezers!" threw in Mikey.

237

"Yeah, and when you do find your pretzel, Dan's gonna lend you his penis enlarger." Cookie had hit two birds with the one stone. He dearly wanted to have the last laugh, especially with the ongoing spat with Danny boy!

"Why does everyone think I have a penis enlarger?" Dan was a little at sixes and sevens why he had been accused twice of owning one in the last couple of days.

"Because you need one!"

"Because your boyfriend likes to borrow it!"

"Because your addicted to dick things!"

"Fuck, man, I give up ..." Dan was tapping out. "You guys win—I'm a penis enlarging, dope peddling, young boy's dream who owns a perverted surfshop for midgets, whores and misfits ... OK? Am I right?"

"Yeah ... pretty much."

The boys merrily continued their bonging on and were enjoying just talking shit. Ronnie Bumbleland presented some pop diva on his Channel 7 TV music show. It was bound to quickly gain the boys' interest.

"She's da shit, bra!" commented Brad as the boys focused on the scantily clad vixen.

"That chick is smokin', brudda!" added Mikey.

Attention turned towards the TV and the room's testosterone levels were understandably nudged as the camera zoomed in and almost disappeared into the fleshy, squishy bits. As arses wiggled and G-strings fell in and back out of the abyss, Porky busted out into a sweat. By the time a hungover Ronnie had come back on after the clip it looked as if he had a banana stuffed down the leg of his pants and there were clear signs of froth starting to protrude from the corners of Porky's mouth.

"Look at Ronnie! He's got a fat!" shrieked Porks.

"Trust you to look!"

"Mate, look at you," exclaimed Brad. "You look as though you just went a round with Mike Tyson. You shoulda come to that brothel with us last night, ya frother." Brad was sporting one of those "I lost a load last night" kind of grins.

He'd been out at the Cross the evening before when he bumped into a bloke who swore he knew him. He couldn't remember the guy from a bar of soap but being the casual lad that he was he went along with it and let the guy shout him all night. At the time Brad was working for one of the local sex shops on the neon strip so he made the guy's night when he offered to take him on a local sex tour. The guy was so impressed at Brad's friendly nature and local knowledge he suggested Brad start "some kinda Kings Cross personal sex tours". He told Brad that there was an art to being relaxed about sex and that Brad had mastered it. Even though Brad thought it was all a bit weird he didn't really care for he was in it for the beer and trimmings, not the conversation. Being the happy-go-lucky kinda guy he was, he was more than willing to see where it was all going. He just kept replying, "Whatever" then indicated he was ready for another beer by raising his schooner and swilling the dregs in the bottom of his glass.

Brad didn't mind putting up with the guy for a free night on the piss; however, the friendship got ugly when they were patronising a brothel in the wee hours of the morning. To Brad's surprise the bloke came barging into the "jungle room", unannounced, whilst Brad was engrossed in skewering what seemed a bleating wild animal on a spit. After all it was called the "jungle room". However what really scared him was the huge double-ended dildo his newfound mate had clenched between his teeth.

The boys continued their babbling, as inarticulate or meaningless as it was. Brad, being restlessly stoned and bored with proverbial Top 40 shitty music clips, was off in his own little world and started channel surfing with the remote being a long bamboo pole. He stopped at a channel screening a newsflash bulletin. Apparently a large rogue kangaroo was terrorising people in outback Queensland. The camera panned the two households which had been subject to the appalling attack.

One of the victims, an elderly woman, was quite emotional, as expected, in front of the interviewer's microphone. "I was hanging out the washing when I heard the beast come up behind me. I turned around and the kangaroo punched me in the face and knocked me to the ground."

Brad had become absorbed in the story whilst the others weren't taking much notice. They were still discussing g-strings and Ads's barbie.

The victim of the kangaroo's vicious assault continued. "I could tell by its eyes that he was out to kill me. I mean, I'd never done anything to a kangaroo before ... why would he want to do that to little old me?" The interviewer held the microphone even closer with one hand on his hip, as though this was cutting edge stuff. "If my Bazza hadn't been there with the shovel I probably wouldn't be talking to you now."

"What?" thought Brad "Is this all for real?" He suddenly took on the interviewer's persona and asked, "Was there any hint he was trying to rape you? I mean, you do look a bit like a kangaroo—a big, fat, old one!" He chuckled to himself and continued, "Maybe he just wanted a paw-job?"

In his state of higher stoned consciousness Brad was pondering the kangaroo's side of the story. He imagined that the roo was obviously just getting back some for his own kind. After all, they'd been fucked over since whitey arrived. Come and see the lovely furry kangaroos in Australia through the sights of a .303. Drive over a few if you like, but just make sure you have a massive bullbar so you don't hurt the car. Brad was now thinking that this kangaroo had good reason to be pissed off. He toyed with the idea that this Kanga could have been trying to lead some kind of revolution. His imagery about hostile animals was now expanding. Animal Farm was coming to the fore. "Four legs good, two legs bad!" Had Napoleon sent this kangaroo as an indication of things to come? Would "Beasts of Australia" be their new anthem? Cows with guns and pigs with pitchforks were revolutionary old hat ... however Kangaroos packin' Uzis tickled his stoned fancy.

He all of a sudden needed a Coke. "Who wants a Coke? My shout if ya go down and get it ..."

"Fuck, man, I feel like one of them too," said Dan.

"Me too," said Porks.

"What is this? Coke time or sumpthin'?"

"No way," spat an alarmed, on the ball JB. "Were you guys watching the TV then?"

"What?"

"It's subliminal, mate. They're fuckin' brainwashin' ya on telly." JB had seen a news clipping somewhere the week before alerting him to the situation at hand.

"Nah ... really?"

"Yeah, ya dumbfucks, haven't you heard that's what they've been doing? Flashin' frames with Coke and stuff on them so all of a sudden you want one!"

"Bullshit!"

"No bullshit! Don't you listen to 'Suicidals', you gay fuck?"

"Oh shit, yeah ... 'They're fuckin with me subliminally' sick track, yeeew!"

"I know that song, 'Flashing pictures on my screen, shown too quickly to be seen'. Right?"

"Fuckin' Coke!"

"Yeah, well, I still want one."

There was a knock on the door and when there was a crew in the room the last one to say 'paxt' was obligated to open it. This was a ritual shared in the 'hood over anything which required an effort, kinda like musical chairs. It was also in the rulebook. Dan, Cookie, Mikey and JB had blurted it before the knock had ended. Brad was still spinning in lala land but his conditioning had him spit 'paxt' out before Porky, whose grotty mouth was occupied wrenching a cone, had a chance to.

"Hoped you wiped ya fucking mouth before you pulled that!" said Cookie.

There was another knock this time a little louder and bolder. Dan thought it sounded a little suspect.

"Answer the door, fatso," remarked Dan. "And blow that smoke out the window. It could be the johnny hoppers." The boys automatically hid the mix and bong under the table.

Porky spluttered the smoke out the window where it was consumed by the languorous, steamy street fumes. A police car drove past. "Take that," he murmured as he took the opportunity to try to spit on its roof. "Shit. Fucken missed."

A voice bellowed out from behind the door. "Are you guys suckin' each other off or are you going to open the fuckin' door?" Immediately everyone recognised Trotter's demeanour.

"Comin'," yelled Porky as he strode towards the door.

Dan relaxed and pulled the billy and utensils out from under the table. Porky opened the door and Trotter walked in. Trotter was still dressed in his tradie's clothes. His top and shorts looked like they had been wiped over by Andy Warhol's paintbrush a few times. He was an abstract masterpiece. He was also drenched with sweat which indicated how hot the day was outside.

"Goin' to Ads's in a coupla weeks?" asked Dan.

"You could at least ask me if I want a billy first before you start talking about sumthin' fucken else!" Trott had worked the morning outside in the hot sun on some terrace house in Paddo and not being too fond of work, like the rest of the boys, was glad it was finished for the day.

"Sorry, mate, how rude of me." Dan packed him a cone and promptly passed it over. "Here ya go, mate. Get that into yer."

"Cheers, Dan." Trott didn't waste any time and smashed it like his life depended on it. "So I heard Ads's havin' a BBQ next comin' up, aye?" he said in a slightly squeaky voice as thick smoke bellowed from his lungs.

"Yep."

"Well, I suppose I'd better get my amp fixed that I blew last night, aye." He slammed the bong down on the coffee table, rolling his head around from the dizzy spell that had engulfed him. He pulled up a bit of carpet to plonk his disorientated body down on.

"Shit, yeah !Ads's is going to go off! I'm so keen to offend the new neighbours." Brad was a huge supporter for the cause of playing and creating havoc especially if it meant sticking it up yuppies who had just moved into the area. Garage cum gutter music at its best, at its most underground, with a bunch of drunk blokes slagging and spewing themselves into local cult status. The reverb equalled any filthy seismic activity rocking Bondi.

"Yeah, well, Curl and I are going to have a jam this week in Ads's garage with Mikey and Brad ..." He turned to Brad who was packing himself a billy and delayed finishing his sentence until he had Brad's attention, "that's if Brad wants to show up!" Brad had failed to show up to rehearsal the arvo before and Trot wasn't happy.

Ads's garage so happened to be "Stiff Arms" jamming room and his barbies were a great place to go ballistic. The boys always dug Brad's fat bass whilst Mikey B smashed away at the well-worn drum kit. A new recruit, Curl, accompanied Trott on guitar. He was a good mate of Trott's from Newcastle. He resembled a Teddy boy, rode single fins and loved getting off guts, so he went down well with the Bondi brethren. He loved playing rockabilly and added another dimension to the band. His hair was always slicked back like Elvis and he was always wearing sneakers and a flanno. He had only lived in the 'hood for a short while but being a friendly guy who surfed well meant he was well liked.

Brad blew out his billy smoke with the words, "Sorry, Trott, I got stuck in the Cross with some fuckin' weirdo."

"Yeah, well, don't fuck us around again. We had the room booked at Newtown so it cost us and who do you think had to fuckin' pay!" Fair enough Trott was pissed off. Occasionally the band would head into Newtown to use a sound studio in King Street for a bit of fine tuning and for four proud working class bums it was expensive for the privilege.

"You guys want to play at the 'Bergs for the preso at the end of the year?" asked Dan.

"Yeah, for sure. Were you gonna ask someone else?"

"Nah, and I know it's a long way off but I just wanted to make sure you aren't on a world tour or somethin'."

"Is the Pope Catholic? I mean, does Oz dog shit in the shop?"

"Not any more, not after I rubbed her face in it and threw her for six enough times."

"Yeah, of course. We'll just have to ask Lofty and the boys when it gets a bit closer but it should be sweet," replied Trotter. "We've probably got a few gigs there before then anyway."

"For sure."

The week was turning out to be a slow one. No waves meant the boys were bored shitless. As always, there was whatever you wanted to indulge in staring menacingly in your face. This led to results that were hard to comprehend at times. Like pinballs being flicked into the game of chance, people came and then were suddenly gone before you knew it. Even guys who had lived in the area for donkey's would vanish in the blink of an eye and the stories of where they went or what happened varied so much you'd usually be none the wiser. The boys kept tight and knew just to keep moving. Drug overdoses, murders, runaway tactics, kidnaps, extortion and the like took its toll on the "Valley". The bottle was constantly in a spin and you never knew if it would stop and point at you. The smart ones tried early to gauge their limitations but no-one could really ever predict their fate—there was no crystal ball and sometimes your number just came up without warning. For that was the life the fast lane dished up and nobody was willing to have it any other way!

Dan sat in his shop reading *Tracks*, the surfer's bible. It was the *Tracks* of old, resembling the *Sydney Morning Herald* in looks and texture. It was always a great read back then, filled with colourful stories, characters and plenty of readers' feedback. It was an ongoing melting pot revolving around surfing discussion, debate and predictions, cutting edge in sub-cultural thinking and design and sprinkled with the added spice of comedy with Captain Goodvibes and Lash Clone serving up abrupt, derogatory lessons on surf, sex and life and not necessarily in that order. Actually, Mary Jane from Newtown met Lash Clone at Bondi in 84 and she believed he was "very charming". She posted this in *Tracks*

243

herself that same year describing Lash as a suave, sexy gentleman to which all editorial staff could only take a back seat. "Making Kempes and Carroll seem tired," she revealed. One could only wonder what the editorial staff thought of such remarks but it is a great example of the freedom of speech and unbiased content of the *Tracks* of old. There were always a few copies of "the bible" in the dunny out back of the shop and the boys got full value out of it by using it for toilet paper if there was no Sorbent.

All of a sudden, like an intruder in your face, a squeaky, clean cut, Brylcream-combing, puppy-faced kid was standing in front of his counter wanting his attention. Dan turned the music down and before he could get a word out the kid slammed a Bible down on top of the glass and asked if he wanted to buy one.

"Go easy, mate, that's real glass. Cost me a lot of money ..." Dan could only start the conversation off with a joke, after all he kinda hoped the kid had a sense of humour, because by the time Dan had got through with him he was gonna need one.

"I can sell you insurance for that counter, or if it gets broken I can offer you a loan for a new one. I'm not only a Christian who spreads the word of Jesus but I'm a bank clerk and insurance broker as well."

Dan instantly thought this guy was Satan himself. A self-righteous, God-fearing, insurance peddling, banking thief. "Well fucken aye, let me just come over that side of the counter so you can fist me!"

"Excuse me, sir, but I don't think that language is appropriate."

"Oh, really?" Dan turned his head around from one side to the other as if he was looking for somebody else in the room. "Well, I can't see anyone that looks as though they own the shop so maybe the person who owns it is ..."—he paused for a sec—"me."

"You don't look as though you could possibly own this shop," said the Christian.

"Why's that?"

"Well, you smell of pot, look like something the cat dragged in and swear like a welfare cheat."

"Well, one thing I can say about you, mate, is that you're good at descriptions, but unfortunately this rude, stoned pussy owns the fuckin' shop so you'd better hightail it outta here before I stone yer to death."

"You really need a reality check, mister."

"Please call me Dan the fucking Atheist."

"OK, Dan." The punk was amazingly prudent in the face of danger, not that Dan would go to town on such a spiffy, skinny clown but his bulletproof Jesus vest gave the kid bigger balls than what one would think his clean, mummy-ironed, white undies could contain. "But you won't go to heaven not believing."

"I believe, mate, believe that you shouldn't be waltzin' in here and carrying on!"

"But I'm offering you salvation."

"You're peddling shit and offering me dollars, and if my memory serves me correctly Christians aren't supposed to lend money!"

"What do you mean in saying that, Dan?"

Dan let a bit of his Christian history studies at Waverley College's library come to the fore. "Well, Christians aren't supposed to lend money, ummm, what was your name?" It wasn't the first time he'd used this denouncing strategy on a Christian, and it wouldn't be the last!

"Peter."

"Yeah, well, you ain't supposed to lend cash, Peter." He paused again. "You're not 'Peter the Puller', are you?"

"Stop being vague and insolent, sir."

"It's Danel to you, like Danel Boone was a man."

"OK, Daniel."

"Danel."

"Yes, OK. However you want to pronounce it."

"Danel."

"OK, I said ..." "Skinny boy" was getting a little frustrated. "Can you clarify your former statement about how I'm not in a position to lend you money? I help with loans at the State Bank every weekday so please elaborate."

"Why do you think 'Shylock' was a Jew in the *Merchant of Venice*?"

"Gee whiz, that's going back a bit. You can hardly expect me to know that ..."

"Well, Mr Smart Fuck, it was because Christians were never meant to lend money. It's in your fucken Bible, mate, if you cared to read it properly."

"Such language ..." He fidgeted with his Bible for a moment. "OK, here's some of your own back then." He put his best angry head on and fired away, "You're full of shit!"

"Well, go and wash your mouth out with soap and water right now, you naughty little boy!"

"How dare you think you know anything about Christianity and the Bible!"

"Actually, I was just reading *Tracks* before you came in and started preaching shit to me."

"Well, get your facts straight. Christians are people worthy of lending money, we are fair and honest ..."

Dan cut in. "Fuckers! Fair and honest fuckers, that's what you are! You should read a bit about Christian history before you pledge allegiance to such a paltry religion. Going to sleep during mass ain't a good enough reason to call yourself a do-gooder!"

"What would you know about religion? You've probably never been to church in your whole life."

"And never want to! Fuckin' hypocrites, all o' you! All religion sucks!"

"Please explain?"

"Where do you want me to start? You're a banker, right?"

"Yes."

"And you charge interest?"

"Of course. That's what bankers do."

"In 1179 The Lateran Council ex-communicated Christians who lent money with interest and throughout your religion this practice was heeded as taboo." Dan had always been dirty at the Brothers at the "college on the mount" and had searched the school libraries especially to get some wood on them. He liked throwing this mud on anyone who asked for it and this skinny lad who was a mile up Jesus' bum deserved a drenching.

He looked a little unnerved from this unexpected serving. "What atheist told you this?"

"You think anyone who calls your bluff is a kook, pal? Your loan interest payments were detested by the Franciscan and Dominican orders, and those Christians who fucked up were thrown out of the paedophile club. Now stuff that in yer pipe, ya fuckin' naïve idealist."

"That was obviously a long time ago if at all what you say is true, and times have obviously changed."

"Oh, sure, Mr Puller, get your hand off yer cock ..."

"Excuse me, please refrain from cursing. It doesn't credit the conversation."

"Oh, right. Christians are nice caring people, right?"

"Of course they are. We make solemn affirmation that Jesus was the son of God and that his benevolent ways and the Ten Commandments are our enlightenment."

"Then why the fuck did Christian crusaders slaughter Muslims and the like in their mission to plunder precious metals all over eastern Europe? Can you tell me that one?"

"You're quite a moron, you know."

"They killed and ripped everyone off to take all the shit back to the church's hierarchy, all in the name of the big fella, God!"

"You really are deluded."

At that moment Trotter waltzed in sideways like a twisted demon on acid, sidestepping imaginary shaped shadows, like a strange Monty Python caricature. Maybe he thought he was in a scene of "The Meaning of Life". He had been catching Mr Skinny Runt's Bible-babbling rave at the doorway where he had eavesdropped enough for him to want to do some of his own pummelling. He rose up behind the kid like a genie manifesting from thin air after a few hundred years trapped in a bottle and blurted, "See the guy's throat that your talking to? Well, he calls it his cock highway!"

"Oh my goodness!" shrieked the square brainwashed punk. He was now copping it from the front and behind.

"Getting sandwiched now, are we, aye, Peter?" Dan's words rang out like a church bell summoning the townsfolk that they were in danger.

"Kinda like a coupla priests giving little Johnny some from both ends, aye, Petey?"

"My goodness, you two are in serious need of salvation." Peter was now starting to sweat. A lonesome angel in a bunker full of hell. "No religion is perfect but Christianity does serve as a good vehicle to praise God and our wellbeing on this planet!"

"Yeah, good point, Pete. What time do you want to meet me at the dunnies?"

"You will burn in hell, Dan, and no-one is going to help you!"

"Don't know about that, Petey boy. Hollywood George might be able to ... actually, he reckons he can get VIP tickets for upstairs. What about you, Peter? Can't ya have a word to the big fella for me? Or at least his offsider who polishes his pearly gates? C'mon ... just for me, mate ... can't ya scam one for us? I mean, you sound like you're in his good books!"

"For both of us, Petey boy?" Trott threw in. "I mean, it sounds

247

like you've got a few gold stars next to ya name. You've given him a few tugs!"

"I will vow to say a prayer for you both and can only hope that God pities your disbelief and blasphemy."

"That's very big of you, mate," said Trott. "Public dunny is down towards the 'Bergs. See you there in five!"

The beat-up kid headed for the door—he'd finally had enough.

"And I hope you're wearing your 'crucify me' undies." The kid almost turned around in despair to stage one last protest but knew it was best to keep walking. "Yeah, so I can bring me hammer and give ya a good fucking nailing! Now, fuck off!"

Speed Bump

Dan was wandering down near central on George Street doing a bit of window browsing after a feed of Laksa at a delicious Indian eatery the boys would patronise at times. It was a benefit living close to the CBD that the guys relished. There was always a new and tantalising restaurant popping up around the city somewhere and it was inevitable that it wouldn't be long till word was out after its discovery. On this particular day he happened to pass a hock shop and noticed the 7'6" Brewer gun that he'd lent Alex a couple of years back smack bang in front of his face. It was propped up against the window with a price tag of 200 bucks dangling from a piece of string that had been taped onto the rail.

"What the fuck!" he spat out as his mind projected visions of punching Alex unexpectedly in the face. His blood started boiling and he felt flushed. Not only was he angry at his cousin's impiety but he cursed the fact that he'd been so desperate he'd sold it for a fraction of what it was worth. Sure it had been a couple of years or so, and he'd kinda known that he was probably never going to see the board again, but the way it was staring him in the face, with its fine almost sensuous curved rails in a shitty pawn shop, was somewhat stirring to say the least. Like a long-lost girlfriend bare, exposed and propped up like a sleazy hooker in Darlinghurst, he felt anguished. He went inside and tried to reason with the guy behind the counter that it was stolen but the guy just fobbed him off and said, "That's not my problem."

He promptly headed back to the shop to ring up his aunt and see if he could locate his misfit for a cousin. "Hello, Aunty Maureen. Yeah, it's Dan here. How are you?"

The formal "how you doing?" and "how's life treating you" questions bounced backwards and forwards until Dan thought it appropriate to ask, "So, have you seen Alex lately?"

There was a moment's silence followed by, "He's inside."

Terrific thought Dan he could now have a word with his boofy cousin and vent some of his anger, "Great, Aunty Maureen. Can you call him so I can have a chat with him? You know, it's been a while and ..."

His words were cut short. "No. I mean, he's inside the clink."

"Oh shit. I didn't know that. Is he OK? How long's he been in there?"

"A little while now, Dan, but he's just the same. Just another chapter in his colourful life. You know, someone should write a book about him."

"Yeah. It'd be a whacky read, I reckon." He'd promptly calmed down the displeasure within. Payback was already upon Alex—he didn't have to do anything, though he knew jail was generally never too hard for menacing Alex. He had a lot of mates in there and would still be up to his mischief which was what he thrived on. It suddenly dawned on him what he'd just said and hoped his aunt didn't misinterpret it as him having a go at his cousin for whackin' it in his arm once too often. "I mean, he is pretty silly at times!"

"I've always wanted to write a book about what happens over this way, Daniel. You know all these 'Bra Boys' are a wild bunch. I mean, have you heard about Big Lee biting the head off that poor little budgie down the Seals Club?" Dan tried not to laugh. Lee was a mate of Dan's and his bird-chomping episode had become folklore in the history of Aussie east-coast surfing. In front of a few hundred patrons the big fella pulled out a budgie on stage and put Alice Cooper's blood curdling show to shame. "And that 'spit the winky' thing ..."

"Spit the Winkle, Aunty Maureen."

"Yes, that's it. Well, oh my God, I was driving down past the Northie car park the other day and there was Lee's younger brother Barrie perched on top of a car, and I thought what's he doing up there? I slowed down and saw a hose or something and then he bent over and started spraying excrement over the car behind me!"

"His reputation's sure is growing, Aunty Maureen!"

"What? As a bum sprayer? Heavens, Dan, no wonder Alex is twisted hanging out with blokes like these."

"They're actually pretty nice blokes, Aunty Maureen, and surf really well."

"Tell that to the person who was driving the car behind me. I mean it was a nice, new looking, white Corolla."

"I heard the spotty poo look was in these days ..."

"Oh Dan, I just hope they had their passenger window up."

They both had a chuckle. It was hard not to laugh at Aussie off-beat humour. Paul Hogan, Aunty Jack and Norman Gunston all had it down to a tee. The boys were just emulating their heroes.

"Well, where is Alex? I'll have to go and visit him."

250

"He's up north in Grafton lock-up. A mate of his, that Johnny, yes that Johnny, well, he got done with some hard drugs and they had my phone bugged and Alex tried to leg it and that's as far as he got."

"Yeah, he's got a few mates up there, hasn't he, Aunty Maureen?"

"Smackies, all of them, I know he's not an angel but I know he's not a thieving junkie and see ... see what happens when ya start hangin' out with lowlifes!"

"Oh, I'm sorry to hear all this ..."

"Well, don't be. What's done is done, but I'm sure he'd love ya to visit him at some stage. He's probably been in there a couple of months now.Just wish he was in Long Bay. Be a lot easier for me to pop in and see him."

"Yeah, sure." Dan drew a deep breath. "Well, OK. then, and don't hesitate to give us a ring if you need anything and if you talk to Alex ask him to call the shop." Dan hesitated for a second. "Actually, don't ask him to do that. Best if I send him a letter and drop in next surftrip I'm up at Angourie."

"That sounds good, Dan." She paused briefly. "And Dan, please don't tell everyone, I mean. Like, don't tell your mum and that. He's only in for 6 months and he'll be out soon enough."

"Mum's the word—oops!" Both of them had a little chuckle. "Actually, it's not the word. I'll just shut my mouth, Aunty Maureen."

"God bless you, love."

"Talk soon, Aunty."

"Bye."

"Bye."

Dan knew of the notorious Johnny. He was a mate from over Bronte way who had fallen into bad habits during the 80s. He was a good mate of Alex's and the infamous standover brute TK and they caused quite a bit of havoc together. Some guys wore balaclavas but these kinda guys basked in the criminal celebrity status that came with not wearing one. A distinguished reputation, you might say.

Johnny had always been a good surfer and his absence in the line-up was noticeable over the last few years. He was a streetwise knockabout guy. Six feet tall and well built. He was out of your typical 70s surfer mould with flowing shoulder length sun bleached locks and a definition that made the girls go weak. Being bred at Bronte Beach he was a keen surfer throughout his childhood. He competed in the local boardriders with Storm and Jay Carter, the Millar brothers, Reg, Gaza, Cronk, Chunky and the rest of the hardcore boys during the 70s, and usually made the finals. Behind his clown-like smile he was a very smart individual. He had a dry humour about him that had to be admired, for it made fun of the dark and desperate. He'd seen most things from the inside out. Been there, done that or at least tried not to do that, so as you can imagine most things didn't faze him. He could therefore negligently make fun of crass situations. His education at the school on the mount, Waverley College, obviously hadn't gone to waste. As when having to apply himself during his earlier years, and one could only wonder what he might have achieved in life if he had ever taken it seriously. Being a beach bum at heart, it wasn't long before he was dismissed for a renegade by his teachers and the label non-conformist sat well with him so he jigged school every chance he got—a rebel enjoying the lifestyle of the sand, surf and sun. It was only a matter of time till he'd meet the disreputable wheelers and dealers hanging about the periphery of the beach. He was quick-witted and adept at talking the talk and for those reasons he was an attractive partner to the many criminals in the area. He was a tall foreboding man with a cheesy grin and hard features depicting the intimidating manner he was capable of when needed. His physique was now understandably a bit on the lighter side from when he was clean and at his surfing zenith in his younger years.

However, the new decade hadn't brought any reason to change his evil ways. 1990 might have signalled a new enlightened beginning to many but Johnny's life was heading directly to jail—do not pass "go" and do not collect two hundred dollars. You see, he hadn't been caring about anyone's salvation, let alone his own, and had blindly headed into another one of life's many speed humps. The misery of being a heroin addict didn't help, either.

A few months before, he'd been travelling between Sydney and the North Coast which was a haven for people wandering aimlessly through life. It could hardly be called soul-searching though one wanders usually with some kind of plan in mind. During this particular time in his life a more sinister intention of ripping off a good crop that someone had worked tediously and secretly to bring to fruition was on his mind. The buds he stumbled upon he found smack-bang in the middle of a sugar cane plantation outside Grafton. The sale proceeds supported his misery and provided a bank to help him delve into the sale of heroin. It wasn't long till he was doing a rip-roaring trade. His operation was simple. Upon purchasing the product in Sydney he would drive up the coast capitalising on anyone sharing the same problem. On a couple of trips Alex, and his other Bondi hoodrat TK, would head up to enjoy the small trip away and get stoned together. Being brothers in crime the boys loved each other's company, especially when things were going well. They had an uncanny knack of covering each other's arses as soon as their cracks starting exposing themselves.

On contemplating a solo trip to Coffs Harbour Johnny took the privilege of flying up since he didn't like driving that far from Sydney by himself. Back in the day domestic air-flight didn't have the scrutiny or security as we know now after George Bush's war on drugs so travelling in the sky with merchandise was common. The banana plantations greeted the descending craft and Johnny smiled on touchdown. It was all so easy. He rang his anxious client from a payphone near the airport and set up the transaction. Unbeknown to him he was also being set up. To him the business with the customer seemed to go as planned. He dropped off the merchandise, collected the agreed amount in crispy redbacks and had a friendly hit with his sycophant. A desperate addict will always talk up to his dealer. Flattery will sometimes put more in the spoon and Johnny, being only human, liked what he was hearing and obliged. The hit was so big that both men tried valiantly not to nod off. Time passed quickly and Johnny awoke to find his mate snoring through clenched teeth. It was a lovely day outside and by looking at the sun he knew if he didn't get an act together quickly he'd miss the late afternoon return flight. Grabbing the landline he made a call to a "ho" named Debbie, who was his squeeze at the time, so she could pick him up around 6pm from Mascot domestic terminal. He tried in vain to wake his mate who wasn't budging for anyone, so he grasped his backpack and headed outside in haste to hail a lift to the airport.

Upon arriving back in Sydney, Debbie ,who he used to refer as his "juice extractor", was waiting with open veins in her arms. She was also keen for him to go and see his mate Phil who he had to cut the money with. She was a typical parasite and wanted some money from the proceeds so she could go shopping. They drove to a close-by residence in Botany and Debbie was told to stay in the car while he went inside and divided the loot. On counting the cash it came up short so Johnny got back on the phone to his Coffs client and started spitting out all sorts of incriminating verbal.

The D.E.A. were happy with their new evidence on Johnny and moved in on him 3 weeks later when he was chilling at a friend's house west of Macksville. So with the phone tap tape in hand the police took him to court where a different hammer came crashing down with a big thud. Three years with a minimum of two, possibly a little shorter depending on his behaviour whilst serving his time.

Another chapter closed in Johnny's life and a new one started as he was whisked away to Cessnock Prison in the back of a meat wagon. It wasn't a new experience for him so he didn't feel apprehensive in what was in store. He sat quietly in the back of the steel mobile cell with his mind ticking over about what he could and should have done to avoid capture. Pulling up in front of the gates he felt a sudden depression. It had taken a while but the loss of freedom had finally sunk in ... again. As he passed through the welcoming, sniggering guards he remembered his last stint inside and braced himself for the change of culture.

"Ah, inside again, where the dumbest are the toughest and the smart stay quiet." Nothing changes in confinement.

Three weeks into his time and he innocently walked into a cell only to see an acquaintance stuffing stolen clothes into the back cavity of his TV set. The prisoner was a stupid motherfucker taking risks that could ultimately lead to leaving the facility in a wooden box. This particular wannabe was on his way to Bathurst after giving a dirty urine sample two weeks prior so he knew he wouldn't be sticking around for any investigation to find him guilty. He thought taking a few inmates' clothes before his departure was a simple exercise. Thieving anything inside was not a healthy practice. Unfortunately for Johnny, another prisoner walked past seconds later and saw the two of them in the room. Fuckwit hadn't quite finished closing the secret compartment and it looked as though both of them were in on the act.

It was another instance of being in the wrong place at the wrong time.

Before John's arrival at Cessnock he was told by Alex to say "Hi" to a man named "the Bull" but, only being there a couple of weeks, he hadn't got around to doing it yet. He'd been occupied in coming down, basically dealing with the wreck that he'd become. Alex had got to know "the Bull" through Dan and his old man, Ted, who was one of the biggest punters in Australia. Ted was a larger-than-life character and used to rub shoulders with all walks of life at the city and provincial racing tracks. "The Bull" had become good mates with him over the years and was indebted to Ted for all the winners he'd tipped him. As Ted was a family man he kept at arm's length from most of the hardened criminals, but he didn't mind their presence and was happy to help if he could without getting too involved. "The Bull" was an underworld figure linked to the disappearance of several people and as much as Ted liked him he knew watching the horses parading was about as close as he wanted to get. Ted knew it was smarter to keep his distance, because like most of the questionable identities that frequented the racecourse if you got too close sooner or later they were asking you for favours that could wind you up in a lot of trouble.

"The Bull" was well-connected with the 50s, 60s and 70s old school and grew up good mates with the Italian mafia that ran all the baccarat in the city and up at the Cross. He was so connected he met Dan Testa, the first US mafia killer that landed on Aussie soil in 64, courtesy of his killer contractors. It wasn't so surprising, then, that his best mate was a loaded gun. He was smart and, like most organised crime figures, protected by keeping company with both sides of the law, including influential detectives. A couple of close personal badges were Derek Robertson and Freddy Brown who were always being mentioned in books and High Commissions.

Dan had struck a chord with him as a young grommet whilst running around race tracks for his dad. "The Bull" had taken a liking to a young well-mannered Dan and had even mentioned that if he ever got into trouble to give him a ring and "he'd sort it out". Dan had introduced Alex to him at the beach when they bumped into him one sunny day whilst he was training with one of Sydney's first personal trainers, George Daldry, on the soft sand. Being Dan's cousin meant Alex was immediately on good terms. Alex had then trained a couple of times with Dan and "the Bull" in the CBD at the City Tatts club. It was here, during the week, that George trained his faithful line-up of professional sportsmen, detectives, hardened crims and anyone connected with this tight circle of influential Sydney folk. He didn't settle for

255

second best and he pushed everyone to their limits who had the guts to train with him. Needless to say Alex gave it away fairly quickly—the 45-floor stairwell run against the clock just about killed him.

Any smaller time crim had the utmost respect for "the Bull" as he'd already done the hard yards and was where they wanted to be. However anyone who had crossed his path figured quickly that they also had to be very wary. He was a figure who walked with plenty of intent and in the underworld notoriety was the essence.

Alex knew "the Bull" was in Cessnock when Johnny was sentenced and knew he'd be connected and probably running the joint. It was only natural to pass on such handy information to his mate. He'd always been in awe of "the Bull" and knew if Johnny dropped his, or Dan's, name especially, that he'd take an instant liking to him.

Word travelled quickly and it wasn't long till everyone knew the story about the two thieves and their cavity in the telly. Johnny had tried telling someone the real story but it wasn't quick enough and the wannabe was transferred to Bathurst leaving Johnny behind to face the music.

His wing of the jail was three floors high and the shape of a quadrangle. Being on the top floor Johnny could peek over the railing and watch the bowel movements of the jail. He was dead certain that it was just a matter of time till he had to deal with his fate and face a hostile jury.

So one afternoon he was called into a room across from his cell on the opposite landing. Inside were six of the jail heavies playing cards. To Johnny it was obvious that the reason behind his summons was the chance to explain his, what seemed beyond doubt to them, guilty actions. Anxiety of the consequences had small beads of sweat accumulating on the hairline of his forehead. No matter what he said it wasn't going to steer them off their purpose to cause him grievous bodily harm.

And so proceeded the most violent bashing you could imagine. As he groped and pleaded his innocence, all six men whaled into him with fists, elbows and feet. He tried desperately not to drop and covered his head with his arms. The more he resisted the more berserk the mob attacked. Johnny was by no means a slouch even with his indulgent heroin habits, so he could fend them off to a degree, but the onslaught became so intense he slumped onto the floor. With a prying eye, through an opening slit between his shielding fingers, he saw the rope to be used in tying him up. He was a fighter and used all his hard-earned defensive skills while they struggled to tie him up. The sight of a pair of pliers generally used in "the can" to cut off people's fingers conjured a survival mode from deep within his spirit. He wanted to yell but needed every bit of energy to fend off the onslaught. He kicked out at the pliers and they dropped on the ground in front of him. In a miraculous chain of events he lashed out again heeling them under an adjoining door which was the entrance to a smaller room where cleaning utensils such as mops and brooms were stored. His luck continued as the sinister weapon became wedged. The attackers couldn't retrieve it for the life of them or the possible death of Johnny. After gallantly taking as much as his body could handle the brave, innocent victim started losing consciousness. They continued their FA Cup kicking finishing him off with the odd vertical stomp.

Awakening a short time later he managed to grasp the situation of what had just occurred and with his never-say-die attitude realised he had to hastily get back to his cell. His welcoming party had vanished and there was only one coconut standing at the door. Johnny actually made it to his feet but the coconut put an end to that by king-hitting him and dropping him back on the cold, concrete floor. Amazingly he didn't black out. With blood leaking out from every orifice and possible fractures he lifted himself off the slab and commenced crawling on his bloodied hands and knees back to his own four walls. There was urgency in his efforts and fortunately for him his cell was on the same level.

As he dragged his beaten body along on its miserable journey he received assorted kicks and blows from anyone interested in venting their own disapproval. Every movement made him wince. The pain factor was excessive and all he could do was bear it and try to breathe. It was excruciating as his ribs were surely cracked or broken. The pain signals to his brain receptors were overloaded and his body was now in uncharted waters. He didn't know whether he would live to see another day.

A screw locked him in his cell thinking he was OK and didn't require any special treatment. Johnny lay horizontal in a state of painful uncertainty. His khaki greens felt starchy, rigid, as though they were at attention, and made his resting state even more uncomfortable. Time ticked by as if he was in some bad dream. He heard voices—they were ushered in and out of his mind by some kind of mad keeper that had taken up residence within him. "Don't you hear them calling, Johnny? You're a dead motherfucker. They're gonna kill you, kill you good!"

A while later he heard his cell being opened and a few more screws arriving to escort him to hospital. His injuries were going to require a lot of medical treatment and the authorities didn't want him dying while he was still their responsibility. After stitching his head and face up and taking some initial X-rays, the hospital wanted to leave him in overnight. They wanted to do further tests on some heavy bruising around his skull and were still suss on some of his rib damage. The screws had other ideas and wanted him back in jail for some interrogation to find out what happened and who was involved. As a sign of integrity to his fellow inmates he gave no-one up. He then astonished the guards by refusing to go into protection. He knew he was a target but he was no dog and he opted to take the long shot in with the mob and clear his name.

He was then told to sign a waiver after refusing to go into protection, withdrawing the state from any responsibility in case he was maimed or killed the next day. Johnny was going back into hell, for in his mind he knew he was innocent. He was in the right and he felt compelled to act and stand up for himself.

He was accompanied back to his bunk, flanked by guards who thought they may as well be carrying a coffin. As he awkwardly hobbled back to his prison residence he was subjected to cat calls and death threats from above, below and anywhere else that his ears could tune into the crazed abuse. As he reached his lonely cell all he could do was lie down on his bed and try to tolerate the constant throbbing all over his body.

He awoke the next morning blind, both eyes completely shut from the massive swelling his face and skull was experiencing. The entity within was bordering on insanity—it seemed like he was about to lose his worried mind. He was hoping someone would be smiling on him that day and the rat pack might leave him alone. He was hoping that they were thinking that the pure hell of nursing his severe injuries was enough punishment for the moment. At least till he was feeling a bit better ... then they'd probably think it would be appropriate to hurt him some more. Drag things out a bit—after all, everyone had plenty of time on their hands and they weren't going anywhere in a hurry. Measuring the day would be hard. He felt it slipping into grey and clung on.

The bang from the screws to wake each inmate up and unlock their doors was getting closer and he contemplated what the new day was going to administer. Being on the top floor his cell was pretty much the last to be opened and he knew other inmates were already outside walking around. He felt like he was bleeding in a pool of sharks who had nothing but going in for the kill in mind. The first click of his cell door had an old Bondi mate Mick entering and protecting him from any incoming prisoners who wanted to earn some respect. You see, in jail you get judged for what you're in for. Not many criminals gain respect on the outside so they generally try to find it on the inside. Killing a supposed dog—thief—gains you a lot of brownie points. They would be lining up to put Johnny out of his misery.

Mick naturally wanted to know what was going on. They were old partners in crime who had started their careers together back on the "Mount". Johnny managed to string a few sentences together telling his old mate that he was innocent and wanted to see the man they called "the Bull". There were a couple of inmates circling outside and Mick had to make sure JC wasn't stabbed before he had returned. Fortunately "the Bull's" cell was only a few doors down from Johnny's so it wouldn't take Mick long to fetch him. As he exited the narrow doorway he mentioned to the thugs outside not to touch Johnny as he was getting "the Bull" to deal with this. It was enough to make them slightly hesitant and delay sticking the knife in the bedridden victim. As they observed him lying still and defenceless they asked him what he was still doing there. They obviously were trying to work out why he hadn't sought protection. As JC started mumbling they peered over their shoulder in anticipation of "the Bull" arriving. He didn't disappoint and was there within seconds with Mick and the coconut who king hit JC winging it behind him.

As "the Bull" stood outside the cell door he gave the two intruders the icy-cold and they both fucked off. He told Mick and his Islander mate to wait outside and he made his entry. JC didn't want to look up but managed to gauge a shape through his crusty slits for eyes. It seemed large and he only hoped it wasn't a big galoot ready to pummel him again. The rounded figure moved towards him and all he could do was wait in anticipation of what might happen next.

"You wanted to see me, son?" came a deep voice. He could hear an inquisitive nature about this person that was missing from any of the inmates that he'd previously tried to describe his innocence to.

Johnny couldn't really move much but he did manage to raise his head slightly and mumble, "If you're the man they call 'Bull' then yeah, I did ..."

"What you want to disturb me for, son?" The large-framed shape sat down on a stool near him. He sat sideways like a priest in a confessional box about to listen to someone outpouring their sins. "Blokes have died for less."

"I was told to say hello to you ..." Johnny grimaced as he tried in vain to sit up somewhat.

"Stay down, son. You look as though you need to." There was a slight pause as Johnny rested his bruised and broken head back down on the bloodstained pillow. "So who is it exactly that sent their greetings?"

Johnny flashed on one of his favourite on-screen scenes. The deep lament in "the Bull's" voice, his powerful aura, his demeanour and positioning resembled the scene in "Apocalypse Now" when Brando is seated in profound conversation with a defenceless Martin Sheen. He could only hope he was to experience vindication along the same lines that was delivered by Brando in the movie.

"Young Dan from Bondi and his cousin Alex, sir."

"Are you serious, son?" "The Bull" turned his head and was now staring at the helpless beat-up messy shell of a man that Johnny could have been passed as. "Why didn't you speak up earlier? I mean, if your a friend of young Dan then I hope you haven't done the shit that has everyone in the joint hot on yer."

"I didn't do it."

"I hope you're telling the truth ..."

"Why would I wanna walk into this hole again without protection if I did it? ... Ahhhh ..." Johnny was speaking too quick for his dented face to deal with. His facial muscles were still dark purple and cramping on occasions.

"OK, son, slow down a bit." He observed a cup with some water in it on the floor. "Here, have a sip of this water." "The Bull" reached over and lifted a nearby cup to his swollen lips. "Slow, now." Johnny took a small gulp and coughed as the H_2O slid down his sore, dry throat. It was as if his passageway had snubbed the action of even trying to put anything down there.

"So, you're trying to tell me that you didn't do it and you've come back in here to try and clear your name when you know you could be killed without a fucken question asked?"

"Yes, sir."

"Don't call me 'sir'; that shits me. 'Bull' is just fine."

"OK, 'Bull'."

"That's better." "Bull's" face had started smiling while, behind it, his jail-weary brain was ticking over. He was liking what he was hearing. "You are either one dumb motherfucker or a brave man with big balls."

Johnny grimaced but had to spit out "The second one" quickly as to seize the moment before "the Bull' might continue his sentence.

"Are you for real, son?" "The Bull" paused as he had to pass judgement on what had happened first before he could get too carried away with the newcomer. "OK, then, take your time. But I want you to explain to me why you're not the thief everyone thinks you are."

Johnny did take his time but went into explicit detail of the sequence of events that went down that fateful day. He didn't have to act or plead to convince "the Bull"; it was as plain as day to him that Johnny was innocent. "And that's the truth, 'Bull'. I'm no low thief, not inside anyway. I've been inside enough to know the rules."

"Well, I have no reason to doubt you and from now on you are gonna be doing time easy, boy. And what's more being a friend of Dan and ah ... what's his cousin's name again?"

"Alex."

"Yeah, well, being a friend of theirs is gold, mate, because young Dan's old man had a lot of time for me at the track back in the day and Dan's a great kid."

"I used to surf with him lots." Johnny coughed again. He tried to clear his throat from what felt like a bit of coagulated blood then continued. "I'm from Bronte and used to surf the southside beaches with him."

"Did you know his uncle played for the Roosters?"

"Sure did, 'Bull'—one of the best hookers in the 70s," spluttered the curled fetus shape on top of the bed.

"Fuckin' oath! I used to watch many a game at the 'Sportground' and 'Cricket Ground' and he was a great tackler. And you know he could win a ball ... you know young Dan was a hooker for McCaulay and Waverley and his uncle Paul used to coach him a bit. He's a good kid, young Dan. I'm happy you

brought his greetings with you—he was a good little player too!"
"Bull" was really enjoying Johnny's company now. To think he
was a surfing friend of his young mate Dan put a twinkle in his
eye. "I went and saw one of his games down Queen's Park and he
never lost a scrum. I mean, that was back when you actually had
to hook for the ball, not like these days where they just put the
thing in the second row. I mean, what's with that shit?"

"Why bother havin' a scrum ..." came a coarse reply. Johnny
throat was harbouring noxious mucus and other nasties. It would
be a few days yet till he was speaking without pain.

"That's right, son, why do they bother? It was tough back then,
those scrums and that. I mean, guys broke each other's jaws and
got off scot-free and stuff. And what's more they'd have to turn up
to work Monday morning no matter how sore they were! Yep, a
different game these days, son." "Bull" stopped abruptly.
"Actually, what's your name, mate? I don't wanna keep callin'
you son, that's all."

"Johnny."

"Well, you're all right by me, Johnny, and any man who walks
back into this forsaken shithole to prove his innocence against all
odds is a pretty brave man."

"Thanks, 'Bull'."

"Yep, your gonna have a good reputation when I tell the boys
the truth of the matter and I just want you to know that from now
on in here everything's gonna be OK. You just do your time bein'
smart and I'll personally look after ya!"

"Thanks, 'Bull'. Dan said I could count on ya."

"He's from good, hard stock and you're one lucky fella! I'd be
buying him a lottery ticket when you get out—he's just saved you
from the wooden overcoat!"

"I'll be buying him two, mate," winced Johnny.

"Good lad. Now, I'll be on my way and send someone up to
make sure you've got what you need and you're OK. Don't want
any of the gorillas payin' ya a visit before everyone knows the
truth."

"That would be very nice of you, 'Bull'. Mick's a good mate;
he'll look after me."

"Yep, he is a good kid. Certainly saved your arse." "The Bull"
was satisfied; JC was to be OK. "Just tell young Dan his Uncle
'Bull' says hello."

"Sure will, thanks," finished a relieved Johnny.

"The Bull" hopped up from his stool and left the small cell. Johnny's throbbing mind at last was at ease. He tried to open his eyes to get a visual happening but they weren't opening in a hurry. Mick walked in after "the Bull" had given him the "she'll be sweet" thumbs-up and was happy about the outcome.

"You're gonna be OK, big fella," said Mick.

JC managed to let out a faint, "Thanks, mate."

"I'm gonna sit down next to ya here and talk shit to ya until ya fall asleep and then I'm gonna not leave ya alone till everything's back to normal, whether ya like it or not!"

"Thanks, mum," snickered JC, and with that he replaced his mad keeper with a contented one and eventually dozed off—to the sound of Mick's waffle, of course.

Bali Bagus

Fitzy entered Dan's surf shop with a certain mystique about him. It was 10am and the morning light appealed to his imbalanced state of mind as it shimmered on the street-front window. The spangles of the pane sparkled bright and flickered in time with his twitching neurosis. It would seem the stimuli emitted by the sheet of glass held clandestine answers to obscure questions that had never been asked.

As he approached the cluttered counter Dan knew his old mate had been having a rough time of late. The grapevine of Scum Valley moved as fast as the rip at Third Ramp on a big day. Stories rocketed over the Bondi airwaves like an overhead F14 fighter aircraft on Australia Day. There was definitely skill involved when avoiding being wrung out and hung up to dry on this gossip highway and as Fitzy's mental scaffolding seemed to be made of vermicelli he couldn't define any of it, let alone stay clear of it. A recent psychedelic odyssey had made him fair game on the grapevine of late. He'd been sized up like a big buck in the sight of a seasoned hunter. His acid trip had recently run him off the rails, tipping him headfirst into a very shallow sandbank.

"Have you got a job for me, Dan?" Fitzy was straight to the point. He was still messy though he had started the regression back to somewhat normal.

"You keep pulling it together and I'm sure I can promise you something, mate."

"That would be pretty cool."

"Want to see you back in the water, though."

"Of course and I'm back at mum and dad's." He paused slightly as one of his eyelids tried to close on him. "You know, just taking things quietly." He continued as his shutter was held at bay by a virtuous twinkle in his eye that wanted to take back control of his life. "I've been out there for a couple of months and they're pretty stoked I'm comin' good."

"Happy to hear that, Fitz. You know I'd be stoked to have you working here, but as I said, just keep it together and you can probably start next month."

"Thanks, Dan. Knew I could count on you."

"If us Bondi guys stick together none of us will get stuck, now, will we?"

"Uck, yeah!"

Dan liked to think he was always there for any of his mates who needed support and hoped they saw it likewise. His grandfather and dad had drummed into him that you're nothing without your "five eights". His dad once mentioned when Dan was still at school that if he ever heard of Dan dobbing one of his friends in then he would belt " the livin' Christ outta him". Dan's childhood world was full of culture that protected Aussie community values. There was no place for political correctness.

Fitzy had been stuck with a valuable friend of the narcotic kind, the one that sticks with you till your health is shot to pieces, you're stoney broke and you've run out of real friends. He knew it was time to put it all to bed, for the time being at least. Dan could see the pain in Fitz's bloodshot eyes—he was tired of the merry-go-round and wanted his sanity back. That was all Dan needed to know in order to give him a chance of self-redemption. Troopers fell on the frontline but it was the ones who kept getting back up that you had to respect.

Dan's shop had only been opened a few months and his good mate's demise seemed to indicate the first crack in Stirling's supposed bulletproof empire. Fitz had always pulled a lot of clout at the beach and being a hardcore local surfer, good looking and exceptionally talented, he was very well liked. His charisma was a huge asset to Stirling's enterprise as most guys were happy to buy boards and surf gear off him. Being such a smart A student with a modest personality and complementary brazen cutback, he was well respected and it was quite extraordinary to see his metamorphosis into spiritual drug whore after leaving high school. Even though he was fast becoming a veteran at losing his mind, it had been a rough road for him and it had rattled him throughout his youth like a topsy-turvy tinny between "the heads" in a southerly buster.

His family couldn't figure why the cable had snapped inside their incredibly well-liked son but when he commenced coming home "high" at 4am in the morning they knew it wasn't good, especially when he started pulling ice cold INXS vinyl out of the fridge freezer. When questioned as to "why?" he replied, "To keep 'em fresh, of course!" And in doing so he'd whack them straight on and turn the stereo up as loud as it could handle, as if to wake up the whole of North Bondi. It was puzzling as everyone loved him and seemed caught off-guard by his sudden transformation.

He was a gentleman in and out of the water, and as much as his new tripping identity made him a source of entertainment and laughter, it was kinda sad how far he had actually flown over the cuckoo's nest!

He was still managing to work his retail magic at Radford's little shoebox shop; however his quivering twitches had increased and his signature blood vessel in the middle of his forehead was on the rise. It was only a matter of time, tick, tock, tick, tock. It was as if the indulgence and excitement going down nearby in Dan's newly opened domain had provoked his lustful appetite and his mind was more than ready to go on another mindless or mindful adventure, depending how you saw it. He definitely didn't feel comfortable working for Stirling's newly employed staff who seemed to take satisfaction in giving him grief. The untamed rebel within was just biding time waiting for pretty much any reason to lift open the rusting lid on his "paint the town red" tin.

This particular time he'd only started bit by bit. This meant he showed a little discipline eating one trip each day at a time, but soon enough, the growing temptation, and the fact he was freefalling, led him to swallowing the rest of the sheet in one mouthful.

Understandably a spiritual warrior fuelled by drugs eventually wore thin at work. He was a huge asset to his boss but being so bent he wasn't much good to anyone. Obviously, to Stirling, getting rid of him would affect his local credibility but there was nothing else he could do. His main local man was frying in his own fat and his gooey yolk was running everywhere. He had no option but to give him the boot.

Experimenting with drugs, and the amount consumed, is something man has never mastered, let alone a kid from Bondi. Some people become demoralised, others enlightened in an ashram somewhere in Tibet or Byron and others end up in padded cells, for the chemistry between man and substance is purely medical by nature. Drugs affect people differently and lead people down different roads. The road that Fitz was heading down this time out was full of hallucinatory heroes and demons. Half a sheet of acid would take him to the perimeters of the universe and show him things that man was a thousand years away from discovering.

Pretty much to everyone's dismay, things had once again

started falling apart for the curly blond Bondi idol. To him, it was the start of another familiar but surreal astral journey. Exhilarating but perturbing, it was a willing frontal assault on his personal world. A reoccurring encounter of the myriad volumes of "All I know is that I know nothing" that he visited when he felt the urge—a trapeze act aiming higher and higher and rocking the once-solid foundations of his youth.

He'd been living in a first floor unit under Jack Thompson's joint down south on Campbell Parade. It was next to the old Laundromat which was directly opposite the two tall pines on the hill. It was just up the strip from Dan's newly opened shop and only a little stroll further on to the shoebox. He was sharing the unit with Sonny Webster who could see the gaping fissure tearing away at Fitz's thin moist tissue but felt hopeless in trying to help. All he could do was embrace the avatar's world as it entertained him with a kaleidoscope of spiritual madness.

When Sonny mentioned his altering personality he'd blurt, "That's nuthin'! You should see what I'm gonna do next!! Yeeeeewwww!" And then punch cone after cone till the mull bowl was empty and he'd have to go out looking for more. All Dan could do was watch his mate in a constant state of flux, changing from Dr Jekyll to Mr. Hyde at the drop of a hat, and hope things straightened up for him.

Fitzy smeared his "tripping balm" all over Bondi and the rest of the world with gay abandon. And if he didn't make you feel greasy then he could sure make you feel queasy. And if that wasn't enough he could "get on to some of the filth for you". For the world was seemingly revolving around the Zen master and his art of making nonsense. "Sam I Am" had nothing on Fitzy!

Sonny could only look on at the grave situation at hand as the acid took over his mate's consciousness. No-one was going to stop him! Sonny and others tried in vain to make things a bit more normal for him and encourage him to stop the self-destruction, but again he didn't listen to a word they had to say—there was a new vortex for him to explore.

Soon funds dried up. The vibrant guru became extremely attracted to his flatmate's mull bowl. He had found quick salvation in Sonny's benevolence and his lending rate of zero interest on zero payback. It was all good as Sonny couldn't deny himself the experience of living with the irresistible flower child even if he had to sponsor him. It was hard not to become fascinated by the acid king's presence. Like any good acid king he had a way of making people feel good about themselves and under his tripping veil was still a true mate with a heart of gold.

The guru relished his tripped-out spirituality and became almost fearless towards convention as if it were a gesture of good faith for all the boys who he regarded as his army of followers. As the days passed his new-found energy naturally drew a lot of attention from everyone in the community. He'd turn up all over town and manage to party with whoever and with whatever was at hand. His new consciousness had virtually stripped him of any responsibility in his life and he'd decided the sweet yummy bits of what was on offer were rightfully his, likening them to offerings for his sacred shrine. His shrine of excess was completely empty as anything offered was promptly consumed. The boys loved him for it! He was a magnetic maverick, making it up as he went along!

The "Guru show" was so over the top security guards and bouncers would either love him or hate him—there was no in-between. He therefore got thrown out of a lot of nightclubs and dole offices. It was hard for edgy steroid types to relax and let him work some of his guru magic on them. They also got fed up with him asking for durries and letting him in for free. Watching him getting turfed was a spectacle in itself. He was never aggro and generally it was only for having too good a time. If he didn't try to get back into the den of iniquity through some tight dunny window or obscure back, dim-lit entrance he would wander off down Oxford Street, or wherever the coloured lights were blinking, and shazam with all who crossed his path. The sound of music was hypnotic to him and became an obsession. Wherever there was a beat, he knew he had to get to the middle of the dance floor. He had become kinetic—a high-energy, loosely-wired entertainer. His trip had sent him into a higher consciousness where he could comfortably sit and talk shit to anyone for hours. There was a certain undefined skill to it. Not that anyone would want to sit and listen for that long, especially when he started raving about the amount of strychnine in "beavers" and "micro dots". But rejection wasn't a deterrent and he constantly tried to speak to plenty of people leaving a lot of them bewildered. Anyone who would bother listening copped a serving of lunacy. At times it would seem as if it all made sense. It was almost as though they could ignore the fact he was wearing a floral dress over a full length steamer and ugg boots in the middle of Summer. There was integrity and meaning in what he said but it all seemed to lead around to that one question, "So have you got any mull?" Were these the teachings of Alan Watts and Timothy Leary or where they just crazy, funny excerpts from the "Book of the Nonsense Guru"? The boys regarded the teachings in his book as an incredible act to follow. Way more worthy than any sage before him. Limitations seemed non-existent.

A Fitzy week was a lifetime for most other people. His mind was detached from conformity and he was trying to get to the guts of life by cutting through society's flesh. Here, there and everywhere. This boy wasn't going to miss a trick. He had become a spiritual clown walking a path through the big tent of the "Eastern Suburbs Circus" searching for action and a mull bowl full of mix.

"Bring it on!" he would yell in a hoarse voice as he'd pull cone after cone. He was a drug-taking machine. He seemed to gravitate towards any mirror or bong that was in the process of being used. He had an uncanny knack of walking in just as the bag was being pulled out. How could anyone refuse to engage "the life of the party"?

Somehow, through all the craziness, he produced a ticket to Bali out of his back pocket one night and showed Sonny. No-one quite knew how he got the ticket. It was miraculous but others thought something was fishy and to this day have been none the wiser. What was even more unbelievable was that his passport had accompanied it. Sonny knew Fitzy was completely inept of organising himself to walk up the road let alone go to Bali so he kept tabs on him all week and kept singing to him the classic Peter, Paul and Mary song "You're leaving on a big jet plane" in the hope the tune would stick in his head and he could actually take on board his upcoming holiday.

On the eve of Fitzy's departure Sonny was slightly panicking for his mate's sake. He really didn't know whether Fitz would make it to Bali or not.

"Are you capable of getting yourself to the airport in the morning?" asked Sonny. They were both sitting comfortably punching cones in their unit's lounge room. The glow in Fitzy's eyes resembled the sun setting on the units of North Bondi out their front window.

"Got a new haircut," he replied, pointing to his new golden

spiralling mop of hair. "The advanced studio's kinda style and I bought a tape too so I can listen to music over there."

He had spent twenty dollars on a Genesis tape which he could buy the next day in Bali for two bucks. Being an Indo veteran Sonny couldn't help but laugh.

As the night traffic sped past the open window Fitzy screamed out into the night "I LOVE BONDI!!" with a fiery look in his eye. Sonny wondered whether he was contemplating surfing Ulu or thinking about whether Sonny would pack him another one using the party cone, instead of the little cone that "wasn't even touchin' the sides".

They bantered on a bit till nightfall dropped. Sonny was thinking that his mate might just get it together in a civil way, get a good night's sleep and get to the airport with some kind of normality the next morning. Wrong!

"I'm outta here. Gotta hot date with destiny!" He obviously wasn't thinking a few hours ahead to his departure the next morning. He wasn't even thinking a minute ahead. All he knew is that he had to get on the street amongst it. He thrived on the Campbell Parade strip at night. Neon lights charged his senses.

Sonny tried in vain to stop him. He told Sonny "not to wait up" for him and disappeared outside, closing the door with a bang!

Sonny packed a cone for himself then started packing his friend's bag. He knew what to throw in and he'd definitely need a rain jacket as February was still rainy season in Indonesia. Sonny came from a big surfing family and all his six brothers shared an affinity with G-Land. Having travelled there for years through the 80s, the brothers had countless barrels to rave about. Sonny was a true Indo warrior and wanted Fitz to catch the plane in the morning and not miss the experience, no matter what state he was in. Maybe Fitz could find some kind of deliverance there because he sure wasn't finding it in Bondi. Going to bed he pulled the sheet over him and hoped his mate would find his way home in time to leave the next day. He started thinking of Indo and fell asleep with images of perfect lefthanders in his head.

He woke up early and as he opened his eyes started wondering whether Fitzy had made it home. He jumped up and headed for the lounge room in anticipation. As he entered the room he immediately felt hot and flushed as the heater was on and there was a body slumped in front of it. He instantly knew Fitz was safely back and smiled on thinking the airport was now a possibility. He also had a chuckle that his mate had turned the heater on as it was still summer. He headed back to the bathroom, washed his face and grabbed his glasses from the bedroom.

Upon re-entering the lounge room he could now see a lot better. It was obvious that Fitzy had been off his head when he got home, dragging the heater out and crashing out in front of it. Dan thought it was lucky he hadn't burnt the joint down. The element was fanning a red, warm glow around the room. On closer inspection it was evident to him that Fitzy had cooked a large part of his lower back. His back was blistered and Sonny thought of how lucky he was that the fire didn't catch onto one of his golden curls. He laughed of the thought of Fitzy ablaze. He patted his snoring friend on the shoulder and tried to stir him with, "Good morning."

After that didn't work he started shaking him but his mate wasn't budging. It was like he was set in concrete.

Change of tactics. "Fitzy, today's the day you're going to Bali." He used a tone similar to a tone a caring parent would use when trying to coax their beloved young child to go to pre-school. "Leaving on a jet plane?" He sung it as more as a question this time round.

He had an hour to get Fitz's shit together and was resolute in making it happen. Sonny had Fitz's boards and bags packed ready to go and all he had to do now was wake him up. As Sonny made them both coffee the slab on the floor started responding to the barbecued nerve endings on his back. With a shriek he cried, "Fucken b-Jesus! Who fuckin' dropped their ciggy on me?" He sat up abruptly and automatically shook his head, then slowly panned the room blinking often, like a broken shutter. He became distracted by the sight of the bong he had fallen asleep next to. "How convenient," his brain thought as it overrode any pain associated with cooked flesh. His eyes were full of crust and he found it hard to light the cone but as usual he managed.

"Drugs are just vehicles designed to drive me further," he splattered as he exhaled. "Whooooooaaa!!"

It was tough being on the frontline and blister burns were just part of it. After all this was just another painful experience in another day of his tripping life.

"Drink this, Fitz. I made it especially for you ..." said a tentative Sonny. "So you can manage to get the plane to Bali." He studied Fitz's azure eyes to see if there was any hope of pulling it off.

Fitz turned around and stared at him as if he had never met him before. There was a short silence then he blurted, "I can't forget me Genesis tape!"

After a few sips of the hot brew Fitz decided it was a good day to go to Bali. Sonny continued his diligence and rang a taxi. As he closed the door of the cab he could only hope that Fitz would make it to Kingsford-Smith let alone arrive in Kuta.

One of Sonny's elder brothers, Marty, was in Bali at the time with none other than Bondi's resident madman, Pottsie. Marty was an Indo legend and his amazing 10-second barrel at G-Land was captured on film and was the first wave on the Billabong's "Surf into Summer" video back in the late 80s. He was out of the blond surfie mould and had a harem of chicks chasing him in his younger years. The third in line in a dysfunctional surfing family of six brothers, he was open-minded and like all of them very artistic. They all took after their creative parents, their dad being a sought-after picture framer and their mum was everything from a bronze sculptor to a screen printer. Their abode in Dover Road, Rose Bay was full of family artwork and was where John the eldest and Garret, the next in line, started shaping surfboards. Garret was now one of the most sought-after shapers in the world which was an indication of the kind of talent the family was capable of.

Marty was good mates with Dan and the boys and was well liked. He'd surfed with them since grommet days and they were all Bondi boys through and through!

He was in Bali living like a king because he was still on double-dole back in Oz. Marty's de facto had left him and he was cashing in as the full amount of the double dole was being deposited into his account. Sonny was helping out, putting Marty's dole cheque in every fortnight at Bondi Junction. He would then deposit the proceeds into Marty's Bank of Bumi-Daya account in Indonesia. Every fortnight for three blissful months, Marty felt like a millionaire. It was a brilliant piece of deception, one that most politicians would praise if it wasn't biting into their own pie.

Being the introvert that he was Sonny used to wear Marty's clothes so it was easy for him to take on his brother's persona. Dressing up was all part of the challenge of becoming his brother which he passionately enacted every two weeks. He enjoyed playing the part and he became good mates with the staff and security guards who he imagined as other actors. The same security guards that Fitzy always got on so well with. One time when Sonny was standing in the dole queue Trotter was a few positions behind him and yelled out, "What ya been up to?"

Sonny replied, "Working hard," all the time smiling at the security guard. He then realised he'd fucked up with his lines and prayed it hadn't diminished his chances of his imaginary Oscar. Judging by his overall performance in his latest role he was at least in with a chance of winning best supporting actor in the "Fitzy goes to Bali" saga.

Marty and Nigel were hanging out in Seminyak at "Doggo's" place, "Gardenia". "Doggo" was a wheeler and dealer from Maroubra who had thrown a bunch of money into a losmen during the early 80s. Bali was pretty damn cheap back then. He was a hell man who charged Indo in the early days. He was constantly surfing big waves all over the planet and was a regular down Cronulla Point and "the island" when home in Sydney. Plenty of southside surfers knew him so he always had heaps of crew staying there. His Balinese partner, Wayan, was a kickback dude who enjoyed helping the dozens of troops that passed through during the year in search of swell. Most of the arrivals were from either Bondi or Maroubra. Mixing these two crews was like mixing Arack with Arak which then equalled a crew hell-bent on pushing the limits and taking their chances. Most were guerilla surfers in their prime taking on anything that was worth taking on. On the land, in the bedroom, when dealing with the law or messing with the ocean, it was all taken in their stride. Most were all-round watermen, wrestling with sharks, spearing and foraging the shallow reefs for food, escaping venomous sea snakes, diving to depths unimaginable to help increase their lung capacity and of course surfing ocean slabs the size of mountains. Basically all things bringing their mortal bodies in touch with King Neptune's realm were high on their priority list.

Marty and Pottsie were in Bali for the same reason that Fitzy was about to arrive. In the 80s and early 90s Bali was a magical paradise for surfers. Mainstream tourism hadn't caught up with it yet so it was still a land rich in customs and full of freedoms. You didn't need a motorbike licence or a helmet, there were no road rules, the waves were uncrowded, Legian and Seminyak were still rice fields or jungle and the general small time development was confined to Kuta and Sanur. Hash was cheap and easily available, a lobster cost four bucks, a Bintang beer cost 50 cents, a board carrier from the road at Ulu cost a couple, losmens also cost a couple for each night and massages from Indonesian healers such as Pak Jagarah cost a measly dollar fifty. A surfer who was classified as a bum in Australia could go to Indo with a few hundred dollars and live for a month like a king.

For the boys it was the best place on earth. They used to take Mushies and go on little adventures. A favourite was watching planes land as you lay on the tarmac of the Kuta runway. After dark was the best time to do it because of all the amazing hallucinations brought on by the flashing landing lights. There was obviously no active Jihad back then because there was no fence surrounding the airport and after parking your motorbike adjacent to the airstrip on the beach you could walk up the volcanic boulders supporting the structure and lay smack, bang in the middle of the jumbo highway. You could look up into the cockpit as the plane moved just 20 feet overhead with the roar of the engines thundering through your body. The flashing lights and the look of terror on the pilot's face usually gave you the meanest head-rush. Bali was still fairly untouched and the environment provided an unlimited playground for all surfers. It had all the ingredients to lure the boys back religiously year after year.

The first indication to Marty and Pottsie that Fitzy was actually on the island was when they stumbled across a crumpled passport on the dirt road in Doggo's front garden. As Pottsie alighted his motorbike he picked up the creased book for a closer inspection.

"What the fuck?" he remarked. "It's someone's passport."

"Poor cunt!" said Marty. "I'd hate to lose me passport in this joint. Maybe we can get it back to 'em."

Marty was now looking over Pottsie's shoulder full of curiosity.

"What is this shit?" Pottsie was commenting on the drawings and poetry scribbled over the back pages.

Marty's face contorted puzzled by the gibberish. As Pottsie turned the pages they were adorned by floral motifs and poetry which didn't make any sense.

"Who the fuck owns this?" laughed Pottsie implying that

whoever owned the passport was completely crackers.

As he flicked the pages towards the front they both waited with bated breath to check out the photo. Pottsie found it difficult to open the photo page because the crease was worse towards the front cover. As it was revealed they needed to squint to see the mug shot because of the arvo glare. A millionth of a second later they both fell to the ground hysterical. It was their mate "Fitzy". His blond curls and blue eyes were unmistakable.

Pottsie, being a bit of a Nazi, drew humour from the situation by simply knowing that Fitz was fucked up. He liked to describe it as friendly masochism. Over the years countless frontline surfers had lost it down Bondi so it was smarter to be amused by their situation rather than become too sensitive. Marty was rolling from side to side laughing for all kinds of reasons as he knew Fitzy all too well. He knew this was a serious situation but on the other hand had to get the funny side out of his system before he could grasp what was really happening. He knew that there was work to be done if their mate was to ever get home to Australia. Both boys knew that as soon as they finished their roll on the grass they'd have to find their mate before the rest of Bali did.

Several days passed and they hadn't caught sight of him. They had only heard vague sightings of "a crazy blonde man with no fear". The talk conjured up images in the lads' heads of Fitzy giving the Balos back some of his own homegrown spirituality. Fitzy's spirituality could have passed as a bemo named "Desire". If he desired it, he took it. The boys were certain he was creating carnage. They knew he was "out there" and hoped he wasn't heading towards Canggu jail or something worse.

As the boys surfed uncrowded 6-foot Uluwatu they wondered if Fitz had even figured out "whether there was any surf in Bali". They wondered if he had even seen the beach yet, let alone know where Ulu was. Concerned about his welfare these thoughts and many more constantly ricocheted round their minds.

One afternoon they were riding back through the chaos of peak hour Kuta after surfing some solid Padang when they spotted him in the distance. His blond locks bobbed through the loud, crowded street, as he cruised along on his green Kwacka 125. Marty sped up and courageously negotiated through somewhat heavy traffic to where he was within a couple of lengths of him to have any chance of making himself heard.

"Fitzy!" he yelled at the top of his hash-tarred lungs. After having to compete with all the other Asian sounds the street had to offer, his words entered the targeted earhole. Marty could only hope it wasn't about to fly out the other. Fitz turned his wobbly head around, ever so slightly, his chin fitted snuggly in the cradle of his shoulder. Marty's cry had registered somewhere in the convoluted mass of grey and white matter that Fitzy's cranium enclosed. It was enough for him to spare a quick glance as he searched for the source that had him unnerved and seemingly rattled. The glance shot straight through the boys as if they were just spectres and not materially of this world. It was useless—they were dealing with the mind of a lunatic. With flared nostrils and fucked-up eyes resembling gigantic red sauces his senses became fully paranoid sending out warning signals like a tilted pinball. He set his sights back on the maze of road in front of him and took off. As he hit the throttle he put his bristly chin down on the rusty tank as any crazed speed demon does to minimise resistance, and powered off. As he weaved through the horses and carts, the packed bemos, the startled pedestrians and the beat-up dogs he was taking every chance on offer, like a game of Russian roulette. He disappeared in a cloud of dust and the boys wondered how many more bullets were in the chamber.

He was wild. His spiritual holiday was starting to get out of hand like a yacht in a tropical storm trying to navigate uncharted waters. He had lost or given away his boards and what little money he had brought with him. He was now having to bend the rules in order to eat, drink and be merry. He wasn't letting go of his Genesis tape and had it taped to his leg for safe keeping. It was all just fun and games for him. He was unaware of any dangerous repercussions his actions were leading him into. He was like a docile innocent who had lost his mind. His intentions were true enough but his methods were lacking. After all, you can be as good a bloke as you like, but you still gotta pay the rent. Originally the Balinese welcomed him, loving his carefree spiritual attitude—up until they realised he had no cash whatsoever, then things started turning pear-shaped. It was a sight to behold—the Fitz was taking them to the cleaners. No-one could ever deny the Balinese an earn but Fitzy could sure teach them a lesson on how to scam properly.

The locals were venting their anger at Doggo because he was known as the closest person to them who knew Fitzy. He was telling them to stay calm and he'd sort it out for them. Wayan was stressing telling Doggo that "Fitzy's life was in danger", and the locals were now going to "use black magic to hurt him". And a machete or two just to make sure.

In all his glory he'd made a habit of casually wandering into the many warungs and bars that frequent Kuta and ordering up big time. Lobster and prawns were on his hit list, washed down by a few bottles of Bintang. After filling his belly he would casually stroll off to the toilet never to be seen again. Within a few days of arriving he had several escape routes sussed. There was no conscience, just a "worldwide cheque" that was due to land in his bank account "any day now"—an ingenious excuse that had a lot of the locals scratching their heads.

A couple of days after the last sighting Marty and Pottsie witnessed another messy scene. It was mid-Legian, Jalan Padma was scorching hot and Fitzy was beaming in the distance. Dressed in only a sarong and Genesis tape, and sporting his trademark tripping grin, he was preaching his word at anyone in his line of fire. The boys could just make out his curls from afar when a somewhat rather annoyed Balo leapt out of a bemo at him. As the boys strode closer it was clear the Balo had a big knife and was clearly intent in shoving it in his guts. Marty and Pottsie broke into a sprint fearing the worst.

The super aware bit of Fitzy's tripped-out mind tapped him on the shoulder just in the knick of time for him to duck under the first swing. After yelling "Steady, matey!" he could see there was a lot more in store so he legged it as fast as he could. His pistons pumped straight past the boys running in the opposite direction and into the hazy traffic behind them. There was nothing they could do, for it was 40 degrees and they were as stoned as fuck on some sick hash. They also didn't want the locals hassling them after he got away.

"Greased lightning!" commented Pottsie who was trying not to laugh about the absurdity creeping into the picture.

"Un-fucking-believable! I wish I had my fuckin' camera," was all the ever inspiring film artist Marty could manage saying. Both guys were then silent for a while in amazement of their friend's situation.

He was gone again, without a trace. The boys were obviously only going to see a few select acts of this touring international circus and were resigned to the fact that the clown couldn't be stopped till he was subdued and the tripping curtain in his head shut down. So far any efforts to pull him off-stage had been futile and although they weren't prepared to ruin their holiday thinking about it, they were asking themselves a few questions on the matter. Unfortunately questioning this kind of crazy shit doesn't always provide rational conclusions so they decided it was better to go and relax and wait for more sightings.

They decided a refreshing fruit juice was in order and headed to the original "Bobbie's Warung" only a few metres away. They really needed a break from the sad reality of worry that they were harbouring about their "lost cause" friend. And it was as if "Shiva" was watching over them, because their prayers were soon answered.

Rich was just another lad magnetised to the "Island of the Gods" in search of the "Holy Grail" of surfing. He was a suave kinda guy whose private school manners had him in line with the gentry of the eastern suburbs. He wore a dark shoulder-length flickback hairstyle and had designer looks that woulda had a few chickies wet behind their beef curtains. As noted, Bali in the early days was the number one destination for all the Bondi crew, as well as most of the other Aussie surfers who ventured off our shores looking for surf adventure. The 80s' surfer was still considered unconventional and as Bali was raw in culture and big in waves it suited a surfer to stay for months on end, getting lost in a world of primitive pleasure. Surfers back then embraced the natural beauty and would never have thought of changing a thing. It was a paradox that the surfers' hedonistic lifestyles and the pure customs of the Balinese were symbiotic. The sub-cultural smiles of easy-going surfers seemed to fuse with the same untroubled smiles of the indigenous people and both enjoyed each other's company and friendly outlook.

Marty and Pottsie thanked the lovely, smiling Balinese waitress, "Makasi", who had just brought them their fruit lassis and sat them down on their bamboo table. Inside the turbo-fanned, crowded warung they'd found a bit of sanctuary from the humidity outside. "Bobbies" was a popular haunt with visiting surfers and had been for years—a hub of surf activity where stories of perfectly-ridden waves echoed from table to table.

As Rich strolled in with all the self-confidence of a used car salesman, everyone was slouching around, seemingly surfed out, a little sunburnt and jaded from the rocks of good hash everyone was puffing on. Marty was sipping on his tropical drink as Rich cruised towards him using his fancy hand jive and the nod of his head to greet anyone's stoned eyes who'd bothered looking up from their nasi goreng. He was grooving so much that it seemed he was there to enchant them. He winked at his Bondi mates' table like a pro in the middle of his routine and for some reason walked straight on by. His show was headed to another level as he'd spotted his co-star for his next act, a live monkey. The poor animal was attached to a rusty old chain at the back of the joint seemingly bored with the world of captivity. Rich thought of it as an opportunity to stir his audience and he took it on like a star on Broadway. He bent over to embrace the small creature as if it was one of his long lost buddies. By this time he could feel the diners' glazed eyes as they watched his glowing stardom in anticipation of the unfolding scene. As he looked into the cute primate's tiny human-like eyes his overconfidence obscured the pending attack. Marty and Pottsie, with the Fitzy episode now long behind them, watched tentatively, closely aware of the obvious outcome. As the star raised his hand to pat his furry little friend, the monkey leapt up and mounted his face like a scene from "Alien". The monkey bit down on his scalp prompting him to scream in pain. He stood upright and instinctively started pedalling backwards. The show had turned comedy and the starring role had just been upstaged by his supporting jungle brother. Humiliating fits of laughter spasmodically resounded around the little warung as the monkey rubbed his hairy arse on Richard's bottom lip, just to rub salt into the wound. As Rich's retreat continued the chain was pulled taut and he fell to the hard ground with a thud. Subsequently his head broke free of the monkey's vice like grip and the monkey retreated to the crowd's hoots and applause. Needless to say Rich's ego had taken a hit—he turned around and saw a sea of cackling faces. Marty and Pottsie had needed a good laugh and now had tears rolling down their suntanned cheeks. The monkey even started laughing hysterically and pointing his bony little finger at his victim. A shattered Rich could only scramble for the door with blood trickling down his forehead. The pantomime was now over and the star exited stage door right.

A day later the Australian consulate rang "Gardenia" and said that he was concerned for the welfare of some Aussie guy running amok on the streets of Kuta. He asked that if anyone knew him to keep him off the streets until they could fly him out otherwise the authorities were going to throw him into "Bangli" which was where the old Bali crazy farm was located. The very same day

Fitzy unexpectedly surfaced at Gardenia looking for his "worldwide cheque". Marty and Doggo seized the opportunity to contain him and offered him hospice till it arrived.

It was hard to explain to Fitz why he had to be kept under lock and key but the peace pipe subdued him enough that he didn't really care. Occasionally he would go missing for short periods of time returning with a couple of large Bintangs under each arm.

"Gotta have me mother's milk!" he would argue. No one knew where the money for the product was coming from and no one bothered asking. The lad seemed oblivious to all the havoc surrounding him.

The consulate arrived upon hearing of his capture. He restated how important it was to keep him off the streets because he had pissed off so many people that they wanted blood. A flight had been arranged for him the next day and he asked Marty to change his ticket and accompany Fitz home to which he benevolently agreed.

The following day the consulate turned up again at Gardenia. He seemed sincerely concerned about Fitzy's welfare and probably concerned about any bad press if an Aussie were to be stabbed by an angry mob in Kuta. Like a valet attendant the official personally ushered Marty and his captive into a bemo waiting outside, ordering the driver not to stop anywhere en-route to the airport. He slipped Marty a couple of pills to administer to his tripped out friend to calm him down before the flight. After a couple of days with his lunatic mate Marty didn't even consider giving them to Fitz and swallowed them himself.

As Marty passed through customs with his bag and boards in tow the pills started to kick in. Upon Fitzy's persistent request Doggo had given him an "Island A Classic" surfboard to take back to Oz with him. With the board under his arm and a ciggy hanging out of his mouth he followed Marty through customs wearing only a pair of board shorts and a Genesis tape. No shoes, no shirt, no bags, no ticket or passport and definitely no sanity. Customs had already been notified and knew the situation so he was sweet to go straight through.

Everything was going smoothly until they got into the air where probably the worst case scenario started to unfold. A couple of cautious gay QANTAS stewards were ignoring his requests for beer. Marty pleaded with them to give him one which was the least Fitzy required to keep him calm. Amazingly he was tolerant with them for the first half an hour, not uttering a word in protest. Marty was surprised to see him handling things so well under the conditions. Then suddenly out of nowhere the inevitable happened and he erupted like a spewing volcano.

He stood up with his signature vein popping out of his head and let rip. "Right. I've fucking had it with you, you, you and as for you!" Lava rhetoric was getting sprayed throughout the cabin at any steward within range. The original powder-puff stewards were now shaking in their nervous little skins as they didn't know what to do. "I get naught from you, you and fucking you!" The cabin went silent. "Where's my fucking beer and ya better make it snappy!" he screamed, scouring the plane but he couldn't see any of them—they had absolutely shit themselves and ducked for cover.

Fitzy stood tall looking straight through anyone who met his glare. Almost immediately one of the senior cabin crew came rushing down from first class to address the volatile situation.

"Look, I'm sorry, sir, but you're going to have to sit down," he said as Marty wished he'd had his camera again. He panned over the other passengers' reactions and was spewing he wasn't filming it all. The feature in-flight movie was "Greystoke/Tarzan" which everyone had lost interest in. They were paying attention to the real Tarzan who had just ripped pieces off the gay glorified waiters in the sky. All he wanted was a beer, specifically a cold can of Foster's, that's all!

Marty started to giggle at how ridiculous it all seemed. The pills were working a treat and he wondered where it was all heading.

Fitzy explained his dilemma to the senior steward who told him he'd be right back and his beer was on the way. This had a calming affect on him immediately. The senior steward returned promptly with the co-pilot. The co-pilot began telling him that "everything's going to be all right".

Tarzan replied with, "Mate, get me Bill Coleman on the phone and quick!" Bill was a long serving QANTAS captain. His three sons were also employed by QANTAS as stewards and the family had lived next door to Fitzy's parents in North Bondi for years. They all grew up together surfing Third Ramp. Fitz then rattled off the boys' names to prove they were personal friends. "OK, so you know Chappy, Wes and Corky. Well, I've played footy for Bondi United with 'em and we've all surfed together since we were fucking grommets so get me Bill on the phone now. He's been with you pricks for years!" The cabin was completely quiet. You could have heard a pin drop. Everyone was transfixed on "the prince of apes" who was deemed a much better entertainer than his Hollywood counterpart. "And while you're up there grab me a can of bloody Foster's," he continued, "or ya better make that two!"

The co-pilot acknowledged his demands and returned to the cockpit. A couple of minutes later he appeared, much to Fitzy's delight, with two cold cans of Foster's. His head suddenly transformed into a different person. The sight of two cold cans approaching had stopped the molten lava flow in its tracks. His vein popping eruption was now cooling at a rate of knots in anticipation of the amber fluid sliding down the back of his dry Sahara throat. None of this scene would've happened if they had just listened to him in the first place. Needless to say the perpetrators hid in the galley for the rest of the flight.

The co-pilot was a champion who understood diplomacy when dealing with the public in general. He gave Marty a reassuring look as if to say, "We are going to get through this." By that stage Marty had taken enough responsibility for his mate and believed it was the co-pilot's turn.

"Listen, mate, I've just had a chat with Bill," commenced the co-pilot. "He said to say 'Hi'. He's in Tahiti at the moment." He was staring Fitz in the eye, confident he was in control of the situation. "He told us to give you whatever you want and he'll see you back home in a couple of days."

As Fitzy cracked open the first can of beer the co-pilot's words seemed to be sinking in. Marty was impressed at how professional the co-pilot was in handling the situation.

"We're currently flying at 30,000 feet and the flight is going to take about another four hours so enjoy your beers and try to get a little shut-eye. If you need anything you know where I am—I'm up the front there." He was so convincing about everything Marty didn't know whether he had talked to Bill in Tahiti or not. He was like the great white hero who had the knack of calming the untamed beast and Marty thought there could also be a place for him in the Tarzan sequel. Within no time Fitz was totally relaxed and then it was smooth sailing all the way to Kingsford-Smith. Marty closed his eyes and got some well deserved shut-eye.

Touchdown and it was another beautiful morning in Sydney

town. Again customs had been pre-warned so they knew what to expect. The pilot had radioed ahead and informed officials of an incoming Tarzan with long blond curly locks and big blue eyes who was wearing only board shorts as a loincloth and a Genesis tape. The order was given to "open the gates and let him through"!

Using a customs baggage official as a ciggy caddy, he bludged several tailor-mades whilst waiting for his surfboard to appear out of the baggage carousel. The longer he waited the more agitated he became. Marty sensed that another violent eruption was about to happen so he moved to the other side of the conveyer to try and avoid being classified as his mate's travelling companion.

"If my board lobs with a fucking ding on it I'm gonna go nuts!" he yelled venting his anger at some female official who was the closest target at the time. It looked as though it was her first day on the job. She was wearing an immaculately cleaned uniform and her fresh juvenile face was beaming with "the first day on the job" glow. A first day that Fitz wasn't going to let her forget.

"Me mate Doggo gave me that board so I don't wanna see any fucking dings. OK?"

All the young girl could do was smile at him. After all they didn't train her to deal with a crazed Tarzan-like, drug-affected, spiritual warrior during her first hours at the job.

"Oh, look ... me board's been fuckin' dinged by you pricks!" The surfboard came out with a little scratch on the tail, prompting Vesuvius to erupt again. He was ropeable but customs didn't want anything to do with the spewing mess. "What's Doggo gonna say about this ... huh?" The customs girl reassuringly smiled at him as if to say "everything will be all right", not really knowing what she should do. "Have ya got any resin?" Fitzy asked her.

As he passed through customs spraying insults Marty moved over to another line to try and give him the slip. He caught Marty out of the corner of his eye and screamed, "These cunts are fucked! They dinged me fuckin' board. Doggo's gonna be spewin' at me ..." Again he had the crowd's attention. "I'll be waiting for ya, Marty, when ya come through on the other side. You didn't bring any of that hash with ya, did ya?"

The last comment had Marty slightly blushing as nearly every custom agent's ears pricked. Poor Marty was given the third degree with every inch of his belongings inspected. Customs had to deal some payback so Marty was detained for no less than three quarters of an hour. By this stage he was feeling a little dazed and confused and was hoping the worst was over. All he wanted to do was get home and have a snooze.

Fitz was waiting for him in the passageway between customs and the public exit which added to Marty's confusion. Marty had been ages in customs and wondered what he had been saying to all the tourists passing him before they entered Australia. First impressions stick and one can only imagine what they thought after encountering a lunatic as they entered the land of Oz.

"Everything all right, Marty?"

"Yeah, thanks, mate." By this time Marty was exhausted.

As both men strolled out of the customs exit amidst the crowd was Fitzy's parents. The look of apprehension on their faces was quite evident. An underlying look of relief also appeared as they set eyes on their boy. Approaching his parents he yet again transformed, this time adorning the best face he could find.

"G'daay, Dad. G'daay, Mum. How are ya?" His first line seemed normal. "Had a fantastic time—wait till you see the presents I bought for ya!"

Marty tried not to laugh at what had just been said. He thought, "Here is a guy with only a pair of board shorts on, and a surfboard under his arm, telling his parents that they should get excited over the presents he was going to give them. Was he going to give them the 6'4" Island A Classic surfboard and ask them to use it in turns?"

Realising the time and effort Marty had just put in to get their son back safely they thanked him with open arms. They were so stoked their son was back in one piece. If Marty hadn't helped his buddy they would have had to fly to Bali to get him. The least they could do is offer Marty a lift back to Bondi. He gladly accepted though he felt a little uncomfortable about the atmosphere of a crazed son around his straight parents.

As the car headed towards Bondi, Marty let out a sigh of relief knowing that it was the last leg of an eventful journey. He was glad to be on Australian soil and excited about seeing Dan and the boys back in Bondi and telling his story over a few coldies. Everyone in Bondi loved Fitzy and knew the acidic reasons behind this new trip he was going through. He was a hard line trouper—a local rugged enigma who everyone cared about. He was, after all, one of them. Marty knew the boys were going to cherish this latest story and add it to their Fitzy collection.

As Fitz's dad took the old shortcut behind Maroubra to avoid the morning's peak-hour traffic his son had one last thing to say. "Hey, Dad, wait till you see the painting exhibition I'm going to have." It was absurdness at its best ... the car took on an uncanny silence in anticipation of what was to fall out of his mouth next. "These Balinese paintings I bought, they're incredible."

The suspense in what he would say next gripped the car. His dad knew it better left alone but his curiosity couldn't help itself. "What do you mean, son?"

Like it was perfectly logical he finished with, "They move!"

Radar Love

It had been a long day in the shop and Dan had shut up at 6pm and headed out back to his comfy lounge to relax with a beer and a bong. He was just getting used to the hectic pace and constant happenings that accompanied his new surf shop lifestyle. Little Oz dog had been accepted with open arms by the local crew and most had become familiar with her cute looks and likeable manner. She had become the furry, four-legged board club celebrity as well as Dan's best mate. He was relieved he'd been successful in getting her quickly into a routine of shitting outside. His tactics of rubbing her face in the smelly presents she had left under clothing racks and elsewhere in the showroom had paid dividends.

Besides that little indiscretion she knew she was loved dearly. Dan cherished her loyalty and she had become his shadow. He fed her every evening on either fried chicken, left over gourmet takeaways or cans of "My Dog". The generic "Pal" and "Chum" brands just didn't cut it with Dan's sense of smell or Oz dog's palate. After a plate of what they had to offer, little Ozzy's farts could make your eyes water and set you off dry-retching. After serving her up half a bowl of left-over Braised Beef and Black Bean Sauce from the Golden Dragon Chinese restaurant in Curlewis Street, Dan was interrupted by someone knocking loudly at the back door.

"Hey, Dan, it's me, Cookie ... open up!"

"Yeah, hold your horses ... I'm comin'!" Dan slid the latch back and swung open the wooden gate.

Cookie looked at him and smiled. "What? Don't tell me I've caught you here by yourself for once? Whatcha been doing?"

"Well, actually, I've been trying to have a pull for a few weeks now but again it looks like you caught me before I could get one away!"

"Shit! Sorry, mate. Not that I'd want to help you or anything ..."

"My life's been a whirlwind since I moved in here, if you haven't noticed ... I don't have time to scratch my arse."

"Has it been getting itchy?"

"Term of expression, mate."

"I know. I just thought, you know, since we're on dick jokes and stuff ..."

"Funny guy ..." Dan said with a smirk then with a quick rub of his salty surf-crusted face he continued, "There's about twenty guys leaving their boards here ..."

"I know. I'm one of them!"

Dan's living space had become headquarters for a lot of his mates and their antics. His shop had become an underground haven for a team of mad boardriders who lived on their wits and ran wild on the streets. There was never a dull moment as they touched base with the shop as if it was their last bastion in the war against conformity and the encroaching yuppie sect. "Yeah, well, you know how it is ... Hollywood's got nuthin' on what happens 'round 'ere, so let's sit down and savour the serenity with a gurgle from the bong before anyone else comes knockin'."

"You read my mind, mate. I've really started to chillout these days." Cookie was becoming a cruiser—getting closer to thirty had seen his playful side reserved for six days a week instead of seven. "Oh, and by the way, didya ever get that big 'gun' back that you lent Alex ages ago when he said he was headin' over to surf Lurline Bay?"

"Why?"

"Supposed to be a big swell comin' and I'm thinkin' about headin' down the Island with a coupla mates. Gonna stay at Don's cabins."

"Well, you won't be borrowing it unless you buy it back from the fuckin' hock shop I saw it in last week."

"Uh oh, don't tell me ..."

"Yep ... cousin Alex doin' what he does best!"

"Fuckin' aye! You spewed at him yet?"

"Bit hard—he's inside again and I won't be seeing 'im again for a while."

"Serious." Cookie's reaction was bordering on the mundane. "What'd he do this time?"

"You mean you haven't heard?"

"What? You think I am his bitch or somethin'? I haven't seen him for months. He didn't even return my calls when I was trying to get him to come over and belt some fuckwit for me."

"He's a kook!" There was a tinge of anger in Dan's voice as he was grappling with coming to terms with his cousin's frequent fuck-ups. "I think the last time I saw 'im was up Oxford Street near the Freezer and he was looking worse for wear and hanging with some seedy, smacked-out slut." He finished packing a cone for himself and wrenched the living daylights out of it. "You know, Cookie," he commenced as a billow of thick smoke left his lungs and became part of the atmosphere, "he is my cousin but I'll be fucked if I can sort him out."

"Well, it seems he's fucked up again, aye, poor cunt."

"Well, it seems he's been throwing too much of his weight around these days. He brings it on himself."

"Yeah, I heard that. He's kinda built up a reputation with some of his mates. Just the norm over Maroubra around his mum's joint."

"I should be dirty but it's nothin' new. Someone should write a book about him—they'd make a motsa, fair dinkum!" Dan packed himself another bong. He felt disappointment and compassion but these ambiguous emotions were being undermined by his frustration of how he wanted his dorky relative to "wake up" to his misgivings that kept landing him behind four walls. "It's hard to change a leopard's spots, Cookie, and for Alex they're on for good with a permanent marker, fuck it! The silly boofhead getting pinched again—shit ... I'll have to go and see him ... he's up at Grafton. He got pinched doing some dodgy shit with JC from Bronte."

"JC?"

"Yep. JC was up to his usual no good and Alex got roped into it when they had me aunt's phone bugged."

"Fuckin' Grafton! They coulda put him a bit closer."

"Yep." Dan had figured he'd head up in a couple of months. "Got caught tryin' to leg it up that way."

Cookie was thinking that's definitely a surf trip visit. "I'll come up with ya and we can visit Grubbo at Yamba and surf the point with him and Devo."

"Sounds like a plan." Dan's surfing-saturated brain navigated his thinking towards timing it with a summer cyclone spinning out of control off the NSW north coast. "We'll wait for a decent swell and head up in the Torana!"

The next morning Dan was walking up the hill towards the hut with Porks, Big Ads and Getz. They had been out for the early and being summer they had been in the water a couple of hours and it wasn't even 7.30am yet. It was a Saturday morning and the beach was already out of first gear and moving along through the rest of its transmission. "George had a fitness pack running the soft sand before leading the charge and swimming a couple of lengths of the beach between the two rocky headlands. The red and yellow clubbies were dragging ski boards towards the water's edge in anticipation of having to save a few throughout the course of the day. Plenty of sweaty joggers huffed and ran just above the high tide mark along the white crescent of sand. All these fit people in preparation for a clean start to another lovely day almost gave you the impression Bondi was a healthy place. They reflected the Aussie pop beach culture's better side. The boys opted to surf and generally stayed clear of its parade.

Dan noticed a lone young girl sitting on the browning summer grass further up the hill. The lads chatted about the waves they had mastered in their surf and Big Ads was telling Dan that he definitely wanted to be in a heat for the next boardriders comp. As they drew closer to the fair maiden a couple of sly comments slipped out. Dan remained quiet and examined her mood in detail. He could see she was in the doldrums and doing some soul-searching.

As they passed her by Getz couldn't help blurting, "Show us your pig bite!"

"Fuck, Getz! That's a bit harsh," objected Dan. "Obviously you've been getting' nought from that hell sort you've been hangin' out with!"

"Fuck you. When did you become Mr Loverboy?"

"After he started suckin' Oz dog's tiny dick!"

"Yeah, Ads, I've been following you and Lindy's lead!" Dan didn't bother crossing Campbell Parade with the boys. He'd witnessed the girl shed a lonely tear and felt for some strange reason an obligation to find out why. It was as if his genes were circulating within the same romantic veins as Brando, Bogart, Elvis and Jimmy Stewart. He felt a chivalry take over his body, pumping him to put his best foot forward.

He backtracked and asked, "What's a pretty girl like you doing in a place like this?"

Her sullen eyes staring out to sea were the only expression on her blank face. As much as they seemed to search the horizon they were only dim receptors to what was really going on inside her fragile eggshell mind. Her head turned towards Dan as if being wound on a slow moving cog. She glanced up at him and pressed out a distressed smile.

"Wow! You are one unhappy angel."

Her mousy looks and long dark hair were aloof on the wind, her heartbeat irregular with the inconsistencies of love. She sat alone, gutted of feeling.

"C'mon. I'm sure you're twice as beautiful when you manage a real smile." She turned her look back towards the distant Pacific Ocean and he countered by moving forward a little back into her peripheral. "Look, I know something's up and I couldn't just walk past and not want to help in some way." She wiped another tear from her eye. "Hey, I'm not here to harass you. I mean, when I see a girl as pretty as you down on her luck I can't just walk on by. I mean, I'm not saying I have any answers either but if you'd like to talk to someone I'm more than happy to listen."

"But I don't even know you," managed to creep past her sensitive lips.

"Sure, I know that, but it don't mean you can't get to know me. I don't bite and I would definitely never think of hurting such a beautiful girl like yourself!"

"I'm not beautiful!'

"Whooaaa! Hold up there ... that's right, you're not beautiful—you're absolutely gorgeous!"

"You don't know me."

"That's true ... but we have a chance to share the moment and change that. Whaddya reckon?"

"I don't feel like talking."

"And nor you should if you really don't feel like it ... but I know that when I'm down it's good for me to talk to someone and get it off my chest." She swivelled her head around once more. "Don't you know it's dangerous to swallow one's pain and it's a lot better to let things out? Works for me, anyway."

"What? You think you know what I'm going through?"

"Well, no, I suppose I don't know what's going inside your pretty head, but what I do know is that your hurtin' and I'm offering you a chance to ease your pain."

She looked back towards the ocean and for a brief moment looked up at the blue sky. "I don't need your sympathy."

"OK, then, I know you probably don't but I was only offering you a shoulder. You looked like you were in need of one."

"Thanks."

"Look, I know I don't know you or what's happening and I'm sorry if I seem to annoy you rather than be of any help." Dan panned the warm beach landscape as if to find his mojo. He wanted so badly to assist and influence this delicate young princess. "But you have to remember your reflection on this given moment is

yours and only you can change that." Dan's approach was similar to
a knight's duty though inside his head bouncing around he had
several reasons for his actions. He was up for the challenge to
sweet-talk his way into her heart, the love game being significant to
who he was and his own indulgent self-esteem. New-found
friendships made him feel alive and any extra trimmings were a
respected privilege. For he was generally a pretty together cat. His
love sensors had been touched by the old movies his dad used to
watch with him and the many crooners who starred in them. For he
believed all men had a percentage of what he considered "charming
genes". Gentlemen were to be revered and respected the world over.

"Look, I appreciate your sincerity but please respect my
privacy." The girl wasn't quite ready to divulge any of her sorrow.

"As good as done."

"Thank you."

"Just one last thing before I leave you to your sadness."

"And what's that?"

"Can you please tell me your name?"

"Sandra."

"Well, I'm Dan and I own that surf shop across the street on
the corner and all I can hope for is that we cross paths again real
soon."

She turned her vulnerable head around again but this time all
the way around so she could get a look at Dan's surf shop with the
big suspended Malibu out the front. She seemed a little impressed.
"You own that?"

"Yep, and I live out back!"

"Cool! I might see you around, then."

"That would make me very happy, Sandra. You have a good
day now and I hope you feel better sooner rather than later."

"Thank you, Dan."

"My pleasure." And with that he trotted off across Campbell
Parade, surfboard in arm, with a spring in his step.

Later in the day he was finding it hard to get someone to mind
the shop for the night, so as a last resort he scoured the hill for any
grommet worthy of the responsibility. There was a Hordern "Rat"
party to be experienced and nothing was going to hold him back.
Dan thought the Hordern parties to be a wormhole of decadence
and wouldn't miss one for the world.

During the 80s the boys were entertained by patronising clubs
and pubs throughout the city. For young adventurers from Bondi

and the suburbs, "town" was where it was at. Besides the many
dance clubs on Oxford Street and in the Cross, the city had a vibrant
"live music" scene happening. Places like the Trade Union Club,
the Tivoli, the Landsdowne, the Annandale, the Hopetoun, the
Manzil Room, good old Selina's at Coogee, and the Phoenician
Club, just to name a few, were full of rowdy stalwarts of the
independent music scene. The boys were up to their necks in the
hullabaloo of late night drinking, noise complaints, riots and the
general air of seediness these iconic venues provided. Bands like
the Lime Spiders, Died Pretty, Happy Hate Me Nots, the Birthday
Party, Spy vs Spy, Mi-Sex, the Oils, the Damned, the Angry
Samoans, the Beasts of Bourbon, the Divinyls and a million more
domestic and overseas acts used to grace the stages and the boys
had their pick of where and who they wanted to see. But the 90s
were giving them different options and the Hordern was leading the
charge with dance parties and girls on MDMA.

Young Beau and Reg were just walking up the hill to the hut
where they had stashed their clothes after a marathon grommet
session on the left shorie.

"Hey, grommets!"

"Hey, Dan."

"How was it?"

"A couple ... but Starman's just paddled out with Grotto and
Sutho so we knew it was best we paddle in."

"Yeah, well, at least you're learning ..."

"Yeah. We were gonna get Big Ads to get his Uncle Johnny
onto 'em," Beau jokingly replied.

"What about ya ring ya mum from the shop and organise
looking after it for the night with Oz dog?"

"Oh! You sure? Don't know how good we'd go if a six-foot
Maori came through the door."

"I'll just put a sign up saying no six-foot Maoris allowed!"

"OK, then. Can we ring Scoots and get him to help mind it?"

"Sure."

Groms minding the shop whilst Dan and the boys partied was
becoming a regular occurrence. They'd enjoy the freedom of
doing what they want while their parents thought they were
having sleepovers at each other's house. They were already little
scammers asking their parents for money for the movies all the
while intending to buy a foilie to get stoned on. They'd laze
around like stoned puppies and watch a bit of TV till they got

293

bored and then start getting restless and looking for things to do. They couldn't help but find their way into the shop, magnetised by the thrill of new skate decks and surfboards. They had a game going where they'd sneak into the shop then dress up from the gear on the racks and act like mannequins in the front display window. Totally smashed out of their brains they'd try to stand perfectly still and fool passers by. Some streetwalkers wouldn't notice them but others would walk ten paces by then ask themselves, "Were they for fucking real or what?" and then double back for a closer look. Needless to say, laugh-outs were enjoyed by both the grommet mannequins and the pedestrians cruising past.

The Hordern Pavilion next to Moore Park in Sydney has always been a hub of excitement for music worshippers. International acts have always played there on their tours around Australia and Cookie even bopped around to Gary Glitter there in the 70s. The "house parties" that gripped the underground dance floors by the short and curlies in the late 80s were a new phenomenon, attracting toe hoppers from every nook and cranny across Sydney. They were the new happening thing at that time and were so below the surface they slipped under the police radar for the first couple of years, making them a haven for eccentric behaviour.

The movement began in Chicago in 1977 when a new club called "the warehouse" opened its doors. The guy who opened it was Frankie Knuckles, also known as the Godfather of House, and it was where he started experimenting by mixing disco classics and new Eurobeat pop. This is where "house" and "acid house" got their names.

House music was deeper and rawer when compared to disco and more designed to make people dance. Slowly synthesised sounds that introduced drop-outs and dub-ins, that had never been heard before, emerged throughout the 80s.

By the time "house" had reached the Hordern there was ten years of growth and refinement behind it. As the music was originally targeted at creating harmony between race, colour and sexuality it was adopted quickly by the gay community and raised as the baby they'd always wanted. But its roots hadn't just been confined to the US, and a ground movement of "house" had pockets synonymous with Chicago and NY popping up all around Europe. The avant-garde Hordern dance parties were originally planned by the UK "house" clergy who were happy to come down under and pump up the volume. They brought with them a shitload of MDMA and, in collaboration with their fag mates residing around Oxford Street, they flooded the craving houses of the beat boppers across the insubordinate landscape of Sydney.

By the late 80s the boys had started frequenting the Hordern parties and other clubs, such as Kinsela's, the Kardomah, the Freezer, the Cauldron, the Metropolis and a new club called Ziggurats where house beats were taking over the airwaves. The Beach Club at Bondi had been quick to jump on board as well and basically by the early 90s most clubs were plugged in to the haunting repetitive beats that had taken over the dance floors of the world.

Coco was on stage with two vixens. They danced as if floating upon thin air, their bodies extensions of the rhythmic beat. The long wooden stage was royal ground, built for rockers and artists who had made a name for themselves all over the world. Coco was up for the occasion and showed the sea of thousands why he was making a name for himself as the Latino spice-sleaze of dance clubs around sin city. One could only have imagined him at home practising, in a tight leotard, on his mum's tiled kitchen floor, gyrating like he had a pungent South American hot meat dish down his pants. He was a man of heat and passion, hot and sexy, with fancy footwork slippery to follow. At times it made your "high" mind just boggle. There was no soul doubt about the kid—he was at one in his universe entertaining any of the masses who bothered to look up and witness his sensual show.

At that moment Dan, Porky, JB, Euge, Getz and Danzig were making their own way down towards the stage, pirouetting around hot chickies as they danced in trance. Aesthetically and spiritually, "house" had organically formed out of the need of the oppressed to build a dance community. To these Hordern faithfuls it had become the main reason for living. It was all they socially needed or ever wanted. It was as if the movement was their "calling".

"Does it get any better!" screamed an entranced Dan.

As the boys got lost in the wave of euphoric emotion the club resembled an earthquake shaking the repressive crust of square-assed thinking. No-one was straight and no-one ever wanted to come back down! Empathy reigned and the cable that connected sentient beings was being pulled tight as they put their hands up in the air! Girls oozed sexuality as guys strengthened into rapturous playboys losing any hang ups that formerly restrained their full bloom. The MDMA swept the crowd off its feet and into the Hordern's mesmerising orbit—open arms, open lips, open minds and open legs. The captivating audio and lighting was nothing short of divine as it trounced the club's senses. Everyone was feeling the love.

"Gotta hit the dunny. Meet you guys back here in five," yelled a squirming Danzig.

"Let the lad through!" shrieked JB. "He needs to drop the kids off at the pool!"

"Nah, mate," was Danzig's quick reply, as if doing a poo was some kind of despicable act. "Bustin' for a piss, mate!"

"OK, Danzig. Don't trip over 'Trough Boy' ..." joked Getz. "Trough Boy" was some fuckin' depraved weirdo who liked patronising urinals face down or up, depending on his mood and whether he'd brought his snorkel.

Danzig strode off and got sucked up by the swirling crowd.

"Plenty of 'starship troopers' in here, guys!" cried out JB. Everyone had to scream to be heard.

"Whaddya mean?" asked Porks.

"Mate, just look at all the arsetrenouts in 'ere," interjected Dan. "Fuck, bra! As if we aren't gonna have a ball! All these beautiful women ... shit, bra, if that's our only opposition even you might get a root tonight, Porks!" Dan and the lads were starting to peak. They'd all dropped a couple of E's before at the Windsor in Paddo and were now experiencing waves of meltdown.

"Been telling everyone for months!" screamed Getz, pleasuring in his rightful prediction. "There's always sex on tap here, 'Vanilla'!"

All of a sudden a bunch of guys and girls came shuffling through the crowd dressed in nurses' and doctors' outfits. They were spraying bottles of liquid mist on the clenched teeth of everyone they managed to pass by. Onlookers saw what was in store and didn't hesitate to take a hit.

Getz yelled, "Line up! This shit's the guns!"

The boys opened up their mouths exposing their ivories and let the squirting begin. Each took a hit and looked at each other waiting for a rush. As the medical procession disappeared into the maelstrom everyone started breaking into fits of laughter. The boys enjoyed the surge as they just kicked back for its two-minute high and let the big beat lead 'em.

As Danzig waltzed into the public dunnies all kinds of pungent smells invaded his sensitive nose. He caught a glimpse of himself in the smudged mirror which seemed precariously stuck on the wall over the grotty wash basin. He kinda frightened himself. Not wanting to look at that person again he continued towards the urinal canal where a smiling, piss soaked, snakelike body was wriggling in the putrid wash. Danzig scanned the rest of the large public toilet to check out whether any other person was reacting to the spectacle. Most were cool, in love with the moment that MDMA had provided them. He suddenly thought, "Fuck it" and strolled over to the mess in the waterway. Positioning himself directly on top of this sad excuse's head he unzipped his fly and lobbed his manhood out. It drooped like a little trunk and Danzig looked down to make sure "Trough Kid" was going to cop a mouthful.

Just as "Look at you, ya pasty punk!" came out of his awaiting mouth, Danzig unloaded his full barrel over the guy's pearly whites.

"Take that, ya cunt!"

"Sex is fun," gurgled the boy fountain. "Even if it's bad it's fun!" Gurgle, gurgle.

After the boys were able to focus after their medical experience Dan continued, "I hope those guys weren't mixing whatever was in that bottle with any bodily fluids!"

JB instantly starting spitting, endeavouring to clear any remnants of the unknown mist outta his mouth. "Is every fucken guy in here besides us gay or what?"

"Most of the guys in here are 'vagina decliners' and we have our pick of the thousands of girls lookin' for dick?" replied Getz.

"Yep, As long as they aren't lesbians, mate, we're in!"

"Doesn't look that there's any swamp donkeys amongst 'em, either. They're looking all pretty shit hot!"

Danzig wobbled back like a lost boy taking in the new and mysterious.

"What's up, Danzig? Looks like you've seen a ghost." Eugene had noted Danzig had possibly experienced something life-altering. It wasn't hard for your life to be changed at one of these parties where it seemed anything could happen!

"Did you bump 'Trough Boy' or what?" yelled an excited Getz.

All Danzig could do was shake his head. Trough Boy had

297

changed another person's life.

"See, Porky. If you don't pull a root in here tonight we are gonna have to tie you up and throw you in the dunnies next to 'Trough Boy'!" cried Getz.

"Yeah and call you, the 'Son of Trough Boy'!"

The night wore on and each of the boys went their own ways in search of decadence. Sometimes they'd cross paths again but the fun just wouldn't let up and they'd just keep following their noses on whatever scent they had picked up on. Girls weren't backwards at coming forwards either and the love drug made it easier to find a root than in a brothel.

Dan found himself dancing with several girls till a quaint distant figure caught his eye. She was dressed in a longer dark dress than most and the way it hugged her curvy body had him captivated. He danced towards her until he was within a metre of her. She was dancing by herself and fobbing off any guy who tried to engage. As he drew close his senses became overloaded with her sweet perfume and her erotic presence. His radar love had been fully activated. She swayed to the beat and unexpectedly looked up into his bedazzled eyes. It was Sandra. His heart missed a beat. She grabbed and pulled him onto her, kissing his lips with a passion and fervour that blew the top off the Hordern. He was higher than he'd ever been before and instantly in love with this temptress. He was lost in the moment and she was seemingly letting go of someone else and filling the void. She held Dan so tight he thought he might shit himself. He clenched his butt cheeks and got lost again. He thanked God that it was only wind and he let it escape in periodic increments as to not blow his trumpet too loud.

The beat was hypnotising and for that moment they both showered in bliss with no comprehension of time. It didn't seem to need grasping. They held close together like a knotted bow and moved as one with the music. There was no need to anticipate anything as both free-fell into ecstasy.

A while later Dan led his newfound love towards the exit. They propped up against a wall for a second and watched the crowd of bodies bopping and shaking, elevated into an eruption of harmonic emotion.

Moose and his mate Terry and another big Samoan, Bobby, were stationed as security guards at the front doors. Not that they ever had to control the huge crowd of kids absorbed in the pleasures of a rapturous love scene. They generally had scams going on where they made a bit of extra cash. This night they had a secret stash of longnecks and since the bar had sold out they were swapping them for grams of coke and business was very good. Moose sighted Dan and his girl and strolled over to say hi. He didn't bother saying anything and immediately stuck a small spoon up Dan's snog. Dan promptly hoovered the crystal down the back of his throat, smiled at Moose as if to say thanks and continued petting with his girl.

"All good, Dan?"

"Yeah, thanks, mate!"

"How many eccys you swallowed, Danny boy?"

"Oh, a few. Why?"

"Just don't eat too many or you'll end up with EBT!"

Dan wasn't really up for a conversation but he managed to spit out, "What's that?"

"Eccy Bowel Rot!"

"OK, I won't. Thanks!" and with that Dan grabbed his fair maiden and headed outside for a taxi.

Out on the street the scene looked like World War 3. Busted up frontliners with "Wham" haircuts and smudged mascara harlots were scattered around like lost marbles. The people of the night were quivering in their skins commencing the process of coming down. Some were trying to make sense of their soaring, drug-soaked minds but it was in vain as it was just another passing moment of another passing day in another passing orbit. The high regrettably was always going to end, unless they had more goodies in their pockets and were ready to hit the day club. It all came under the banner of "limitations". Some people knew theirs; others were going for broke; others were still exploring the unknown corners of their brave new world. There was a cultural beat revolution happening in Sydney and the rumblings of the underground were happily leading the charge.

Dan and Sandra held each other's hand tight and flagged a vacant cab.

"Where to, mister?"

"Bondi, please, mate."

As the cab drove down Bondi Road and passed the white perimeter fence of Waverley Oval, the sun was getting on with its job and hoisting itself upwards in all its golden glory. Dan looked into the sexy eyes of his special princess and if needed could write a rhyme about her. Infectious adoration spilled out of his worshipping eyes. Jammin' with this lady was the only thing on his mind.

"Girl, I adore you." She gripped his sweaty hand harder. "I can take you from wherever to wherever you are!" If she was willing he felt like he could move mountains for her or at least make her wanton and wet. The game of love had ceased for they were both rendered submissive by each other. A passionate romp of marathon proportions was in the wings and they were just going with the flow and letting the cosmos clear the path to an eruptive orgasm. Dan's bed was only minutes away and as they flirted heavily in the back of the cab it almost wasn't needed.

"Where in Bondi, sir?"

"Campbell Parade, just down south across from the hill, please, mate."

"No worries."

"Owww!" She'd bit Dan on the lip as if he shouldn't be focusing on anything but the task at hand.

"Here you go," said the cabbie as he pulled into the kerb. The sun was casting a morning-after halo over both of them. Their pores exuded an emotive aura as they waltzed around to the back lane locked in like a heat-seeking missile on target.

Beau woke up to Dan knocking hard on the back gate.

"Hey, you grommets, let us in!"

The grommets had been sleeping on board bags on the floor though Beau had moved onto the lounge after Oz dog had curled up next to his face and started farting.

"Yeah ... coming!" Beau said as he rubbed a bit of crusty next-morning "pot eye" out of his sockets.

Dan looked his prize up and down and was hooting as loud inside as the continuous whistle-blowers at the dance party. She was about the same size as him 5'7" and casted into her dress like a fine sculpture. She had nothing to hide, she was delicious and he was filled with excitement as he couldn't wait to rip her clothes off like her eyes were telling him to do so.

"Open the gate!"

"Hold your horses. Gotta finish putting my pants on."

"Who's that?" asked Sandra.

"Couple of groms who have been holding the fort."

"Little troopers, aye."

"You could say that."

300

Beau opened the gate and the lovey-doveys entered. Sandra panned the underground den of iniquity and it made her go slightly weak at the knees. She loved grunge and the abode stunk of it.

"OK, grommets, out."

"But it's only 6am, Dan."

"Yep, that's right. I've got some official business to attend to so take your gear over to the hut and have yourself a nice day!"

The order had been given but the three of them had a bit of a giggle at the "official business" line. Reg and Scoots jumped up to attention and they all grabbed their boards and gear then high-tailed it out the door.

"And thanks for coming, and make sure you pop around after lunch. I've got some stickers for ya!"

"OK, Dan. Thanks."

Dan closed the door as his vixen pinched his arse.

"Where's your bed, baby?" She couldn't quite contain herself.

Dan picked her up like a newlywed, walked her into his stock room and with the strength of Samson hurled her up onto his loft. His elevated lair had seen him slay many a dragon, but as he used to say, "you have to slay a few dragons to get to the princesses", and his pork sword was at last through the scary woods and into the fortress. For him this fair maiden was way overdue!

They necked and tore each other's clothes off like wild beasts, all the while perspiring like their bodies were on fire. They became absorbed in licking and sucking the clammy secretion off each other's naked body. Hands groped, legs wrapped, tongues flickered and orifices were explored—foreplay at its best! The lion's den roared with erotica. After her satisfying fellation he returned the favour and went down on her like an anteater ravaging a nest of termites—crazed MDMA junkies in a heightened sexual union making a hell of a racket!

Bangs and knocks peppered the back gate but it was shut with good reason. The boys would have to wait to collect their boards to go surfing. By the sounds coming from the back storage room most of the visitors got the picture that Dan was in the process of raising his kundalini and had a laugh at the enthusiasm involved in its erection. A couple of the boys gave a hoot and a holler but the sexual culprits were unaware of anything except the flooding of their erogenous zones in Dan's tiny, sticky room. The callers would have to wait out in the wilderness until the job was done.

Dan hammered her like their was no tomorrow and that's what she wanted. The princess was being murdered and she could only scream for more. The lovemaking went on and on like a marathon and no position was left out of their repertoire. After a couple of hours and giving her the pleasure of multiple orgasms, Dan knelt up straight like almost at attention as if he was in some kind of militia and shot his RPG across the smooth barren wasteland of her back. He let go of a war cry that shouted he'd finished to the rest of the world and then, with an empty tank, promptly slumped on the sweat filled sheets alongside his slain princess!

A Hero Returns

"Yeah, Johnny, always happy to be of help."

"Well, you and Alex pretty much saved my life!" Johnny was trying to cram as much as he could into his 3-minute Cessnock jail phone call. "It was touch and go for a while but I pulled through with only minor injuries, though me face needs a bit more surgery!" Johnny had lost a tooth and probably been carrying a cracked cheekbone but was generally on the mend.

"Shit, man! You'll have to cancel those modelling appointments ..." Dan couldn't help himself. "I'll ring Chadwick's and tell 'em!"

"You haven't changed, aye. You're still a little smart-arse, Danny boy!"

"Suppose you can still do a bit for full face burqas and helmets."

"You little shit, don't make me laugh. I'm still achin' a bit."

"Thought the only thing you'd be aching from in there is a sore bum."

"Don't get so jealous, now. I can bring around a few mates when I get out and they can break you in if you like?"

"No thanks!"

"Anyway I owe you a lottery ticket ... no, actually 'Bull' said I should buy you two!"

"But what would your boyfriend think?"

"Ha ha ... wait till I get outta here ..."

"No seriously, JC, 'the Bull' is a top bloke ... but, fuck, man, don't get on the wrong side of him."

"What? You think I'm new to the game? I know that, mate. Anyway, tell the boys I said 'Hi' and if you talk to Alex tell him not to drop the soap and that I miss his ugly head!"

"You know 'em, mate. Big 'Hi' to 'the Bull' and look after yourself in there."

"Too right, Dan. Later!"

"I'll get a wave for ya."

"Thanks, mate. Drop in on someone for me!"

"See ya, brudda."

And with that Johnny gathered his momentary happy thoughts of freedom and hanging at Bondi with the boys and headed back to his 4 × 2 cell. Dan put the receiver down and envisioned how trading places with Johnny would pretty much be hell on earth. Sure, Dan sold a bit of pot here and there but he was old enough now to know that he never again wanted to take a risk that could see him wearing Khaki greens.

He looked over at Oz dog who was snoozing under one of the clothes racks and said, "I'd better go and have a bong and celebrate my life in Bondi." He refused to say "freedom" because he didn't think anyone was really free under the control of bodgie politicians. Plutocrat puppeteers made sure of that.

He looked over towards the hill in hope of roping a grommet in but being Monday morning they were possibly all at school. He was feeling a little sore and hung over from the weekend's party. He couldn't remember how many eccys he'd dropped or how many cones he'd managed. The sex he'd shared with Sandra was like a few hours in the gym, but a bit more pleasurable. Pummelling her was sure better than using an "Abs Cruncher" or a "Flabbuster vibrator" though he could have put to good use a vibrator if there was one lying around. "Fuck, Ozzie. If Monday had a face I'd punch it!"

At that moment Big Shano walked into the shop. "Morning, Dan."

"Morning, Shano." The reply had a wobble attached to it as Dan tried to steady himself on his counter's high stool. Shaky Mondays were common and Dan had in mind a visit to the Diggers' steam room later that day to sweat the muck off him and exchange stories about weekend antics.

"You haven't got those sunnies on for nothing, have you?"

"Better off not going there ... but you do already know that my body is a nightclub."

Big Shano was a bit big around the gut but he was a gem of a young bloke and a dedicated board rider. He wore thick rimmed glasses and being in his late teens still had a few pimples to deal with. Overall he was a pretty clean looking kinda guy, with his combed hair cut above his collar and over his ears, his pearly white teeth smiling at you like a set of perfect piano keys and the whiff of "Old Spice" circling his orbit. He was also very well mannered, though those who knew him well were aware of a jovial pervert underneath his straight bubba-boy face. There was no evil intent and he was just another horny young devil wrestling with his bubbling testosterone. All straight men are admirers of the female anatomy and if they ever tell you any different then you're talking to someone who sucks cock!

Dan actually thought Big Shano was a real asset to the shop on the occasions he had him stand in and work for him. The big guy really enjoyed selling surf and skate gear and it reflected in his good sales, even if Elle wasn't returning to buy a bikini in a hurry.

"When are you putting the heat draw up for next weekend?"

"Steele's coming around today and we are going to have a little chat and sort a few things out, but it should be up on the window by tomoz."

"Cool. Can't wait. My little brother Luke wants me to put his name down, if that's all right?"

"Sure, mate. Here's the book."

"He's only a cadet."

"That's OK. We're gettin' a few cadets joining up."

"Wow, that's great! It seems to be really moving right along, Dan."

"Sure is, mate. Actually, a few kids from Bronte have just joined."

"Who's that?"

"Yeah, well, good old Porky—you know, the legend old dude from Bronte who drives the garbo truck that Alchin works on—yeah? Well, he came in and signed up his two boys Luke and Vaughn, and Bluey Graham from Bronte Surf Club came in as well and signed his two, Aaron and Koby!"

"That's unreal! Those guys rip! Wow, Dan, the team is starting to get some good talent in it."

"Yeah," Dan said with a tone that mimicked "Why wouldn't it!"

"And what about all the Bondi guys starting to make a name for 'emselves? Shit, man—Mikey B, Josh, Brad V, JB, Getz, Jamie and Leon are all fucking ripping! We're definitely gonna have a good team for the Quiky Tag Team this year." The streets of Bondi were merging.

"Oh, yeah. I forgot to mention that McIver's just joined ..."

"No way! He rips."

McIver was a young goofyfoot who had moved to Bondi a few years prior and had been lying pretty low though his surfing was turning heads. He'd fine-tuned his style growing up surfing Pipe with Derek, Davey Cantrell, Liam, Mickey Nielsen and the rest of the Hawaiian boys. He was aloof in many ways but his zest for life and surfing made him an asset in any boardrider team.

305

"Yeah. I also heard young Chandler and Cam from over Bronte way and a couple of ex-McKenzie boardriders have joined too!" Big Shano almost had some froth coming out of the sides of his mouth—it was obvious he was just as excited as Dan about the club's early magnetism.

"Yep, forgot to mention them. The club sure is pullin' 'em in, mate! All the guys Stirling's elite team didn't need. Geez, I'd have to say we've got between about 60 to 80 guys in the club already—maybe more."

"Well, I'm so keen for this Sunday, aye."

"Yeah, Shane, get down early and help me with setting up, aye?"

"For sure!"

"And after the comp Ads's gonna have a barbie in the arvo so we can all get shit-faced!"

"That's sick!"

"Yep, and Trotter and the 'Stiff Arm' boys are gonna be jammin' some sick tunes there so we can go mental and break all the rules!"

At that point in time, Faye, the lady from the council, stuck her head in the door and humbly asked, "You're not busy, are you, Dan?"

Dan immediately gave her his instant attention. "No way, Faye. Please come on in. I've always got plenty of time for you."

She stepped inside and walked over to the counter. Big Shano politely moved aside so she could talk directly to the newly appointed "Youth Liaison Officer".

"Thank you." She acknowledged Big Shane's etiquette. She formally crossed her hands in front of her as she wasn't yet completely comfortable in understanding her street culture portfolio and underground surroundings. It was at times daunting for such a refined lady. "You don't mind if we have a chat, do you?"

"Of course not, Faye. I'm happy to talk to such a lovely lady any time."

"Sweet talkin' the ladies as usual," smirked Shano whilst giving the immaculately-dressed Faye a wink.

Faye started blushing as any middle-aged lady would.

"Hey, whooooaaaa, pull up, matey." Dan quickly put Big Bubba Shane's comment on the rack. "Don't believe anything he says. Actually, I just met him. He reckons he's just come out of the closet and I'd say he's probably jealous that I'm not falling in love with him!"

Faye's blush was only temporary and a sly grin couldn't help emerging from her delicate mouth. She might have been 40-something but she had obviously been a good sort and a good sport when she was younger.

"What?" burst out of Bubba's gob. "You really have a dirty mind thinking up shit like that!"

Dan composed himself, shone a big smile at Faye and turned his tap charm on again. "I don't have a dirty mind," he paused for an instant and his smile grew wider as he looked into Faye's hazel eyes. "I have a sexy imagination."

It was back to blushing for Faye. Kinda the colour between a tomato and a beetroot.

"So, what do the council and police think of my new responsibility and position as far as the Bondi kids are concerned? I hope I didn't shock them too much."

Faye was glad the wheels of conversation were back on track, for council matters were the reason why she had visited Dan in the first place. Though Dan's mind was still as flirtatious as the day before and he even thought if he possibly got a few drinks into her she might just submit! His eyes couldn't help but wander down and look at her neatly-packed cleavage.

He lapsed back into an ogling deviant till Big Shano derisively ejaculated, "You lost something down there or what?"

Dan corrected his day-after eccy goggles and could only keep smiling at her kumquat cheeks and puzzled eyes. He noticed what a pronounced piece of art her nose was, narrow and pixie-like. It reminded him of this Russian girl he had shagged in the toilet at the Freezer about 6 months earlier. "Shit," he thought to himself. He hoped he could stop his current thought patterns and mentally groped for higher ground to prevent him backsliding into the blubbering, debauched state that ravaged his mind the day before.

"I am so sorry, Faye. I got hit in the head by my surfboard yesterday and I'm kinda getting dizzy spells and it's a little hard for me to focus at times as well."

"Oh, you poor dear. Don't you think you should go to the doctor's?"

"Under control. If I don't get any better by lunch time I'll head down there and get it seen to."

Big Shano amazingly kept a straight face and decided he'd

heard enough, excused himself politely and told Dan that he'd drop in later.

Faye continued, "Well, look, Dan, I've only dropped in to tell you how proud I was of you at the January meeting. I'm sorry I haven't made it in any earlier but I've been very busy at the chambers, and I did actually drop in a couple of times but you were out."

"No worries, Faye."

"And I was hoping you could make the next one that they are scheduling in a few weeks towards the end of March."

"That shouldn't be a problem."

"It will be on a Monday night."

"That'll work for me."

"And do you know that the suggestion we brought up about the big skate ramp has been agreed upon and they will start work on it in the next couple of months."

"What? Really? That's unreal! Wait till I tell the lads about that—they're going to be stoked!"

"Yes ... and you should also know that the head sergeant down Bondi Police Station likes you too."

"You serious?" Dan was a little flattered. It was usually the opposite when it came to the men in blue. "I thought that old guy was pretty cool too! I surprisingly saw him nodding his head when I told that other copper to lay off the young kids smoking pot, and told him that it was just a passive drug that did them no harm compared to alcohol. I mean, you know, kids don't want to go fighting or causing havoc when they're stoned. They just wanna watch the footy on TV or go surfing. I mean, I probably shouldn't have told him to stop ruining their lives by giving them a criminal record but I suppose it just slipped out. What's done is done."

"Don't worry. Harl is a wise old policeman and he knew what you were saying was pretty much hitting the nail on the head. I mean, he doesn't make the laws and he is a compassionate man who's seen it all, Dan."

"I find it hard to believe that he agreed with that."

"Yes, and so did I. I was quite impressed by your bold nature, Dan."

"Well, I didn't really mean to be bold, Faye. I just told them how I saw it."

"And that's why I chose you as the voice for these kids down here—they need someone like you to pull them all together and they need the council to help them with recreational facilities to keep them active and interested in other things besides crime."

"Thank you so much, Faye, for having some faith in me."

"You're a real man, Dan. You stand up for what you believe in and I like that in anyone."

"Wow, Faye! You're too kind."

"Just happy to be working with someone like you." She held out her dainty hand. "I've got to go but I'll be in touch again real soon."

He gripped it softly and couldn't help but kiss its fine texture. "Thanks for stopping by again."

"Love this shop—it's the real Bondi. See you again. Bye!"

Dan watched her walk out into the street—she looked sleek from behind. An older Ferrari ... but surely still a damn good ride!

He looked over at Ozzie who sensed his attention and opened one eye. Dan loved dogs and they loved him. Oz was his one real constant amongst the tumultuous uproar his life had become.

Dan loved a particular canine story that had become part of Tibetan tradition involving one of their great monks Asanga and he really believed it to be true. The story explains that Asanga spent years meditating and visiting heaven where he received teachings from a future Buddha named Maitreya. It was said that Maitreya manifested generously in the form of a dog and met Asanga as such before his incarnation far in the future. Maitreya adopted the form of a dog in order to encourage depressed and scared people to rise above their fears and develop trust and faith in other sentient beings. Dan liked to think that the story is why dogs are a man's best friend!

Steele arrived around 3pm and before entering the shop saw H-Man taking in the rays at his 322 bus stop office. He managed to hoot a loud coo-eee at him before disappearing off the street. Dan was still comfy behind his dark sunnies listening to some Bob Marley to help subside his easing jitters when Steele sauntered in.

Steele was living northside up near Palm Beach where he remained focused on trying to keep up with the new kids on the block like Slater, Potts and co. He would float through Bondi on occasions but it was easier being at arm's length from the distractions that "Scum Valley" hurled at him. The waves were better up that way and the number of beaches offered more variety.

He walked over to Dan with a box under his arm.

309

"About time you showed up," said Dan. "What's in the box?"

"Sex wax. I was over Bronte at Storm's and he gave me this for ya. He said you ordered it last week."

"Stoked! I was getting low on that shit and you know what it's like if someone walks into a surf shop and you don't have any wax to sell them!" Dan took the box off him and commenced to slide it under the counter.

"It ain't a surf shop!"

"That's fuckin'.right!"

Steele looked around the showroom and nodded his head as he digested the surroundings.

"Wow, Dan, this is great!"

"Thanks, mate."

"No, seriously, and you know I've been in surf shops all around the world and this shop has a vibe as underground as you can get."

Dan was a little dumbfounded. He held Steele's praise in high regard and it was very satisfying hearing it from such a surfing statesman. The day just seemed full of compliments and Dan was hoping his head could fit through the door come closing time.

"Whaddya want from me?"

"Nah, I mean it. This is how surf shops should be."

"That means the world to me, brudda."

"Yeah, well, I can see you're just being yourself and trying to help the locals and especially the young kids with the club and that's where I'm at too!"

"Yep, and as long as I can pay the bank back and feed me and Oz dog I'm happy as Larry!"

Both men believed in what they were doing. There was no money in it but it sure felt good. They both had some big plans in mind for the club and the fact that it was so much fun being part of their local beach's new emerging crew was a blessing. The challenge ahead was to turn a fairly green club into one that could hold its own against some of the best clubs in Australia. Steele and Dan were up for it and were quietly confident their keen, talented boardriders could pull it off. Expectations were high but both lads had the chemistry to make good things happen. And if they didn't, no biggy, but no-one was going to die wondering!

"So, I'm hoping I can get in a heat for this Sunday. Need some practice before I head off to California for the Cold Water Classic."

310

"As I told you before, mate, it's only for guys that can surf!"

"I know you're worried I'm gonna kick your butt!"

"Stay away from my posterior."

"So what's been happening with the club? How many names are down for the weekend?"

"Shit, bra, I'd have to say about 75 or somethin' like that, and for sure there'll be a few put their names down through the week."

"Well, sounds like things are coming together."

"Mate, you should see some of these guys surf. They rip!"

"I'm gonna get out there now and hopefully check a few of them out."

"Feels good you being home here, mate. You know you're a hero to a lot of the kids?"

"It's good to be home, mate, and with the club up and running you can expect me down here a lot more. I have been thinking that when I'm not on tour and home over Palmy some of the team can come up and train with me. I've got a great pad over there with a gym and good training program and the waves are so much better than down here."

"I'm sure you'll have plenty of takers. These kids are chompin' at the bit to surf with you."

"I was even thinking if things go well this year we can even take 'em to Hawaii in December and really blood them."

"That would be fucking awesome!"

"No reason why we can't do it, especially if we want these kids to improve and come of age."

"I couldn't agree more. Let's just see how it rolls this year and if we make it there, good and proper. If not, we'll make it the year after. It's good to have goals for these kids—it will keep them focused.

"Shit, yeah, Dan. I've got a good feeling about the club's future. It's kinda like our destiny to look after these grommets."

"Mate, tell me about it. I've got 30 of their boards parked out back and the traffic is that full-on I can't even have a pull in peace."

"What? You been caught trying?"

"Mate, I don't even have time to lob it outta me pants!"

Both lads had a laugh and Steele headed out back of the shop and got himself psyched for a wave and went surfing.

The weekend rolled around pretty quickly and Dan refrained from hitting the town Saturday night to make sure he was up bright and early for the contest. Beau, Reg and Trott had slept over at boardriders headquarters and the grommets made cups of coffee whilst the elder of the tribe mulled up for brekkie.

"Looking forward to today—kinda like a triple whammy," said Trott as he passed the bong to Dan.

"Whatcha mean?"

"Well, we've got the comp, then Big Ads's barbie and the cricket's on as well." Australia had won the first Benson and Hedges final against Pakistan and if they were to win the one-dayers for that summer all they had to do was beat them later that night at the SCG.

"Yeah, well, Kerry Packer's a fuckin' legend!"

"Fucken oath. If it wasn't for him and Channel 9 we wouldn't be watching anything tonight. Just hope Ads's mum's OK with us taking over her lounge room. I mean, in between beltin' out tunes we can be watchin' the Aussies beltin' the sambos!" Trotter would be entertaining the crew with the "Stiff Arm" boys and would only be able to watch snippets of the final.

"She'll be cool. She knows what we're like! Anyway, we can always wobble back here for a quiet couple and an update of who's smashin' those Pakis for six!"

"Fuck, Jonesy's 83 not out on Friday night was spectacular."

"For sure, he's gotta get cricketer of the series!"

"You'd reckon. I think he's smashed over 400 runs so far, though O'Donnell has been doing some damage with the ball."

"True, but if Jonesy can make a good score tonight he's odds-on!"

"Just as long as we smash 'em, who gives a fuck!"

"Well, if we can repeat last Friday's effort we're a huge chance. Winning by 7 wickets has gotta fire 'em up to finish 'em off!"

"For sure. Wonder if Mikey and Brendan are donning the pads?"

"Ha ... who's gonna play drums and sax if they do?"

"Wasim and Saleem, of course!"

The tent was erected by many hands next to the hut and as Dan wrote up the heats on the blackboard the cadets were already showing up in numbers so it looked set for a 7.30am start.

The Bronte cadets at first were a little apprehensive to mingle with Reg, Beau, Scoots and the rest of the Bondi grommets, choosing to sit high and wide of the tent up near the pines. There was definitely some ice to break but as soon as a few of their heats had been run they all gathered around the blackboard in anticipation of results and the team started bonding. Just like most kids, it only took a little time till they were occupied in amusement with each other and carrying on.

Steele arrived around 9am as he had to drive down from the peninsula. He wasn't partying as he had an ASP contest in a week over in the US. He waltzed into the mob with his board and took his position next to the hut. He immediately got down to business asking JB how big and often the sets were rolling in? It was a fickle summer's day swell, north-east and passing the headlands, but it was big enough to see 3-footers push into the shallows of the bay.

"I'd say three foot every few minutes,' JB replied. "There's a couple behind the reef but Dan has put the contest flags up down second ramp on the little right hander."

Steele rubbed his hands together in delight. As a youngster he loved surfing that bank and he relished being back at his home beach and participating in a club contest. It had been a couple of years since Dan and Stirling had fallen out and everyone was enjoying the fact club contests were being held again. Everyone, that is, except Stirling and a couple of his loyalists.

As the contest hill became a mass of local surfers and their supporters, the main opposition observed the event from across the street and seemed slightly shocked at the numbers actively taking part.

A few of the elite RBS surfers and their mates went surfing but most of them steered clear of the event. It wasn't as if they didn't want to mingle with their mates competing on the hill, but more to do with the fact that they were sponsored and felt an obligation and loyalty to Stirling's surf shop and successful club. After all, their RBS club was still at the top of its game and it was hard to fathom that any new Bondi boardriders club could ever challenge them for the title of best club at the beach.

"Bloody try-hards," was all a hungover BP could manage as he strolled across the parade dragging his ciggy. He flicked it in the general direction of the event and strode down to the sand like he owned the joint. He paddled out near the contest site and dropped in on anyone practising for their heat. It was his way of showing his discontent towards any local who seemed to ignore that "Rude Boys Surfing" was the superior club in the area. RBS team mate Dobbo joined him with some other tight crew and made it difficult for anyone else to get a wave. A few cadets couldn't cope with the onslaught and paddled in, complaining about the targeted attack back at the contest site.

"I'll paddle out there and fucken' smash 'em!" said a seething JB.

"C'mon, Jason, let it ride," interjected Steele. "They'll get what's comin' to 'em." Steele was now the club captain and had a responsibility that the club do things right.

"But they're pickin' on our grommets!" added a huffy Porks.

"Let them carry on like knuckleheads. It'll mean that when we eventually get our chance to beat them in the Surf League the taste of victory will be so much sweeter." Steele's logic rang true.

"You reckon we can beat them one day?" asked Porks.

"I believe we can, but the less ammunition we load their already half-cocked attitude with, the better. Believe me, I am quietly confident we can—all have to do is stay humble and achieve things step by step."

This was exactly what Stirling and his club was dreading, though most of their egos couldn't admit that a club full of bums could actually challenge them. They were right that the new club couldn't compete with them any time soon but what Steele and Dan had in mind would take time. Great teams don't happen overnight and they both knew there was a lot of work to be done.

Stirling rankled at the thought of the new club becoming successful. The circle of compassion of the new boardriders was encroaching on what he had already laid claim to. It made him feel uneasy. It threatened his progress at the beach and seemed to already be straining some of his local relationships. Surfers now had a choice and he now had a real fight on his hands.

A vanguard of forgotten surfers were at last making their mark, christening their home turf—just like the cheeky Oz dog cocking her leg up on anything worth squirting, they were certainly making the rest of "Scum Valley" know it was their beach too.

Even Big Ads surfed in a junior heat, unable to ignore the tremors of the new movement. The local boys were having a field day! Mikey B and his brudda Brendan, Brad V, Trotts, Eugene, JB, Dan, Steele, Getz, McIver, Porks, Cookie, Ken-san, Big Shano and little brudda Luke, Shane P, Fordie, Jamie, Leon and the scores of others from Bondi and Bronte finally had a means for the local streets to be recognised. The local lads cheered and jeered each other as they vied for placings and club points and all that made the finals were all glowing in the accolades of their fellow boardriders.

Laughter, coo-ees, shakka shakes, brudda calls and solid handshakes threaded the boardriders all day. The contest scene was as much a celebration as it was a competition.

"You know, Dan, this club is already a success," commented Steele during a brief minute that they were able to share in private.

"I reckon it's got some great potential."

"Yeah, well, you know I talked to Stirling and asked him to merge his club with ours?"

"And?"

"Well, he's not here, is he? Could you imagine how strong we'd be if we all pulled together?"

"Sure." Dan knew that he was right but also knew Stirling would never even consider joining forces. Obviously olive branches weren't part of his nature. He then asked Steele a question that had been on his mind of late. "Why did you want to surf for us, mate?"

"Mate, it was easy. A boardriders club has to put club contests on for all to compete in. What good is a club if it doesn't give the young kids an open chance to perform and hone their skills? Everyone deserves a bite at the cherry!"

It was late February and Bondi's summer was in full swing. All around them the surfers, skaters, joggers, musclemen, bikini ladies, promwalkers, drug addicts, hustlers, musicians, lifeguards, Icebergers, westies and tourists added a bit of city soul to the beach. To the boardriders everything again seemed how it was supposed to be. It was fitting that the contest resembled the centre of the beach and everything else was revolving around it.

As Maori Pete and his Brazilian beach soccer contingent kicked their ball around the high tide mark, they paused and cheered as the Open final's contestants passed them by and readied themselves to do battle. Time for talking had ceased and it was now time to let their surfing do it for them. This was the expression of freedom, of creativity, that they had longed for as a club in a competitive arena.

By the end of the day Steele had won the open final and the

315

hearts and minds of the club. Most of these younger guys had grown up with surfing posters of him stuck on their bedroom walls. Most of them were still in awe of meeting their hero.

There had been over 100 guys surf in the comp and it had blown most expectations for six, just like Jonesy was gonna hit the Aussies to victory that night against the Pakis. Sure, Dan was the anchorman of the boardriders but Steele was the star and he sure inspired the boys and made them feel valued.

All had flowed smoothly except for a couple of minor incidents. One of the lads had accidentally shot the window out of a passing car from the Britannic Mansions after missing a bikini-wearing buttocks. It was an action that brought the coppers down looking for the culprit but the bb gun bandit was never found. There was also a bit of a punch-up on the beach with a Pommie backpacker. Nothing too serious but he wasn't going to mouth off again at the boys any time soon—till he found his teeth, anyway. But besides that it all went according to plan.

Trott, Mikey, Brendan, Curl and Brad V had left the contest site early to get things ready at Big Ads's for the BBQ. A few of the grommets and young Kathy had done the surf shop proud earning a few hundred bucks that would enable Dan to pay the bank and a few creditors the next day. And as the tent was folded most of the crew were either buying cases or substances of other kinds for the party to follow.

Someone running past yelled at a busy Dan, "Have to make this a habit, mate!"

"A habit of happiness!" he screamed back.

He felt a great sense of satisfaction and he reflected back on his life and how the journey he'd travelled to make it to where he was right at this moment was nothing short of remarkable. One thing for sure is that he knew the way forwards hadn't always been straight ahead. He'd gambled everything on this bet and observing the contest site and the joy it'd triggered it seemed to him that it was destined to pay off!

New and old grommets were emerging into the light. It was as if the beach had completed a cycle and was now ready for a new beginning—as if an enema had just taken place relieving the stagnation and the Bondi boys were now recharged and ready to rumble. Sure, there was still a long way to go but the foundation was laid and it was solid. He whispered to himself, "Thunderbirds are go!"

"Stop daydreaming and talkin' to yerself, ya poof, and let's get this shit done!" said a huffing and puffing Porks. Just folding a tent had that affect on him. "There's a party at Ads's, if ya haven't noticed!"

"Sorry, mate! Don't want you to have a heart attack and keel over on me now."

"That's right. Who else would be there to chew the fat with ya if that happened?"

"Oz dog!"

"Yeah, well, she does like spare ribs, I suppose."

"And Pork in Plum sauce."

The boys finished packing up, gave each other a high-five and marched across Campbell Parade stopping cars as if they felt obligated to let everyone know that this was their town. As they made their way towards boardriders' HQ at the back of the shop, Oz dog loyally followed a couple of steps behind.

As Porky grappled with one end of the bulky tent and Dan with the other he managed to utter on his heavy breath, "Fuck, wish someone'd give us a fucken hand!"

At that moment Steele seemed to pop out of nowhere and obliged. "Gotta stop fillin' yourself full of pies, Porks."

"I swear I'm on a diet. You know ... I mean, I've only been smashing party ones!" he joked.

"Yeah well, if they're from the Flying Pieman, mate, who can blame you!" remarked the lionised hero.

Porky seemed it fit to mention his delight in Steele's return in the Captain's presence. "Happy to see you made it home and is one of us again, Steele. Don't ya reckon, Dan?"

"Yeah, mate, it's gold!" Dan was also beaming about the sequence of events that had led to his dream being realised. "But that was never in doubt, Porky.

"And why's that?"

Dan turned to Steele, winked, then answered with, "Because you can take the boy outta Bondi, mate, but you can't take Bondi outta the boy!"